THE OMEGA POINT

BEYOND 2012

THE OMEGA POINT

WHITLEY STRIEBER

TOR®

A TOM DOHERTY ASSOCIATES BOOK
NEW YORK

THE OMEGA POINT

A Tor Book
Published by Tom Doherty Associates, LLC
175 Fifth Avenue
New York, NY 10010

www.tor-forge.com

Tor® is a registered trademark of Tom Doherty Associates, LLC.

ISBN 978-0-7653-2334-7

First Edition: June 2010

Printed in the United States of America

0 9 8 7 6 5 4 3 2 1

ACKNOWLEDGMENTS

I would like to thank my editor, Robert Gleason, whose support and skill were essential to the writing of this book.

I am also grateful to authors Robert Bauval, Michael Cremo, Laurence Gardner, Graham Hancock, William Henry, Rand Flem-Ath, Andrew Collins, and many others for their research into lost human history, and to Robert Allen Bartlett, Joseph T. Farrell, David Hudson, Robert Cox, and others for their explorations of the mysteries and path of alchemy, and to so many more whose work has led me to the new vision of the human past and future reflected in these pages.

The pioneering work of Richard Firestone, Allen West, and Simon Warwick-Smith on the catastrophe that struck our planet twelve thousand years ago also informed my story, for which I am grateful.

I would also like to thank Anne Strieber and Paul Canterna, whose expert insights and thoughtful support made this book possible.

Any mistakes or inaccuracies are my own.

Strong evidence exists that planetary transformations of the earth are being caused by highly charged material which has broken into our solar system from deep space.

—Dr. Alexey N. Dmitriev,
IICA Transactions, Volume 4, 1997

WHITE POWDER GOLD

In Greek mythology the quest for the secret of white powder gold was at the heart of the Golden Fleece legend, while in biblical terms it was the mystical realm of the Ark of the Covenant—the golden coffer which Moses brought out of Sinai, to be housed in the Temple of Jerusalem. The substance was said to confer extraordinary powers on the user, including, among many other things, the power to move in parallel dimensions of spacetime.

—Laurence Gardner,
Lost Secrets of the Sacred Ark

And I saw the dead, small and great, stand before God; and the books were opened: and another book was opened, which is the book of life: and the dead were judged out of those things which were written in the books, according to their works.

—Revelations 20:12

THE OMEGA POINT

PROLOGUE: THE PAST

12:04 AM EST, DECEMBER 21, 2012
TV STATION WBUL, BUFFALO, NEW YORK

Marty Breslin sat at the desk watching the cameras watch him, waiting for his nightly few minutes of local fame. "How's the remote?" he asked Ginger Harper. They had dropped a number of feeds lately, although not on him, because weathermen normally don't do feeds. But he was horrified at the idea of being left under the lights with nothing to say. Even when he had something to say, he had nothing to say, so a dead teleprompter was a terrifying thought. "Ginger, come back, please. We do have that feed ready to go?"

"We're good down the line."

"Anything unusual actually happening? Anywhere?" There were New Agers out in force around the world, on hilltops, crowding places like Sedona, and swarming by the thousands in Yucatan and Guatemala. Fourteen of them had been iced during a blizzard yesterday on Mount Everest. Even the stock market had gotten quiet today, waiting to see if anything might happen over the weekend. "Hello? Ginger?"

"I was just looking. CNN, quiet. BBC, they're still on the Himalayas story, nothing fresh on the AP. Joke stories."

Across on the news desk, Callie and Fred tossed real stories back and forth. They hit the Himalayas, but the big one tonight was a gang riding the highways disguised as state police officers, soliciting bribes in lieu of tickets. "Sounds like a good business," he said into his mike.

"That it does," Ginger replied.

He'd tried her a couple of times. No-go. Apparently her marriage was real. Well, it was her loss.

His lights came up. "Thirty seconds," she said.

"What're they doing out on the feed?"

"Chanting."

Fred Gathers said, "And now for the latest on the end of the world, let's go to Marty. What's a weatherman doing reporting on a subject like this, Marty?"

And he was on. Magic time. Famous in Buffalo, folks all said hi along the Chippewa Strip. It wasn't Manhattan, but they had the lake. The teleprompter began to roll. "Our thought was, if the New Agers were right and the world ended, it would be a weather story. As in, none. Obviously, weather post the apocalypse is gonna be kind of quiet."

"Okay, so it's after midnight on December 21, 2012. Why are we still here, Marty?"

"Good question, Fred. Tim Burris is on the scene at the Love and Light New Age Spiritual Center in Grover's Mills, New Jersey. Tim, has anybody been beamed up yet?"

"Over to you, Tim," Ginger said.

On the monitor, Burris appeared standing in a pool of light surrounded by figures in flowing white robes. Many of them were female, young, and, from what Marty could see, well worth the time. "Man, I wonder if he's gettin' any of that?"

"Yeah, yeah," Ginger said.

"This is Tim Burris in Grover's Mills, here at the Love and Light New Age Spiritual Center, where I have the Reverend Carlton Gaylord to explain why we're all still here."

He thrust the mike into the face of a tall, cadaverous man whose white robe had a gold choke collar. "We are celebrating the moment that the earth crosses the center of the galactic plane for the first time in twenty-six thousand years," he said. "Nobody said anything about the end of the world."

But that wasn't true! *He'd* said it, and on camera. That was the whole point of sending Tim all the way to Joisey. "Hey! We got that clip!"

Tim waited. Nothing happened. He blinked, then continued. "But isn't this the end of everything?"

Marty said into his mike, "Run the clip, Ginger!"

"It's not in the system."

"Aw, fer crap's sake, find it!"

Burris tried to pull the clip out of the guy. "But you said, uh—we have a clip—" Oh, so lame. There was a reason he worked in this joke station.

"Ginger!"

"It's gone!"

"Tell him, he's dyin' out there!"

When she imparted the wonderful news, Mary saw his face fall, then set with determination. He tried again. "You've been quoted as saying that the world would end tonight at twelve oh one."

"I said that the Mayan prophecy would come true."

Crap! Crap! Crap!

"But the world didn't end! We're all still here."

"The end of the world was media hype. You people. All the Mayan prophecy said was that we'd cross the centerline of the galaxy, and we did." He pulled up his sleeve and glanced at his Rolex. "Exactly four minutes and twenty seconds ago."

"This is so poor, Ginger, he is eating us for frigging lunch!"

Ginger, her voice tight, said, "Go to the scientist clip, then we're back in with the forecast."

They ran the talking head from the university, who explained that astronomers had no idea whether we were crossing the centerline of the galaxy or not, because it was hidden behind dust clouds.

"And we're out," Ginger said. "Two minutes on the break, Marty."

His lights went down. His camera turned off. He tried to control the red-hot rage that was building in him. "That was shitty as hell," he said, forcing himself not to scream. "I mean, we had that guy nailed down, that's why we bought el Timothy a ticket all the way to New Joisey, Ginger, hey!"

Ginger was silent.

He knew that there was no point in commenting further, but he could not shut up. "I mean, have you got your professional screwup certificate, Gin, or are you still an advanced amateur?"

"I found the clip!"

He wanted to tell her to stuff it up her ass, but that would be harassment of some damn kind. "How nice," he said. "Wrap it up for me and I can smoke it after the show."

"To you in five, four, three, two, one."

"And the big story tonight is that lake-effect snow, folks, you got that right, we're gonna get a heavy dose tonight." And so it went, down to the bottom of the hour, and they were out. When he walked off the darkened set, Gin was already gone. Far, no doubt. But where else were they gonna get somebody who could run a board for her money?

Later that night, he was hanging on a bar sucking beer and wishing some kind of dealer, any kind, would show up. Then a citizen came in, saw him, and said, "Hey, Marty. No snow!"

That was Marty Breslin. Batting a thousand.

Dr. Deborah Wilson pointed to a faintly blinking readout from the Advanced Composition Explorer. "What's that spike, Sam?"

Her graduate assistant thought perhaps this was some sort of quiz. He tapped the screen, and the ACE II detailed readout appeared. What he saw confused him. It was ordinary for the ion flux from the sun to vary, sometimes by a lot, but not by this much, never. "Let me run the circuits." What this would do was to determine whether or not there were overloads anywhere on the satellite, or tripped circuit breakers. From there, they could pinpoint the source of the anomaly.

"I've done that," Dr. Wilson said. She was clipped, careful, and very uncompromising. But she had also just told him that this tremendous spike in ions was some sort of real phenomenon, not an artifact.

He pulled up the Solar and Heliospheric readouts. The solar wind speed was 431.5 km per second, the proton density was thirteen. There was a coronal hole at midlatitude, and two small sunspots on the near side. "So this isn't coming from the sun," he said.

"Apparently not."

Energy from deep space, then. It had first been detected in the late nineties of the last century by Russian astrophysicists, but it wasn't considered a significant factor by their American counterparts.

As he spoke, his voice rose an octave, which he just hated. "But this can't be." He cleared his throat.

"Except that it is."

And there it was, entering the solar system right now, the sudden increase in intensity unmistakable. And his instructor was waiting. "I think it's a wave of energy from some sort of extrasolar event, perhaps an archaic supernova."

"Why archaic?"

"Well, obviously, there's a lot here compared to the normal range of solar output, but I'd think that a close supernova—that would be, um, even more energetic."

"Unless we've been in the distant corona since 1997, and this is the leading edge of the real stuff."

There was something in her voice that he didn't like. He looked up, met her eyes. "You're scared."

"Supernovas happen."

"But—my God." If this was the leading edge of a supernova wave, it could end life on earth. "This isn't possible!"

She reached across his cluttered desk and did something that she had never done before, and, in fact, was probably not appropriate conduct. She touched his hand. She started to speak, then stopped, and her silence said everything.

It was possible. It was quite possible.

However, when their findings eventually became a press release, it didn't exactly cause people to go rushing into churches begging God for deliverance. In fact, the story appeared in *The New Scientist* as a single paragraph. It showed up on Space.com for a couple of days. Various scientific blogs commented on it, more or less in passing.

Still, though, the energy level in the solar system quietly began to increase, and it kept increasing. Nobody noticed that the ion flux had begun to rise at exactly one nanosecond after midnight on December 21.

Nobody would ever notice that, but the story of what was happening to our solar system would grow and grow, until it became the most important of all stories, the greatest story, and, in a sense, the last story.

1

LUCKY BOY

David Ford had never flown in a private jet before, but it seemed almost inevitable that the superexclusive Acton Clinic would transport its new chief psychiatrist this way. The thing was small and louder than an airliner, but it was also swift and plush, if a bit worn. The sweep of leather was cracked here and there, and the carpet was tight from many steps.

Mrs. Aubrey Denman sat opposite him. She was the board's representative, all angles and desperation, narrow arms, a neck like knotted rope, her face an archaeology of lifts, so many that she appeared to have been transformed into a waxwork of herself. Her laughter was all sound and no expression. She must be seventy-five, maybe more.

The jet was claustrophobic. There was absolutely no wasted space. In the galley, a cadaverous servant in a blue blazer stood at the ready, his eyes emptied by a lifetime of waiting.

She was so rich that she had not only a plane, two pilots, and a servant, but also the plane was working.

So here he was in this really amazing situation, thirty-two years old and moving straight from his psychiatric residency to a good job in a time when there were no jobs of any kind.

"Dr. Ford, I want to take this opportunity to give you a little additional information."

They were in facing seats, knee to knee in the compact cabin. "I would appreciate that very much."

"First, I must apologize about the plane."

"It's wonderful, and I'm so grateful for the ride. It could've taken days otherwise."

"This is a fifty-year-old airplane. The only one I have that works. The newer ones—the electronics are ruined, they tell me."

The sun, of course. Always the damned sun. He noted the implication that she had a number of planes. Extraordinary.

She seemed to brace herself, like somebody bracing for a crash or waiting for an explosion. But when she spoke, her tone was casual, almost offhand. "You do know that Dr. Ullman was the unfortunate victim of a fire."

Something had opened the position, that had been clear enough. He had not asked, and nobody had explained. "I'm sorry."

"He was living in the town. Unfortunately, the fire service in Raleigh County has deteriorated. They were too slow."

It seemed odd to leave information like this to a moment when he was already on his way to the facility, as if the knowledge might have changed his mind. "It was an accident?"

"We assume."

"Is there anything else I should know? I mean, why are you telling me now?"

"You understand that your quarters will be on the estate?"

"I've been told that I have Herbert Acton's personal suite."

"Which is one of the most extraordinary interior spaces in this country. In the world, for that matter."

"That I was told. I'm fascinated. I tried to find pictures online, but—"

"No pictures. We're not the Donald Trump sort." She smiled a little. "Mr. Acton met girls in the bedroom you will use. Of course, you're a bachelor." Now her face became as hard as flint. "He wasn't."

Could she have once met Herbert Acton there? He'd died in 1958. She'd probably been a girl then, a teenager.

She burst out laughing. "It's just brilliant, you're going to love it, young man."

She reached for her drink—they had both been given highballs by the waiter—and as she lifted it to her lips, a blue glow appeared around her arm. She looked at the glow for a moment, then tossed the drink away with a little cry and an electric crackle. David noticed the same glow along his arms, and felt a tingling sensation. He thought, *This thing is about to blow up,* and his heart started racing. The waiter rushed to pick up the glass, blue fire shimmering along his arms and back.

"Ma'am, it's Saint Elmo's fire," he said. "We've got incoming solar energy again."

She looked pained. "We should have taken the car, Andy."

"Impossible, Ma'am. Too slow, too dangerous."

David glanced down at what he supposed was the New Jersey Turnpike far below. There was no sign of movement in the long, gleaming snake of vehicles. He said nothing.

She jabbed the intercom. "What does this Saint Elmo's fire mean? Is it going to cause a crash?"

"We're trying a lower altitude."

"I hate these damned solar flares. It's hideous, all of it. Hideous." She twisted about in her seat where she sat, a spidery old creature in silk and diamonds. She looked at him, suddenly as intent as a snake.

"Where's it all going to end, Doctor, do you know?"

"It'll fade away eventually."

"That's one opinion. But perhaps you haven't seen this."

She handed him a document in a beige folder. When he opened it, he saw red classified stamps.

"I can't read this."

She waved her fingers at him. "You'd better."

"I haven't got a clearance."

"Don't you understand, David? That doesn't matter anymore. All of that's gone."

The paper was only three pages long, a quick series of paragraphs. It was from the chairman of the National Security Council, directed to the president.

"Where did you get this?"

"Oh, for God's sake, young man, read the damn thing!"

According to the paper, the solar system was entering the atmosphere of a supernova—information which was hardly classified. Everybody knew it. But then came a more shocking sentence: "The last time we passed through this cloud 12,600 years ago, debris from the body of the exploded star impacted the glaciers. An area of the great northern glacier, the Laurentian ice sheet, was transformed from ice to superheated steam in under a second. This area was as large as Rhode Island and the impact resulted in enormous icebergs being thrown as far afield as New Mexico. A storm of smaller pieces created the million craters of the Carolina Dells."

Still, he was not surprised by this. Since the publication of Firestone, West, and Warwick-Smith's *Cycle of Cosmic Catastrophes* in 2006, it had been a generally known, if debated, explanation for the abrupt end of the Ice Age.

He read on.

"The ice melted so rapidly that the entire North American continent was flooded. In North America, all human life was destroyed. Elsewhere, man survived, and the catastrophe gave rise to all of the world's flood legends."

He looked up. She had knocked back his drink. She regarded him out of shadowed, appraising eyes.

"Does any of this ring a bell?"

"Sure. It's one of the theories about why the Ice Age ended. Why it would be classified, I can't imagine. It's been in the news for years."

"Read on."

"As our last advanced civilization was being destroyed by the upheaval, scientists made detailed observations of the stellar debris field. They mapped it and found it to be irregular in shape, and it became clear that we would reenter it in another twelve thousand years. But they could not pinpoint the exact date without taking extraordinary measures.

"There is evidence that they created some sort of substance that enabled them to see very accurately into time itself, and actually looked forward into the future to determine the precise moment of reentry.

"Whatever this was, it is why later users were able to draw glyphs of modern military equipment at the Temple of Hathor in Egypt. But more importantly, some truly exotic use of it may be why certain people, such as many of the priestly class in the late Mayan period, simply disappeared. They went elsewhere in time physically.

"So far, our efforts to determine what this was have failed.

"In any case, its use enabled the people of the past, at some very distant point, to make the exquisitely careful observations that pinpointed the precise date that the danger would return. They marked this as the final end of the world.

"However, they also understood that mankind had much history to live before that day came, and they realized that all of their learning centers, clustered as they were along shorelines that would soon be under hundreds of feet of water, were doomed. They created a calendar now called the Zodiac, that measured the ages. This was further refined as the Mayan Long Count calendar, which revealed the exact moment the solar system would re-enter the cloud.

The tone was ponderous with official importance. But there was a problem—it was based on an absurd notion.

"The ancient civilization they refer to—I assume they mean Atlantis? Plato's little speculation?"

"What do you remember?"

"About Atlantis? Nothing. It was before my time." His contempt was growing.

"Please keep reading, young man, if you don't mind."

As the jet sped on, its old engines blaring, its airframe shuddering, he returned to the document.

"The beginning of reentry was first detected as an increase in cosmic background radiation by Dimitriev in 1997. Then, precisely on

December 21, 2012, as the Mayan Long Count calendar suggested, an unusual spike took place. Since then, the density of the field has continued to grow, and all indications are that this will continue, possibly for thousands of years, with unknown consequences. In fact, the solar system is headed directly into the center of the cloud. In a very short time, we will begin to actually see the core of the exploded star, and it will be flooding Earth with radiation."

This last paragraph had changed his opinion of the document. In fact, he was eager now to know more and flipped the page—and sat staring at the back of the folder.

Mrs. Denman took it from his hands.

"Let me ask you this, David. Do you recall Herbert Acton? Bartholomew Light?"

"I want to know more about this document. Because if this last part is confirmed—"

"It's confirmed. Please answer my question."

"Who confirmed it? How?"

"The way you give me the space I need to address that is to answer my question."

"I know who Mr. Acton is, certainly."

"But you recall nothing else? No childhood memories?"

"Of Herbert Acton? Mrs. Denman, I was born in 1984. He'd been dead for—what? thirty years or more."

"Charles Light, Bartholomew's son?"

David was mystified. "No, I don't remember him. Should I?"

She reached over and touched his face, drawing her fingers along his cheek. It was an oddly suggestive sort of a thing to do, and David was embarrassed.

"As far as you're concerned, you were never at the home of Herbert Acton?"

"No."

She regarded him. "No memory at all?"

He shook his head.

A small, sad smile came into her eyes.

"There were thirty-three families, all associated with Herbert Acton in one way or another. Your family was one of them."

"My family?"

"Your great-grandfather sold Herbert Acton the land the estate is built on. That connects you."

"A very tenuous connection."

"You remember nothing of your childhood?"

"I remember my childhood perfectly well. I was raised in Bethesda. My father was a GP. He was a good doctor and I've been trying to be the same."

"But you don't remember Charles Light? Or the class? Or Caroline Light?"

"Absolutely not."

She smiled. "You will meet Caroline, and when you do, I'm sure it'll all come back to you. In any case, you were hired because it's time, and you've been carefully prepared."

He absorbed this last and most mysterious statement. When she had originally interviewed him, she had a list of obviously professionally written questions about medical qualifications. Frankly, she could have gotten them from any hospital personnel department, or even a book. He had thought her interview technique a poor one and had doubted her qualifications to select a physician provider for any decent sort of mental health facility. Now he really doubted those qualifications.

He'd also had the sense that his answers didn't matter to her, and even that she didn't understand his discussions of patient evaluation methodologies, the uses of the *Diagnostic and Statistical Manual of Mental Disorders*, his thoughts about drugs to be used and dosing, or, frankly, any of it.

No matter this document, whatever it might actually mean, he had no intention of proceeding if anything other than his professional qualifications had gone into his hiring. It was already a sticking point that she'd come to Manhattan Central and found him, even though he wasn't looking for work. First in his class at Johns Hopkins had been the stated reason.

"If you didn't hire me on my medical qualifications—"

"You have magnificent qualifications."

"Who is Caroline Light? What class?"

"Doctor, you will remember."

"No. I need to know right now or we need to turn around and go back to New York."

"You have nothing to go back to. You've resigned."

That was true enough. For everyone working just now, there were fifty ready to take his job, and his position at Manhattan Central had no doubt been filled within hours of his leaving.

"What class?"

"You were in a class as a child. On the Acton estate."

"That's impossible."

"That's what you say now, but you'll remember."

"Why would I forget?"

"Because if you had not been made to forget, you might have revealed something about an extremely sensitive matter. Any of you."

"*Any* of us? Of who?"

"The class!"

"I don't remember this class, Mrs. Denman, so I need you to explain it, please."

"David, the class is now assembled at the clinic. They will appear to be patients."

"*Appear to be?* Mrs. Denman, please. What am I getting into?"

"David, when you're at the clinic, you'll remember more on your own, and there will be somebody coming soon who'll help you remember everything."

If there was one thing he could not handle and had never been able to handle, it was helplessness. He needed to be in control of his life, and that was at the core of his willingness to take this job. He wouldn't be under control of a hospital administration, he would control one — or so he had thought.

"This is an outrage."

"Yes, it is, David. I admit it. You were always the only candidate for the job."

He could not turn back, that was clear. He did not relish ending up on the street just now. The world was starving and there was no recourse. Professionals were clawing for food alongside beggars.

"You've lied to me. In effect, kidnapped me."

"And who're you gonna call? The FBI?"

He waved the report. "I hope I'm not expected to deal with supply problems and survival issues, because this looks like a horrific disaster. Something way beyond the Acton Clinic."

"You have been trained to navigate us through this. You are uniquely qualified."

"I've had one class in disaster management. I treat psychiatric disease."

"You will remember. Trust me on that."

"Trust *you*?"

"You must understand —"

"I don't understand a thing!"

"Shut up, boy!"

"I will not shut up! I don't understand and I need to understand because you're dropping me into an incredibly challenging situation and at the same time telling me that I've somehow forgotten all the damn rules. Come on!"

The jet shuddered.

"Oh, God," she said. "I loathe air travel."

"It's starting to land, that's all. What am I supposed to remember?"

"David, let's please just get through the landing!"

"What in *hell* am I supposed to remember?"

She sighed. In her eyes he saw something beyond desperation, the expression of an animal that is dying and knows it has run out of options.

But then again, that was apparently the definition of the entire world, if this document of hers was to be believed. Everyone had been assuming that it would be like this another few weeks or months. Surely it would get better.

And surely it would. Earth wasn't descending into hell . . . was it?

As they banked, David could see the trees over northern Maryland brushed with fragile early spring leaf, a dusting of green not quite thick enough to camouflage the reality on the ground, of burned-out houses and strip malls, and abandoned vehicles along the roads.

Off to the west, he saw a large estate, a complex of shale roofs in lovely, manicured grounds. He could see figures on the grounds, a man riding a lawn tractor, two others walking along the curving driveway.

"Is that it?"

She jabbed the intercom. "How much longer, damn it?"

"Five minutes, Ma'am."

She regarded David. "I don't want to die. Isn't it odd? An old woman like me. So selfish."

He wasn't interested in her anxieties. "It's human nature," he snapped, causing her to blink and set her jaw. Well, let her be offended. "I need to get to the bottom of this," he continued. "Tell me about this class. And if I'm suffering from an amnesia, what was responsible or who? Was I underage? Did my parents consent?"

"Of course they did! Your father brought you to the class."

"I'm taking this job as a clinician, not a survival expert or whatever it is you expect me to be. I'm a psychiatrist and that's all I am."

"Think of yourself as a shepherd."

"All right. That's valid. But not a disaster expert."

"You're our Quetzalcoatl."

How tiresome. Since it had been realized that December 21, 2012, actually did have some significance, everyone was an expert on Aztec and Mayan civilization, and their dreary, complicated, and unforgiving gods.

"I am so tired of that stupid fad. Those damn gods didn't mean a thing."

"They had meaning."

"Come *on!*"

"Not in the way people think, of course. They represent scientific principles that have been lost. Human personality types, hidden powers. But you understand all this. You just need to remember, David."

"Remember *what?*"

They came in low over the estate, then banked again, this time quite sharply, resulting in an excellent view of the property.

Behind the shale roofs of what was obviously a very large mansion, stood an austere modern building. The whole establishment was surrounded by high brick walls.

"Is that razor wire on the walls?"

She peered out the window. "Looks like it. We have an excellent security organization. I'm sure it's there for good reason."

"I'm sure."

When they landed, what looked to David like an unusually heavy black car appeared, some sort of Lincoln, he thought. Andy the waiter opened the jet, dropping down the door and lowering the steps. David checked his watch. They'd been in the air for thirty-eight minutes, a journey that would have taken six hours by car, assuming the roads were open. But with all the disabled vehicles around nowadays, it could have easily taken a week, or proved to be impossible.

As they went down the steps, the pilot appeared.

"We need to keep moving," he shouted over the whine of the engines.

Andy was already putting David's bags in the trunk. Mrs. Denman had no bags. She was returning tonight.

David gazed off across the airport. There were a couple of Cessnas in tie-downs. The wreckage of two personal jets—newer than this one—lay piled alongside the runway.

"Get in the car!" Andy barked. David realized that he'd taken on a new role. In the air, he was a servant. Here, a bodyguard.

David jumped in. A moment later, the trunk slammed, the pilot returned to the jet and it took off, making the car shake violently as its exhaust hit the vehicle.

"Jesus, they're in a hurry!"

"There can be shooters," Mrs. Denman muttered.

"How dangerous is this place?"

She looked at him as if he was some sort of a lunatic for even needing to ask. Andy, now driving, did his job in silence.

"I have two hours. The plane will fly a pattern, then meet me back here. Not a good idea to keep it on the ground."

"No, I suppose not."

The car swayed, then picked up speed as it approached the town of Raleigh itself. David had never been here before, but had been told that it was a prosperous and settled community of upscale commuters and local gentry.

By the time they reached the outskirts of the town, the car was doing at least sixty. They accelerated as they went along the main street, tires screaming as they rounded courthouse square.

Buildings raced past on each side as Andy leaned on the horn and they shot through one red light after another.

"What's going on?"

"We call it 'running the town.'"

"But—Jesus . . ."

"There's a lot of inappropriate resentment."

At that moment, the car turned and slowed as it began moving, once again, through the countryside. "Cigarette?" Mrs. Denman asked, holding out a pack.

"I don't smoke."

She put it away. "Neither do I." She sighed.

Soon, David saw ahead of them a pair of enormously imposing gates. They were iron and easily twenty feet tall at their peaks. Across the top were four iron finials. On the finials, David recognized gryphons with their eagle's wings and lion's bodies, familiar, leering forms from the walls of Gothic cathedrals. Gryphons were guardians of the gates of heaven. Worked into the iron of the gates themselves were images of Mesoamerican deities—which was odd, given the age of this place. In the early twentieth century, they'd hardly been known.

"Are these gates new?"

"They're original to the estate."

As they opened and he saw the great house standing off across the rolling, exquisitely kept lawns, he was struck as if through the heart with the most poignant déjà vu.

"You're as white as a sheet, Doctor." She put the back of a long, spiderlike hand to his forehead. "No fever, at least, young man. Memory can bring fever."

"Stop the car."

"Ignore him, Andy."

"Stop the car! I'm not taking this job. No matter what, I'm going back to New York."

The car didn't even slow down, and as they approached the great redbrick house with its wide colonnade and broad terraces, the sense of déjà vu, rather than fading, became more acute.

"You feel it, don't you?"

"I feel very strange and I do not want to go ahead with this. I don't know what's going on here."

She laid a hand on his wrist. "Just relax and let yourself feel it. Memory will return." She leaned back and gave him a smile as broad as a child's. "You'll thank me, young man, when you do remember."

"Just tell me, for God's sake!"

"You have to make the connections yourself or they'll have no meaning. No emotional resonance. You need to find your commitment to your mission in your own heart. I cannot do it for you."

"But you know."

"I know that the class existed but not what you were taught in it. And

I also know that you just this moment remembered being here. It's written on your face."

They pulled up before the portico. David opened the door of the car, which was so heavy that it felt like pushing open a safe.

Walking toward the great house, he found himself profoundly drawn to the sense of order and permanence that pertained everywhere. The docile clicking of the lawn sprinklers, the early green of the trees, the grand apple tree just by the south wall in full bloom—it all spoke of a world that elsewhere had already slipped into the past, replaced by the sense of the posthumous that was coming to define modern life.

But it was also part of *his* past. His own personal past belonged in some way to this place.

Aubrey Denman opened the front door using a fingerprint detector. He'd half expected the great door to be swept open by some sort of butler. Instead, an armed security man in a blazer and tie greeted them. Obviously, his orders were to wait until the fingerprint reader had released the lock.

"Where are the—" David's voice died. He had been about to ask where the patients and staff were, but the splendor of the room he had just entered silenced him. He found himself looking across a wide hall with a magnificent inlaid floor depicting a hunt in full cry. It was marquetry, and yet not too fragile for a floor.

And, incredibly, he remembered: *You slid across this floor in your socks.*

The leaping horses and racing dogs in the floor led the eye to a grand staircase that swept upward as if to heaven itself, drawing the eye further, this time to a phenomenal trompe l'oeil ceiling that imparted an unforgettable illusion of a vast summer sky.

You lay on the landing and imagined yourself among the birds.

"Where are my patients?"

"The patients are in the patient wing. Study the records first, Doctor, please. Then meet them."

"Will they know me? Are they also in amnesia?"

"They're in a state of induced psychosis."

He stopped. "What did you just say?"

"For security reasons, this place appears to be a clinic for the mentally ill. Most members of the class are here as patients, their real selves hidden beneath a combination of amnesia and artificial psychosis. Members of the class who are on staff have only the amnesia, and one or two of them, who will guide the others, retain clear memory."

He turned to her, and on her. "This is totally unacceptable. Who did such a thing to these people? I can't be a party to it."

"You can be a party to waking them up, then, and ending the need."

"This is all insane, the whole thing. Who would *ever* induce mental illness to conceal somebody's—what, their knowledge, their identity? Why was it done?"

"The enemies of our mission are incredibly ruthless and they're going to get more so. If they found the class, they'd kill every single one of them. And you, David, make no mistake. But beforehand they would tear your mind to pieces with drugs and torture beyond anything you can imagine. And in the end, they would obtain your knowledge, amnesia or not."

Never in his life had he struck another human being, but he was tempted to now, as he found himself coping with a disturbing impulse to shake the truth out of this old lady.

"Who are these enemies?"

"Presidents, kings, the rich and the famous, not to mention the members of the Seven Families who control the wealth of this planet."

"I have no idea what you're talking about."

"The more you remember, the more you'll understand. Come with me. My time is short, and I need to show you your office." She touched his hand. "David, you'll regain control of your situation and I know how badly you need control; I wrote your personality profile."

"*Wrote* it? Where is it? How could you write it?"

"I'm a psychiatrist, David, just like you. I managed the mental health of the class."

"You did this to these people!"

Her eyes sought his, and in them, brown and hazed, he saw that hunted expression again.

"How did you do it? What method did you use?"

As if in shame, she turned away from him, and he knew that whatever she had done had been traumatic for all involved, including her.

Causing amnesia was a matter of hypnosis and drugs, but to make a person psychotic must be a ferocious process.

"How can they be released from this?"

"I'll come back, and I'll release them."

"When?"

"We're working on a very exact timeline. But I can assure you that it will be done."

"Wait a minute. What timeline? I need to know!"

"If somebody who knew that was caught, it would be an incalculable disaster."

"Caught? Could I be *caught*? By whom? Who are these enemies? Are they here?" He followed her up the staircase. "Damn it, I want answers!"

She mounted the stairs with the deliberation of a heart patient, her nostrils dilating as she sucked each careful breath.

"The house itself is lived in by staff and service. The patients are in the back, in the new wing."

"Answer my questions!"

"Time will answer your questions."

"Too damn late!"

"At exactly the right moment. Now, please focus on this. You'll meet your staff later, then be introduced to the patients. I want to talk to you about your colleague Marian Hunt before you meet her."

She stopped before an imposing mahogany door.

"Are you ready?" When she smiled, that expression came again.

The office was gigantic.

"I can't work in this. It's ridiculous."

"Nonsense. You ought to be grateful to be surrounded by all this beauty."

It was the size of a ballroom, but constructed out of mahogany inlaid with many other woods. A broad bank of windows looked south, another north, and the walls were lined with shelves and shelves of books, all old, all leather bound. An immense Persian rug filled this end of the room, under an equally huge and ornate desk. At the other was a fireplace fronted by a leather couch and wing chairs. In the paneling above the door were two glyphs of Mesoamerican gods, exquisitely carved, their faces glaring and ferocious.

"Who are they?" he asked.

"What principles do they represent? I haven't the faintest idea."

"I thought you were an expert on Aztec crap."

"Thank you. Each of us knows only what he needs to know."

Unlike the downstairs, he had no sense of déjà vu about this room. He surveyed the library. Every shelf was filled.

"Is there room for my books?"

She pulled down a row of what turned out to be book backs, revealing some empty shelving.

"Your predecessor kept his here."

"Ah. Is the whole library fake, then?"

"Hardly. There are some extraordinary texts here."

She handed him a volume with a gold-embossed glyph on the spine. He opened it to magnificent color plates of glyphs, hundreds of them.

"It's entirely in . . . what is this? Is it Mayan? Toltec?"

She looked at it. "You'll have access to scholars."

"Where?"

"Here. Among your class."

His only choice, he saw, was to just roll with this. There was no question in his mind that, as a child, he'd been to this house. Certainly, he had seen the downstairs. But what this class was all about, and why the security, he could not imagine—or rather, he supposed, remember.

Or could he? There might be vague memories in the back of his mind of the names of the old gods. But it was also true that their names were everywhere these days. And yet, he recalled other children, and being happy here.

He remembered, also, that there had been an enormous security issue.

"We need to discuss Marian Hunt."

"Yes. She's been assistant director here for what, ten years?"

"Since it opened."

"Then surely she was the ideal choice for director."

"She wasn't part of the class. But she doesn't know that and cannot know it; so as far as she's concerned, she's been passed over for a mere boy."

"If the board doesn't have faith in her, perhaps she would've been better off leaving."

"Where would she go?"

A question without an answer. Or no, it did have an answer: she would go nowhere.

"Let me show you the surveillance toys," Mrs. Denman said. "Every patient is available to total monitoring." She pressed her finger against a discreet fingerprint reader embedded in the bookcase beside his desk. Two more shelves of fake books slid away to reveal a very large screen populated by dozens of small video images revealing what he felt sure would turn out to be every inch of the public spaces in the facility, indoors and out.

She touched a button and new rows of images appeared.

"These are the patient social areas," she said. She tapped one of the images, which expanded to fill the screen.

For a moment, David did not understand what he was seeing. Then he did, and he was so shocked that he must have gasped aloud, because Aubrey Denman's bird head snapped toward him, and the expression of fear on her face was almost as appalling as the straitjacket confining the patient.

At Manhattan Central, he'd seen patients under restraint, of course, but not being kept in one of these things. If not illegal, it was certainly a spectacular medical failure.

"I can't allow that," he said.

There were three patients in a sunny, pleasant room. Each one had a nurse in attendance, not surprising in a facility that offered the extreme level of care found at the Acton Clinic. But one of them was in this primitive restraint.

"He's unable to bear . . . anything. At any moment he'll just lose himself."

"Do you know him?"

Her eyes closed, she gave a slow nod, one that communicated a sense of the anguish that her work clearly caused her. "There has been a great deal of sacrifice here, David. Lives sacrificed—the happiness of youth, David—all for the mission."

"Which is what?"

"David," she said, "the future. The *future!*"

She took his hand—snatched it—grasping it as if it was a lifeline in a storm. And suddenly, there came a memory.

He was trying urgently to explain something to a tall man, and to emphasize his point, he had grabbed this man's hand.

"I told him I couldn't do it. I told him!"

"But you can, David." She glanced at her watch. "I'm out of time."

He would have to keep his questions and his considerable doubts to himself. But he did not agree with her optimism, not at all. How could anybody save anything, given what was coming?

Well, perhaps he had a mentor in her. She was hardly the wealthy old fool she had initially seemed.

"You'll be back," he said. It was not a question, and not intended to be one.

"Of course. And I'm always available on my cell."

"I need to get to know my staff," he said, "and the class. Who are my classmates?"

"There will be somebody coming to help you. Until they arrive, don't breathe a word about the class, not a single word."

"I'm sitting on top of an institution full of people who've been spectacularly abused and I'm not supposed to even *say* anything about it? I don't think so." He gestured toward the screen. "What about them, are they members of the class?"

"Two of them. The other is genuinely disturbed."

"And you did this. It's appalling."

"David, we did what we had to. Without security this deep the class would have been found. That must not happen, David, it *must not.*"

"What's so important about them? I'm sorry if I sound callous, but I really need to know why, in a world where billions are dying, a small group of people would need to be so carefully protected?"

She closed the control center. "Call a staff meeting, but I'd advise you to move carefully. After Marian, your next order of business will be to meet Katrina Starnes. Katie. She's your assistant."

"Isn't it rather odd that she's not here now?"

She gestured toward the book backs that concealed the electronic wonders. "She's not a member of the class. She isn't allowed access to this system or to know anything about the inner meaning of this place."

"Which is what? I still don't understand."

"No, of course not."

The moment he had experienced the déjà vu that had convinced him that he had been in this house before, he had made the decision to let this play out. These vague, amnesia-stifled memories he was experiencing were really very strange, and, if they were true, then he was potentially looking at a whole hidden life, and he had no intention of not exploring it.

"I need to know more. A lot more. Are there any records of what we studied in the class? Video? Even just a syllabus. What did we study?"

"I need to leave."

"Oh, wonderful! Leave me with an insoluble mystery and an institution to run during the worst social collapse since the fall of the Roman Empire."

"Your memories will come back to you."

"And if they don't?"

"Oh, they must! Young man, you see the stakes. They *must!*"

A moment later, she was heading toward the door of the office. He was appalled.

"What about Dr. Ullman? Was the fire really an accident? Am I in danger?"

For a long moment, she was silent. Then she said, "David, we don't know. Maybe it was a fire set by resentful townies. Could be. Or it could be something worse."

"I need to know more!"

"You have your security force and Glen MacNamara is very, very good at what he does. Start there."

As she spoke, she hurried away across the large room.

"Wait! The fingerprint reader? How do I get programmed into it?"

"You're already in it."

"Nobody took my fingerprints."

"Of course they did—in class. Your fingerprints, your DNA, we have it all."

She neither spoke again, nor wished him well, smiled—any of it. She simply went stalking off down the hall.

Her hidden timeline was strict, clearly.

"Mrs. Denman, wait! I need help! I need my questions answered!"

Her footsteps sounded on the stairs, quick, clattering away into the silence of the house.

As he heard the enormous car start up outside, he ran down the stairs, but by the time he reached the front of the building, she was already well down the driveway.

He yanked his cell phone out of his pocket and jammed her number in—and got nothing. The damn phone was deader than dead. He glanced up at the spotted, angry sun and threw it down onto the elegant brick driveway.

A moment later, there was a flash, followed at once by a sound so loud that it was like a body blow from a wrecking ball, an enormous, thundering roar.

He had never been close to a large explosion, and so did not know the effects and did not immediately understand what was happening. Then he did.

Shocked, disbelieving, he watched the smoke rising. She had been right and more than right. This place had enemies, and so did he. And he felt sure that they had just taken from him his most important ally.

From behind him, a siren began to wail. No police came, though, no fire department, no EMS. The siren was the clinic's alert system, and it would be the only siren, because the Acton Clinic was alone. And he was alone, and they were all alone.

Not their enemies, though, hidden, aggressive, and lethally effective. Obviously, they were not alone.

2

THE ENEMY

In the disoriented silence that followed, a fireball erupted above the wall from the other side, then disappeared into the roiling pillar of black smoke. The car's gas tank had exploded, ending any thought that its armor might somehow have protected the occupants.

Two white Jeeps came bounding down the driveway, with discreet ACTON SECURITY signs on their doors. They raced through the gate.

Finally absorbing the reality of the situation, David began running behind them. At once, though, powerful arms stopped him. He struggled but he could not escape from hands like great stones.

"You can't help her now."

Then another man ran past them, a tall man in an improbably elegant green crushed-silk suit.

"Mack, stop," the man holding David shouted. "STOP THERE!" Then, more softly, "Shit!"

A small fire truck left the gate, and a moment later white steam began rising, and the sound of water hissing from its pump.

The man holding him released his grip. "I'm Glen MacNamara," he said as David turned around. David was startled by a sense of recognition. He'd seen Glen before. His voice, even, contained an echo of familiarity.

"I'm David Ford."

The patient called Mack came back with his minder, who was introduced by MacNamara as Sam Taylor.

"I'm sorry I manhandled you like that, Doctor," Glen said between breaths. He was pale, his eyes shocked. He looked to Taylor, who shook his head. No survivors.

"The car—you mean Mrs. Denman's car? That's what blew up?"

All three men, Sam, Glen MacNamara, and the patient, looked at him with careful eyes.

"It was a bomb," Mack said.

Aubrey Denman had certainly been right that there was a security problem, but this was far, far worse even than her warning had suggested.

"They've been killed," he said faintly, trying to grasp the catastrophe, trying to understand. But he could not understand, could not even begin to. "Why? An old lady like that? *Why?*"

"Doctor," Glen MacNamara said, "I'd feel a lot better if we could go inside."

Two security guards went toward the gate carrying freshly opened body bags.

"Don't bag them until I've inspected," Glen said. "I'll be back shortly."

Glen insisted on accompanying him to the house.

"I need to get in touch with the rest of the board," David said.

"You'd best ask Katie Starnes about that."

The tone of Glen's voice, his choice of words, brought more recognition. Normally, he would have simply asked him outright if he'd been in the class, but he wasn't about to do that now.

"Glen, you look familiar. Have we met before?"

Glen stared back, his eyes steady.

"We have, haven't we?"

He did not say no.

"And you remember, and thank God. What else do you remember?"

Glen grabbed his shoulder so hard he stopped talking immediately.

"Never speak about it," he said.

"No, obviously not directly."

"Not at all."

As they walked, Glen took something from his pocket, then slipped it into David's hand. David felt a small capsule.

"If you're captured, bite down on it and breathe deeply. It takes ten seconds. No pain."

"But—"

"Do it without fail."

He jammed the thing down into his pocket, and then they were through the main door and immediately confronting a silent, frightened crowd.

Staffers, patients, workers—the whole front half of the house was filled with people. A couple of security men kept them back.

David realized that he was going to have to make an introduction of himself here and now. No waiting on this.

He raised his voice. "Obviously a tragedy," he said. He found himself clutching the cyanide capsule, as if it represented rescue, or needed protection. Then, afraid that it might open, he took his hand out of his pocket.

A sea of faces, eyes wide, silent, looked back at him. Here and there, somebody exhibited inappropriate behavior, grinning, bobbing their head, dancing to some inner music.

But these people weren't really crazy, at least not all of them. Induced psychosis as a means of concealment. And now what was he to do?

"I'm Dr. Ford. David Ford. I'm your new chief psychiatrist. I—we—we—" But what did he say? "The security team will handle this," he finally blurted out. "Mr. MacNamara—here—here he is."

Now, there was a great speech. Very dynamic and take-charge. Idiotic.

"Thank you, Dr. Ford. We've informed the Raleigh County Sheriff's Office," he told them. "Right now, we're assuming that criminal activity was involved." He drew himself up. "There will be an investigation. The perpetrator will be found."

"Was it one of us?" a voice called.

"There will be an investigation. That's all. Thank you."

David said, "Attendants, please accompany the patients back to routine. Back to routine, please."

He went slowly up the grand staircase, into the fabulous painted sky, with its birds and its heavenly clouds.

I made believe I could hear those birds sing.

He had never felt this alone. He had not known that such a feeling—like falling and being buried alive at the same time—was possible.

He entered his office, filling now with evening shadows, as silent as death.

There was one *hell* of a security problem here, and Jesus, he had to be a prime target. That other guy—Ullman—had been burned to death. *Burned.*

His stomach was sharp with acid, his mind racing. He needed a gun, he needed a bodyguard, but how to tell who was reliable?

Then he realized that somebody was in the room. He turned. A lovely young woman had entered and was standing in the doorway, silently watching him.

"Hello."

"I'm Katie Starnes."

That was to be their only introduction.

"Miss Starnes, I want a list of all the other members of the board. And I want us to start trying to get in touch with them immediately."

She stared at him.

"Please!"

"Dr. Ford, there are no other members of the board. Mrs. Denman—she's the board."

"That's impossible!"

"I'm sorry."

"Then get hold of her secretary, her accountant, whoever you can locate. I need to talk to anyone I can!"

"We only have the one number."

"That can't be true!"

"We only have the one number!"

"What about her bank? Call her bank, call her lawyer!"

She shook her head, her eyes full of fear. "We only have the one number, I'm sorry. Security here—"

"Is very damn tight but very damn poor!"

And what were his alternatives now?

That, at least, was one question with a perfectly clear answer: he had no alternatives. He was trapped.

DAVID FORD'S JOURNAL: ONE

I have never been so scared in my life, so confused in my life, so apprehensive in my life. I'd take mood regulators but they're out of supply, and anyway, I can't afford to lose whatever pitiful edge I may have.

The clinic is full of guns, and I have been issued a weapon. It's a compact thing, a Beretta. Can I use it? I don't know, I've never shot a gun in my life.

I tell myself that I don't know enough to matter, that I'd never need to use the gun or the cyanide, but then I look into the well of my own mind, and I know that there is amnesia there, and suspect that a skilled interrogator could break it. Psychosomatic amnesia is nothing more than a refusal to access certain memories, which remain intact beneath the surface.

How, without Mrs. Denman, do I repair my broken classmates, not to mention find them in the first place? There isn't any literature on the induction of psychosis—at least, in the public domain. Probably reams of it in the classified world.

I am keeping up as best I can with outside events, but communications are sporadic. For example, the Internet has been intermittent for days and so far cell phone coverage has not returned since this morning. Given that they're so entangled with the Internet, landlines are unreliable. In the past, they survived all but the most extreme catastrophes. No more.

In a world going out of control, an organization like this is highly vulnerable. We are suffering every kind of shortage, including drugs. For example, we have no atypical antipsychotics left. No clozapine, no risperidone, no nothing. Because of the youth of most of our patients, the lack of Risperdal is particularly distressing. We have Xanax, but that's hardly adequate.

Many of the patients I have met display very structured, relentlessly typical symptoms. They're like actors who have been captured by their roles. I suppose that this is induced psychosis.

It's not that they all exhibit the same symptoms or should receive the same diagnosis—but there is a strange by-the-book quality about them, as if they'd stepped right out of the *Diagnostic and Statistical Manual*.

As conditions deteriorate, what do I do with patients who I know to be imprisoned by artificially induced mental illness? What if the death of Mrs. Denman means that we will never get the information we need to draw people out of their psychoses?

It's late, and auroras are appearing, even this far south. The sun must be literally blazing for this to happen. They are a bizarre emerald green and flickering like a broken lightbulb. Across the room, the shadows are deep, and I dread going through them to get to my bedroom.

And why should I? I don't sleep, how can I?

My head is on the block. I await the stroke of the axe.

3

MACK THE CAT

Michael Graham—who had called himself Mack the Cat ever since he came to be nicknamed "el Gato" by his colleagues at the Mexico City station—drew on the notepad that the doctors had agreed not to look at—but, of course, did . . . as he expected them to. If he was supposed to be crazy, he needed to exhibit symptoms, and doctors loved drawings.

He was encouraged by the ease and success of the Denman operation, which had trapped these bastards like a maze full of rats. She'd been a fool to be so controlling that their whole operation depended on her.

Buried in this place as he was, it was easy to forget that he had been assigned to the Acton Clinic, not committed to it. He was a specialist in stealth, and this was not only a place of interest for his superior, General Wylie, it was packed with exotic security. So he'd been given a false past that would allow him entry, and sent here to find what the general needed.

He tried to be professional and dispassionate, doing his work with clarity and efficiency. But he could not help hating these arrogant people. Filthy half-breeds all, chosen by that obscene fool Herbert Acton to represent the common man.

The common man was the goddamn problem. Blood is what counts, and this was the time to save the best human blood. Let the common man die; he'd shown himself to be a weak, ignorant fool.

The Acton Clinic had looked easy to deal with, but this was among the most difficult situations he had ever confronted, and despite the success of the Denman operation, he was still having trouble making progress understanding exactly what they were doing here—and therein, of course, lay the key. They had a means of survival, or believed that they did. But what was it?

Every night he got an increasingly urgent demand for that information from General Wylie.

He sat beneath the apple tree that grew near the enormous oak at the edge of the grounds, his back against the sweating bricks of the wall, in the shade of the oak and the scent of apple blossom.

The sky was a shimmering electric yellow, and last night the auroras had been intense. So the sense of urgency around here was right. Time was running out.

He was supposed to be not only crazy but dangerous, so he had a minder, Sam Taylor. He sat under the tree drawing a glyph of a *tzitzimitl*, a skeleton demon of the stars that governed the sun at times like this. Death star. Everyone in the world by now was well aware of the fact that this present disaster had begun to unfold during the night of December 21, 2012, and people were obsessed with the Mayan and Aztec religions, and with their calendars and their prophecies. So he was just another stupid patient, chewing the fad.

A lot of people had suspected that Herbert Acton had possessed some sort of secret beyond his uncanny skills as a speculator. He had been approached by occultist J. P. Morgan and by John D. Rockefeller, by representatives of Presidents Harding, Coolidge, Hoover, and the Masonic master Franklin Delano Roosevelt, all without any results. Also by leaders of half a dozen of the truly important human organizations—the Thule Society, the Society of the Illuminated, the New Knights Templar, the Vatican—and representatives of the best and truest human bloodlines, especially the Seven Families to whom this world belongs.

He must have been offered astonishing rewards—but he would have none of it. He lived on his estate and did his business and ignored the world around him. When everyone was sending gold to Germany, seeking to save the bloodlines of the best people from the catastrophe, Acton had spent his time assembling his collection of mongrels and irrelevant, disposable people. After the war, when money had been desperately needed by the Germans to establish colonies in South America to provide shelter for those who had given their loyalty to Hitler, he had funded the ridiculous intelligence service of the Israelis, adding immeasurably to the expense of protecting what remained of the great bloodlines.

Now the children of the collection of mutts Acton had assembled were believed to possess his secrets, and therefore quite possibly the means to survive the coming catastrophe, while the people who mattered did not.

The intensification of the auroras last night, the increasing deterioration of electronics, even the bizarre color of the sky right now—it all suggested to Mack that the climax was unfolding.

General Wylie, commanding from the Blue Ridge Redoubt seventy miles from here in West Virginia, obviously agreed with him, thus the increasing urgency on the radio.

Massive efforts had been made, whole cities built underground in Arizona, in the Blue Ridge Mountains, in the Black Forest and the North York Moors, in the Gran Chaco in Uruguay and the Maule Region of Chile. A hundred thousand people had been tagged for access to these refuges. All well and good, but something more had to be done to insure survival, something beyond present knowledge.

Suddenly, Sam was there. "Doing okay?"

"I'm plotting my escape."

"Ah." He looked at the drawing. "Who's that this time?"

"God of destruction."

"Pretty."

He finished his drawing and then, staring straight up at Sam, ate the paper.

Mack was just getting up to follow Sam inside when he heard a very surprising and very interesting sound, the whine of the main gate sliding back on its hinges.

He noticed that Sam came a couple of steps closer to him. Could this be police, perhaps? If they still existed, that might be inconvenient.

A Mercedes came nosing slowly into the estate. A new victim being brought in? That seemed unlikely at this juncture. To get here through all the chaos in the world took significant resources. Even the rich were more likely to stash their crazies in the attic, he would think.

The car proceeded up the long drive with the grim majesty of a hearse. No, this would not be a garden-variety crazy. This might well be a crown jewel, a member of the hidden leadership, someone whose knowledge had not been obscured by artificial psychosis—that is to say, someone who was in possession of their information and therefore useful.

So there were perhaps now two, David Ford and this new one. And, of course, MacNamara, that bastard. He knew a lot, that one, Mack had always sensed it.

He glanced across at Sam Taylor, who had returned to his bench and his thermos of coffee. Yesterday, Sam had been the victim of a little sleight of hand. He'd never seen Mack trigger the mine with his cell phone. The towers were out of commission, but the radio receiver on the mine was only a few hundred feet away. One of the general's men had buried it two days ago.

So far, there was no suspicion of the CIA officer who'd gone mad in Mexico and started sacrificing drug mules to the old gods.

He lay back and gazed up into the spray of pale pink flowers that crowded the apple boughs, putting on a show of nonchalance. Above and behind the tree, he could see the top of the wall. The gleam of the new razor wire winked down.

He heard the car's engine stop, and he knew that it was about to disgorge its occupant. And, indeed, one of the rear doors opened a little. The driver got out and came around.

A girl emerged, tall, unfolding herself and shaking her shoulders and her hair as if today's sunlight was her first.

She was auburn-haired, tanned, and—well, was the word "ineffable?" There was a sense of air in the way she moved, and yet something about her said that she was used to being in control of her life and her world.

She did not look insane, or even particularly troubled, which he found most interesting.

She paused for a moment before the great façade of the mansion, put her hands on her hips and gazed at it. Well, it was normal enough for a person to be impressed by the row of columns, the red brick of the façade, the imposing doors . . . for a normal person, in any case.

Then, determined and yet hesitant—a complicated human being, he saw that at once—she went inside.

He needed a surname, and right now, but the secrecy of their operation was so extreme this might be hard to obtain. In fact, the secrecy was so deep that these people, who had been together in a childhood class run by Charles Light, the son of Bartholomew, were in a state of amnesia more profound even than the CIA could induce.

They were not insane, but they believed that they were, and *that* was security at its extraordinary best.

He watched the newbie, who had reappeared quickly after her entry into the building. She went off toward the gate, a curving pour of very feminine milk.

She stopped before the enormous iron bars. Nurse Cross strode across the deep green of the lawn and conducted her back to the building. The newbie's sobs tumbled through the air.

Was this just a patient?

As Beverly Cross tried to get her to enter the building, she shook her off and stepped out along the brick terrace that spread so elegantly beneath the front of the structure.

She took out a cigarette. She puffed, he watched. Puff, white smoke, hold the cigarette aside, puff, white smoke, hold the cigarette aside.

And then, quite suddenly, he was surrounded by the color red. All around him, a rose-red haze. Sunset? No, something else. He tried to wave it away, but found that he couldn't move his arms.

That scared him and he cried out, whereupon he felt warmth on his forehead and a voice, young, female, said, "You're fine, Mack, you've just been finishing."

The taste of rubber from the mouth guard caused him to realize that he'd been in shock therapy.

"How do you feel, Mack?" the nurse asked.

As he sucked in breath, the room appeared around him, all tile and dismal machines. Across the way, a hydro tub moaned and splashed. The head of Glenda Futterman bobbed back and forth, as frantic as an agitated waterbird of some sort.

"Mack?"

"I'm coming out of it!" He gazed around at the room. "I'm sorry. I thought I was . . . outside."

"Earlier you were."

"Did I dream about a girl? A beautiful girl?"

"She's a new intake. Very real. You saw her come in."

When he tried to get off the table, Dr. Ford said, "Not yet, guy."

It was so damnable to have to endure their ridiculous treatments, but what could he do? This was the deepest possible cover he could create for himself, and the danger that he might be discovered was too great. So he endured the stupid indignity of taking electroshock treatment that he did not need.

The treatment made him forget a lot of things, sometimes too many things. He kept careful notes hidden in his room, but they might eventually be found, he knew that. So speed was essential. He needed to complete his mission, which had two parts. First, find out whatever was hidden here so well, so that it could be taken and used by the people who mattered. Then, the pleasant part: destroy this place.

4

THE LADY OF THE STARRY SKIRT

External conditions were deteriorating far more rapidly than David had imagined possible, and the problems this was causing forced him to put his effort to unravel the mysteries of this place aside for the moment. The blackened bodies of Aubrey Denman and her failed protector had been given a quick burial at the end of the estate's formal garden.

He went to his windows, gazing out across the green lawn to the two rough mounds of earth. Close to them, an apple tree bloomed. It reminded him of something, but not something pleasant.

"The apple blossom is the color of . . ." What? It was blank, so he left it. But it was disquieting.

A little farther along, an oak spread spring leaves, their pale new green at once reassuring and heartbreaking.

If you did not raise your eyes, all appeared normal and settled and safe. Look up to the top of the perimeter wall, though, and you saw that razor wire. By reading the clinic's activity logs, he'd discovered that Aubrey Denman had not been candid with him about much of anything, and certainly not the security situation, which was far worse than she had claimed—or, it would seem, known.

The razor wire was there because there had been an incursion from the town. People had tried to come over the wall. They'd been forced back and additional defensive measures had been taken, including the acquisition of some very powerful new guns, and thousands of rounds of ammunition.

Look past the wire, though, and a magnificent view of Raleigh County unfolded, the rolling hills brushed now with palest green. Only if you looked closely would you see a blackened house here or there.

The sky was now always that odd color, no longer the blue it had been. Really, not a color, more of an absence of color, a steely whiteness during the day, flickering auroras at night.

The lawn sprinklers came on, clicking smartly. It was a sound from childhood, which the child in him found reassuring, he supposed. But where did they get the water? he wondered. Hopefully, from a well on the grounds.

Katie Starnes's voice came over the intercom. "The new intake's in prep."

"Bring in her chart, please."

When he saw the name on her chart, he was stunned to frozen stillness. He kept his voice as calm as he could.

"What's her state?"

"Agitated. But it's a self-commit, so we're expecting her to be cooperative."

"Expect nothing."

"Yes, Doctor."

Aubrey Denman had said that he would remember Caroline Light, and that she would bring some focus to this whole affair. But it was just a name on a sheet of paper. Seeing her, that must be what would do it.

"Schizoaffective disorder, previously controlled with lithium therapy," Katie said.

He was careful to reveal nothing to her of what the name meant to him, or of his excitement that this was the daughter of their teacher.

He read on. She'd lived a wealthy easy life, it seemed, up until symptoms began to appear last year.

This sounded a troubling note. Aubrey Denman had induced psychosis in the class during their late teens, not last year, or so he'd assumed. So was this a real case of mental illness, some sort of odd coincidence? Or was she simply playacting? Because this report gave no indication that any symptom had been present before 2019.

Sudden onset of mental illness was commonplace now. The whole human species was under extraordinary stress. That was why Manhattan Central had literally been overflowing into the streets. So it was perfectly possible that the daughter of their teacher had, quite simply, gone mad.

But it was just as possible that something else was happening, so his only choice was to play it as it appeared.

The report said that her disorder had begun to break through the lithium, in the form of auditory hallucinations ordering the patient to do various things—paint a picture, take a journey to some irrelevant spot, arm herself with a pistol.

At what must have been astronomical expense, she had made the pilots of her family plane fly her to Guatemala, where she'd chartered a local plane to take her deep into the jungle. What she had done there was not clear, nor had she been willing to explain herself when she returned home.

Herbert Acton and Bartholomew Light had gone to Guatemala in the twenties, and brought back extensive journals, drawings, and maps that filled many shelves in this library.

"I want her housed initially on confinement, but give her full indoor privileges with observation. Outdoors accompanied only."

"Awfully tight supervision," Katie commented.

Caroline Light's vulnerabilities were complex. Whether she was acting or genuinely troubled, with that last name, she was probably of as much interest to the opposition as Aubrey Denman. More, conceivably.

"In my opinion, it's necessary. And keep her surname confidential, please."

"We never use patient surnames in population."

"Not even in her chart. Call her—I don't know—Caroline Smith."

"Of course, Doctor."

Her tone was too neutral. He thought it concealing, but of what he could not be sure.

The door flew open and Caroline Light came striding in, a breathtaking beauty, her legs outlined by her blue silk dress, which fluttered behind her as she walked forward.

He felt a sensation of literal, physical shock pass through him as she got closer. Her eyes were jewels flashing light, her skin tanned but soft, her lips at once held in a tight, angry line and yet ready, almost, to laugh. The eyes, made brighter by the darkness of her full lashes, glared, stared, and mocked all at once.

Behind that complex, challenging expression, though, was a face of heartbreaking beauty, the forehead broad, the eyes shaped for night-time, the nose tapering but not severe, the cheeks full but not so full that they concealed the suggestive curve of the cheekbones.

However, the memory he had hoped she would spark did not come. There was no sense of déjà vu, no poignant quickening of the heart. She was, simply, a stranger.

As Katie discreetly withdrew, she sat down, crossed her knees, and regarded him with pale eyes. Was that anger in there? Amusement? Both?

"At last," she said.

He thought it the most disconcerting comment she could possibly have made.

"Have we met?"

She flushed, then tossed her head like a young mare. He had the impression that she was both furious and hurt.

"Okay, let's do our medical interview. See how good we are." Long hands dipped into a purse made of what looked like some sort of cloud, white and soft. She drew out a cigarette.

"No smoking in the facility, I'm sorry."

She lit it, took a long drag, then expelled two streams of smoke through her nose, an exquisite dragon. She glanced around.

"What is this dump, anyway?"

"The Acton Clinic. Do you often lose track of where you are?"

"I mean the room. Of course I know where I am." She barked out a laugh. "David, are you still asleep?"

He wanted to open up to her, but he couldn't, not without some inner signal, some echo of recognition, and there was none. He maintained his professional posture.

"What do you mean by sleep?"

"You can take your shrink questions, fold 'em up, and stuff 'em you know where."

"Which would be?"

She flipped the cigarette at him. It hit his shoulder and bounced to the floor.

"That was useful."

"David, you're embarrassing yourself and—to be frank—hurting me."

"In what sense?"

"Stop it!"

He was really having trouble here. He was strongly attracted to her, that was certain, but there just was no memory.

"Those images over the door, I'll give odds you don't know what they are," she said.

"I do not."

"Well, I do, because my grandfather was the man who discovered them. *In tetu inan, in tetu itah.* That's Nahuatl for 'father and mother of the gods.' Ometeotl was two in one, mother and father."

"Is this why you went to Guatemala? Are you a believer?"

"What do you think?" Her tone was knife-edged with sarcasm.

"That's for you to say, Caroline."

Her eyes became sad. "You need to remember something, David."

This was a subtle mind, quick and supple, and it was testing him, but in what sense? Was the real Caroline Light trying to find out if he remembered her, or was an imposter trying to determine if he'd been in the class?

"What about myself do I need to remember?"

She lit another cigarette. "Shall we do sex talk?"

"Shall we?"

"Isn't that what you do here?"

"This is a hospital you're in, Caroline. It's a place where people who are suffering come for relief. Which is why you checked yourself in, I would think. What do you think?"

"That I need an ashtray."

"There isn't one."

She flicked ash on the carpet. "This is a Tabriz, probably a Hajii-jalili, and look at the abrash. Gorgeous." She smiled a little, then, and her face became soft with promise. Really, she was meltingly beautiful. "I always wondered what it was like up here. Remember the time we tried to sneak up and old Mrs. Acton got mad and threatened to spank us? She lived to a hundred and three, did you know that?"

"Under the terms of the transfer, we can't alter the décor in these rooms. That's why the rug is still here."

"How strangely colorless you've become, David. You're not in total amnesia, though. I can see it in your eyes."

She stood up and came around the desk. He stood, also, and suddenly they were quite close, and the attraction was powerful. He cleared a dry throat.

"Maybe I've always been a colorless bureaucratic type. By your definition, anyway."

Fingers brushed his forearm, a seemingly innocuous gesture that was surprisingly intimate.

"We know each other, David, and we have made promises, and even if your mind is in denial, your body knows it." She gestured toward the images over the door. "They mark this as a sacred space. Worthy abode of the Plumed Serpent, for example. Quetzalcoatl. Does that ring a bell with you?"

Vaguely, he recalled talk of the Mexican gods in the class.

He cleared his throat. "The situation—the disturbed sun, the coincidence of the dates, all of that—has caused a significant minority of patients to integrate Mayan cosmology into their fantasy production. We psychiatrists used to get Hitlers and JFKs and Napoleons. Now, it's Tlalocs and Quetzalcoatls. So yes, I am indeed familiar with the Plumed Serpent. If I may be so bold, which god are you?"

"I get what you're doing. You're not sure about me. You remember something, but not enough to let down your guard. I could be the enemy."

"What does that mean to you?"

Her cheeks went rosy, her lips parted just enough to reveal the pearl edges of her teeth, the moist pink of her tongue.

Maybe it was the most seductive look he had ever seen.

"David, I want us to be us again, like we were when we were kids."

There was no longer the slightest question in his mind that his decision to house her on confinement was correct. If she was a member of the class, she'd welcome the safety of it. If she was some kind of agent, she'd be contained. This woman had no psychiatric symptoms, and she wasn't even bothering to pretend.

Katie appeared, meaning that he was out of time.

He said, "Caroline is ready to go."

With a dancer's grace, Caroline turned around. Then she whirled back, her cheeks red, her eyes so savage that they sent a shock through him. Caroline angry was a terror.

"That works exactly once," she snapped.

She was very controlling. She did not like to be "handled." And he was just not sure where he stood with her.

He tried a smile. "It's just that it's lunchtime, Caroline."

"Anything raw and bloody. A heart, preferably."

"Be careful, you might get just that."

"Ah. Can I order it? Does this place work like a cruise ship?"

He ignored the question and instead turned away from her in his chair. After a pause, she huffed out, Katie hurrying along behind her.

Katie handed her over to Sam Taylor in the outer office and began to push David's door closed.

"No, Katie, I want you," he called.

She returned. For the safety of Caroline Light, he intended to make a convincing case to every staff member at the clinic that she was genuinely insane, perhaps even dangerous.

"I want this patient placed on priority observation at all times. Her luggage is to be searched by Glen personally for anything that shouldn't be there, and it's to be brought to me. She is to have locator buttons placed in her shoes and clothing, and I want security to put her on the alarm list for any deviation from routine."

Katie's face suggested carefully concealed surprise.

"This woman is in a good deal of trouble," he explained. "She's been poorly diagnosed and inappropriately treated, but that's not the problem. What we have here is a time bomb that's about to explode. In the safety of this environment, surrounded by professionals who can control her, she's going to give herself permission to just plain cut loose."

"I'll get this set up right away." She turned to leave.

"Don't worry, she's not going to blow just yet. But she will, Katie. At some point that anger is coming out, and it isn't going to be pretty."

"Doctor, you have the steering committee meeting."

When Katie had gone, he took a deep breath and let it out. He was drawn to his assistant sexually—not as explosively as to Caroline Light, of course, but he'd welcome company in bed.

He went to the bookcase and pulled down one of the beautiful codices. He really wanted to spend some time with them, if nothing else admiring the artistry. He was drawn to them. He wanted to feel them in his hands.

He drew down another volume, then another and another. They were all different, all huge, and he thought that any one of them might contain more writing than all the known Aztec and Mayan codices in the world.

Then he saw a volume that was not a codex. *The Gods of Mesoamerica* by Bartholomew Light. He took it down. Obviously, it hadn't been touched in a very long time, and the leather cover crackled when he moved it.

He had just opened it when Marian Hunt came in, followed by the executive chef, Ray Weller, Glen, Bill Osterman, the chief engineer, and the other members of the on-site steering committee.

Appropriately enough just before lunch, the subject was to be food resources. Supplying the clinic with the luxuries the patients expected was getting more and more complicated. There had to be cutbacks, followed by the inevitable protests.

As the room filled, he began to experience an acute sense of claustrophobia. He was not used to feeling suspicious of coworkers, and having his office filled with them was surprisingly unpleasant. As large as it was, it felt just now like a coffin.

Katie said, "Doctor, are you okay? Because you don't look okay."

He put a hand on her shoulder and could feel her stiffening and recoiling from the contact.

"Do you think Dr. Ullman was murdered?"

"Excuse me?"

She was surprised by his question—as, for that matter, was he. But she recovered herself quickly.

"He died in a fire," she said, her voice sharp.

He looked around at the assembled group, the concealing, careful faces.

"Very well," he said, "let's get started. We don't have much time."

And then he thought: in truth, we don't have any time. No time at all. In fact, the Acton Clinic, all of us, the country, the world—we are all in the same situation: we no longer have time.

DAVID FORD'S JOURNAL: TWO

I was looking through Bartholomew Light's book and a document fell out, and this document has, quite simply, turned me inside out. Reality is not what I thought. Not at all.

The note is old. It is signed by Herbert Acton. The heading is "Divinatory Calendar" and dated "6.1.1." This is either June 1, 1901, or January 6, 1901, I have no way to tell which.

Now, this next part is important, and I want to record it exactly: I found this note at 11:50 in the morning of May 22, 2020, while paging through the book.

I know it isn't forgery—not because the paper looks old, but for another reason that will become clear after I have recorded the list itself.

The list. In my humble opinion, probably the most astonishing words ever written by the human hand.

On the surface, it is the work of someone with deep insight into modern history. On the surface.

It is a list of the dates on which certain small but crucial events took place in the twentieth century. Each date is accompanied by a stamped glyph, and I found the deities they refer to in *The Gods of Mesoamerica*.

In the absence of the Internet, I have used *Every Day in History*, also in this library, to research the dates I did not know, which was all but one or two of them.

I record them herewith together with the identity of the Aztec glyph associated with each one:

2 February 1910: Entry of Aleister Crowley into the Order of the Golden Dawn.

This was an occult organization. The glyph is the god of the underworld, Acolmiztli, as if this act somehow drew us all into a kind of hell, or marked our passage into it.

28 June 1914: Assassination of Franz Ferdinand of Austria.

This assassination led to World War I. The associated glyph is Ixtab, goddess of suicide. Eater of blood.

13 October 1917: The Fátima "dance of the sun."

This bizarre event was witnessed by thousands. Glyph of Citilalinique, "she who illuminates," goddess of the starry skirt. (And I do recall the remarkable star-covered robe the apparition at Fátima was described as wearing.)

5 January 1919: Foundation of Deutsche Arbeiterpartei.

Adolf Hitler joined this party the following year and it became the Nazis. Tezcatlipoca, god of rulers, death, and the night.

16 September 1922: The last reparations meeting in Weimar.

At this meeting, it was decided to strip all the gold from Germany. As a result, the German mark hyperinflated and the stage was set for the rise of Hitler and his party. Five-Vulture, god of ruinous excess.

30 March 1934: Leo Szilard conceives the nuclear chain reaction.

Szilard was walking the streets of London when suddenly he saw how the atomic bomb would work. Quilaztli: goddess of the Milky Way, whose roar signaled war.

25 January 1938: Fátima prediction fulfilled.

On that night, massive auroras over Europe heralded the beginning of World War II, just as Our Lady of Fátima had warned would happen. The event was associated with Chalchiuhtotli, god of mystery.

This is the last date save one, which is the most shocking of them all.

This is a list of events that took place beneath the surface of history, but which were critical markers in mankind's long journey through the underworld that we apparently entered in 1910.

I have a personal story about one of the events. Specifically, my father knew an elderly priest, Father Thomas Heim, who was among the thousands who actually witnessed the dance of the sun at Fátima. Father Heim had said that the object was not the sun, but something in the sky that was in front of the sun. He said that he could see a ladder on the object, with figures moving on it.

I have never known what that might have meant, but this last date has made it more clear.

It is June 22, 1947. This is the date of something called the Maury Island UFO encounter. It was the first UFO event of modern times, preceding the famous Roswell Incident by about three weeks. It involved the sighting of a number of unidentified flying objects over Maury Island, Washington, by some fishermen. Some strange material fell out of one of the objects and onto the boat of the fishermen.

It also involved the deaths, over subsequent weeks and months, of many of the people involved in the investigation.

One who survived was called Fred Crisman. He was later implicated by New Orleans District Attorney Jim Garrison in the Kennedy assassination. What that may mean, if anything, I do not know, but he was certainly involved with Lee Harvey Oswald.

The point of this list, I think, is to reveal crucial moments in history that illustrate the hidden battle among the higher powers that govern human affairs. We have not drifted into this desperate trap at all, but been led here. Just as the ancient Maya knew when we would reenter the debris field of the supernova, so did whoever is behind the way this world of ours works. And they have been *designing* history, not simply allowing it to happen.

But, of course, my own assumption that this document is old isn't enough to convince me of its authenticity, but the second page is. On this page are just two paragraphs, the first entitled "Citilalinique." There follows an intimate description of Caroline Light: *The Lady of the Starry Skirt, bringer of the light of understanding. She is to be born 25 October 1986 on schedule and sign. Will enter class 1 June 1994 with the others. Pubescence takes place 12 July 1997. Amnesia will then be induced.*

The second paragraph is called "Quetzalcoatl," and it is about one David Ford. *The Plumed Serpent, creator and builder, is to be born 25 October 1988 on schedule and sign. Pubescence takes place 12 July 1992. Enters class 1 June 1994 with the others. Partial induction, no artificial psychosis. Directed to medical career in anticipation of later role. To become clinic director 14 May 2020. Will find this document at eleven-fifty in the morning of 22 May 2020.*

Perhaps I could explain all this away as a clever forgery, except for that last sentence. As soon as I read it, I looked at the clock. It was 11:57 A.M., and it had taken a few minutes to read.

In other words, no matter the ink, no matter the age, the author had anticipated the exact moment I would find it, and could *not* have known this in any conventional way, not even if the document was written an hour ago. So, as I turned over the page, I also overturned everything I understand about our world—as, I am sure, I was meant to do.

The list ends with two sentences: *What I could not do, you must. The judgment has begun.*

Many religions and societies have intuited—or known—of the existence of the great cycles we are moving through, and seen their periodic end as times of divine judgment. All well and good, except I don't think that we should view the higher force that creates and harvests souls on earth as something supernatural.

I don't believe in the gods identified in the document, or any gods, for that matter, and certainly not in myself as some prancing Aztec deity. But I now have no choice except to believe that an extraordinary science, hidden from most eyes, is able to predict the unfolding of time, and that it is in some incomprehensible way connected to the images of these deities—and to me and Caroline, and to this place, and probably to whatever future the world has, if any.

What I have here is a document based on the lost science I am beginning to remember being taught in our class. It operates entirely differently from modern disciplines, for this is a science of the soul, and as such makes use of more than the three dimensions we see around us.

Its engineering built the impossible structures we see from the past, such as the gigantic platform at Baalbek in Lebanon, made of stones so huge that we could not move them to this day, or the fortress high in the Andes at Sacsahuamán, constructed from more than thirty thousand perfectly matched boulders, each weighing at least a ton, and carried thousands of feet from gorges far below.

But it was its ability to see into time that was its most extraordinary achievement—to see into time and, just possibly, to actually move through time.

Of course, I'm going to look between the pages of every book in this room, because I understand very well what I am seeing here. I have beside me on this desk as I write these words a list that is a map of mankind's descent into an underworld where we are still trapped.

I have often reflected on the fact that a single bullet fired from a small pistol by the political simpleton who assassinated Franz Ferdinand led to the collapse of Western Civilization and the destruction of a billion lives.

This list, by including that event, acknowledges its hidden importance, and by associating it with Ixtab, the symbol not of war but of suicide, reveals much insight into the actual psychology behind the events. The old world did not die, it committed suicide, quite literally. It was the mechanical nature of the interlocking treaties involved that amplified that single shot into the vast international immolation that followed, and, above all, the *machinery* of the situation. Once one country had put its soldiers on the trains that would take them to the front, the others were forced to do the same or risk being unable to prevent the army that was already mobilizing from simply walking across their borders.

At its deepest level this is a list of man's enslavement to mechanism.

It is also something else. It announces the coming of a higher power in the form of the UFO, a phenomenon that started with the Maury Island incident.

In 2012, NASA did say that some of them were apparently of intelligent origin, but who has investigated? Who's had time? Maybe somebody, but I never saw any news about their findings, and now it's too late for that sort of thing.

So this higher power has returned to oversee this enormous change.

I find myself in this marvelous, silent room with its tall bookshelves and exotic carved walls, with its mysteries all around me, going deep into myself and finding more and more questions. I am a man alone at the end of time, with a dependent flock to keep, a sort of shepherd.

Before God, I could not previously have imagined a sense of helplessness this profound.

5

QUETZALCOATL

Caroline Light followed Sam Taylor through the lovely front of the house. He'd been described to her as a "minder," and he looked considerably tougher than the nurse who had originally met her, a gentle lady called Nurse Cross.

Coming here had been the hardest thing she had ever done. Leaving her dad, and him so old and the situation so perilous—it had taken all the strength she possessed to turn her back on him. His old driver, Vincent, had gotten her here in just over fourteen hours, traveling back roads, bypassing cities, avoiding the interstates where a car like the Mercedes was a definite target.

And now here she was in the place where the legendary Aubrey Denman had just lost her life—and in certain danger herself.

Dad had wept quietly as she left. She had, too, but not quietly. The last she'd seen of him was that proud old figure, narrow but immensely dignified, standing before their beloved Mayfair, the house Dad's father had bought after being blessed with the friendship of Herbert Acton. Dad's last words to her had been a cavalier wave and a confident, "See you on the other side." The tears, though, had been silent testament to the truth: they were beyond the edge of the age now. Not even Herbert Acton had been able to see clearly into this period of chaos.

The future was on her shoulders now, hers and David's.

They reached the end of the long corridor that split the second story. Before them was a black door locked by a fingerprint reader. It looked like the entrance to a gas chamber or a prison, or the underworld. He touched the reader and the door clicked, then opened onto a white institutional corridor lit by fluorescents.

She needed to seem like just another patient, and saw a chance to do a little acting. She stopped.

"Excuse me, Sir. Mr. Taylor?"

"Ma'am?"

"What is this? Where are we going?"

"Your things are being moved into your room now, and I'm taking you on a tour of the facility."

"Fair enough, as long as I don't have to fraternize with the other nuts." Lay it on, girl.

They entered a large room, and for the first time she saw some of her compatriots. She hadn't seen her classmates since they were children, but she could recognize almost all of them. In any case, she knew their names, so she would be able to identify even the ones who were most spectacularly different.

Being close to them again was every bit as eerie as her father had warned her that it would be. Most of them had not the slightest idea who she was, and those who did weren't going to show it.

David had been expected to remember her immediately. Her mention of Quetzalcoatl had been the trigger that was supposed to break his amnesia.

It hadn't worked, so now what? Mrs. Denman was dead, and she dared not talk about such a subject with Dad on the phone, even if she was able to get through. Obviously the enemy was right here in this place. Could even be this Mr. Toughguy with a heart of gold, for all she knew.

"This is the activity area," Sam said. "This is where we meet friends, make new friends, that kind of thing. There are games, there's a poker game, there's bridge, of course, we have two leagues and an annual championship, there's backgammon, a lot of stuff like that. Also, we have an art room where you can paint or sculpt or do pottery. Actually, we have practically everything."

She noticed a guy ogling her. He had not been in the class, so he was one of the real patients, and his nostrils were actually dilating. What a creep.

"Who's he?"

"Graham Mining."

"If we go by our company names, that makes me Daddy's Little Girl. We have no company. We're post-work."

The patient followed her with his sick eyes. Then, annoyingly, he got up and came sliding over. Big, imposing man with a carefully tuned smile. "They call me Mack the Cat," he said.

She understood why, too. He moved like a jaguar. You wanted to step back.

"May I know your name, Miss?"

"No."

" 'No' is a good name. Easy to spell."

"And it gets the point across. Incidentally, you drool, but cats don't. From now on, you're Mack the Dog."

The smile froze. She wondered if he was marked yet. If not, her guess was that his truth would soon emerge. This was a bad man. Written all over him. So, enemy or not? Bad was certain, the bastard had rape in his eyes. But the enemy—wouldn't he be charming, fit right in? So no, this one was probably just damned unpleasant. Good window dressing for the clinic, though.

Mack the Cat met Sam Taylor's eyes, and Caroline saw that they knew each other all too well. Sam's hand came to her elbow.

"Ma'am, we need—"

"Oh, be quiet." But she followed him. No excuse needed to get away from Mack and his drool.

They went down some steel stairs and suddenly they were in another lovely room, back in the old house. It was large, glassed in, and full of sunlight. There were three patients there, each with an attendant. Two of them were in straitjackets, struggling and growling. The third paced back and forth, back and forth.

She sucked hard breaths, forcing herself to appear calm, but she was seeing Monty Offut who had been so strong and Carl Winston who'd read Greek and Latin, and pacing in a state of paranoid frenzy, Jenny Offut, Monty's sister. They had swung together on the old swing that had been under one of the oaks out back, and dreamed the dreams of little girls.

"This is the old solarium," Sam said.

"I know what it is!"

"You do?"

"I—of course. It's obviously a solarium, you stupid jerk."

She felt him tighten—felt a hurt, a disappointment come from him—and thought that she did not like playing this role of the testy, overwrought neurotic.

But look at the tile floor, at the walls painted with those vines, even the old sunporch couch over there—she'd lain on that couch and gazed out at the marching clouds.

The nostalgia was tremendous, and seeing her friends like this—it was also agonizing.

"I think we need to move on," Sam said. Tough, gentle man.

"Yes . . ."

This had been the classroom, where Daddy had taught them the secrets of the old gods, and given them their ancient names. She was Citilalinique, the Lady of the Starry Skirt, and her work was to bring the light of understanding to an ignorant age. Light the bringer of light. Nominative determinism. Not funny, though. Funny was in the past.

Finally, she could bear it no longer and turned away. She went toward the living room, where you had been allowed to sit and read, but certainly not play or roughhouse, and not endanger the collection of Fabergé eggs that was no doubt locked away upstairs somewhere nowadays.

She had curled up in that chair right over there and read—what had she read? Yes, *The Philosopher's Stone*. She had memorized her formulas and what alchemists called confections, the assembly of the different components that would go into the extratemporal matter she was here to make.

Her father had brought her out of her own amnesia ten days ago. Prior to that, he had been awakened by Mrs. Denman, who had come on a day and at a time that had been specified by Herbert Acton fifty years ago, and showed Daddy a glyph of Huehueteotl, the Aztec god of life and the polestar . . . also the symbol of guidance, but not to the current polestar, not to Polaris. No, when the time came, they would journey toward a new polestar.

"Miss, patients are requested not to use these rooms."

She sat down in her old chair, regarding him with mild interest. Would he drag her out? He certainly could.

"Thank you for letting me know," she said.

He inclined his head. The guardian servant, then. Fine, she could stay.

She let her mind seek back over the events of the past few tumbling, chaotic days.

When Mrs. Denman had shown Dad the image of Huehueteotl, his eyes had grown steady and hard, and he had set his jaw like the soldier that he was. Then he'd embraced the cadaverous old woman, who had left as silently and mysteriously as a nun under vows.

That evening, he had been very quiet, refusing to speak of what had happened. Eventually, he had gone to one of Granddad's wonderful handmade books, the one called the *Book of Silence*. He had opened it to two beautifully colored images and said to her, "Remember."

As she had looked upon Quetzalcoatl and Citilalinique, a whole hidden life had come flooding back. She recalled swinging in the garden at Mr. Acton's house, and Daddy being their teacher, tall and rangy then, full of smiles and remembrance of Mother, and Mrs. Acton, incredibly ancient, looking down on them from the upstairs windows with appraising eyes. She had been the master behind the class, Daddy's teacher, but they only met her once or twice.

Caroline had been ten, and Mom's sudden death had then still been at the center of her life. The night before it happened, it was as if her parents had known—which, on a deep level, not then conscious, they indeed had.

The two of them had sat together in their private study into the small hours, talking in a loving way, touching each other and kissing, and Caroline had watched, and seen a kind of wonder between them, as if they were privy to a miraculous secret that was at once deeply serious and deeply joyous, perhaps the secret of life itself.

Mom had died of an aortal aneurysm, so suddenly that she had not even had time to cry out.

Mom had ascended, Dad had said. She would not be returning to earth again. Dad had explained, back then, that almost everyone who had ever been born was alive in the world now, every human soul returned to the flesh to experience judgment. And, he had added, by 2020—not 2012—they would all be here, all who needed to be.

Mom didn't need to stay, she was finished here, he had told her.

All well and good, but it didn't change a daughter's grief. When there is a death between people who love each other deeply—husband and wife, parent and child—the relationship continues on in the heart of the survivor, and Caroline had told her dad that she wanted to follow Mom, she wanted to go, too.

He'd explained in his gentle way, "You and I are working-class, girl, we stay put. Only the saints and the sinners get to take off early."

Since Mom's death, he'd spent many an evening in that study, reading poems he had explored together with his wife, and Caroline had, in recent years, made a habit of joining him, and they had shared their grief and their love, enjoying their memories.

She recalled once again the images of Quetzalcoatl and Citilalinique, intricately painted, their seemingly bizarre faces going deep into mind and memory. The Mayan and Aztec gods were representations, among other things, of the human unconscious, the purest ever created by the mind of man . . . the unconscious in all its wonder and playfulness, and all its paradoxical savagery.

On softest wings, when she had first seen them, memory had come, bringing with it a love that had been hidden in her heart for years.

She had remembered David.

Now, she recalled watching him curse and, on the wide lawn, trying to fly a kite. She'd laughed until her sides ached. David was so clumsy and so sincere and so very dear to her, and she thought that they had known one another across many lifetimes.

"Daddy," she said to her own secret heart, "tell me how to make him remember me."

When he was awakened—if—he would become their leader, assuming the role and the power of protector and healer. The knowledge that the new world that was coming would rest on his shoulders made her proud of him, and proud to be his promised love.

Except, what if he did not remember? People change, even locked in the amber of amnesia. What if he had somebody else now? There were attractive nurses here and people under pressure form attachments fast. In war, whole lives are lived in days, and this was just like war. It was war.

"Miss, we have a lot still to see. I want to show you the dining facilities and the kitchen. It's quite a wonderful kitchen."

"Sure," she said. The poor guy was practically dancing, he was so eager to get her out of the so-called restricted area. As if she'd somehow damage carpets on which she'd played Monopoly on rainy afternoons.

She followed Sam through a pair of double doors with mirrored windows in them, entering a spotless, magnificently appointed, but very busy kitchen—all of which was new. This had been the music room in the old days. Now, the piano was in what had been the old smoking room, opposite the solarium.

The new kitchen revealed a fine spread of marble countertops and high end appliances. She counted four chefs in toques, surrounded by rushing crowds of assistants. It looked like the kitchen of the *Queen Mary II* back before she'd disappeared in that storm.

"Miss Caroline, this is Ray Weller, our executive chef. He's the one who'll read your preferences list."

"Hello, Ray."

The way he smiled told her that he knew her. So this fellow classmate was not in total amnesia. Dad had said that some would be and others not, but that she was to show everyone their glyphs, because the sight of their particular image would end all amnesia. Those hidden in psychosis, though, were a different matter. They were the stars, the powerful ones, the essentials, the most important and therefore the most deeply concealed.

"We aim to please," Ray said, "so do think carefully about your desires. We can do just about anything, as long as supplies aren't short, of course."

"Now we're going to the art room," Sam said.

She followed him through double doors that led back into the patient wing, but this room was brightened by big windows that overlooked the lovely grounds. There were men and women in paint-smeared jeans and T-shirts, some painting on canvases large and small, some drawing, others creating clay sculptures.

She was satisfied to see a group of potters working industriously, their kiln casting a glow that she found extremely realistic. They were actually firing pots in it, but it was not really a kiln—or rather, not only that. In fact, right now, it was the most important machine on planet earth, because of what she was going to do with it.

An old classmate, Susan Denman, sat reading *The Philosopher's Stone*. She looked up at Caroline and smiled through what was obviously great personal sadness. Her father had told her that, if all else failed, a sufficiently intense shock could often cause spontaneous remission of artificially induced psychosis. The murder of Susan's mother had obviously, in her case, been enough.

Caroline returned just the slightest glimmer of recognition. She and Susan Denman had studied subspace together, learning how to form holographic realities that would be at once in a single place and in all places at the same time—essential knowledge, given Caroline's mission. And Susan would bring the colors and prepare the brushes.

She sighed as she walked, wishing that things were different, that they weren't so hard and so dangerous. Class had been a joy—the joy of their childhoods, and she was so grateful to Mr. Acton and to her dad and granddad for all they had given.

She'd been glad to be recognized by Susan at least, because this business of concealing the group inside induced symptoms of mental disease, and turning Mr. Acton's beautiful home into a fake mental asylum, was even more horrible than she'd feared it would be.

Susan might be awake, but over there, Aaron Stein, painting that horrific thing—what was it, a woman colliding with a gigantic penis?— obviously still needed to wake up.

"What's that guy's problem?"

"Schizoaffective disorder," Sam replied in a self-important tone. Proud of his jargon.

Beautiful, poetic Aaron, so quick to laugh and so full of gentle wisdom . . .

She would soon be painting as well, but it wouldn't be an outlet for mental illness, far from it.

It was essential that it be completed quickly, for there would come a time soon that the chaos would be too great, and it would be impossible to finish it. Even the color of the sky was going to change, and without good color, she could not make this artifact that was to be a perfect confluence of the knowledge of science and the energy of art.

If Mr. Acton's plan worked.

"Let's get out of here," she muttered to Sam.

Another member of the class—a grinning Amy Makepeace—looked

up from a painting of what appeared to be some sort of grim tower, and smiled the too-radiant smile of a madwoman.

"What's your death going to be?" she asked, her tone crisply genial, her eyes button-bright. "Me, I prefer to jump."

At least there was plenty of painting going on, which was an important part of the plan. The device she had been trained in class to create would appear to be a painting, at least at first. Later, as it developed, it would reveal itself to be a doorway through time, and when it did, nobody would imagine for a moment that it was just a picture.

By balancing the artistic skill and scientific knowledge in her mind, all enhanced by the power of the alchemical gold she would make, she was actually generating their escape route. What she would create in this room would look like a painting for a while. But it was not a painting, not at all.

"Ma'am, we want to move on."

"Sure. Gotta cover my cage, I'm too noisy."

"The tower," the woman said, "you walk and you fall." She thrust her grinning face into Caroline's. "And you *fall* . . ."

And Caroline saw an opportunity to reinforce her own feigned symptoms. She pretended to have a seizure, letting herself pitch backward shaking. She hit the floor so hard that she blacked out.

A moonlike face appeared, its demon eyes fearsome. She gasped, then screamed—and the face of Mack Graham smiled, and it was as if the demon had withdrawn—hidden, once again, in its lair in the man's heart.

He helped her to her feet. "I'm so sorry, Miss—"

Do not tell him your name.

Brushing herself off, she scrambled away from him.

"Maybe your medications are affecting your balance," Sam said.

"That's just it! I'm not on any. I've run out so I came here—" She looked around the room. Every eye was on her, and she was looking at gargoyles, at smoldering sex maniacs, at wild-eyed schizophrenics, at paranoids in their sullen corners—it was awful, a gallery of the damned in the faces of people she loved dearly and respected enormously. That brilliant class of wonderful kids were the center of her heart and to see them like this was almost enough to induce actual insanity in her.

She smiled, forced a laugh. "I won't miss that step again," she sang out. "Let's see my suite."

"Of course, Ma'am."

Sam laid an arm around her shoulder, or rather, his big arm came oozing around her with the muscular stealth of a python. She allowed herself to be guided out of the art room and down yet another long institutional corridor.

Ahead was another of the black doors, looming at her like a hungry trap. "Do we have to go back in there?"

"Your suite is there."

"Where does Mack live?"

"Next door, actually."

"No," she said, "no. I need to live in the house, you see. It's what I'm used to. This—oh, my God, it's a prison."

"The rooms are nice, Ma'am. So, please—"

She had to lay it on. She had to continue to seem insane, here. She must not raise the suspicions of that monster Mack, and he was suspicious already, there could be no doubt of that. She pulled away from her minder. "Look, I've made a mistake. I can't do this. I'm going home."

"Caroline—"

"I'm going home!" But now she found herself confronting not just dear old Sam, but David and his assistant, Katrina Starnes. Katrina, the modern name of the Mexican goddess of death.

"Caroline, you need to go in now," she said.

"Please, Caroline," David added—and the lack of recognition stabbed her heart.

"We're still processing your intake," the death goddess said. "Someone will be along to help you with your program in a few minutes."

She had to continue her act.

"I'm free to leave," she snapped. As she tried to push between them, the enforcer laid his thick—and surprisingly gentle—hands on her shoulders.

Drawing herself away from him, she cried out, "How dare you touch me!"

His body blocked her way, but when she tried to get around him, he proved to be as adept as any dancer.

"What's she doing, Doctor?"

"I don't know."

She turned on David. "Get these people out of my face!"

As she tried to make her way back into the main house, Katrina dropped a leather strap around her arms and pinned them to her sides. Even fighting as hard as she did, she could not free herself.

She did a little method acting, imagining what it would be like if this were real, if she were actually mad and being trapped, and terror exploded through her with such intensity that she just burst out screaming, surprising even herself with the ferocity of it.

The sounds of the struggle echoed up and down the corridor, and the cries of other patients were soon added to her own screams. As patients came out of the art room and other public rooms, some of them laughed, their voices warbling high with hysteria, while others shouted for help, or came rushing forward to do battle on her behalf.

Susan Denman watched, amused and appalled at the baroque antics.

But before any of this chaos could resolve itself, she was dragged backward hard, there was a great crash and sudden silence, and she was on the floor looking up into David's dear, empty face.

"Okay," he said, "she's controlled. Now, Caroline, can you hear me?"

She continued her act. "Bastards! *Bastards!*"

"All right, all right. You're angry and I would be, too. Now, I want you to get yourself together, Caroline. Can you do that?"

Despite all that she knew, she could not help being genuinely furious, if not at his ignorance, then certainly at his condescension. "I'm not one of your patients," she wanted to say, "I'm part of your heart."

She managed a choked, "Yes, Doctor."

This was hideous, to see him like this.

"I'm going to have Katrina here release you. Is that all right? Are we able to calm down now?"

"I'm calm! So get me out of this damned thing!"

"Uh, Doctor, is this wise? She's very agitated."

"Do it. But step away. Step *behind* her."

"I'm not going to do anything," she said as Nurse Katrina freed her. "Just keep that other guy away from me. Sam. I mean, what is that, a giant dwarf? A troll?"

"The hell . . ."

"Leave it, Sam. Caroline, we'll address all of these issues in our in-take interview."

"I thought we did that."

"No. No, not entirely. We did not." David pranced toward her, all officious professionalism. He took her elbow and in a moment they were in a small room, sparsely furnished with a cot and a recliner that took up far too much of the space.

"Now," he said, "you can collect yourself. Get in the recliner, it's great! I mean, you talk about relaxing, these things—all the patients just really love them."

"It's a chair, for God's sake." But she sat down. After a moment, she pulled the lever and leaned back. She noticed that the ceiling lights were protected by wire cages.

"What is this, one of the cells? Am I a prisoner, because I better not be. I did a voluntary commitment, remember that."

"This is a safe room. We call it a safe room. Now, close your eyes." He began rubbing her temples and she let herself drift, let the distant sounds of the institution die away, let the world drift and drift . . . on a quiet ocean . . . ocean of silence.

"I have a little something," he said.

"I don't want anything."

"You're very agitated."

"Oh, it's just this sun business! I can't quit thinking about it."

"Take deep breaths, let it go, let the trembling go."

She was trembling? Yes, actually shaking like a leaf. She could feel the dark gods coming, smelling her weakness, coming with their jaws clicking, their obsidian eyes flickering with inner fire. Xipe Totec, the Flayed One, skinned by the sun, dead but alive, and coming out of the bloody mouth of Mack the Cat.

She was aware of movement in the room, the clink of glass. When she opened her eyes, a nurse was there with a small paper pill cup and a glass of water.

"What is it?" she asked David.

"A mild sedative."

"No."

His hands were gentle, insistent. She felt his subtle power and liked the feeling. She saw plumes of red and blue around him, feathers in the wind.

"And he will descend into hell and gather the bones of men, and he will spread them on the earth, and his wisdom will make them dance."

"And that is?"

"The work of Quetzalcoatl. The bringer of peace, the builder of heaven." She saw him in David's eyes, just as she had when they were children, and she had thought him the most beautiful creature that God had ever made.

He touched her temples again. "Take it easy, Miss. Right now, you're agitated. Let's cross this bridge first." He took the pill cup from the nurse and handed it to her.

She pretended to take what she recognized as a Xanax. She did not take it, though. She needed her wits.

"Good. That'll help."

"David?"

"Dr. Ford. I'm Dr. Ford."

"Okay," she said, fighting to keep the pain out of her voice. "Dr. Ford,

I want you to humor me. Indulge a little innocent paranoia. Don't tell anybody my last name. Can you do that?"

He blinked as if surprised, and she wondered immediately how much he did remember. Clearly, he wasn't entirely clueless.

"Patient surnames are confidential. Nobody gets your surname except from you."

His hands caressed her temples so gently, so firmly, that this time when she closed her eyes she did indeed drift away.

Then, seemingly without more than a moment passing, she came to understand that he had not been rubbing her temples, not for some time. In fact, not for a long time.

With a shocked gasp, she opened her eyes. At first, she couldn't see anything at all—and then she could, a line of light floating ahead of her. A line of light . . . which she moved toward.

She understood that she was on a low bed. And naked, she was also naked, or rather, in one of those loose hospital gowns that tie in the back. She leaned down and touched the line of light, running her fingers along it. A faint coolness brushed them—air, she realized, from outside.

Once she understood that this was the door, her disorientation resolved itself and she stood up, feeling for the doorknob. She found it and turned it, but it was locked tight.

She called, "Hello, I'm awake! Hello!"

Not a sound came in reply.

She tried to look at her watch, but couldn't find it on her wrist. Taken. Not stolen, of course, she didn't think that.

They'd overdone this, and she saw a chance to put on a performance.

"Hey! HEY!" She shook the door, then hammered on it.

Nothing.

She felt the walls and found a quiltlike surface on them. She ran her palms along it. Soft. So was the floor, soft, quilted. There was no window.

The ceiling no longer had caged lights on it, but rather flush glass fixtures that emitted a faint nocturnal glow.

He'd doped her with something more than Xanax, that clever David, good at every job he'd ever done. And she'd thought she hadn't swallowed the pill. She hadn't been meant to—or rather, it hadn't mattered. Whatever had done this to her had been in the water.

So, okay, here we go. He wanted crazy, he was going to get crazy.

She backed up, then took in a deep breath and screamed her lungs out.

And—wow, that was something! Her heart was hammering, her body flushing with adrenaline. She did it again, then threw herself against the door.

The padding absorbed the blow without the slightest effect, which was genuinely disturbing and isolating, and made it quite easy to scream more, so she screamed and screamed and screamed, and roamed the cell, hurling herself against the walls, against the door, dropping to the floor and rolling and screaming, and screaming and screaming and screaming. But, then again, that's what a padded cell is for.

She stopped. This was all well and good. She was putting on what must be a convincing performance. But she was also here for serious reasons. She needed to get the arc furnace running. There was a lot of gold to make and only a little from Guatemala to start the process, far less than she had expected to find. And there was the matter of the painting. It would be a meticulous, difficult process, enormously intimidating, and all of it needing to be done on a very tight and very precise schedule.

The whole world had arrived at the border of an unknown country, a rare shadow land that few men ever enter and fewer recall. Already, they were advanced into it, for the death of Aubrey Denman, an incalculable disaster, had not been predicted in any of the writings of Herbert Acton.

This was because he had not foreseen it. Her father had told the class, "There is a period at the end of a cycle of time that we call its omega point, where life itself enters the unknown. An omega point is a dark labyrinth from which only the few will escape." He had smiled then, this gentle and compassionate man, a smile filled with hope and pain. "Be among the few," he had said.

She rattled the door again, and this time it was no game. "Let me out," she shouted. But there was only silence in reply.

This time, when she screamed, it was no act, and she screamed and screamed and screamed.

DAVID FORD'S JOURNAL: THREE

The staff is alerting me about poor Caroline again and again, but I sense that she's taking advantage of the situation to do a little playacting, and I keep thinking that I need to let her do that. Somebody needs to be convinced, I feel sure. But I don't want her to pretend so well that I have to put her in a jacket or shock her.

Caroline is brilliant. But how did she get here through all that mayhem on the outside? Was she helped, perhaps, by the resources of the Seven Families?

I wish that I could have proof that she is the real Caroline Light.

I have about convinced myself to take the risk of opening up to her. Despite the fact that I don't have any recollection of her, I am tremendously drawn to her, and perhaps that is a sort of memory. If we were children when we last met, she would look entirely different, would she not?

After she drank the sedative, I held her in my arms and she felt as light as air, her body slack with sleep, her sangfroid gone. Her vulnerability broke my heart even as it filled it.

Glen turned up nothing unusual in her belongings. Her driver's license seems genuine, for example, but what does that mean?

If she's the real person and she isn't in amnesia, I need her desperately.

Last night, there were monstrous, flaring, leaping auroras. Today, half the face of the sun is covered with gigantic sunspots.

The Internet, TV, and all telephone systems have more or less failed. Even the patient families we have relied on for food deliveries are not supplying us at this time, and we cannot reach them to find out what's happening.

What happens when we eat our last food and burn our last fuel? And when the solar flares get worse, then what? What I need to know is how we survive.

At least Katie Starnes is becoming more at ease around me. She isn't a problem like Caroline, and I would really welcome some development in our friendship. Just friends, though, sexual friends like we had in med school. No commitments, and I don't think she's looking in that direction, either. I hope not, at any rate, because this is no time to involve oneself in hopes for the future.

What's my next step? Where do I turn? I don't have a religion, not even some childhood thing to fall back on. My parents were scientists and atheists, just as I am. But right now, there are only three words that come to mind, that haunt me, that never leave my thoughts for long: God help us.

6

THE SOUND OF BLOOD

Again Mack heard them, pulsating out of the dark, long cries of human anguish. He could open neither his window nor his door, and he wasn't absolutely sure that they were coming from inside the facility. With all the mayhem these days, they could be from the distant streets.

As scream after scream pealed out—but so faint, why did they use all this soundproofing?—his whole body was set to vibrating.

He pressed his intercom button.

"Yes, Mack?"

"Somebody's upset."

"It's the new intake. She's struggling again. We're calling one of the residents for her."

He threw himself on his bed. Damn, what did this mean? He would have sworn she was an actress, no more crazy than he was. But this was one hell of an act, damn her eyes.

He did not want to sweat over some worthless loony, he wanted to sleep. But there would be no sleep, they doled out their goddamn pills nowadays like they were gold fucking bars. Worse. Everybody around here was crawling in gold bars, but they damn well were begging for Lunesta. Damn fucking cheap bureaucrats.

"What's her name?"

"You can ask her when she's in the population."

"Sweet Caroline, I already got that much. Also, the fact that she's a bitch. That came through loud and clear." After tonight's transmission, General Wylie had come back inside of a minute. "Get me the name."

At this point in time, any new arrival was important.

"She might be a bitch, but she's suffering now, Mack."

"Caroline . . . who?"

"Ask her!"

Well, the hell with it, the screaming had stopped, and thank you, God. He turned out his light—and, damn, the flickering out there was incredible. He went to his wire-enforced window. The sky was a flaring, jumping curtain of multicolored light.

He was not making the kind of progress that was needed. They should have put a whole team in here. He hated to admit it, but that was the truth of it. Too late now.

In Mexico City, in the embassy's garden, he had watched the gods dancing in the night sky, watched Tezcatlipoca shift from man to jaguar to serpent, taunting and raging at his brother Quetzalcoatl. In Egypt, Quetzalcoatl was Osiris, the god of resurrection, and Tezcatlipoca was his brother Set, who cut him into small pieces. The Bible called them Cain and Abel. In Judea, the light and dark brothers had been Jesus and Judas.

He identified with Tezcatlipoca, El Gato, the night cat roaming and changing, the shadow cat. That's where his nickname came from. Doing his work, he moved like a cat.

But just as he had planned to begin exploring patient and personnel files, he had suddenly been deprived of his ability to leave his room at night.

They'd found out that he'd been off the premises the night Dr. Ullman was killed. Well, yes.

Now this new director and patient turn up just when it was expected that the Acton group would be putting their leadership in place—and here he was, locked up like a monkey in a GODDAMN ZOO!

He twisted on the bed, as uncomfortable as a man in a rack. And that thought took his mind back down a path it loved to go and hated to go, the torture path.

You look down at the guy in straps and you know that he belongs to you. You lay the cloth over his face, adjusting it a little, drawing out the suspense. He turns his head and Billie Fisk gets it between her sweet knees and holds it steady for you. Then you get the pitcher, you fill it in the sink, you hear the echoing drip of the water on the tiles as you carry it brimming over to the guy's gurney-bound body. It's not a torture chamber or something, it's a men's room with a DO NOT DISTURB sign from some hotel on the door. Embassy basement, where else were they gonna go? Their work was illegal on Mexican soil.

Then you ask your question and you do not wait for the bullshit answer, you start your pour. The body of Ramos curves on the board. Stomach sucks in. Legs pulse. Dick comes up. Feet hammer. Pour and pour. Neck goes from red to purple.

You run out of water. As you are refilling, you ask your question again. This time, he kind of starts in, but you don't listen. You and Billie will work him for an hour, doing maybe twenty pours. When his dick comes up this time, you dig your heel into it. You slip and practically fall on your ass. Billie laughs.

Somebody somewhere reviews the video feed, looking for clues in the body language, piecing together bits of words, all of that, working up a report for whoever.

Drug interdiction, that was the mission.

Thing is, why? Why are drugs even illegal? They're good, they do a search-and-destroy operation on the weak.

Never mind, you did your work and now you are here playing crazy, and, you gotta admit, it's just a little too easy to act that way.

She started screaming again, and that was it, she reminded him of too damn much. "Fuck this, will you shut her up! Shut her UP!"

"Dr. Claire is with her."

Claire Michaels, that floppy little puppy of a shrink. "She's useless! Get Hunt, get Ford! But shut her up, please."

Was this woman actually one of their leaders, or had her appearance at this time been chance?

Hell, that screaming was loud—and maybe it was there to cover some other sound that he might hear, like the hiss of the arc furnace they had in the art room. It was disguised as a pottery kiln but there were elements in there that could generate truly extraordinary temperatures.

But for what purpose?

It had to be involved with time, and the CIA's Acton Working Group had determined that Herbert Acton, like certain ancient Egyptians and ancient Maya, had definitely been able to somehow see forward in time. This explained his flawless investments, which statistics could not. As one of the statisticians who had examined them put it, "there isn't enough chance in all the universe to account for this. He wasn't lucky, he was informed."

In other words, he'd been able to see forward in time. This also explained things like the accuracy of the Mayan calendar. It hadn't been constructed forward to December 21, 2012, it had been written *backward* from that date because they had *seen* forward first, then built their exquisite calendar from the top down, as it were.

Seeing didn't make a difference now, though. The only thing that would matter to anybody right now was physical movement through time.

So that's what this place had to be about.

If this Caroline was indeed one of their leaders, she had some damned important secrets, there was no question about that.

His mission was quite clear, and he didn't need General Wylie screaming down the horn at him to tell him that he needed to confirm her identity and then obtain her secrets by whatever means presented itself. No legalities, that was over and done with.

He had his problem, though, which was his night confinement and his daytime minder.

For the thousandth time, he considered his window. The upper sash, he could get that down a bit, maybe even work his way out. Problem was, there was nowhere to go from the sill. No, the ductwork was his only option. But he needed a blueprint. You couldn't go wandering off through the air-conditioning system of a building this size. You'd be heard. You'd get trapped.

There was a faint beep from his desk. Damn, he was shut down for the night, and here was Wylie back again.

He went for his radio, but he never got to it, because the next moment something completely extraordinary happened. It wasn't as if he hadn't been expecting it. He had. Expecting any damn thing.

What this consisted of was, in quick succession, three flashes that must have been a million times brighter than the sun, flashes that filled not only the eyes but the entire head, as if they had entered every orifice and pore on his body, and penetrated right down to the marrow.

One second, he was going for the radio, and the next the flashes hit. They caused an immediate, powerful, and startling hallucination, a form in plumage, grimacing, its face draped in golden chain mail, skulls strung around its neck, its long, black nails slicing toward him, sparking in the air.

In his surprise, he cried out, he pressed himself against the wall beside the bed.

That had been a damned hallucination of his own adopted god, Tezcatlipoca. But as his eyes adjusted to the sudden change in light, he realized that it was still here, it was real, he could even hear the clatter of its bejeweled robe and the swish of its plumed headdress as it darted its face toward him with the horrible precision of a snapping vulture.

In another instant, though, his revulsion passed. It was as if a fire came into his body, lighting up the cells, causing his spirit to dance within him, and it was a dark and bloody dance.

With understanding, the apparition faded. He had seen a reflection of his own soul in a very special light, and boy, had he felt it. The energy of the damn god of death had come into him. That had been powerful.

His radio beeped again. Goddamn them! He turned off his light and opened the drawer. His little Sony was a masterpiece of clandestine technology, its additional circuits smaller than grains of rice. On the surface, it was an ordinary multiband portable. But it also contained this other component, a high-energy single-sideband transceiver and very careful shielding so that it would not be fried by solar electromagnetic energy.

The small display quickly flashed the decoded message. "General warning. General warning to all stations. Atomic clocks have stopped worldwide. Repeat. Atomic clocks have stopped."

Physicists had theorized that such a thing might happen, as the world came to the end of the cycle.

They had gone past the frontier of reality. And at that very moment, the people who ran this place had started something new, some device that emitted light that drove you to face the truth of your soul.

And here was Mack the Cat, trapped in his damn room.

The end of time had arrived and what did he have to do? He had to goddamn well *wait*!

DAVID FORD'S JOURNAL: FOUR

It's now three o'clock in the morning and I have been paging through every book in this library and I have been doing it for five hours, and I will now record the reason. My search was inspired by those last two sentences at the end of the list. The first one was, "What I could not do, you must."

I interpret this to mean that he could not accomplish time travel, but knew that it was possible, and also that it would be, in our era, the only route of survival. But movement through time—literal, physical movement into another time—how could that ever be done?

When I was in college, the great physicist Stephen Hawking announced that he had changed his view of time travel, saying that he had come to believe that it was indeed possible. Last year—God, how long ago that seems—there was an experiment at the CERN supercollider in Switzerland that projected subatomic particles into the future, which were detected a few millionths of a second later, as they "landed" in time and the rest of the world caught up with them. They had never left time, but rather had moved through it faster than the universe normally allows.

Still, though, can something as large as a human body ever be accelerated like that? Even if this were possible, we'd have to go incredibly far in order to find a world that had healed from the wounds of this catastrophe.

Herbert Acton didn't do it. From my days in the class, I remember visiting his grave, which is on this estate. Mrs. Acton took us there, and now lies beside him, I am sure. They had no children. Understandable, knowing the future as they did.

As impossible as acceleration through time sounds, it may be that it has happened before—not to a human being, but to an animal.

A story that might involve time movement appears in a book called, I believe, *Hunt for the Skinwalker*, by a biochemist called Colm Kelleher. Dr. Kelleher was the manager of the Institute for Discovery Sciences, an organization which sought to bring scientific method to the study of unusual events.

One of these events was the sudden appearance of an enormous wolf on a property that had been bought for the institute. This property, in Utah, was known to be a hotbed of odd events and sightings of the otherworldly.

When I read the book, I recognized the animal to be a dire wolf. It came up to a paddock containing some goats, in full view of the ranchers, then loped away after they shot at it. It went into some tall grass and simply disappeared.

Now, the dire wolf was rendered extinct by the catastrophe that ended the last Ice Age. And yet, here it was on this ranch. The scientists were even able to determine its weight by measuring the depths of its footprints in the marsh where it disappeared.

I think that this animal had moved through time, and I think I know why this happened. First, there was something about the place. There must also be something similar here, and this, I think, is crucial to whether or not we will be able to do it. This house was undoubtedly placed here because this spot is, like the ranch in Utah, conducive to such movements. Why, I cannot even begin to imagine.

Second, I believe that, in its own time, this animal was experiencing incredible fear. Its world was collapsing around its ears. At the end of the Pleistocene, most of Utah was flooded along with the rest of the United States by rapid glacial melt. Like now, the solar system was passing through the energetic remains of the supernova, and this had brought about a planetary bombardment and the complete, sudden, and devastating ruin of the world.

So given pressure extreme enough and the right conditions, actual, physical movement through time must be possible.

How, I do not know. However, my thought is that the class, if it can be brought back to normal, *will* know. They will all turn out to have pieces of the greatest puzzle that has ever been: the secret of time, and how to walk it like a road.

But, for now, I must leave this part of the document behind. If only the class can come into focus before it's too late, maybe we can construct our bridge across time.

I think on this. Come up only with one thought—I have to trust Caroline.

So I go on to the second sentence: "The judgment begins."

What is happening now is, we already know, a repeat of a disaster that happened 12,600 years ago. In that time, the human population of Earth declined by over 90 percent.

After that, there was a long period of silence on this planet. Nothing happened. But then, about seven thousand years ago, heroes appeared throughout the world. The story of the great Egyptian hero Osiris dates from that time, and the stories of India's demigod Krishna and other brilliant heroes, and civilization starts. Throughout its early years, we see such leaders as Akhenaton and Moses, who was perhaps his son, who bring the idea of the single God into the world. In the Americas, the civilizing Viracocha appear and, of course, my avatar Quetzalcoatl. Then, to begin the recently ended Age of Pisces, Jesus, who learned his secrets in Egypt and who was born in a most mysterious way.

I believe that these people were not mythological figures but very real human beings, time travelers from the lost civilization, coming forward to bring its wisdom to a new, still brutal era. The ideas of compassionate life, of the one God, of the promise of resurrection and the means to attain it—these are what they brought.

Just as their pre-Egyptian civilization was being inundated worldwide, they used their knowledge of time travel to leap forward five thousand years and reinvent human decency and goodness. They left behind new civilizations in the Indus and Nile valleys, in the Fertile Crescent in Sumeria, on Crete and in Central and South America.

Even as recently as the early Christian era, somebody knew of the existence of the great cycles and the periodic harvest of souls, I think, and was consciously directing the construction of civilization from a high perspective, with the objective of making more souls that were energetic enough, and light enough, to enter higher realms.

The energy is the energy of love, and the lightness is a lack of attachment to the physical world.

My reasoning that these cycles were known comes from observation of the Western long count calendar, the Zodiac, which measures the slow movement of the North Pole around a great circle that lasts just over twenty-five thousand years. It is divided into twelve roughly two-thousand-year segments, the houses of the Zodiac.

Like the Mayan Long Count calendar, it marks ours as an age of enormous change, although without that extraordinary precision.

The Old Testament was written during the Age of Aries, the ram, and in the Old Testament, the ram is mentioned seventy-two times, more than any other animal. It is the testament of the ram, written by people who knew very well what they were doing. Similarly the New Testament, which appeared just as Aries gave way to Pisces, the fish, speaks of Jesus as the Fisher of Men. The apostles are fishermen. The earliest symbol of Christ is the fish.

They knew and they understood, and they left this hidden record for the future.

Now we have reached the Age of Aquarius, the water carrier, and he is pouring out his water—that is to say, Earth is becoming unlivable.

During the Age of Pisces, the little fish—mankind—was nurtured in the water—the womb of Earth. Now, however, we are too big for Earth to carry and we are experiencing the violence of birth. As Earth becomes unable to support the little fish, she is ejecting us onto dry land.

Many will die now. Souls heavy with greed and cruelty will be unable to rise and will sink down into the core of the planet—the lake of fire described in Revelation.

In the autobiography of Hitler's architect, Albert Speer, he describes his experience after the ringleaders of this spectacularly evil movement were hanged at Spandau Prison in Berlin. They had been executed in a gymnasium, and he and other remaining prisoners were ordered to clean it up after the process was complete.

Underneath the gallows, they found a scorch mark in the floor so deep that they could not remove it.

Charles Light explained to us that this mark was left by evil souls as they fell out of their bodies and sank into the core of the earth, where they will remain until their evil has been consumed. They will return as the merest sparks of essence, ready to begin the eons-long climb from tiny life to intelligence, or, in some cases, to remain forever a part of the lesser world, never again to be granted the chance at change that being an intelligent creature offers.

The evil descend, the good rise—and then there are the rest of us, the little band of perhaps a million who stay. And what happens to us?

I know that we are intended to build a new world, but I also know that nothing is certain. It is clear to me that we are supposed to escape into the future—to go forward to a time when Earth has healed herself.

Somebody else also knows these things, and they want to escape into the future instead of us, and they are here and they are fighting hard.

I'm exhausted beyond words and I feel sick to see the way this whole affair seems to be going off the rails, but my body has betrayed me with exhaustion, and I've got to sleep.

I fall back on the bed. I reach over to the table and take my gun in my hand, and clutch it, holding it over my heart. I close my eyes.

7

DEVILS

A bright light—very bright—brought David's eyes flying open. Before he could think, he had leaped out of bed, but it was gone now and he was blinded.

He stood poised at his bedside, his heart thundering, desperate for his vision to return. When it did, he saw a shadowy form between himself and the window. Instinctively, he stepped back. It didn't move, but he could see in the untidy glow of the auroras that it was something fantastic, feathered, massive, radiating a presence he could actually feel, a kind of immediate, spontaneous joy that made him think of the joy of a child, but also another, more fundamental sense of the rightness and balance even of this terrible time, and he seemed to see a deep secret, that the world rides a wire of balance that man cannot break.

No matter how bad things seem, in some deep living heart, the heart of the universe itself, always, all is well.

It was Quetzalcoatl in all his richness and joy.

The emotions were confusing and powerful and the apparition was so real that he drew away from it—and felt, then, the brush of feathers as the thing came right up to him, its eyes infinite pools of kindness, its soft hands caressing him and, it seemed, dipping into his skin as if it was cream, sliding with a quivering, eerie tension, into him. He twisted, he pulled at it, but it drifted between his fingers like smoke, and kept on entering him until it was entirely inside him. Gradually, the whooshing of its feathers was absorbed in the trembling rumble of his heart.

Gagging, his pulse soaring, sweat and tears pouring off him, he retched, then fell against the edge of his bed, then staggered into the bathroom.

He was heaving over the toilet when a cool hand came under his forehead. Shocked, he jumped back and turned—and there stood Katie in white silk pajamas, her hair loose around her face. He tried to say something but had to return to his vomiting, and she held a damp cloth against his forehead as he struggled.

"Let it come," she said, "let it be."

It was, frankly, immeasurably reassuring to feel her holding him and hear the calm in her voice.

Finally, the feeling subsided. He straightened up. "I'm sorry. I—my God, that light! What was that light?"

She gave him a quizzical look. Not for the first time he saw past her job to the woman, noticing the sensuality of her lips and the seductive directness of her eyes. They were not gentle eyes, but frank ones.

She guided him back into the bedroom. "I think you had a nightmare, David." And also, that was the first time she'd addressed him by anything except "Doctor." She drew him down to his bedside.

"That light—my God!"

"I didn't see a light. I heard you yelling."

"I hope I didn't wake up the whole house." The medical staff were all on this floor. He did not need to be embarrassed. He did not need to appear weak.

"Just me and Marian." She gave him a tentative smile. "I told her I'd handle you."

"I've made a fool of myself."

"You've revealed yourself to be a man under pressure."

"It was weak and unprofessional and I'm sorry you and Marian had to hear it."

She ruffled his hair. "Is there anything else?"

There was, he realized. There could be. But then he had a change of heart. That sort of fraternization was just a bit less bad than diddling with patients, especially in an enclosed situation like the Acton Clinic was becoming. Or rather, had become.

"Thanks for helping me, Katie."

She smiled, he thought, a little sadly. "Not a problem. You're a lot easier than the patients."

"I should hope so."

"Incidentally, if you want to read the paper files, could you please ask me in the future, David? I'd really appreciate that."

"Of course. I was just curious, Katie."

"Oh, hey. You do know how to use given names. Everybody's been wondering."

As if on impulse, she leaned forward, lifted onto her toes, and brushed his cheek with a kiss. He started to speak, but she held her finger to his lips, then waved it. Then she turned and was gone.

The little intimacy had shot right through him, warm and immediate and comforting. The need he had been feeling for a woman surfaced so intensely that he sprang up in his pajamas.

Sitting on the edge of his bed, he took deep breaths, waiting for the desire to subside. He could probably go across the hall right now and have her. That had been a clear invitation. But no, it was a mistake.

And then he thought, *That light was real.* But the hallucination that had followed—dear God, the pressure was really getting to him, driving itself deep. That had been Quetzalcoatl, the Aztec god he was identified with in Herbert Acton's note. Now he was, himself, integrating the imagery into his fantasy life.

Well, here was some pretty obvious psychology: he wanted to identify himself with the compassionate and healing aspect of the dark religion that was obsessing the world, and had long since seduced this place.

He worried about the light. Finally, he called the guard station.

"Did you notice a flash?"

"Yes, Doctor. But we don't know its origin."

"The facility is quiet?"

"All secure."

He padded across his bedroom and gazed out the window. Katie must not have seen it because it had originated on this side of the building.

Standing, watching the grounds pale in the auroral light, he felt a great surge of compassion for this little community whose welfare had been put in his hands.

But then he saw—could that be real? No, it was a trick of light, surely. But then he saw it again, a supple figure moving toward the copse of honey locust that stood between the parking area and the formal gardens behind the house. Was that somebody heading toward the gate?

He watched the trees, their leaves fluttering in the wind. No, he was sure he had seen a woman going toward the gate—a woman in what looked like a hospital gown.

Not a staffer, then. So, a patient. He went back to his phone. "Dr. Ford again. You guys need to light us up, we've got somebody on the grounds. A woman. Heading for the main gate."

"Got it. I'll alert perimeter and send a team out."

As David hung up, the night security officer threw the switches that flood-illuminated the entire property.

A moment later, three uniformed guards, guns on their hips, came up from the gatehouse, and two more from the nearest of the new watch-towers that had been installed along the perimeter.

He grabbed the phone again. "I want a patient census. Every room, including the lockdowns."

"We're moving."

Glen he trusted, and his security team was the best money could buy . . . but, these days, how good was that? He did not want to end up having to call a family that was paying fifty grand a month to keep their patient safe, to tell them that he or she had left care, especially not naked in the middle of the night.

Should he go down and supervise? No, that would send the wrong message. He needed to show his people he had faith in their abilities—

or, at the least, to conceal his suspicions. Only if a patient was apprehended would he go down. If it turned out to be a member of the staff, he'd leave the matter to others.

Still, he might be needed, so he pulled jeans and a sweatshirt over his pajamas, then thrust his feet into a pair of sandals.

His phone rang. He picked it up and Katie said, "Now I see light."

"A possible patient outside," he said. "I thought I saw somebody over by the parking lot."

"Oh, okay. Do you need me again?"

"No, I'm waiting on a census from security. If we've got somebody missing, I'll call you."

He hung up. A moment later, the phone rang again. "We're fully complimented," the security officer said without preamble. "The patients are all in their beds and the staff's all accounted for."

"Well, okay, then chalk it up to inexperience."

The security officer chuckled. "Doc Ullman lit us up twice a week at least. Comes with the territory."

"Boy, does it ever." He hung up. The flash of light, the bizarre hallucination, the person outside—were they all somehow connected?

Thinking back, he thought maybe he recognized the woman. That flowing hair—maybe it had been Caroline Light. But she'd been so extremely distraught—or acting the part so well—that he had moved her into a padded room, which meant constant surveillance, so surely she hadn't managed to just stroll out.

He sank down onto his bed. He was absolutely exhausted and dawn was not far off. But before he went to sleep, he had to face some facts. First, there had been that flash. It couldn't have been an aurora, they weren't that bright. Maybe an exploding satellite, but then surely Katie would have noticed it, too. No, he thought that the flash must have come from below his windows, either from inside the building or from the grounds in front. From Katie's room on the back, it must not have been noticeable.

Then had come the hallucination of Quetzalcoatl. It had been very vivid, but his overwrought and overtaxed mind was the explanation for it.

He was less sure about the presence of Caroline Light outside. That had seemed real. He had been awake, standing at the window.

He decided to look in on her, and not rely on the surveillance system, but do it personally.

He went quietly into the corridor. All the doors were closed, including Katie's. Even so, a glance up at the surveillance camera at the far end of the ceiling made him wonder who might be watching him besides the guard station, or if anyone there might be part of the opposition.

He came to the door that led to the patient wing, swiped his right forefinger across the reader, and waited for it to unlock. But as he waited, he heard sounds coming from the part of the recreation complex that was in the old house, which included the art room with its tall windows, and the music room. Somebody was playing the wonderful old Steinway that was there.

Immediately, he changed direction and hurried down the service stairway that led from this back hall to the pantry below. At the foot of the stairs, he stopped and listened. No question now. That was Beethoven's *Appassionata,* and the pianist was superb. The only problem was that it was nearly five in the morning, and the public rooms were closed.

As he passed through the patients' dining area and the sound grew more distinct, the superb musicianship made him think that it might be a recording.

At the door to the music room, though, he saw a vague figure sitting at the instrument.

It was a woman in a nightgown, her hair down her back.

Caroline?

No, the hair was straight, not shimmering and flowing like Caroline's. The woman was wrapped in an enormous robe. As she played, her body moved gracefully. She was easily good enough to go on stage. A member of the class, then?

He knew that he should not approach this person without support personnel equipped with restraints, and he hesitated—whereupon she stopped playing.

"I'm not dangerous, Doctor," she said without turning around.

He knew the voice. It was Linda Fairbrother. No wonder she had been identified with the god of music. He wished he had her glyph with him. He could test the process. If it worked, he'd awaken the whole class. The time for waiting was past, he sensed that clearly, and he was going to trust his instincts now.

"Linda," he said, "I think there's a time for this. Another time."

She resumed playing.

"Linda, we need to stop now." Slowly, carefully, he moved closer, until he was standing directly beside her. "Linda, we need to stop."

She played on.

There was another of the terrific flashes. In the second or so that it filled the darkness, Linda Fairbrother seemed to turn into something else, a complicated creature full of flaring colors—her god, or, as we call it now, her subconscious. And then the light was gone and all he could see were two red dots. But the music never stopped. She didn't miss a single note.

Unlike him, she had not startled. So she was expecting the flash, she must be.

"Linda, what was that?"

He put his hand on her hand, dropping the music into discord.

She stopped, and in the silence, he heard something unexpected— a hissing noise that had been covered by the sound of the music . . . which, he thought, was meant to have been covered by it.

It came from the art room.

"Linda," he said, "what is that?"

She sat staring into the dark, silent.

"Linda, I need you to step out of here because that sounds like a major gas leak, and I've got to—"

Another flash, and again he was looking at the fluttering, dangerous, wonderful deity of music.

Whatever was happening in the art room had to be dealt with. He went to the wall phone and snatched it up, only to find that there was no dial tone. Wonderful.

He called back to Linda, "You can play, go ahead and play." He didn't need this one to be wandering right now. But the music did not start again and he had to prioritize. Clearly, the possible danger to the whole structure took precedence, and he pushed his way into the art room.

At once, his eye was drawn to the kiln, out of which there glared an unearthly blue light. Here, the hissing sound was a roar. There were figures clustered around the furnace—it was no kiln, that could not have been more obvious. They were wearing welder's masks.

"Excuse me!"

As if in a nightmare, nobody seemed to hear him. He went right up to them, but here the light was so intense that he had to shield his eyes.

"This has to stop!"

He saw a big square tray from the kitchen's baking department. On it was a measure of white powder, and two of the concealed figures were carefully pouring it into tiny jars, mixing it with a liquid. Others took trays of the jars toward the kitchen.

A yellow flash so bright that he was ready to believe he'd been blinded forever this time came out of the furnace. In it, though, he saw something completely unexpected, not glowering Aztec gods but a beautiful field, a green and smiling land, incredibly detailed. It was there for only a second, but it was as if he was actually in this field.

Then it was over—and there was a smattering of applause. Applause! And still they were acting as if he wasn't there at all.

An instant later, he saw the face of Caroline Light three inches from his own, the eyes tight with anger, but also—what was it? Humor? The kindness, he thought, and the danger of the gods.

Then the room was filled with clouds, beautiful, soaring clouds just becoming visible in the light of the predawn. Clouds . . . he was looking up at clouds.

Dear heaven, he was in bed! He was in bed and those were the clouds of his ceiling, one of the many trompe l'oeils in the mansion.

As if the mattress was on fire, he jumped out and onto the floor. But nothing was on fire. He was simply alone in bed at dawn, that was all.

But no, that couldn't be. It could not be. That had not been a dream, nobody dreamed that elaborately, it wasn't possible.

He was still in his jeans, anyway, so he went back downstairs.

There was nobody at the piano and the kiln was dark. But, God, how disorienting. What had happened to the time?

Exactly.

Whatever they had been doing with the kiln had affected not just the brain, inducing hallucinations, it had, he thought, done something to space-time itself. Warped it, twisted it, sent him racing across the hours from three o'clock until dawn in just seconds.

He went to it, opened it, and thrust his hand into the firing chamber. A faint warmth was all he felt, exactly as if it hadn't been fired since yesterday.

But he had seen Caroline Light in here, and Linda Fairbrother had been in the other room playing music to cover the sound of the super-intense fire.

They'd made some sort of powder, he had seen it. And they had also been fools, because everybody in the place must have noticed the flashes, except for the staff in the four bedrooms on the far side of the building, and maybe them, too. Maybe Katie had lied.

What a hell of a situation. What was real? Who could be trusted?

Those people could. That had been the class, and Caroline had been there. They could be trusted. But who were they?

She must be waking them up. Of course she was, they'd been taught to use the glyphs and she was doing it.

Not all of them, though, and not the ones likely to be needed the most, they were still trapped in their various insanities.

It was while they were making that powder that space-time had gotten all twisted. So the opposition was going to try to take it. Therefore, blood-shed was coming.

He took the stairs leading to the second floor of the patient wing, running up, then through the door and down the hall to the central nurses' station.

"Nurse!"

Nurse Fleigler came up from behind her small, electronically dense station.

"Doctor?"

Behind her was a bank of screens. Cameras covered each room from two directions. A computer continuously analyzed sounds, and immediately warned her if there were any screams, breaking glass, thuds, any sound suggesting violence. It also warned her when a room became too quiet.

"You're up early, Doctor."

"What kind of a night?"

"We had a security check. Some lightning flashes. Aside from that, it's been quiet."

David noticed movement in Mack Graham's room.

"What's four doing?"

It was perfectly obvious that the man was engaged in sexual self-stimulation.

"This is the third time tonight. He claims that he's entertaining me."

"He's been in there all night?"

"Absolutely."

"Have any confinement patients been recorded outside of their rooms tonight?"

She shook her head. "What's the matter, Doctor?"

Could those have all been staff members? But no, he'd seen Caroline—or had he?

"How's Caroline?"

"I've got a good sleep signal. Normal breathing pattern. REM sleep."

"But she was agitated earlier, after Claire left her?"

Fleigler nodded, her plain, broad face registering sadness and, perhaps, a degree of accusation.

"The poor woman — she did not like that locked door."

"I want to see her tape, if you don't mind. Just roll it back to, say, three, and play it for me."

The screen flickered, then flashed, and he saw what at first appeared to be a static image, but the status readouts confirmed stage four sleep, heart rate fifty-seven, breathing regular.

There was a flicker on the screen. "What was that?"

"What?"

"Roll it back."

She did so. The flicker repeated.

"Run it slow."

He watched Caroline sleep. Were the flickers caused by the flashes from the art room, or were they edits that concealed Caroline's comings and goings?

"So everything's been quiet? Definitely?"

"Quiet, Doctor." She looked up at him, her brows raised in a suggestion of question.

On his way back to his suite, he came face-to-face with the fact that mystery was piling on mystery, and he was drowning.

Using the fingerprint reader on his door, he entered his suite. He returned to the window where he had seen Caroline disappearing under the trees. Ripped clouds sped past the low moon, and, to the north, lightning now flickered. The east was red with dawn.

He tried the Internet, but it was useless. Finally, he called security.

"How many of those flashes did you record?" he asked.

"Two sets of two each."

It was still over an hour to breakfast, and he was profoundly exhausted. He threw off his jeans and T-shirt and returned to bed. It was so very strange to draw these gorgeous silk sheets up around himself in the context of the world as it was. There was jeopardy all around him, but the bed was here, the sheets were soft, and the mattress even somewhat tolerable.

He closed his eyes and began to drift . . . and found himself having to will his mind away from the image of the woman running in the night, and thoughts of Caroline Light.

He redirected his longing toward Katie Starnes. Her dark Gaelic eyes and cream-white skin were well worth a few moments of presleep contemplation. He shouldn't have been such a damn fool when she'd offered herself. He needed to fix that.

He wondered what Katie actually knew about this place. She hadn't been in the class.

It was as this thought was forming in his mind that he slipped through the invisible door into sleep. His breathing became more steady, his shoulders relaxed, his lips parted slightly. After a moment, his body turned onto its right side, entering its preferred sleep position.

The dreams were immediate and once again he was facing the kiln, watching it flare with that amazing light. Then the broad clearing once again spread out before him. There was thick grass. A distance away was a tall oak, its leaves spring-fresh. Beside it was a thickly blossomed apple tree. In fact, the scene looked very much like the clinic's grounds, but in far, far better days. Caroline Light was there, standing near the trees. She gestured to him, smiled and gestured again.

He thought that this sight of this woman in this place was the most beautiful and compelling thing he had ever seen.

Then there was a crash, followed by a long, retreating rumble, and he was again in bed. More crashing thunder and, coming with it, more flashes, but ordinary lightning this time.

He opened his eyes. Seven ten by the clock. More than an hour had passed in a sleep that seemed to last only a few seconds. Outside, thunder roared and bellowed, and lightning flashed.

The first thing on his agenda this morning was yet another staff meeting, more bad news about supplies and infrastructure, he supposed.

He thought that he needed to understand more about that powder. He needed to gain the confidence of the makers.

He should damn well remember it from the class but he didn't . . . or did he?

Gold? Was it connected with gold?

Rain struck the tall window behind him, crashing torrents of it, and the great house groaned from the pressure of the wind, and the eaves mourned.

Exhausted, confused, and deeply, deeply afraid, David prepared to meet his day.

8

EXTRAORDINARY MINDS

Nurse Beverly Cross and Dr. Marian Hunt came in at the same time, taking seats in the huge office. As David greeted them, he came around from behind his desk. The office enforced the formality of another age.

Nurse Cross gave him a weak smile. She looked exhausted, her eyes hollow.

"You lit us up," she said.

"Sorry about that. I thought I saw a patient in the grounds."

"We have trouble after a light-up. The patients need support."

Bill Osterman, the chief engineer, arrived.

"We have a supply problem," he said as he came in. "Critical low oil and there's nothing in our pipeline."

"Okay, Bill, is there any other supplier we can try?"

"We need to start thinking in terms of a shutdown, to be frank."

"How long do we have left?"

"On full use, four days."

Nobody mentioned the flashes or the activity in the rec area, and he felt that the omission must be intentional.

"All right," he said, "the first thing to do is reduce air-conditioning use. Drop it back to the sleeping areas at night only. The rest of the time, it's off. How much more time does that give us?"

"Another forty-eight hours, maybe. So say a week."

It seemed a great gulf of time, a week, but that, he knew, was just an illusion. What would he do when the generator shut down for good? How would they run the well? And how did you manage a building full of crazy people at night without the use of lights, let alone monitoring equipment?

"I want max possible power down, then. No air at all except in confined spaces where we can't do without. No lights except emergency lighting and as needed for patient control."

Bill nodded. David didn't ask him how much longer this regime would give them. He'd do that later, in private.

Ray Weller arrived announcing that he would be reducing portions and simplifying meals until he could get more reliable deliveries.

"Supply fell out of bed," he said, "everybody just stopped coming and communications are so bad, I can't even tell you why."

On food, they had five days.

With the nurses, handlers, counselors, and other personnel, there were now twenty-one people in the office.

"All right," David said, "obviously we're in serious trouble. Can we send any patients home?" He turned to Glen MacNamara. "I assume we shouldn't even try."

"From what we can tell, it's a probable death sentence. I asked that new intake. She said she was lucky to be alive. She's worried about her chauffeur, not to mention her father back in Virginia. Terribly worried."

He remembered Charles Light as young and vibrant, bursting with sheer joy because of the value of what he was teaching. What charisma, and what a man to have for a father. She must be beside herself.

David decided to try to deal with the unspoken issue in the most straightforward manner that he could.

"Let me be frank. I observed people in the art room last night doing something with the kiln that was producing extraordinary flashes of light. I couldn't tell who it was, they were wearing welder's masks. But I think more than one person in this room knows what I'm talking about, and I'd like an explanation."

Marian Hunt said, "What I find interesting was that you were down there at all."

"This place is my responsibility, Marian. And I think that the new intake, Caroline, was out of her quarters at some point last night."

"She was confined," Marian said, "on your orders."

"And your tone says that she shouldn't have been."

"She showed no signs of violence."

"She was distraught. She needed to be controlled. Supported." Also protected, but he certainly did not intend to add that.

He could see the color rising in Marian's face. She was looking at it entirely from a professional point of view, from which standpoint he'd obviously made a misjudgment.

"I was with her for a time. Claire and I spelled each other. Doctor, to be frank with you, it's not appropriate to bring procedures you learned at a public facility into this environment."

"Doctor, if you don't mind, I'd like to continue this outside of staff."

She nodded. He continued playing his role.

"Mr. Osterman, I need you to deal with that kiln. I want it moved out of the art room." Actually, he was terribly excited by what had been done. Even if he was still only peripherally in the picture, progress was being made and that was the first hopeful thing he had known since he'd realized the true import of what was happening.

Claire, who had been shaking her head, now burst out, "That's a therapeutic tool! I want an explanation!"

"It's being used in an unauthorized manner by unknown parties in the dead of the night, which is a damn good explanation, in my opinion."

She gave him what he interpreted as a condescending look. Katie Starnes crossed her legs and smoothed down her white skirt. The silence in the room deepened.

"Leave the kiln," he finally said. He was no actor, and the whole process involved made him uncomfortable. But he had no choice, obviously, not until more was known.

It was time to shift subjects, and he turned his attention to Katie.

"Is there any word from Maryland Medical Supply?"

"They're expecting to ship day after tomorrow. But even if the shipment gets through, we can expect massive shortfalls and no-ships on most drugs."

"So, basically, we're in a tailspin. We're going to have to cut to the bone. As far as our therapeutic service is concerned, it looks like we're headed back to about the mid-fifties, before there were even any tranquilizers." He looked to Glen. "Given that we're leaving the kiln as is, I want the recreation area patrolled regularly at night, but if you find anything unusual, don't intervene. Call me."

Glen's eyes told him that he understood. The workers at the kiln would be carefully guarded.

"And nurses, if you have patients missing from any confined setting at any time, I am to be informed personally and at once. Is that clear?"

Nobody spoke. Finally, Claire said, "Well, I think we have our marching orders."

As far as they were concerned, he'd gone too far. Never challenge a nurse's professionalism, not if you expect peace in your hospital. He tried a little diplomacy.

"Obviously, circumstances are presently working against us, so I want us all to stay as focused as we can on our mission, which is to keep this institution running, which means working together as best we can. But, if I am going to manage this place, I am asking you, please, to cooperate with me. We have a terribly hard time ahead, and we also have this security issue, given what happened to Mrs. Denman."

"Here," Katie asked, genuine surprise in her voice, "a security issue in the clinic?"

"With the town," he explained hastily.

"Well," Katie said, "I don't know about the rest of you, but I'm doing my best."

"We all are, and we're certainly willing to carry out your policies," Marian Hunt added.

"And the kiln is just a kiln," Osterman muttered.

The meeting concluded on what he could only see as a sour note. But why wouldn't they be sour? There was nothing positive here, it was all supply problems, security problems, and, because of the subterfuge he'd had to engage in, a lack of faith in their new boss. But any opponent in this room would have to see him as being nothing more than what he appeared to be—an inexperienced and overbearing supervisor.

Marian lingered at the door. Their eyes met and he nodded, and she returned.

She said, "David, we need to talk about some additional matters."

"Don't resign, Marian. Remember that I didn't pick me, Mrs. Denman did."

She sat down before the dark fireplace.

"If it's all the same to you, David, I won't dignify that with a response."

"I'm sorry, I—"

"Don't say you're sorry. You say that too much. It makes you look weak." She smiled a little. "Do you know that T-shirt? I think Mack wears it from time to time. "'Graham Mining, Where the Weak are Killed and Eaten.' Do you know that?"

"I haven't seen it."

"He's in the art room now," Katie said. "He's got it on."

Marian waved her hand. "The point is, if you appear weak, Acton will devour you."

"Is that what happened to Dr. Ullman?"

"As far as we know, the fire was set by townies."

"And yet one day later you put Mack under confinement and gave him an armed guard."

"I did that because he's potentially violent."

"Not because he killed Dr. Ullman and you know it perfectly well?"

"I do not know it. It could've been the police themselves, or even the firemen. We are hated here."

"I've noticed."

"Understand it. Live it. It is the central reality of all our lives. This is the palace, still splendid in the middle of a ruined and starving world."

What was her point? And speaking of Mack, he was due here for a session in a few minutes.

She continued, "I want to agree with you to an extent, David. Oh, not about the conspiracy business. You saw lightning, or some sort of static effect. Who knows these days what nature might toss at us? And patients go downstairs at all hours." She held up a hand. "I know it's against the rules, but you don't tell people like this to follow your rules. You ask them."

"But they—"

"I'm sorry, but I'm not even interested in what they were doing. They do all sorts of odd things. Most of them are geniuses, which I'm sure you've noticed. Or have you?"

"Don't patronize me, Marian."

"Trust them, David! What they are doing here, even who they really are, most of them—well, we're not sure, none of us. But we serve their needs. We feed them and protect them and give them shelter and psychiatric support. They're far, far beyond most mortals, including you and me. Did you know that most of them can learn a new language in a couple of hours? And ask them to recite something for you sometime. Anything worth reciting. They'll know it, almost certainly. Give them something to read, then ask them to repeat it a couple of days later. It'll come back verbatim. Engage them on the most complex topics, you'll be amazed."

"Like what—Aztec culture?"

"Most of these people are as interested as anybody in ancient Mesoamerica. The difference is, they understand things like the Nahuatl language of the Aztecs, and their philosophy, and Mayan mathematics."

His mind went to Acton's list sitting right now locked in one of the drawers of his desk. He did not want to feel as if he was drowning, but that was exactly how he felt. He knew that Marian was not an insider, Aubrey Denman had told him. So he would not open up to her, no matter how familiar with the situation she seemed.

Mack Graham was on his way, and there wasn't time to continue this. All he could do was to tell the truth of his feelings.

"Marian, I'm moved, I have to admit, by your loyalty to the patients."

"David, in this place nothing is as it seems."

"What does that mean?"

"It means that you may never fully understand them or what they're doing. But trust it, David. We all do, we just trust it." She came to her feet. "I have patients, too," she said. "Linda Fairbrother had a very difficult night. A painful interruption, as I understand it. She has a compulsive need to play every note in precise sequence." Her voice rose a little. "But some insensitive fool touched her hand—*touched it*—and disturbed the flow of her music and that has injured her."

"I'm sorry," David said.

"Yes," she responded, "you are." And she left.

David fought the pain that her sarcasm brought. He should not have interrupted the patient. It had been insensitive, even unprofessional. You empathized, you did not control . . . unless, of course, you were a kid who was just plain out of his depth.

To regain his composure, what he needed was information. If he just understood the basic realities of this place better, he could be more useful. Or, frankly, begin to be useful at all. He looked to Katie, who remained as still as a wary bird.

"Katie, you've been here for, um—"

"Four years."

"As a psychiatric nurse who has been working with Dr. Hunt for that time, what do you make of this conversation?"

"Are you putting me on the spot, here?"

"I'm asking for your professional opinion."

"As a nurse, my opinion of her is that she's a conscientious and effective doctor."

"And me? How am I doing?"

"David, to be completely frank, you're taking longer figuring things out than I would have thought."

"I can't figure anything out!"

"You can figure out what you need to figure out, which is how to support these patients. Just concentrate on their needs, David! Who knows what they're *doing*? We can't understand, we don't have the minds for it. What we can do is provide a hug or a pill when needed, and a sounding board. Let them go where they want to go, be there to catch them when they trip. That's all we can do."

His buzzer rang, and at the Acton Clinic, you did not keep patients waiting.

9

ORME

Mack appeared in a silk jacket and trousers, moving with that curious precision of his. As he slid into the patient's chair in the nook that David had reserved for these sessions, David thought that he looked not like a mental patient with a severely distorted grasp of reality, but like some sort of vaudeville performer.

"We could become cannibals," Mack said.

That certainly sounded like symptomatic production. He settled in for a real session with a real psychiatric patient . . . for once.

"What makes you say that?"

"No eggs at breakfast, therefore Acton is having supply problems. We could send raiding parties into the town."

"Do you think cannibalism is a good idea?"

"I'm crazy, so of course I do. I want to know about the new intake."

"You'll meet her in the common areas."

"Social Register?"

"I wouldn't know, Mack."

"Let me tell you about her. She's at least thirty. She's a self-commit who's been having very serious second thoughts. And last night, when she was screaming in that so very pleasant padded cell of yours, and you went to observe her, you got, shall we say, sidetracked."

What was this? Had this patient overheard something? Or had he been behind one of those welder's masks, perhaps—another confinement patient being let out at night?

"Expand on that."

"I think there are lots of surprises in the Acton Clinic. Right answer?"

"Therapeutic interaction isn't about right answers. It's about opening doors."

"You see the sun this morning?"

"Have you seen the sun?"

"My point is that it looks like it's had a bite taken out of it. The sunspot is gigantic."

"What does that mean to you?"

"To me? That I won't be alive in six months. Like you. Like everybody."

"Are you sure?"

"Of course I'm sure. Incidentally, the new intake—what's her surname? Where's she from?"

"We're back to the new patient?"

"I just like to know who's here. Who I might be dealing with. The world of the obscenely rich is not a large one. She and I might have played doctor as kids. If so, I'd like to renew the acquaintance."

"Being in the CIA makes you rich?"

"Being the heir to Graham Mining makes you rich. I served my country for a dollar a year. And I was retired mental, okay? Is that what you want me to admit? That I was humiliated and ended up in this idiotic place, spilling my innermost secrets to a kid? Dr. Ford, I want just two things from you. First, I want to know the name of the new intake. I want to know who I'm living with. Second, I would like you to review my file and see if I really need to be on confinement."

"You don't think you should be?"

"Of course not! I don't understand it at all."

"Dr. Hunt did it because you have anger issues. Your daytime rights aren't affected."

"Except I have a goddamn armed guard when I go outside!"

"Armed with a tranquilizer gun. After Dr. Ullman passed away, you were very, very angry." He did not bring up the fact that Mack had been AWOL at the time of the fire.

"Something was wrong that night, Doctor. And something was wrong last night, is wrong now, and has been wrong for weeks. And I don't mean the sun or the economy or any of that crap. I mean that something is wrong *here*. Something is happening to this place, and yes, it scares me and when I am afraid, yes, I have an anger problem. Like those flashes last night? What was *that*? I had—" He stopped, shook his head.

"You had?"

"I don't know. A dream. Not pretty."

"You think the flashes were a dream?"

"Hell no, but they triggered something."

"Can you describe it, Mack?"

"Um, sure. A demon. I saw a demon."

David strove to maintain the therapeutic context, but at the same time was acutely aware of his own reaction to the flashes, but what he'd seen had hardly been a demon.

"You want to ask me something, Doctor. Go ahead."

Mack was certainly perceptive. "What do you know about the flashes?"

"They're making an ORME, and that's pretty damn disturbing."

"An ORME?"

"An orbitally rearranged monatomic element. Gold, would be my guess. The legendary philosopher's stone."

Those two words, "philosopher's stone," would ordinarily have evoked in him the quiet contempt of the scientist dealing with an ignorant member of the public who was silly enough to believe such twaddle.

That was not how he reacted now. "Go on."

"It's being made in their arc furnace. The 'kiln.' Look inside sometime."

"I have. It looks like a kiln."

"Not at night, Doc. That's when they install their tungsten filament, and you're looking at three thousand degrees sustained."

"Isn't that rather a high temperature?"

"Not for them. And this new lady, she's their leader, I think. I think things are going into overdrive. She, um—God, you know, I've forgotten her name."

"Caroline."

"Haven't we done this? Maybe the flashes erased my memory. I mean her last name. Is it Acton?"

David remained impassive.

"Is it Light, then? Is she a member of the Light family?"

Mack was fishing hard—too hard, David thought. He would not forget this. "Let's get back to ORME," he said. "It's what?"

"An orbitally rearranged monatomic element is an element that's not entirely confined to three-dimensional space. It's torsioned into hyperspace. You eat it, and you extend into hyperspace, too."

The philospher's stone . . . they'd been taught about it in class. *"It's not just for philosophers and it's not a stone, it's a white powder."*

"And extending into hyperspace gets you what?"

"You're outside of space and time. So you can see the past and the future. You can . . . maybe escape. Move around time or through it faster. Except, of course, for the problem."

"Which is?"

"It's total bullshit. All ingesting a heavy metal is gonna do is screw with your kidneys."

"That would be my best guess, too."

If a man's stare could express the hunger of a tiger, Mack the Cat's poisoned eyes expressed it now. At that moment, the session bell chimed softly and he leaped to attention and saluted. "Hup!"

David recalled Katie's comment that Mack alternated between incipient serial killer and charming boy.

After he left, David slid aside the wall of book backs that concealed his electronics from patients. He keyed in Mack's code, F-0188, and the system began following his transponder. David watched him go down the wide hallway past Katie's office, then down two flights of stairs, the system automatically shifting from one camera to the next as it followed him.

He went into the art room where a number of other patients were painting and one was sculpting.

David closed the monitors. This was the very picture of a compliant patient.

He had fifteen minutes before his next appointment, which was Linda Fairbrother.

He pressed his intercom and said to Katie, "I'm going down to the art room to observe Mack. I'll be back in time for Fairbrother."

As he was closing his monitoring system, he saw Caroline Light sitting at an easel in the art room. Again, he pressed the intercom. "I see that Caroline is in the population."

"Dr. Hunt said to release her."

He went into the outer office. "But she's under constant supervision?"

She gestured toward her bank of screens. "Absolutely. Sam's on the job, watching her and Mack and keeping them apart."

"Oh?"

"Mack has expressed interest in her."

He was tempted to issue Sam a real gun and live rounds. He would immediately reinforce to Sam that he thought that Mack was potentially quite dangerous to her.

"Let Marian know that I'll expect to discuss Caroline's progress toward the end of the day. We'll need to make a decision about where she sleeps tonight."

Frankly, he hoped that she would fake more evidence of disturbance and justify another night under confinement—not that it helped, given her hidden power to apparently come and go as she pleased. He'd assumed that she'd had help from the staff—probably Fleigler—but now who knew, maybe she'd just walked through the walls.

This substance they were making—even the process of creating it affected the mind profoundly, and look what had happened to him when he drew close. He'd been somehow—was the right word "overcome"?—yes, overcome, and what had taken place next? He thought that they had probably carried him to his room.

But the state he had been in was not sleep, it was darker and deeper than sleep. Had he been outside of time, somehow? Was such a thing truly possible?

In any case, if just the manufacturing process was that disorienting, perhaps the substance was potent indeed. He could certainly understand why the group making it had been wearing welder's masks.

White powder gold . . . it had been discussed in class—discussed a lot. He could see Mr. Light sitting on the edge of his desk speaking about it. Could see but not hear.

God, but the fog of amnesia was maddening. Maybe Katie knew more than she was saying. Maybe there would be some trigger to memory if he just talked about it all. "Katie, what's your impression of what happened last night? Please be frank."

"You were overwrought. It could happen to anybody."

Not helpful. "Did I go out? Were you aware of that?"

She was silent. Then she reached out, her hand tentative. For a moment, he still hesitated, but when she began to withdraw it, he took it. They remained like that for a moment, and he felt that her hand was warm and small and very soft.

A moment later, it was over, and she turned away and busied herself with her files. He went down to watch Caroline and Mack, and try to feel his way a little further down the dark passage that was life at the Acton Clinic.

10

MAYHEM

Mack sat near Caroline Light, watching her paint the most strikingly realistic painting he had ever seen. She was just beginning, but it was really very odd. It wasn't photographic, it was beyond that. The light shimmering in the meadow, the glow of the tiny flowers and the green of the grass—it was just uncanny, and what a very mysterious thing for her to be doing. What would a painting have to do with anything, no matter how it appeared?

He had calculated every word uttered in his session with young David, controlling not only his own answers, but also the doctor's questions, until finally the truth had been revealed. At the instant that the young doctor's untrained body language—crossing his legs, glancing away— had revealed the correctness of his guess that this was Caroline Light, a bolt of pure fire had shot through him, forcing him to will his face to impassivity and idly straighten his tie while he was actually brimming with triumph inside.

It was Caroline Light, and my, but she had fooled them all, hadn't she? Rich, neurotic playgirl. And all that screaming and crying last night—she was an excellent actress.

No matter how good she was, though, in the end he was going to squeeze out every morsel of information she possessed, including how to make white powder gold that worked, and exactly what to do with it that would lead to escape from this hell.

They might not be able to save all the people in all the redoubts, but they could certainly save the Blue Ridge, which would be enough to start mankind again on a far stronger footing. No more corrupt bloodlines, no more inferior people, not ever. A new world.

He was eager to get to his room and let General Wylie know she was here. He needed orders and support personnel. There must be no mistakes, and if there was resistance from the security guards when he took her—as he had to believe there would be—he had to be certain that they would not succeed in stopping him.

"Don't," she said.

Was she speaking to him? Surely not. He was thirty feet away, hardly looking at her.

She turned toward him and challenged him with a stare. "You. Don't."

"Excuse me?"

"Go away."

"I'm sorry. It's your painting. The life in it—"

"I don't think looking at pictures makes men drool like dogs, Mr. Dog."

Why did she care so much? Why was she so concerned about a *picture?*

He was so maddeningly in the dark.

"Hello? Are you deaf?"

"I'm terribly sorry."

He got up from the chair and moved out into the larger recreation area. He strolled up to Sam.

"I guess that didn't work," he said, trying to sound affable.

"Not her type, Mack."

"Yeah, I was halfway across the room."

"You were staring pretty hard."

"Look, I'm going to take a little siesta. Wash her outa my hair."

Sam nodded.

"Um, would you do me a huge favor and not turn on my room." He tugged at his crotch.

"I hear you. I'll hang out in the hall. Monitor off."

They went together up the stairs to the living area. "You used to only be with me when I was outside. I feel kind of oppressed."

"Glen's orders. Supertight security from now on. Thank whoever did Dr. Ullman."

"Townies. Nothing to do with us nice, sweet patients."

"But you were out that night. Unfortunately for you."

He went into his room and closed the door. He couldn't lock it, of course. That could only be done from the outside.

Immediately, he went to his drawer and got out the radio. Using the keypad on the modified TV remote that controlled it, he tapped out a few words: first, "Caroline Light has come. Need immediate action."

He waited for the faint tone that would indicate that his message had been received. The set on the other end was monitored twenty-four hours a day. For security reasons, they had no set transmission times. He looked at his watch. The sixty-second window came and went. Still no acknowledgment. Following protocol, he transmitted a second time, then once again waited.

This had to work, it was too important not to. But the sun was awful today, maybe even the single sideband system they used was gone.

Again he transmitted, and again there was no response.

Okay, he was panicking now, feeling that same sense of being trapped that regularly woke this claustrophobe up nights. Angrily, he shut down his equipment. He told himself that it was a lot harder for his simple system to detect their signals than vice versa. So maybe they'd gotten the message. Maddening. But he had to take risks now, and one of them was to find a way out of this room after lockdown. It was urgent that he gain the freedom of this place as soon as possible.

Sure, he could enter the ductwork, but he needed that blueprint, which meant another excursion into town and a search of the building department's records.

Once he could get out of this room, cover would also require confusion, and he thought he knew how to cause it. The townies lusted after this place. They stayed away because of the guards. He understood the system, though, and he could provide them with a plan. If they were desperate enough, they would come. There would be a battle, and he would use it as a cover to capture Light and wring the truth out of her. Maybe Ford, too. He'd been appointed supervisor of this place, so he had to be high up in the leadership, also.

He stepped out into the hall. Sam sat half asleep in a tipped-back chair in the nurse's station. Good, he would leave him behind right here and now.

"Hi, there," Sam said.

Shit! "Well, I think I'm looking at a walk."

"You want to go out in that? Have you seen the sky?"

"I'm crazy, remember."

Sam was not happy about it, but he stuck to his orders. Don't control the patient, follow the patient.

They reached the bottom of the stairs and crossed the art room.

"Jesus," Sam said.

Mack also looked toward Caroline Light at her easel, and this time was even more awed. It looked more like she was opening a window into a beautiful forest glade, a real one—but not in the here and now, because her sky was normal.

Although he needed to discover what, if anything, this strange talent of hers might mean, he didn't pause long. He wanted no more trouble from her, and he had his plan, and he would find out everything.

At the end of the room, there were broad glass doors that led into the side garden. Glass, but thick as steel. Sam unlocked them with his fingerprint reader, and he and Mack stepped into the white glare of the sun.

"We don't want to be out here, Mack, I'm telling you."

"It's incredible."

"Don't look at the sun."

"I'm careful, Sam." Mack held up his hand, observing through two cracked fingers. The damn thing was devoured with sunspots, a great, jagged, flaring mess.

Sam was doing the same thing. "Come on, let's go back in, Mack."

"Just to the apple tree. Five minutes." He had to get Sam out of sight, just for a moment. He went down to the formal garden, where there were some tall laurel bushes, just trying to bloom. Their slick, dark green leaves were thick, and the path between them was concealing.

People sense things, and in particular, they sense danger. You need absolute control over your body language, your breathing, everything, if somebody who is guarding you at close range isn't going to become wary as you attack them.

"I just want to stretch my legs," he said. "I just do not get why you're on me at all, let alone inside."

"Personally, I like you. I think guarding you like this is bullshit. But hey, I got a paycheck to be concerned about."

They were in the formal garden, Sam just behind him. Ten steps later, they were at the most concealing point, surrounded on both sides by large tea rosebushes in fitful bloom. From here, Mack could see only the top edge of the guardhouse at the corner of the south and west walls.

He took a quick step aside, then one back.

"Mack?"

He wasn't called Mack the Cat for nothing, and before Sam could turn around, he'd enclosed his neck from behind, lifted him in his iron-strong hands, and made a quick spinal adjustment that would paralyze him for about two hours. This was an "in and out" technique he'd learned in the Black Magic program, an offshoot of the MK-Ultra mind control experiments and Nazi medical discoveries. MK-Ultra had been plastered all over the media back in the 1970s and decisively shut down, but not Black Magic.

Sam dropped like a bag of ashes. Mack lifted him and arranged him on a bench. Maybe the mouth tried to open. The eyes stared into his, pleading. Mack said nothing. Sam couldn't move, but he was still conscious.

"You'll be fine, buddy," he said. Except, not with your boss, not so fine there.

Now he would work his way to the low area in the wall near the service gate that led out onto Route 16. Sam had been a piece of cake, but
this next maneuver was going to be seriously dangerous. The guards
were a bunch of nervous kids, and nervous kids were hair-triggers.

The old gate he was headed for hadn't been opened in a long time,
and it was on the opposite side of the property from the town. So it had
one, maybe two guys on it. He could do two, no problem.

He moved through the garden, strolling casually. Let them think
that Sam was sitting on a bench sipping his usual cup of coffee.

When he came to the end of the garden, he stopped. Ahead and to the
right was a hydroponic greenhouse. To the left, the disused road to the
service gate crossed a clear field of grass, nothing to shelter him at all.

So, okay, speed would shelter him. He strode out of the concealing
garden and onto the road, heading for the gate. A moment later, the
guard came out of his little station. He wasn't dressed like the ones near
the house, in discreet blazers. This guy was in full battle dress, helmet
and all. He carried an automatic rifle on his shoulder . . . and a paper-
back in his hand, a finger holding his place open.

Mack pushed away the thought that it would be easy. You take that
approach, you are dead.

As he drew closer, he smiled. "Hi, there!"

"You need to stay away from the wall, Sir."

"I'm just getting some exercise."

"Stay away from the wall."

Mack moved closer to him. "Sure. No problem." He kept going closer.

"You need to return to the garden, Sir."

"Sure." He started to turn. Then froze. Looked more closely at the
guard. "Man, that can't be an M14A SOPMOD."

The kid shuffled. "Yeah, it is."

"Jeez, can I just come close enough to get a look?"

"You're Mack Graham. You have a minder."

"Oh, come on, take it easy. He's got a sore foot and he's over there
sitting down. Don't make him get up, he won't like me anymore."

The guy smiled slightly, then ported the rifle. Mack took three quick steps toward him. The kid was trained, but not so well that he recognized Mack's movements as an assault setup.

A quick rap to a point just between and above his eyes and he went down. As he doubled over, Mack grabbed the rifle out of his hands and set it down back in the guardhouse. Then he pulled the kid in. He'd be unconscious for only five minutes tops, but there was a difference: this maneuver blew out the short-term memory. The kid would not recall that Mack had even been here. He'd assume that he'd fallen asleep and try to cover that with his superiors. Mack would have done the same thing with Sam, but if he woke up in five minutes and found his charge gone, he'd raise hell. He needed the time he'd get out of Sam to put distance between himself and the clinic.

He reached up to the roofline of the guardhouse and pulled himself up. No question but that he could be seen from here, so he had to keep moving. Not a problem, though. The guardhouse was only two feet higher than the roof, so he was sliding through the razor wire in a couple of seconds.

For a moment, he teetered on the narrow edge that topped the wall, then dropped down onto the far side.

Still not out of danger, though. He had to move fast now, to get into the cover of the woods that spread across the wild portion of the Acton land. A hundred-foot perimeter had been created between the wall and the trees, and so recently that the stumps were still bleeding.

Only one thing to do, now: cross it and trust to luck that nobody would see him from the two other towers that watched over this particular spot. In fifteen seconds, he was in the shade of the trees. He waited. No alarm. So he headed deeper.

The storms of earlier had gone, and the air was clean, faintly tanged with smoke. One thing solar electrical energy this intense did was to cause spontaneous fires in wiring of every kind. There were houses and buildings burning all over Raleigh County, no doubt.

He moved off deeper into the forest, taking a long, curving path among the trees, one that he would use later to guide townspeople to this vulnerable spot. He would bring them back, a great number of them, and they would come to kill, and while they did, he would do things to Caroline that would definitely bring the information he needed. Black Magic had many tricks up its sleeve, many tricks, and some of them caused amazing discomfort and amazing confusion, and some of them could hypnotize your adversary into becoming your slave.

He wondered who would break first, Caroline or dear little David. His money was on David. That Caroline was beautiful on the outside, but the interior was tough. David was nervous, rule bound, and insecure. Start pulling his skin off, he'd tell you every damn thing he knew.

He found Route 16 and sped up his progress by jogging. It was no trouble for him. In his condition, he could jog for hours.

Not until he came to the outskirts of Raleigh did he slow down. In that time, he had not seen a single car or a single person. The town was quiet, too. Very damn quiet.

He moved on, dropping back to a walk as he passed Raleigh Mortuary Services and the Dairy Queen. There would be a mayor. Some leader. He would find him. They would talk. And mayhem would come to the Acton Clinic.

11

THE NIGHT WALKER

David and Katie sat together in the living room of his suite attempting to get some kind of idea what was happening in the outside world. The Internet was still down, and, in any case, when it had been up, the Spaceweather.com website had been too swamped to be accessed. Toward one in the afternoon, the television signal had failed, both on cable and satellite. Prior to that, though, the stations had not had much information except endless repeats of the FAA statement that all aircraft were grounded and Homeland Security's warning to remain indoors.

Katie turned on the radio, trying to find a station. Voices drifted in and out, sounding as if they might be emanating from a land of dreams. But most of them were probably from Baltimore, fifty miles away.

Security was working frantically on the surveillance system, which was blowing circuits left and right due to massive atmospheric electrical overloading.

Katie picked up the small radio, raised it above her head, then slumped. She put it down.

"Just when you need them, they're not there."

"People are looking to their own lives."

"David, how bad is it? You know, don't you? You understand these things."

"It's certainly the most intense solar storm since 1859. Sunspots, a huge solar flare, and an intensely energetic coronal mass ejection. So it's inevitable that the satellites would be gone, but many of them are programmed to shut down during incidents like this, so they could come back. On the other hand, even well-insulated power grids are going to be collapsing all over the world. Even here in the U.S., if it keeps up."

"But it's not what people are saying, surely? It's not the end of the world?"

Before he came here, he would have brushed off the claim as having no scientific basis. But even though he now knew the truth, how do you tell another person a thing like that?

"We need to be prepared for anything," he said finally.

She looked doubtful, turning away, then glancing back at him.

"I think it's the last thing they would admit. The panic would be incredible. People would claw their way into every hole in the world. Anyway, how can they tell us?" She gestured toward the radio.

"Let's keep focused on the clinic. That's our responsibility."

"Okay, fine. Nothing was delivered today, David. And I can't reach Sysco, I can't reach UPS, FedEx, Maryland Medical, anybody."

Outside, the auroras were dancing.

"I do think we need to close all blinds and curtains."

"That won't keep out radiation, will it?"

"Actually, it'll help. Gamma rays aren't very penetrating and the walls are thick. The roof is made of tons of slate. The weak point is the windows. And I think we need to minimize guard patrolling. Keep the men in sheltered areas."

"I think this place is going to collapse. In fact, I think the whole world is going to collapse."

At first, she had seemed welcoming, but no longer. She was totally focused on the welfare of the institution and its people, and he thought at once two things: she's right to be afraid; but then, can I rely on this woman? Her file was equivocal. It was hard to know exactly what her relationship with Dr. Ullman had been, and there were a number of years in her timeline that were not accounted for. If they were going to go through a crisis, he would like to know about those missing years. In fact, he'd like to know more about the entire staff, especially the security personnel. He needed to know who the class could rely on and who not.

The intercom clicked. "We have a code blue in Room 303."

He hit the reply button. "Is the cardiac team in motion?"

"Yes, Doctor."

"I'm on my way." As he left, he called back to Katie, "Do you know which patient that is?"

She was right behind him. "I'm not certain."

As he ran across the flyover to the patient area, he could hear voices ahead. The nurses had just wheeled the shock wagon into one of the rooms. David saw that they were working on Linda Fairbrother. Her skin was cyanotic. David's initial impression was that the woman was dead.

The nurses performed efficiently, but not like code blue teams he'd seen in operation at Manhattan Central, where they did a cardiac arrest every few days. Then he saw that one of the defibrillation paddles was on the wrong side of the woman's chest.

"Hold it," he snapped. He could hear the whine of the defibrillator loading.

"It's gonna fire!"

He grabbed the paddle and placed it correctly. Just as he pulled his hand away, the system fired off and the patient convulsed. A moment later the computer said, "No response. Reload. Ten seconds."

He would let it go through two more cycles, then pull it off. He saw that he'd have to inform the Fairbrother family that their patient had expired. But how, given the state of communications?

The third round came, the body convulsed again . . . and the heart started. "Stable rhythm," the computer said. "Defibrillation complete."

The staff wasted no time moving her to the facility's small infirmary. David wondered what this was—a natural event or the result of some sort of attack?

"We need to get this woman into cardiac intensive care," he said.

"Raleigh County EMS isn't responding," one of the nurses said.

"Did you call the hospital's main number?"

"Doctor, I called all five hospitals in the area. No response."

Katie said, "I told you, David, it's all coming apart."

Anger put a bitter snap into his voice. "Maybe it is, but we're here now and we have a heart attack to deal with." He felt the full weight of this place and all these people on his shoulders just now. "I'm sorry," he said. She did not deserve his spitting words, it wasn't her fault.

He went down the corridor and through the door into the main patient area with its wider hallway and its expansive suites. People had heard the activity and were coming out. As Linda was moved past, they watched in a silence that was quite unlike what would have happened, say, at Manhattan Central. Frankly, these people were much more contained than he would have expected, and he wondered if perhaps Caroline was secretly waking up the class. He hoped so.

"All right," he said to the largely calm and silent group, "Linda had a minor cardiac event. Please return to your rooms now."

William Moore, one of the genuine patients, gave him the most menacing look, lips a set line, body language suggesting that he'd like to pounce. Then he grinned from ear to ear.

"You're a bureaucrat," he said.

"I'm your doctor."

"The bureaucracy of medicine is the machinery of death."

David stopped himself from automatically moving into a therapeutic stance with this patient and said simply, "We can talk tomorrow."

"With you? You're a waste of space."

"All right, then, with Dr. Hunt or one of the psychologists, as you prefer."

Leaving the patients to the nurses, he went into the infirmary.

Linda Fairbrother was lying quietly as Marian Hunt applied leads to her chest from the EKG machine.

"They're coming for me," Linda said.

"Who is?"

She snapped her jaw shut.

He would once have thought that this was yet another patient struggling with inappropriate thoughts, but as she was a member of the class, he wasn't sure what was meant. He wanted to ask her more. He remembered those two glyphs on her record. There was something special about her.

"Linda, tell me what's troubling you? Who's coming for you?"

"I got a message." Her fist closed on his shirtfront and she pulled him face-to-face. "I don't think Tom can go." Her voice dropped to a whisper. "Never tell anybody this, but he has this blackness on his back and side, and it's growing."

David's mind went to the notion of judgment. Could those who had done evil be actually, physically marked? It seemed impossible, but all the rules were changing now. Perhaps bodies were becoming mirrors of souls, our flesh no longer concealing our truth. But what had Tom Dryden ever done, that innocuous little man? All he could think was that people tend to keep their evil acts secret.

Marian came up to him with the EKG tape.

"This is normal," she said.

"Can we e-mail it to a cardiologist?"

"If the Net comes back. But we'll get a normal report, no question."

David looked at the tape. He had been assuming that this was an episode of sudden arrhythmia death syndrome that had been interrupted by timely action.

"No Bruguda sign," he muttered, "no fibrillation."

"No arrhythmias at all, in fact."

"I think we need a deeper study on this woman. Hearts don't just stop. And we want her under close observation until we can get her into a cardiac unit."

"David, I've been exploring unexplained cardiac arrests. *Bangungut* and familial long QT syndrome are possibilities."

"And *Bangungut* is?"

"A type of nightmare so intense that it can cause death. Common in parts of Asia."

This staff was out of its depth. No specialist would even bother to think about something so irrelevant.

"And familial long QT syndrome? Any symptoms?"

"There's no heart abnormality or defect. A little crud in the arteries, nothing to get excited about."

"And how do we know this? Do we have documentation?"

She paused for a moment, then said more quietly, "She's presented this way before."

"So was there follow-up?"

"Of course there was follow-up! We could get out of here then. She was worked up at Raleigh County. The heart muscle was healthy."

"So she can stop her heart at will?" He looked down at her. "Can you do that, Linda?"

"I'm afraid you won't let me go home. I have nightmares about it." Her eyes bored into his. "I'm not like the rest of you. It's time for me to go home."

"Linda, normally you'd be free to leave. It's just that current conditions make that difficult. Nobody's holding you against your will."

"Doctor, when the time comes, I will have only a couple of minutes. And all these doors in this place—oh, God, how I hate the Acton Clinic!"

A voice came from the doorway. "We'll take care of you," Caroline Light said. She addressed David. "When she wants to go outside, let her."

"So now the patients are the doctors. Fine."

"Will you wake up, David!"

"I'm awake."

Linda said, "Caroline, let him be."

"He's an idiot! He won't wake up!" She strode in, got right in his face. "Wake up," she shouted.

He looked past her to Katie. "Nurse, get this patient under control."

Caroline slapped him so hard that he saw stars.

For an instant, there was rage and he grabbed for her wrist. But then he stopped. His mind had gone silent. Clarity came.

"What was that supposed to be," he muttered, "a Zen slap?"

"That's exactly what it was." She turned and stalked out of the room.

"Confine her again tonight," he said.

"Oh, shut up," Marian replied.

"*What?*"

"Will you people stop!" Linda said.

He was appalled at himself, realizing that he was doing this in the hearing of this patient. It was grotesquely unprofessional. Katie was right, the world was falling apart, and not just the outside world. He drew an unwilling Marian Hunt out of the room.

"Hold your tongue in front of the patients, Marian."

"Then show some competence."

He paused, struggling not to explode in her face. "Keep her under observation for the night."

"They're all under observation all the time," she muttered as she headed off the floor. "Want her *really* locked up now? Maybe cuffed to her bed?"

"She doesn't like you," Katie said after she left.

"Who does?"

Katie's expression said every silent thing that her lips did not, and suddenly the crisp, worried professional was replaced by a warm, compelling woman.

She turned to go back to their side of the building, and he followed more slowly as she strode on ahead.

He was hardly disappointed to find her in his sitting room. She had just dropped into one of the big wing chairs that stood before the fireplace, once again tuning the radio.

"Pick up anything?"

"News from WBAL. It's huge, what's going on. Satellites are not coming back, power systems are down all across the world, the Internet backbone is fried. We won't see the Internet again for years."

As suddenly as suppressed fears will do, all the terror that he had been containing inside himself boiled to the surface and he uttered a single racking sob, then immediately stifled it, but not before she started in the chair, and looked up at him, her face registering surprise.

"Katie, I'm sorry. I'm on edge."

"Well, yeah." She rose out of the chair and stood before him, her eyes cast down.

They were in each other's arms so suddenly and so naturally that David hardly registered what was happening. It was just *right*. But when she lifted her neat heart of a face and he saw her lips open slightly, he did think about it. What he thought was that fraternization like this never led anywhere good, and then that he was tired of being the person who had thoughts like that. Caroline Light had accomplished a true Zen slap. He recognized the need for change.

She was looking up at him, waiting, and he did not do what he had been about to do, which was to turn away. Instead, he kissed her, and as he did he felt the hunger for her change from something he could control to something he could not control, and he had never felt such a flood of gratitude and desire, not in all the kisses of his life.

"Oh, God," she said, breaking away.

"I'm sorry."

She shook her head, then threw her arms around him. Her throbbing life pulsed close to him. When his body responded, she laughed a little, her eyes shimmering, and pressed closer. He found himself wondering again if she had been Dr. Ullman's lover—and threw the thought out like the rubbish that it was. What if she had, what did it matter?

Life was not about things like that. Life was about this moment, here, now.

This sensitive woman broke away. She returned to her place by the fire. "What's that called?" she said. "Absence of affect? We see it in patients."

"Katie, no."

"You're just sort of a cold fish by nature, then?"

"I was hardly feeling cold." He went to her, reached down and took her hands. He drew her up to him. She came, but leaned against him as a child might, expressing affection without yearning.

What had been broken here, and so suddenly? And by him, or by her? He put his arm around her waist. Tentatively, he moved toward the bedroom. She came without the protest he expected, but when she sat on the edge of the bed, he saw in her face for just a moment a haggard expression. She was exhausted, but she was here.

"I'm sorry," he said.

"You were suddenly just so distant. What do you think about when you do that?"

"Do I do it often?"

"People around here say you have no emotions. That you're—well, that you're heartless, David." She took his hand in hers, and for a moment they sat side by side, two awkward kids.

He went to her top button.

"I'm scared, Katie."

"Not of me."

He unbuttoned it.

"Of taking on a job I can't handle. And from a murdered man in a place where murders happen."

She opened her blouse, then reached around and unsnapped her bra. Her breasts tumbled out in a pale perfection of curves. Then she put a hand on his belt and glanced up at him. He found the shyness flickering in her eyes profoundly erotic.

She drew down his zipper. Laughing a little in her throat, she said, "You're going to tear these pants," and she drew him out into the coolness of the air and the warmth of her hands.

Her nakedness was exquisite. Certainly, she was among the most beautiful women he had ever touched. She was as pure and smooth as cream, and when they lay back together, he sensed that he was forgiven, as if whatever had almost driven them apart had with kindness and grace been put aside. The only flaw she possessed was a brown shadow along the back of her neck, and as he slid his hand along its smooth coolness, then kissed it, it tasted faintly of ash, perhaps a faded suntan. And yet, it was odd, not really a color at all. He'd never seen anything quite like it, as a matter of fact, a color that wasn't a color, that seemed more like a shadow being cast from within. Maybe it was something bizarre to do with exposure to the sun.

"Have you been outside?"

"When?"

"Recently? Say, the past three days?"

She sat up. "Why do you ask?"

"Just don't go. There's a lot of radiation in the atmosphere."

She kissed his nose. "I've wanted to do that."

"Kiss my nose?"

She hugged him, and they fell together and he tried to love her with skill and care, to be for her what he believed women wanted, drawing from his not very wide experience, which was of mostly equally unsure nurses. Many a hospital was full of exhausted, brilliant kids exploring not only the challenges of medicine, but also those of the heart.

When he reached up and turned off the bedside lamp, the room filled with greenish-purple flickering so intense that he had to close his eyes against it. This had been a long, hard day, and one that seemed to have become night very quickly. But the hour was eight by the clock.

She reached up and turned the lamp back on, pushing away the demented flashes. "Let's not let it spoil it," she whispered.

The lamp was another treasure, graceful girls sleeping, satyrs with erections leaping. Perhaps the only piece of pornographic glass ever produced by Louis Comfort Tiffany.

Coming together seemed so completely right and so completely innocent, and as his body filled with the pleasure that she had for him, the burdens that he bore slipped away like soldiers into a morning mist.

He knew that he would be too quick with her, and tried to slow his pace, but the energy of it burst through, and as his body was swept by the familiar tingling waves, he looked down into her face, into the happiness there, and could only think that, glowing in the soft light of the bedside lamp, it was the most beautiful of faces.

Then his body swept all thought away and his loins shuddered and his blood hummed, and the glorious, dying explosion came, and she smiled and was excited, too, at least that's how she appeared, and he came to rest on her and in her.

They shared a silence that was marred only by the twisting of the wind as it worried the eaves of the old building.

"Have you noticed the scene on that lampshade?" she asked, her voice full of warmth . . . and, he thought, a certain triumph. He had thought himself the seducer, but this Katie was a clever woman.

"This is the room where he took his mistresses. He had dozens of them, you know."

She came up onto her elbow, then kissed him on the cheek, a tentative sort of a peck. "David, you have got to be about the cutest guy who ever came here."

"I thought you really did not like me."

She kissed him again, this time on the edge of his mouth.

"Please just melt a little, okay, David?"

Then she kissed him full on the lips, pressing him down into the thick and giving pillows. He opened his mouth, letting the kiss penetrate, enjoying her sudden aggression.

They swam together across the gulf of the night. He let himself be intoxicated by her, and, drifting between sleep and wakefulness, he made love to her again. Toward dawn, he slept deeply.

It was then that the dreams came, his mind flowing so seamlessly into its own reality that he had essentially no idea that he was, in fact, dreaming.

The first one involved the opening of the bedroom door. Although, later, he understood that he must have been asleep, he seemed to hear a click, and to sit up and look toward the door. However, nobody came in. Instead, a shadow appeared a few feet in front of it, a human shadow. Or no, it wasn't a shadow, it was more solid than that. He watched it move forward, and thought that it was something that was coated in a darkness deeper than any normal darkness, and felt emanating from it what he could only describe as a wave of hate. His first impulse was to push away from it, and then next thing he knew, Katie was shaking him.

He looked up into her face, dark with night shadows, alive with light from the flickering sky.

"You were having a nightmare," she said. "You were really going strong."

"I saw somebody in here."

"What? Paranoid about a place like this? What *could* be the matter with my beautiful man?"

They laughed together, but he felt little conviction. That had not been a nightmare, it had been a whole level more intense than that. It had been a classic pavor nocturnus, a parasomnia disorder. Classically, also, he had felt as if he was still awake, when actually he had been deep in slow wave sleep.

"God, what if I'm hypoglycemic? That's all I need."

"You want a test? I can look for one in supply."

"Nah, it's not that. It's just stress."

"You're the doctor." She slid close to him, and they kissed, and he felt that she could not only inspire him sexually, she could be warm and comfortable in the night, and he began to drift off again.

He did not drift off, though. Instead, when he heard her breath change to a sleep rhythm, he found himself growing uneasy. He was lying with his back to the room, and he began to get the impression that this was a mistake, because the figure—or was the word "phantom"?—was still there.

Finally, he turned over and looked out into the room. The door was securely locked and chained, and there was no other way to get in here. Or was there? In an old place like this, especially a room where mistresses had been entertained, there might be hidden access.

Then, without seeing anything specific, he knew that the presence was approaching the bed. Despite the fact that his scientific mind could not for an instant believe such a thing—knew it to be impossible—it appeared that a vividly alive but invisible presence was now standing right beside the bed.

He knew that this was a return of the pavor nocturnus, an effect that was common with this type of sleep disturbance, but that did not change what he was feeling, and now he noticed a very strange sensation, a vibrating coldness that moved across the skin of his chest. He looked down at his nakedness, and saw a flurry of goose bumps rise where it was touching him.

There was somebody there, he knew it. But he couldn't *see* them.

Why not?

This was some sort of schizophrenic hallucination, it had to be. But he didn't possess any genes for schizophrenia, and none of the single nucleotide polymorphism associated with delusions.

So, was there somebody actually in here?

He raised himself up on his elbow. Beside him, Katie moaned softly.

He fumbled for the lamp, finally turning it on—and thought he saw the door slip closed, and jumped up and ran to it and threw it open.

The hallway was empty.

A vivid dream, then.

The next thing he knew, he was standing at the window, the one that looked out over the parking area and the trees. Overhead, an enormous object, brilliant with lights, moved majestically past. It was no plane, this thing, and it was absolutely massive. Gigantic. And behind it was another, and above them two more, and then he raised his eyes and an awe of surpassing power captured him, for he saw hundreds and thousands of these gigantic things, stretching off into the sky until the sky itself was swallowed in auroral discharges.

Then he was inside one of these things, surrounded by columns of light that he somehow knew were living beings, ascended to great heights of the heart, and filled with love so intense that it seemed to thrust him back into early childhood, and he saw his mother and father on the beach at Cape May, Dad calling out, Mother lying with cucumber slices on her eyes, Jack the terrier barking, a tiny girl singing general praises of the day.

They were angels, a fact which he seemed instinctively to know, and he felt absolutely naked in their light. They were so deeply right and so deeply true that he cried out, or imagined that he did, for they also radiated a sense of joy and purity that was without the slightest question the most glorious, the most innocent, and the yet the most awesome emotion he had ever known.

He felt also, though, a certain sadness and he lunged at it in his soul and demanded that it leave him but it did not leave him, far from it, for the next thing he knew he was in darkness absolute, crushed by waves of sick terror. The most glorious of all dreams had turned in an instant into the black and formless mother of all nightmares.

He was moving past stone, down some sort of deep fissure. There came a sensation of heat. Soon, the rock around them was glowing and the heat had become a horrible pain, more like being sanded than burned, but it was hideous. Again and again he threw himself against the walls, back and forth, back and forth, but there was no escape.

Objectively, he knew how serious a seamless, absolute break with reality like this was. Stress induced, yes, so vivid it was the next thing to psychosis.

He went deeper, and as he did the heat rose and he writhed and fought, hammering his fists and kicking, reduced to the frenzy of a panicked child.

Cries came around him, and he could see forms embedded in the walls now, bright, blazing human shapes, and they were all crying out their innocence, but they were not innocent, he could hear it in their tone, a despairing cacophony that bore within it the discordant note of the lie.

A new pain joined the fire, a very definite pain in his right wrist.

And there was somebody yelling, and again and again he was hammering his wrist against the edge of the bedside table, and the exquisite old lamp was bouncing.

Gasping, he wallowed in the sheets, then held his wrist. Jesus God in heaven, had he broken it? No, just the skin, but he had hammered the devil out of it.

"What happened . . ."

The room was normal, everything quiet. His clock said six forty-five. "Katie?"

His bed was empty. She was gone, and he had to ask himself if she had ever been there.

He knew this imagery, of course. The Christian heaven and hell. So he'd dreamed it, that's all that had happened, and no matter how vivid, it had been, in the end, just a dream. A symptom of stress, perhaps, but not the psychotic break he had feared.

A sudden voice from the little sitting room beside his bedroom startled him. Male, but who was it? Nobody on staff sounded like that. He threw open the door.

"Excuse me—"

He recognized the voice of *The Today Show*'s Craig Harding. They were in the window at Rockefeller Center, and people were looking in on them. So the solar storm, also, must have passed and the satellites had switched on again, and the world had resumed. As he dressed, he listened hungrily to the news, which was basically about all the disruptions. But they were disruptions, not the end of the world.

He allowed himself to hope that Mrs. Denman's white paper had been wrong.

In his luxurious marble shower, he imagined that the foaming body shampoo was washing off the madness of the night. For sure. If the solar storm was gone, life would return to normal very quickly now.

By the time he was striding down to the staff dining room for breakfast, he had put his dream aside.

As he descended the stairs, Glen MacNamara stood waiting for him.

"We have a patient missing."

He absorbed this.

"Sam Taylor lost Mack."

"When?"

He paused. "Yesterday afternoon."

"*What?* Why wasn't I informed, Glen?"

"Nobody was informed. Sam was knocked out."

"But Mack's on lockdown! Surely the staff noticed this when he didn't turn up at lights out."

"Sam asked for time while he looked for him."

"All night?"

"He let me know about ten."

"Glen, it's seven o'clock in the morning and the director of this institution is just finding this out?"

"Doctor, I didn't see the need to wake you up. What could you do? This is my issue."

David was about to really get into Glen MacNamara, but the truth was that he was right. He couldn't have done anything to help.

"Okay," he said finally. "Could Mack pose a danger to us?"

"It would be damn surprising if we ever saw or heard anything about him again. If you want me to guess, I'd say he won't last a week out there. It's hell, Doc. I'm telling you, from the smoke columns I see and all the infrastructure problems, folks are tearing each other apart." He gestured toward the dining room. "Toast, bacon, coffee, and Gatorade. In here, everybody's outraged. Out there, it would be a feast."

They went in together. As he crossed to the buffet, Katie came close to him, discreetly touching his hand.

"At least that scumbag is gone," she said quietly. "Nobody cared for him." She brightened. "And anyway, the cable's back and the sun looks better, and I've got a feeling we're getting past this thing."

Mrs. Denman's paper had warned that the solar system was headed much deeper into the supernova's debris field. Much deeper.

The truth insinuated itself into his mind. They had not come to the edge of the storm at all.

This was the eye.

12

GOLIATH

Caroline woke up on her first morning in the general patient popu-lation in a state of intense unease. She didn't actually wake up, because she hadn't slept. She'd lain there with her eyes closed, worrying, primarily about David. She had a letter for him written by Herbert Acton, but it was not to be handed to him until he remembered his past, and to her that meant remembering their time together, their shared innocent life.

Herbert Acton had warned about this period right at the omega point, that it was too unsure for him to see into it clearly, so his instructions about these final days were vague.

Beyond the borders of history, which is where mankind was now, nothing was certain, and as the evil came to understand their fate, their efforts to escape it were going to make them incredibly dangerous. Many of them would actually want all of mankind to be destroyed, if they were destroyed.

David had remembered a lot, she could sense that. But if he did not remember her, he was not on mission, and time had run out.

Intending to confront him late last night, she had gone to his bedroom. She had hoped to feed him some of the potent white powder gold they had created in the arc furnace, and see if that helped.

Oddly, the door had been unlocked. When she slipped inside, she had discovered why: Katrina Starnes had come in before her, and was sharing his bed. Carelessly—or perhaps out of an unconscious desire to broadcast her conquest—she had failed to pull the door closed.

She had never been warned about him falling in love with anybody else, and she was appalled and deeply saddened.

She had stood there, her face flaming with embarrassment, her heart wretched, her mind at a loss as to what to do now. They were too involved with each other to notice her, and she had quietly retreated.

When she'd returned to her room, all she could do was cry into her pillow.

The first thing she'd done waking up this morning was to arrange an appointment with him. "We'll need to squeeze you in," Katie had said in concealing, velvet tones, "but I think I can get you fifteen minutes."

Katie was no fool. She sensed a rival, and no way was Caroline getting any more of his time than that.

Well, Katie was going to be hurt and there was nothing Caroline could do about it. She'd been hurt herself last night, hurt terribly, watching them in their pleasure.

She had been assured by her father that David would remember everything the moment he laid eyes on her. If there were any gaps, she could show him his trigger, which was an image of Quetzalcoatl.

Neither thing had worked, and she was no longer able to contact her father for further advice, not unless the phones returned, which they had not. So she waited now, sitting with her hands folded, watching Katrina bring David his morning coffee.

As Katie crossed the room, her body spoke to Caroline of its conquest. And by the way she laid the cup near his hand, with a too-furtive glance toward his lower extremities, she knew that she was remembering him in his passion.

She fought back her anger and jealousy, but Katie sensed her feelings and her eyes darted at her, and there was between them a moment of daggers. Then Katie went flouncing out, her cheeks brushed with rose . . . and Caroline was horrified to glimpse, just above the edge of the young woman's neckline, a telltale shadowy darkness from a mark concealed below.

Katie was judged! Caroline felt actually queasy—physically ill. This was the first person she'd seen with a mark, but there were going to be a lot of them, she knew that.

At the omega point, bodies ceased to conceal souls, and some became like light and others like darkness and others—workers like her and the rest of the class—shouldered the burden of life and kept on.

It was hard to be so evil that there could be no redemption, so what terrible things had Katie done? She looked like a sweet young nurse, the last person you'd expect to see in such a situation.

She didn't seem in the least uneasy, so maybe she hadn't yet noticed the discoloration or didn't understand it. But she would notice it, and come to understand it, and when she did, the evil that she was concealing was going to explode to the surface, because this woman could not be what she seemed. Hidden beneath that pretty surface, there lurked a monster.

Then she was face-to-face with David.

"Thank you for granting me my freedom," she said to him, after Katie had gone. "How is Linda?"

"She had a mild heart attack. She'll be fine."

"Will she?"

"You think not?"

"I don't think anything. I asked a question."

"Which had implications."

"I don't do implications. I say what I mean."

He sipped the coffee. His prop, in lieu, she supposed, of a pipe.

"David, do you have any idea who I am?"

"Caroline Light."

"Why did I come here?"

"The same reason people usually come to the hospital. You were suffering and you wanted relief."

"You know more than that. Do you know we were childhood sweethearts?"

"I know about the class. I know who you are and I know about . . .

something. The gold. Sort of. But I'm lost. And I don't know you. You're like a stranger who's sharing a compartment on a train or something."

"I need you to wake up," she said.

He gestured with the coffee cup. "I'm wide awake."

"I'm going to say something," she told him, "and you can take it however you're going to take it."

"Okay."

"I dreamed you made love with Nurse Katie last night. I dreamed I watched you."

So much blood drained out of his face that he seemed to turn to wax.

"You feel a need to tell me this?"

She decided to force the matter even further.

"I saw you tangled in blue sheets, in the light of a beautiful Tiffany lamp—so sexy, I didn't know he did erotics—and, oh, God, I felt such incredible jealousy, because, David, you need to face the truth, and the truth is that even though we were children when we made our vows, they counted, and even though you don't remember right now, last night you were cheating on me!"

The waxen face slowly filled with the color of a deep flush. He blinked rapidly. He picked up his pencil and put it down. Then his chin lowered, his fingers stopped toying with the pencil and grasped it tightly. There was an odd sense that they were moving down a tunnel, racing away from each other. She feared that she had made a major mistake.

He jumped to his feet, came out from behind the desk, and stood over her.

She felt the menace in it. She said, "I'm sorry I slapped you."

"I am, too. It hurt."

"I'm a punisher. It's a fault. But you're hurting me, David, you're hurting me terribly."

He loomed and she could feel him suppressing his own violence. Then he strode across the room and threw himself down in one of the sumptuous chairs that stood before the fireplace. He was muttering, and she could not hear the details.

"I'm sorry," she said, going toward him. "I've touched a nerve and I'm very sorry."

Slowly, his head turned toward her. His face was sunken and gray now, skeletal with fury.

"Will you please tell me which member of my staff allowed you access to my bedroom?"

"I—nobody. The door was unlocked."

"Damn you! *Damn* you!"

She tried another sort of shock. "You have a mission, David. Face it! You have to lead us out of this mess."

As if the chair was burning him, he leaped up and strode away again. She realized that he knew. Inside himself, he knew it all. It wasn't that he couldn't remember, but that he couldn't face it.

"Were you also out the first night you were here?"

What should she say? One of their fellow classmates had released her from her looked room, and she had gone to fetch the tiny amount of ancient white powder gold she had brought with her. She had hidden it near the gate until she was sure she wasn't walking into a trap. That gold was star stuff, what NASA had found when they went searching for stardust, and what was found in the crop circles of haunted England. Without a little of the ancient material, new material could not be made.

He returned, a stalking lion. "How stupid do you think I am?"

"David, the whole nature of reality is changing and there's work to do. You have to accept this."

"And I suppose the ridiculous, bloodthirsty, mad Aztec gods are coming back, too, and we're all going to be sacrificing children soon!"

"The gods don't exist."

He gestured toward the glyphs above the door. "A couple of days ago you sounded like an evangelist."

"The old gods are the mythologized principles of a lost science. As human knowledge declined after the last cataclysm, science became myth, and myth became religion. They ended up worshiping subtle principles as meaningless gods. That's all religion is. Worship of the powers of a science that existed before Egypt."

He glared at her in silence.

"David, you know this! We were taught it. We sat side by side."

He looked long at her. "Yes," he said softly, "I know." But he seemed to sink into himself, his face growing ugly—eyes bloodshot, cheeks seething purple, lips twisted back—a face savage with amazing depths of rage.

"Now wait," she said helplessly, "it's all right." How soft and full of grace that face had been when he was a boy of twelve. "Be as little children—"

"I'm an adult!" Seeming to overcome something deep within himself, he pulled away from her and stalked off again. This was a cage and he was an animal.

"David, all you have to do is embrace your role. Then you'll see how important our love is."

"We were kids. The loves of childhood don't survive."

"Our bond is essential to our mission, and it was meant to survive."

"Well, I've remembered a lot of things, but not that."

She came close, and he did not stop her. "Start again then."

"Now? There's no time. Not for feelings."

"All this pacing you're doing—you're trying to run away, but you can't, David. There's no place to go."

"There had better be, because we have very little food left and almost no fuel, and I don't know how to save the situation."

She did something she had last done in the basement of this very house, when they were still just kids. She kissed him . . . but not with the gingerly innocence of those days, not this time.

For a moment, they were frozen like that. And then, slowly, he pulled away from her. His face was popping sweat. She slipped close to him, and drew her arms around him. They became as still as statues, two people in the ancient, tentative posture of unfolding love.

She lifted her face, and found him looking down at her, and felt the same delectable weakness go through her that she had known when they were innocent.

"Let me show you something," she said.

For an instant he closed his eyes, and his face was as narrowed and sculptural as an old painting of a saint enduring martyrdom. When he opened them again, they were on her, boring into her.

"What's going on?" he asked vaguely, muttering as if in a dream.

They lay on the floor, going down by mutual consent, saying nothing.

Then, suddenly, his lust came and he tore at her clothes, his eyes wild, his body thrusting, she thought, uncontrollably. In another moment his pants were off and he was pushing, seeking, and she turned a little, opened her legs a little, and the shock of his entry into her was by a thousand light-years the most intense experience she had ever had in her life.

He arched his back and cried out, his teeth bared, and then drew himself out and she tore at him, grabbing his thighs, and he entered her again, and this time it was more than sex, it was beyond all physical experience, it was the moment of death amplified to a great, roaring, abandoned surrender of body, mind, and soul.

They lay, then, in soft grass, and from the billowing woods nearby there came birdsong.

"Oh, God," he whispered. "Oh, God, where are we, what is this place?"

"This is the future," she said, "if you want it. But it takes love. To come here takes fear, but to stay, there must be love."

He thrust and thrust and thrust, and every time he did, a wave of heart-stopping pleasure shot from her curling toes to her shuddering scalp. Then he kissed her, his tongue like fire boring into her and setting everything inside on fire, and the birds made their music, and a soft breeze caressed them, and the sun crossed the sky and went low, and in the long shadows, they heard, like distant bells, the secret harmonies of the human soul.

It ended then, in a series of declining thrusts. Surely now he would remember their love, and they would gain from it the energy they needed to pass through the time gate and not fall back.

There was no sound that marked their inevitable descent back into the familiar world, nothing but a gentle, subtle change from cool, pliant grass to the old rug they'd started their journey on.

"It was your painting, Caroline, the one you're doing in the art room. It was like we were in it."

"Yes. We went there."

"Then it's not a painting."

"No, it's a navigation tool and it worked just as it's supposed to. We couldn't control our movement, though. We fell back. You and I should be able to cross easily by now, to prepare the way for others."

"Why can't we?"

"There must be love, David."

His hand withdrew from hers. He sat up.

She saw that he'd enjoyed himself with her. Lust, though, was all that it had been for him, the lust of a soldier on his way to die.

She was down to the final card, she saw. No matter Mr. Acton's instructions, she must play it now because if she didn't, she would lose him here, now, forever.

Without love, the journey across time—the physical journey— would last no longer than it had just now, the flicker of a eye.

"I have something for you," she said.

She drew her purse open. This letter, in its fading envelope, had come to her from her father's hand, as he had wished her well on her quest. "My knight," he had said, "with no armor. My beautiful girl." Being held by her father, this man in profound transmutation, was the most sacred experience that she knew. She feared so for him, off there in the Virginia countryside with no guards and no guns.

"This is for you," she said. He looked down at the envelope. Then back up at her. "It's from Herbert Acton," she said. "It was written over a hundred years ago."

He took it, then turned on the magnificent desk lamp, in which

Louis Comfort Tiffany, himself a master alchemist, had reproduced, as if they were a swirling rainbow, all the colors of alchemical transformation, from the black of the ground through red to creamy white to green and yellow, then to the radiant white of monatomic matter and the ruby red of super consciousness, to the violet of night and wisdom, the color of the Great Elixir itself. In the lamp, fairies danced.

As he opened the letter, the dry old paper crackled. For a cold instant, she feared that it might turn to dust. Anything could happen now, in these enormous moments, beyond even the reach of visionaries like Herbert Acton.

He read in silence.

"What does it say?"

"You don't know? I thought you'd know."

"It's never been opened before, not since the day Herbert Acton wrote your name on it and sealed it."

In his eyes she saw flickers of the Great Elixir, shimmering and shuddering faintly, living violet in the blue that had long ago captured her heart. She allowed herself to hope.

He read aloud, "'David Ford, this will come to you from the hand of the woman you love. Surrender and learn. But quickly, David, for nothing is decided. Goliath follows her close behind.'" He made a little sound in his throat. "That's all." He held the letter out. "And there's today's date."

"'From the woman you love,' David. He knew what was supposed to be between us."

"Caroline . . ." His voice faded. Then she realized that he wasn't looking at her anymore, he was looking past her.

When she turned, she found herself confronting Katrina Starnes and waves of hate unlike any she had ever felt, and she knew that this was the pure hate of darkness and, even worse, the hate of a scorned woman.

"I was just leaving," she said faintly.

"Oh, no," Katie snarled. "Fuck him again. Fuck him on the floor, you rich, spoiled filthy *bitch*."

"Now, wait."

"I've been waiting all day. And hearing!" She turned on David. "You sob a lot, asshole. Sob with pleasure. You sound like a complete jerk when you're fucking, did you know that? And you're even worse than Marian says. You're not only a self-centered piece of shit, you're an incompetent doctor. If we could get out of here, or we could get the goddamn phone working, your license would be history. And it will be. Because when this is over, you're going down, Doc." Now the jewel-hard eyes returned to Caroline. "Like his dick? Tell him to wash it next time, between fuck toys." Her voice dropped low now. "Guys like him—human garbage—they end up in pieces. Be warned." She strode out. "There's a list on your desk, Doctor," she said over her shoulder. "The patients you missed, the problems you ignored."

Silence followed. Hardly above a whisper, he said, "It's dark. We've been here all day."

"An uncontrolled move through time."

"I have a problem with her now, Caroline. Big problem."

"I have to go work on my painting."

"I know."

Their eyes met, and their hearts danced, but it was a slow dance, full of sorrow and full of fear.

She wanted to stay with him but she could not stay with him, there wasn't time. She left, moving quickly down the halls, intent on her task.

Neither of them was aware of the other eyes that watched them via the surveillance system, Katrina's eyes, or the true intensity, the towering fury, of the hate that was there.

DAVID FORD'S JOURNAL: FIVE

I've always moved too fast with women, and now I've got two of them on my case. It's happened before and I've always been ashamed, and I feel that now.

Caroline Light wants my love but I just do not feel anything there. Katie wants it and, again, I just want the comfort of her body.

Both women are furious at me, of course, but I'm dealing now with a new issue, and they're going to have to wait their turn. To be frank, I believe that I know what Herbert Acton did to look into the future.

Educated as I am in modern science, I have always viewed alchemy as the first primitive fumbling of what became chemistry. However, what I now suspect paints a different picture. Alchemy, as we have known it through history, is the degenerated remnant of a chemistry far more advanced than what we have now.

The shibboleth has always been that the "philosopher's stone" is supposedly capable of turning something like lead or iron into gold. In the Middle Ages, mountebanks went about in Europe using sleight of hand to convince the wealthy that they could do this, with the intention of fleecing them.

There is a truth behind it, though, and it is the explanation, I am convinced, for Herbert Acton's abilities. And, in fact, as I write this, I feel a sort of déjà vu again, as if the words are a kind of echo. I would surmise that this is information from our class, being drawn through the amnesia.

What this ancient science concerned, I believe, were manipulations that are presently far beyond our ability. It was able to see into the future, and, I think, holds the promise of actually enabling physical movement through time—an orderly, organized version of what happened to that dire wolf in Utah.

I have made a most interesting discovery about this room. It contains a time machine—not one that can enable physical time travel, but one that can facilitate the sort of seeing that Herbert Acton was so expert at. I think of it as a time telescope, and it stands on this desk, the Tiffany masterwork that is far more than a desk lamp.

It was the alchemical colors that revealed the lamp's true purpose to me. The master who created them understood the uses of light frequencies, and when I close my eyes and let the colors wash across my forehead, I am able to see brilliant images of the future. In other words, the legend of the crystal ball or the magic lantern is about lamps like this.

Accelerating vision into the future—perhaps bodies, too—need have nothing to do with arcane contraptions like supercolliders. It has to do with changing the temporal frequency of the body, and that can be done with light.

You look into a color of the type produced by this lamp until, when you close your eyes, it fills your head—and then, after a few moments, you will see what for me are flickering, indistinct visions, but which for a master like Herbert Acton must have been exquisitely detailed images.

Even with my limited skills, though, I have seen the future, and, frankly, I am terrified. Not because of what is there, but rather what is not.

In my mind's eye, for example, I can see this room as it will be later tonight, empty, the darkness flickering from the auroras.

Then something else happens, involving strange light rising in the east—a piercing violet object in the sky. And that light—the color is like that of the Great Elixir, a light frequency of great power, both creative and destructive.

No sooner does this light wash in through the windows than all light disappears. It's not night, it's another kind of dark entirely. When I tried to see into it, it almost seemed to want to suck me in, as if it was in some way hungry. I think that I was seeing the absence of reality itself, the absolute emptiness that surrounds the universe, that is, what exists before light has come and after it has faded, beyond the limits of time.

In other words, we are almost at the end of time, probably just days away, or even hours.

And yet, it's not the entire and complete end, because something else is there, a glimmer in the black ocean.

I think this is the beginning of new life on earth, thousands of years from now.

And getting there is our goal, and it is why Caroline refers to her painting as a navigation tool. As she paints, she is looking in her mind's eye at a specific spot on the Earth of the future, the place she briefly took me to. Once the painting is finished, everybody who sees it, and is properly prepared—no doubt by consuming the substance they're manufacturing in the arc furnace—will supposedly be able to navigate to the point in time it depicts.

I have also seen our world as it is right now, and what I have seen has almost made me sweat blood, because hell is unfolding here, and it is far, far worse than I imagined. Even as desperate as we are here at the clinic, compared to what's going on outside, we are a splendid palace shining in the middle of a wasteland.

For example, the farm belt all over the world is a gigantic desert of brown, ruined crops. I sailed from Iowa to Texas on the lamp's magical wings, and saw nothing but stubble and burning cities and long lines of dead cars on the roads, and everywhere bloated, dead cattle, and people in their millions cutting and eating the carrion meat.

Also, I saw ever more of the huge objects that I glimpsed out my window the other night, drifting over the face of the land, lingering over cities, marching in enormous platoons across the suffering world. I saw them drawing people into themselves in vast numbers, but I could not see what was happening to them. I do remember, though, that it was beautiful. Were these the biblical elect, then, those who have finished with earthly life, being raised up? Or was it something else, the harvest of mankind, perhaps, as slaves or as a DNA pool?

I could see what was happening, but there was nobody to tell me why.

I have also seen people cutting themselves to the bone—literally butchering themselves—to get rid of the strange quasi-physical shadows like the ones on Katie's neck and probably on Tom Dryden. I fear that I know why, and I fear for them both. Katie seems a good person and Tom is innocuous, but we do hide our darkness, we humans.

Taken together—the vision of the lake of fire from Revelation, and these two encounters with those huge objects, I think that what I am seeing is the beginning of a legendary event, the actual, physical judgment of man.

At the thought, my guts congeal, my heart overspeeds. This whole planet is on death row, and I feel it not only as a member of human society and a man responsible for a lot of lives, I feel it personally. I am the one whose energy will enable us to take our first step across time. That's why I am identified with Quetzalcoatl who was, among many other things, the god of new beginnings.

My impulse is to throw myself into my work, and I have a lot of work to do. My primary immediate responsibility is clear: be sure this place is not destroyed before we've completed what we've been put here to do.

I wish that I could say that I was confident, but I am not confident at all. We know literally not a thing about whoever killed Mrs. Denman, and until we do know that, everybody here is in danger, and so is our mission.

Undoubtedly, somebody has at least an inkling of what we are going to attempt, and wants to take our knowledge and use it in our stead.

I look to Mr. Acton's final letter to me. It warns David that Goliath is coming—in fact, that Goliath is here now. But who is Goliath, a person, a storm, some new fire about to be spit from the sun?

No doubt Goliath is many things, but one of them must be that violet light—the highest color of alchemical growth and also the color of ultimate death. The light is an incredible poison, and it's coming. But it isn't the only aspect of the giant. Goliath has servants.

As I am apparently David to this Goliath, it's worth asking just how I sling my stone into his forehead. The light must come from the supernova that was mentioned in the document Mrs. Denman gave me to read. Maybe we're getting close enough to it to see its core as a distinct stellar object.

A supernova's core emanates sterilizing sheets of gamma rays.

As I sit here, night is coming on, the worst time.

I go to one of my majestic windows, to the glowing, bizarre darkness. Frankly, when I looked into the future, I was surprised that I did not see that the sun had gone supernova. Such things happen all the time, with one stellar explosion blasting nearby stars with so much energy that they explode, too.

I cannot see around to the east very well, but it looks as if there is a violet-purple tint off beyond the limits of my vision.

This distant star—previously unknown to science—is, in reality, what controls life on earth. I know from modern paleoastronomy that light of this monster first washed the earth forty thousand years ago, leaving a huge swath of the planet, from Australia through southern and central Africa, empty of large, plains-dwelling animals. They died because they could not hide from the gamma rays. It came again during the end of the last Ice Age, and once again, the plains-dwelling animals, the mammoths, the mastodons, and so many others, were decimated.

So violet is the highest, and therefore also the most dangerous light, and as I sit here looking into my lamp, I ask for direction, but get only silence in reply, and darkness in my mind's eye.

Purple is the light of evolution. But evolution also means death. Ask the dinosaurs—and ask, also, mankind. Are we destined to follow them into final species death?

We have reached the end of the game. The rules are cast aside, but still we play on, deep into the night.

And I am left with the question, What is my stone, what is my sling? How do I slay Goliath?

13

THE TRACK OF THE CAT

Mack had moved swiftly through the countryside, but thought better of entering Raleigh during the day. He needed to work fast, but he also had to stay alive, and that was going to take some care. For all of his skills, anyone with a good rifle and a good eye would be a danger to him. He wished that he could have brought the young guard's rifle with him, but if it had been gone when he woke up, even though he would have had no memory of what had happened, he'd have known that something was wrong and raised the alarm.

Hiding in a barn, Mack hadn't rested, he hadn't been able to. When so many people were waiting on you and things were deteriorating this fast, the tension was appalling.

After the sun had at last set, he climbed down from the hayloft and surveyed the farm. It was as quiet as it had been when he'd come here. He needed food and, above all, water, so he decided to take a chance on the house.

He'd had a great deal of field training, so he knew how unsafe it was to expose yourself to dark windows, but it couldn't be helped.

It was pointless to conceal himself, so he just strode forward.

When he returned to the Acton Clinic, all exhausted and apologetic, he would use the same technique. He would let them lock him in again. The window was hopeless, but there was an escape route through the air-conditioning ducts in his room, and one of his jobs in Raleigh was to go to the county building department and look at the plans of the patient wing. He had not killed yet, but when he got back there, he was going to do a good deal of that, and a good deal of information extraction.

By the time he reached the house, he knew that it was empty.

The fridge was warm, but there was a half-finished bottle of Coke inside, flat and hot. He drank it all. The water taps didn't even drip when he turned on the faucets, so he got a pitcher out of the cabinet and banged through the house to the nearest bathroom. There was water in the toilet tank, which he pitchered out and drank. Down the hall, he saw a woman's legs in the doorway of a bedroom. The rest of her was sprawled out of sight.

He left the house and found a pickup in the garage but its electronics were fried so he headed off down the road on foot. With the setting of the sun, the sky had turned an odd pinkish-purple color, something that was new. Pinkish purple, with long, shimmering sheets of green auroras cutting through it. Beautiful, indeed, and so could death be beautiful.

By the time he reached the outskirts of town it was full night, and now it could be seen that the odd color of the sky was centered on a faint thickening brightness low on the northeastern horizon. What was it? He knew little about astronomy, but it had the look of something that the world would come to wish had not appeared.

Most of the houses he passed were dark, but some contained faint, flickering glows of candlelight, and one or two the brighter light of oil lamps. He had no real plan, except to see what he could do to stir these people up against the clinic. They hated it, of course, but they needed leadership to go up there and cause mayhem.

As he drew closer to the town center, he was stopped by something he had not seen in many years, not since his days in Mexico, when drug cartels sometimes did it to terrify locals into serving them.

On a street lamp about halfway into the town, a man had been hung . . . and, he noted, hung badly. The body was covered with blood from the neck, because they'd hauled him up without tying his hands, leaving him to struggle with the knot while he choked. Ugly way to do it, probably because they were clueless about the process. Under the body, dogs snarled at one another as they licked the blood in the street.

A number of storefronts were burned out, and he could smell death in the air. More dogs could be heard in the darkness, and as he passed the ones beneath the hanged man, some of them gave him a predatory appraisal. Once a dog has tasted blood, it is dangerous, always. Not wanting to have to fight off the whole pack, he gave them a wide berth, and did not meet their eyes.

You could give a dog a heart attack by shattering its muzzle with the right kind of blow, but six or seven dogs would keep you damn busy, and you would absorb damage.

Ahead, there was a restaurant showing a flicker of candles in the front window. Inside, he could see the shadows of many people. Good, this was what he'd been looking for. Desperate people band together, at least when they still believe that they might have some way to save themselves. Only later, when they understand the hopelessness of their situation, do they turn on one another. In another couple of days that would happen here. In fact, he was probably lucky that it hadn't already happened.

He went to the door and paused, evaluating the crowd. There were men, women, and children present, so this was probably some kind of survivorship gathering. Safe enough.

He stepped in. Voices rumbled around him, angry and desperate ones, and the children were crying, many of them. A few were playing.

"We're real hungry, John," a male voice said. "You gotta find a way."

"We need to do some urban foraging," the man in front, probably the mayor, said.

"We've scoured the town, goddamn it," somebody shouted. Rage. Terror. They were just about to turn on one another.

Mack took a breath and raised his voice. "Excuse me."

They froze like frightened mice, then turned all at once. Suspicion in the faces. Women swept their children behind them. He was acutely aware of the fact that the room was full of guns.

He held up his hands. "Hey, I'm unarmed." He looked from face to face, smiling just enough but not too much. His next words were crucial, and he had thought about them carefully.

"I just escaped from the Acton Clinic."

An immediate murmur, more suspicion in the faces. All expected. He was playing them.

"I'm not a crazy, okay!"

They quieted down a little.

"Let him talk," the man at the front of the room said. He was pudgy, but his eyes were hollow. That was one famished fat man up there. He must be almost crazy with hunger, probably dropping ten pounds a day.

"I'm an assistant chef."

A guy with a deer rifle said, "What do you mean, you escaped? Why does an assistant chef need to escape?"

"That goddamn place is a palace! There's tons of food, *tons* of it. They've got enough to feed their damn psychos for a year. It's enough to get this whole town through this thing—I mean, if there's another side to it, God willing." Then he stopped. Time to let it sink in. Time to let them chew.

"How much food exactly?" a woman asked.

"Try a hundred dressed hogs, forty beeves, maybe a quarter ton of prepared meats, not to mention a whole huge basement storage area full of canned goods for long-term use. That's a damn Versailles palace up there on that hill, and they have no right to keep all that food just for a bunch of loonies. No right, not when good, normal people who are the backbone of the country need it! That's why I escaped. I want to help people who need help . . . folks who're healthy and normal." He laughed, made it bitter. "That palace up there is full of people who this world doesn't even need. But it needs you." He pointed to a little girl peeking out from behind her mother's dress. "It needs her."

"They got more guns than we have, man."

General assent.

"Yeah, I know. You've gone up there and taken a few shots, I know that, too."

"I did that," the same voice said. He stepped out of the crowd. He was a young guy, about thirty. He had a preteen boy in tow who looked as tough as he did. "I'm two tours in 'Stan. I was on rotation stateside when this thing started. And if we try on the Acton Clinic, I can tell you as a soldier that a lot of us are gonna get wasted."

Mack let silence follow that statement. They needed to taste their fear, then be pulled out of it. "How long has it been since you folks got anything to eat?"

People looked around at each other. "Three days," the man in the front said.

"Okay, I had three squares before I came out. I think it was the steak that made me make my move, eating it, knowing that at least some decent, normal folk down here could be eating what the crazies were gobbling. And the patients get a lot better than we do. It's like a damn cruise ship up there."

Another voice rose, this a kid of about fifteen. "Mister, they signal. They use SSB code bursts. I pick them up on my scanner. So they could signal for help."

That brought an uneasy murmur. Of course, the kid was worrying about Mack's own code bursts, but no way could he say that.

"Those are probably just signals to their rich families, arranging for more supplies. Now listen to me, I know the place from the inside out and I've got the kind of training you need for an op like this. Special Forces. Afghanistan. Pakistan."

"Unit?" the guy with the rifle asked.

He'd done this sort of thing many times before, and it actually felt good to do it again. "Night Stalkers," he replied easily. "160th SOAR." One of the many answers he had to the many questions a CIA field officer gets about his identity. You always lie, even to your friends.

The guy started to be impressed, but then he asked another question. "How'd you end up in the kitchen?"

"Oh, I was on security, all right. But we got shoot-to-kill orders last week and I told Glen MacNamara that I could not do that." He looked around the room. "You all know who Glen is?"

They knew. Like any town living beneath the walls of a castle, they were obsessed with what went on inside it. Except they did not know about this food, of course. Naturally not, because it didn't exist. But their imaginations and their eagerness to hate the palace made them believe it in without question. In truth, the clinic was just about stripped of food like everyplace else—except, of course, for the redoubts. If he had wanted to be straight with them, he should tell them how to get to the Blue Ridge underground facility, but he had no intention of doing that. There, they would find food enough to carry this town for five years. Yeah, and give the food of the pure of blood to this gaggle of human trash? Not gonna happen. The pure of blood were the future of the world, or it had no future.

"What I need to do is for you folks to get me the building and ground plans for the clinic from the buildings department, then I can lay out a professional plan of attack for you."

"Mister, they've got SOPMODs in there, I've seen them. And bigger stuff. Lots of it. Plus those cannons that make you feel like you're on fire. The best we can do are a couple of assault rifles and this kinda stuff." He ported his deer rifle.

"Except you're gonna have me in there, and you're gonna have a Ranger plan." He addressed them all. "I can't tell you that nobody's gonna go down, because that's not gonna happen. There will be casualties. But you will win. That I can tell you, because that's what's gonna happen."

And when they couldn't find the food, they would first slaughter the bosses, and when they still couldn't find it, they would fall victim to their own rage, and they would lay waste to the place.

They got the blueprints he needed, and together they laid out a good plan of attack, one that would actually work. "This gate," he said at last, pointing to the disused back gate on the grounds plan, "will be unlocked. After your feint draws them to the front of the grounds—and they'll all come running, they're not that well trained—then you just send your main force right through that gate. You get inside the grounds, they are toast, people."

They worked out a schedule, and at midnight, he began his journey back. Crazy ole Mack was just about done in, starving and filthy. Mack was sorry. Mack was coming home.

14

THE HAND OF DARKNESS

On the night side of the earth, most of the lights—the cities of New York and London and Paris—had gone dark, and the atmosphere glowed softly purple against the strangling void. The International Space Station swung through its orbit in darkness. Inside, the bodies of the crew floated, one or two hands fisted, most touching the air as if it was something miraculous, their fingers carefully extended. The bodies appeared old, the hair gray with frost from the suffocating carbon dioxide of their own breath, which is what had—mercifully and gently—killed them.

Along the face of the night far below moved the great, glowing objects, working faster now, sliding just a few hundred feet above the suffering land, seeking with probes beyond human knowing, signals from our souls.

They had an enormous task before them, because one of the most improbable truths about mankind is that the vast majority of people are good, and would not need to sink away into the long contemplation that draws the evil, ever so slowly, to face themselves.

Had we not been rendered soul blind by the catastrophe that destroyed our pre-Egyptian civilization, the coming of the great objects would not have been mysterious to us. But it was mysterious, it was very mysterious, and the immense, drifting shapes only added terror to terror, and people hid, and hid their children, and dared not look upon these machineries of rescue.

Aboard, this caused neither surprise nor concern. If you looked into the workings of these machines, you would find that they were old and worn, full of humble signs that they were somebody's home.

In this immense universe of ours, worlds die every day, so the objects and their crews were always busy, flashing from one catastrophe to the next, harvesting the spiritual produce of planets in cataclysm with the industry and care of the good farmers that they were.

David had been watching these objects in his mind's eye, when he heard screams.

They were not cries of madness but of pain—no, agony. Terrible human agony was involved.

"Katie," he called as he went through the outer office, but she was already far along the hall. As he reached the top of the grand staircase, he saw her at the bottom, turning toward the back of the building and the patients' activity area.

He slid along the broad mahogany planks of the priceless floor of the front hallway, his stomach churning and congealed. Was there fire down there, or somebody being torn apart by some escaped jacket case, or had one of the dociles suddenly gone berserk?

He went through the empty dining room with its splendid crystal and silver laid out already for tomorrow's breakfast, and then to the steel door that led into the patient wing.

The uproar was coming, as he had anticipated, from the activity area, which was filled with a white, chalky light unlike any he had ever seen before. Was it radiation from the sun? But why only these windows? So, no.

Katie stood in the doorway, and David stopped beside her. For the first moment, a scene of true terror often makes no sense to the eyes, and that was the case here. What David saw were crowding black silhouettes, all pressed up against the barred armor-glass windows that, at better times, let sunlight flood this space. Then he realized that they were patients, all peering out the windows.

In among the figures was somebody moving quickly, racing back and forth and screaming, and then he saw her run like a mad thing through the parted crowd and leap at least six feet into the air, hurling herself against the outside doors with a horrible crunch.

"Let me through," he shouted as he went toward her. Katie remained standing, transfixed.

As the crowd parted, David saw two injured people on the floor, Sam Taylor and Beverly Cross. Sam cradled his right arm. Beverly looked up from a swollen face as he passed.

"Careful, David," she said, "she's real bad."

It was Linda Fairbrother.

Caroline was near her. "She's breaking herself to pieces. David, help her!"

She leaped at the door again, then bounced back and hit the floor with a sickening slap and lay still, a lovely woman covered with bruises, her nose a mass of purple flesh, one eye swollen closed, in the glaring white ocean of the light that shone through the windows and the glass of the door.

"Linda," he said, kneeling beside her shattered body, "Linda, I am here to help you. I can help you."

"Let her out," Caroline cried.

From outside, there rose another sound, low at first, then gaining strength, finally becoming the enormous howl of what must be the largest siren in the history of the world.

As it grew louder, Linda's body stiffened. Then her good eye swam to the front and stared up into the light.

"David, get back!" Caroline drew him away from Linda.

As if being drawn by some sort of invisible rope, she rose up, knocking him aside in the process. Then she ran toward the door, gathering speed fast. He leaped at her, felt his head and shoulders connect with her body, noted the rigor of extreme panic, then felt himself thrown aside like a rag.

While he tumbled helplessly against Caroline, Linda slammed against the door, hammering it with her hands and shrieking, then leaping against it again and again, so fast that the sound of her body hitting the thick glass was like a series of cannon blasts.

Dear heaven, he had never seen a symptom like this, never in his life.

"Hurry," Caroline snapped.

If she was going to survive, he saw that he had to open the doors, but if he did, other patients would certainly go out into that light and God only knew what it was.

"All right," he shouted, "everybody across the room. Staff, help me here—get them back—all of you, get back, give her space."

Caroline made a gesture, and everybody moved back. David made note of this. Even the staff were watching her for instructions.

Linda leaped up and began slamming against the door again, jumping four or five feet into the air each time.

"Do it, David! Let her out!"

A haze of blood appeared around her, and as the air filled with the smell of it, he went close, shielding himself as best he could, and finally managed to swipe the fingerprint reader.

It didn't work.

"Keys, my God, I need keys!"

Again Linda hit the door, again and again. Caroline and Linda's desperate, tear-streaked lover, Tom Dryden, tried to control her.

"Glen! Glen MacNamara, I need keys!" David looked desperately around the room. "Get Glen, somebody!"

The siren came again, rising, wailing, a soul-whipping sound that turned Linda into a human piston, driving her again and again and again into the thick, unyielding door.

"Doctor," Tom shouted, "sedate her! Get a damn shot in her!"

Then Glen was pushing through the crowd, his dirty white shirt soaked with sweat. "I was afraid we'd lose that damn locking system," he said as he thrust a key into the door and threw it open at last.

Linda went racing out, her body lurching from broken bones, her face now a purple blotch, unrecognizable. Tom followed her into the light, laughing and eager, and both seemed almost to be dancing, their anguish transformed in an instant to lilting joy.

David followed them, and when the light struck him he was suffused with an exquisite sensation, at once physical and emotional, a surging shiver of delight that was coupled to poignant nostalgia, and he thought, *This is how we're meant to feel, this is the aim of life.*

He saw in the light a ladder hanging down—and it was old, with bent rungs, but made of silver metal that gave off a gorgeous glow.

He remembered his grandfather's friend's description of the thing that Father Heim had seen at Fátima, and knew that, even then, they had been preparing.

Linda dragged herself, a white mass of bone protruding from her left leg, her fingers crazy from breaks, her breath coming in warbling sighs as she sucked air past swollen lips and broken teeth. Tom assisted her, an arm around her waist.

"You look to the injured in there, David," Caroline said. "We've got this under control."

As Linda was flooded by the light and her body became white with it, she began to reflect its whiteness. He saw her bones melt back into her skin and her face grow normal again—but then more, it was a shining face, full of the joy and energy of some higher world, and David had the sense that he was in the presence of a great and dignified being that was returning home.

Before his eyes, this ordinary, humble patient was transfigured into a being of grandeur, naked in her physical perfection, ascending in the healing flood of light.

An obscure sort of sorrow flickered in his heart then. Caroline's hand slipped into his, and he knew that she had the same question, Why not me?

Other patients came out like pilgrims to a shrine, wandering as people do in fog, blinded by the light, calling out, their voices echoing dully. Some of them raised their arms as if asking for deliverance.

In the next moment Linda, the light, the great object that had produced it—all were gone, a majesty ascended into the turmoil of the sky.

An instant later, there was a devastated, earsplitting shriek and Tom Dryden collapsed in a heap in the grass.

More groans filled the silence, sounds of deep human misery and despair.

"Don't," Caroline called out to them. "It all balances out."

Tom got up and came shuffling closer. "We were going together," he muttered. "Together!" He jumped a couple of times, snatching at the air.

The others were milling now, peering into the violet sky, still calling to the emptiness.

"Please," David said, "we need to get inside, this is not safe."

As they went back in, he said to Glen, "If this recurs, let any patient out who wants to go. I don't want them beating themselves to death against the walls."

Glen nodded.

Most of the patients were clustering in small groups in the activity area, talking among themselves. Tom Dryden cradled his chest and swayed back and forth, his eyes closed.

David said to Claire Michaels, "Can you attend to him, please?"

"Of course, Doctor," the resident replied. "Tom, do you want some Xanax? You can have a dose, Tom, if you need it."

"The sins of the world belong to us," he said, "the sins of the world."

"Why do they belong to us?" Claire asked him as she gently led him away. If the world ever returned to what it had been—if that was possible—she was going to develop into an excellent clinician.

David approached Katie, who was wiping blood off Sam Taylor's forehead.

"I'm sorry, Sam," David said.

"I'm the one who should be sorry, Doc. I lost my patient."

He was referring to Mack, of course. Frankly, David was glad.

"That guy was no loss. Katie, how's Bev Cross?"

"All right," she said, as he moved deeper into the recreation area, then the art room.

Caroline was sitting under the light of a lamp she had pulled close to her easel, once again painting with quiet concentration.

Going toward her, he caught sight of Katie following him with her eyes.

"I'm fine," he said to Katie.

"I know you're fine."

He heard anger and stopped. He went to her.

"I am. I'm fine."

"We've now lost two patients, first Mack leaves and then this. That's the sort of operation you run, Doctor." She turned away from him, started toward the hallway.

He caught up with her.

"Katie, you need to pull yourself together."

She froze, her head bowed.

"Me? I don't think so. You're screwing a patient. Another patient is AWOL and probably in danger if he's not already dead. And now this third—I can't even begin to imagine what's happened to her. But I do know one thing. You're not competent."

"I can't quit. Where would I go?"

"David, I think last night was wonderful and I think we can be important to each other, and maybe this is the only chance for either of us to taste real love. But not if you screw the patients."

He looked over at Caroline, who was painting steadily. Katie saw this, and drew away from him.

"Go play with your toy, then." She stalked out.

"Katie!"

"I'll be in the infirmary with the injuries."

When she was gone, Caroline said, " 'Also when they shall be afraid of that which is high, and fears shall be in the way, and a man goeth to his long home—' Do you know it?"

"Of course I know it. It's from Ecclesiastes."

"Did you know that the Bible is a scientific document?"

"I don't see that at all."

"You're soul blind, therefore blind to soul science. You're afraid of yourself, David. The long home of Ecclesiastes is the shadow of the soul reaching back across time, looking at its life and its previous lives. You need to open to yourself, David."

"I am, I'm remembering an enormous amount. I can even use Herbert Acton's lamp."

She put down her brush, leaned closer and whispered to him, "We need to try a very serious dose of the gold. Take an injection."

"It's a heavy metal. You can't inject that."

"What we make isn't a metal anymore at all, or even really connected to the physical world like other elements."

"Gold is gold."

"No, this starts with some of the ancient substance, so it becomes a hyperelement. In its pure form, it's so light that it levitates."

"It's hardly ancient. You just made it."

"We made it correctly, starting with a little of the ancient material, to light the path for the new gold."

Her hands came like a fluid, and framed his face, and the love in her eyes was so intense and so naked that he felt embarrassed for her and looked away.

"David, you have to face our love. You need its energy."

Furious, he pulled away from her.

"Goddamn it, *shut up*! What fatuous nonsense."

Lowering her eyes, she quietly returned to her easel.

He looked around the room at the milling patients. He had to control this situation first, but he had to get out of here, he could not bear another moment with this woman. He felt nothing and she felt a lot and it was just extremely disturbing.

"Patients are to go to their quarters now and remain in their rooms until the breakfast bell at seven," he announced.

"Excuse me, Doctor, you're needed." Ray Weller had come up to him.

He stood there in a dirty apron, Glen and Doctor Hunt with him.

"We need an emergency meeting," Ray said. Then, more softly, "We're in trouble. Big trouble."

That was obvious, but why say it in the hearing of patients, even in a whisper?

"In my office in five minutes," he said. Then he went to Claire, who was talking softly with a group of patients. "Time to shut it down for the night," he told her. "We're going to have an administrative staff meeting. We'll all be in my office."

Claire raised her voice. "Okay, boys and girls, beddie bye."

There were none of the usual groans and protests, David noted. People simply got up and began moving toward the door into the patient wing.

"This is a danger sign," he said to Claire. "They're in shock."

"Yeah," she replied.

"I want two people on the monitors tonight."

"Doctor," Glen said, "the system's down, and it's not coming back until we can get a new motherboard."

Without its computer system, this place was in its death throes, especially when it came to security.

He waited until the last patient had gone, leaving just Caroline. The only sound in the room now was the faint rustle of movement when she dipped a brush.

"You need to go," he said.

"I can't stop and you know it."

"You can't work in the middle of the night, alone."

"Especially in the middle of the night, alone."

Glen stood in the doorway. He nodded sharply, urging David to come. Obviously, there was an immediate problem and he could not stay here longer.

"Someone will take you to your room," he told Caroline. He would send one of the orderlies down immediately. She must not be left alone, not ever.

He followed Glen up what had once been the servants' stairway at the back of the original house. They rose into the magnificence of the upstairs hallway, its elegance speaking of an orderly world that had entirely gone.

They arrived at his office to an uneasy murmur of voices. When he entered, silence fell.

Glen's eyes went to the sitting area in front of the large fireplace. In one of David's wing chairs sat a filthy, bedraggled man, his clothes torn, a badly skinned elbow protruding.

"How did he get in here?"

Katie's response said it all: "How did he get out?"

Mack the Cat had come back.

DAVID FORD'S JOURNAL: SIX

Caroline says that I have to face our love, but what can love possibly mean in a situation like this? How many people die in, say, sixty seconds right now? Millions, no doubt, in a world that is disintegrating this fast.

Apparently, she wants me to remember her in a way that I do not remember her. I want her physically. Of course I do, who wouldn't? But this love of which she speaks seems to be some sort of a bridge, and I don't understand why that would be true.

It's quite clear how the gold is supposed to work, but I am not finding any change after ingesting it. Perhaps she's right and I'm not taking enough, but there is no way I'm going to eat a heavy metal. Supposedly their preparation no longer contains any elemental gold in metal form, but how can that be? It's an element, it's going to be there.

I've remembered a lot and understood a lot, but the situation that's unfolding now really eclipses more or less everything. It is true that Herbert Acton anticipated this, but his vision did not penetrate into the actual event or surely he would have left us more clear instructions. My best guess is that this is because things are now so chaotic that looking into this era would have been like looking into dirty water or dense fog.

So we're on our own, and I think that it is very clear what we're going to have to face. That document of Mrs. Denman's was right, I think. The solar system is going through a very dirty and dangerous area of space, and the sun and all her planets are taking a terrible pounding.

I think that it will be too much for mankind. Certainly, civilization is finished. If this lasts much longer the way it is, our population is going to plummet massively. If it should intensify, then I think we are going to go the way of the dinosaurs—unless, of course, Caroline's wonderful painting can somehow save a few of us. But it will be a very few, won't it, just a tiny elite? In itself, that troubles me. Why should it be us and not, say, the great scientists of the world or the great saints, or simply the children?

So where does love come into this? Why does it matter anymore? I want to spend time with Katie and Caroline. I want to take every bit of pleasure from life that I can, while I can.

I have made a decision. If we cannot take the world with us, then I am not going myself. It isn't right for just the carefully chosen to live while the rest, equally deserving, do not.

And yet, I am talking about my own death, here, and, in the end, if I have a choice, I know that I will try to save myself. It isn't a moral choice, but an instinctive one. I am not a hero, and I don't fully understand this business of calling me a leader.

When I was a boy, Charles Light tried to drill my specialness into me, my brilliance, my natural ability to take control of situations—all qualities that he saw but that I did not.

And yet, and yet . . . it's true that I understand a great deal of this. I understand why the gold works, but not, perhaps, why it doesn't for me.

I think that the best thing for me to do is to keep striving to save my patients, and give Caroline the space she needs to accomplish her work.

So far, there has been no further sign of the presence of our enemies. Does that mean that they've been swept away in the chaos? Perhaps, but somehow I doubt it. It has crossed my mind that Mack, the former CIA agent, might be one of them. He takes an inordinate interest in Caroline and her work.

He's among the patients who display genuine symptoms. Paranoia, among other things. I can see the violence in the man, and I know that he has the skills necessary to enable him to enter and leave this place, and to infuriate Sam by neutralizing him the way he did, a professional handler like him.

In any case, he bears watching, I suppose, but the reality is this: events are going to overtake our enemies just as they are going to overtake us and, very shortly now, the whole world.

15

THE RED STAR

Mack selected from the tools he'd stolen over time and brought into his room a screwdriver and a small knife. They'd given him a meal of canned corned beef hash and potatoes washed down with tepid water, but it sure as hell beat gnawing on raw potatoes and drinking toilets in abandoned farmhouses.

What was important here were two things. First, he'd seen from the snow on the screens in the nurses' station that the surveillance system was down. Second, he'd had a close look at that painting of Caroline Light's, and nobody—no ordinary person—could create a work of art so detailed. As incredible it seemed, he could most safely conclude that she was somehow creating another reality in the medium of oil on canvas, and that had to mean something, and he intended to find out what in holy hell it was.

He got up on his desk and stood, using the screwdriver to open his air-conditioning vent. It would take a real mastery of the human body to get around some of the turns, but he intended to try.

Out the top of his window, he could see auroras spinning complex madness tinted blood red. This was a change even from last night, and it unsettled him and made him work faster.

Then he noticed something very odd indeed, that made him look out into the grounds.

It was light out there, even brighter than the auroras and a full moon would make it. But this was not the moon or the tinge of auroral light.

This was the glow of something else, something that he could not quite see around the corner of the building.

There had been reports of strange ships in the sky, and he'd overheard mention that Linda Fairbrother had been taken up in one. Absently, he ran his finger along the shiny dark spot that he'd noticed just below his neck in the shower the other morning. Was it tingling? Perhaps. He feared that it might be a melanoma, but they were supposed to be irregular and this thing was perfectly round. Growing, though, no question there. It had an odd texture, not like skin, but slicker and more featureless, almost as if it was covered by a film of some kind. Also, at the center, where it was darkest, it wasn't like color at all, but more an absence of color. It was really the strangest thing he'd ever seen on a human body and he needed to get it cut out, no question.

Faint voices drew him back to his window. Now there were people down there. Guards and staff were out on the lawn, their forms lit by an eerie violet glare coming from a source that was blocked to his vision by the corner of the building.

Normally, his ability to concentrate on his work was prodigious, but this unsettled him. He'd witnessed a woman burned at the stake by the Taliban in Afghanistan, and the wild, abandoned agony of her screams had left him, already claustrophobic, with a creeping horror of suffering death by fire.

He hammered on his door. Hammered again. Finally, he started kicking the hell out of it. His relationship with Nurse Fleigler was not pleasant, and it had not been improved by his recent excursion.

"What do you want?"

"What the hell's going on? What's that light out there?"

"Nothing."

"Come on, Fleigler, I'm a paying customer here."

"Nobody cares. We don't like you. You're a creep."

"Please, Fleigler, gimme a break. What's everybody looking at?"

"You haven't earned any breaks. Sam's still got a headache because of you."

"Fairbrother did it!"

"Sam says you used some kind of a hold on him. Paralytic."

"All right, I will kick this door"—he gave it three wall-shaking wallops—"until you tell me what in fuck's happening out there!" He started in again, and, frankly, he could probably pop it off with a few more body blows.

"All right already! If you must know, it's this really bright speck in the sky. Deep violet-red speck. It's weird and I'm reading my Bible, so good night."

Jesus God, what was it? The townspeople were supposed to be coming up, but who knew how they'd react to this? They were hungry, that was for sure, but this could frighten them into hiding.

It could be emitting energy, too. What if it totally killed his radio?

He had to face something here: this situation was deteriorating too fast, and changes in tempo were dangerous to missions like his. Unless some luck came his way, he was not going to succeed.

He went back to the desk and started scraping the paint away from the screws that held on the vent above it.

"I know you by your name," he muttered as he worked. "You are Wormwood, come to collect the blood of man."

He dissected carefully, so that there would be no evidence of anything when he returned. He'd seen the look in Glen McNamara's eyes, baleful, the look of somebody who was just about an inch away from damn well blowing Mack Graham away. Sam, too, for that matter.

Had Caroline Light secretly taken over? She had to be above the terrified Dr. Davey-boy in the pecking order. That guy was a wet-behind-the-ears fool.

One nurse—Katie, that one—might not be on the side with them. She had a black spot, too; he'd seen it under her turned-up collar. He did not want to think about the damn things, though. What were you going to do about cancer now? And yet . . . something deep within him told him that this was not cancer. It told him that he'd be better off with a melanoma the size of a pie plate.

Then a welcome interruption to his thoughts: the grill came loose. Working carefully, he took it off and laid it on the desktop.

He had his route traced with measured care, every turning calculated, including the ones so tight that pushing too hard might snap his bones.

No doubt to save fuel, they'd turned off the air-conditioning an hour or so back, so the ducts would be stifling and he would have to hurry or potentially face heat stroke.

He lifted himself and raised his arms, drawing his shoulders together until his bones sighed. To get his head into the space, he had to turn it to one side with his arms straight out before him. Then he worked the rest of him in, twisting his hips until they were at a diagonal, which gave him just enough room to wriggle forward.

He felt his claustrophobia acutely now. If he got stuck in here he did not know how he could bear it. Just inches in, he knew that he was already essentially trapped, in the sense that he could only squirm ahead, not back. Lying along the duct, he began working his way around the first bend he had seen in the blueprints.

If he was successful, as far as the clinic was concerned, Caroline Light and David Ford would just disappear. Before they died, though, they were going to learn some new things about themselves, and what the human body can endure. If he failed, he would either suffocate in the ductwork or get back here and reseal his vent and nobody would be the wiser.

At the first turning, impossibly sharp, he felt his body growing warm from the effort of the stretching, then growing hot. He pushed against the aluminum corner in the smothering dark, and knew that his skull was being compressed really severely, because a storm of crazy images—a girl with a mouth like a cave laughing, a man dancing slow and burning, a dog serenading a dead child—began gushing through his mind's eye as his brain was constricted, and bands of pain whipped his temples.

He lay along the duct gasping, his body an agony of muscle knots and popping cartilage.

A push with his toes brought some release to his head and his twisted hips. Another inserted his upper body into the larger feeder duct, giving him a pulsing rush of blood to his brain and a surge of relief.

He edged ahead now, pushing with his toes, thinking only of his objective. Another turn and he was above the nurses' station. He worried that his movements would make too much noise until he heard the faint scratching of Fleigler's iPod, which she was playing at its usual deafening level over her earphones. She must be trying to drown out reality. Good for her, good for him.

Finally, inching along, sweating, his eyes closed tight to minimize the feeling of being trapped, he reached the even wider sloping duct that led down to the air-conditioning system itself. Here, he could move easily and therefore go much faster. But when he pushed himself into the duct, he went into an unexpected slide, which resulted in a series of booming sounds. Worse, he went slamming headfirst into the fan, and would have been sliced to meat if it had been turning. As it was, he ended up with a painful gouge in his forehead.

The blueprints showed an access hatch here that was used to clean the fans, and he felt for it, his sense of confinement growing as his fingers sought edges that were not there.

Unless he found it, he would be trapped. There was no going back up that slope, which was far steeper than it had appeared in the blueprint. His heart sped up and he began to need to take deep breaths, but the air was foul. Without the system running, he thought he was in danger of suffocation, and it was not just his fear of confinement working.

He fluttered his fingers along the smooth duct, seeking for edges, finally touching a seam. Yes, oh, yes, he felt along it, felt hinges, felt the simple flat latch, pushed it—and it was tight, too tight to move. Wriggling, twisting, too frantic now to care about the noise he might be making, he got a quarter out of his pocket and slid it along until it stopped against the tongue of the latch. Pushing, he finally felt a shift, heard the rasp of it, felt it moving more.

Cool air rushed in and he found himself almost weeping with relief. Carefully, making as little noise as possible, he slipped out of the ductwork and into the dim basement.

Listening, looking around him, he detected no other human presence. Very well. With a predator's quick and silent stride, he moved toward the stairs and ascended them.

Here was the supply room, its shelves mostly empty. Good, this would outrage the townies. Hopefully, they'd tear the place apart. He went to the door, then paused. He was watching the strip of light beneath it, because it was flickering.

So was somebody there, or was it the flickering of the sky tricking his eyes?

No choice but to find out, so he grasped the door handle and turned it slowly, making certain that the door did not creak as it opened.

Before him spread the kitchen, with its long row of gleaming stainless steel ranges, its ovens, its broad cutting tables. Stepping softly and quickly to the knife wall, he pulled down a cleaver, a nice one, beautifully weighted, sharp as sin. So he would be the classic madman with a cleaver. Except he knew how to use things like this.

What little of him that might have been decent, might have felt mercy or relented, now slipped into memory, became unreal to him, and finally went out like a dying candle.

He felt full of the dark, and was in a curious way comfortable in it, like a man who has entered a cave that appeared dreadful from the outside, but who, once inside, becomes used to its terrors.

He strode across the kitchen, pushing through the double swinging doors into the dining room. Here, all was elegance, the crystal stemware flaring with the wild light from outside, the silver seeming to jump on the place settings from the glowing sky.

It was different tonight, the auroras pulsating rather than flashing, and there were long streaks of light in the tops of the tall windows that surrounded the room. Now, meteors.

At the door of the dining room, he paused. Beyond this point, anything could happen. He went out to the broad corridor that led into the beautiful front rooms of the house. It had been a long time since he had been here in the flesh. Except for visits to their shrinks, inmates rarely got past this door.

"Excuse me."

Standing at the foot of the stairs was a security guy. He was six foot three and fully weaponed.

Mack smiled. "I've lost my way."

"Identify yourself, please."

He took a step closer, at which moment the guard's eyes flickered and Mack knew two things. He'd been recognized and the cleaver was spotted.

In the split of an instant, Mack stepped up to him and swung it, and his head went wobbling off, hit the stairs with a wet thud and came rolling down, coming to rest at the feet of the crumpling corpse.

Human bodies contain an amazing amount of blood, and there was no way to stop the ocean of it that was pumping out of this man. Mack picked up the head and took it to the coat closet that was concealed under the wide staircase. He shoved it onto a shelf, then dragged the body in, leaving behind a long, streaked trail of blood.

When morning came, they would certainly find this, but in the night, with all that flickering, it was hard to see exactly what was going on with the floor. So, unless somebody slipped in the mess, he had a reasonable chance that it would not be discovered until morning.

The stairs were open to him, and he thought he might alter his plan and try Dr. Ford first.

He took them three at a time. Surprise was essential.

Hallways led to the left and the right, then a central one, arched, where Mr. and Mrs. Acton's suites had been. On the left were the old nurseries, now offices.

Moving along the central corridor, he heard nothing. The doors were thick and all were closed. He stopped at the one with the DR. DAVID FORD sign. Behind it lay his office, his reception room, and his private rooms.

He put his hand on the doorknob and twisted it very carefully, so as not to make the least sound. After an eighth of an inch, he met resistance. The damn thing was locked, which was a setback, although a predictable one. He was going to have to find some basic tools, a coat hanger or a long, thin screwdriver, if he was going to get through a thick, well-made door like this silently.

As he leaned against it, trying to see if he could hear the tumblers as he moved the handle, he heard voices inside, faint but intense. The door was so closely fitted that you couldn't even see a line of light under it. Leaning against it didn't help, the voices remained indistinct.

For all he could tell, whoever was in there might come out at any moment. His bridges were well and properly burned. If he was found here, something permanent would be done to him. These were kindly people and he could not imagine them killing him. But they were desperate, also, and desperation causes unexpected behavior.

Initiative was slipping away from him. He'd thought it was possible that he would not unlock the secret of this place in time. If so, then his duty was clear: he must prevent it from being used at all. If the purest and best could not continue, the whole species had to go extinct. No third alternative was acceptable, not to him and, he was certain, not to the people in the bunkers.

He went back downstairs and threw open the recreation area doors and went through it to the art room, and there it was in its magnificence, the painting. And the damn thing was gloriously, superbly finished. Caroline Light had painted a great masterwork in a day. He didn't know a great deal about art, but he knew that the technique was immeasurably accomplished.

Even in this bizarre light, he could see a lovely meadow just after sunset, behind it a woodland, and in the far distance the western sky still glowing orange. Just an amazing thing.

As he peered into it more closely, he noticed that he became physically uncomfortable. He found himself rubbing the dark place on his neck, which seemed to be getting hot.

Swallowing the pain, he continued his examination of the painting . . . and realized something. For all the realism of this thing, the sky was wrong. Or was it? Yeah, the constellations could be off. He wasn't aware of exactly how they should look, but it wasn't like this. Then, as he watched, he saw that the painting appeared to be changing. And that was the damnedest thing he had ever seen. The glow in the sky was fading. That *was* a sunset.

But then this wasn't a painting. It was—God, what was it, a window into another world? Because there were no auroras there, no purple sky.

He thought: I could go through. Just climb through. To hell with his goddamn duty, this was a chance to save himself. He extended his hand toward it—and his skin immediately got so hot that he snatched it back.

More carefully this time, he moved his hand closer, and the closer he came, the more the heat in his body increased. Gritting his teeth against the pain, he touched the surface of the thing.

It was like touching the edge of a column of air.

He pressed a little deeper, and could feel, on his palm, a subtle change in temperature.

It *was* a door, damn right. So he was going through and screw them all.

He extended his arm, and immediately felt such furious agony in the discolored area on his neck that he had to stop. He threw himself back away from the thing, rolling, writhing, forcing his screams back into his throat. The dark area hurt like hell. He could smell burned skin.

Clutching his shirt, he smothered what seemed to be a fire that had started spontaneously in his flesh.

These people were full of tricks and goddamn them.

He raised the cleaver. Then stopped. What would happen if he struck it, would it blow up in his face or what?

He looked more closely at it, being careful not to try to touch it again. You could see the places where the canvas was tacked to the stretcher. The back of it was just—well, he pushed the edge of the cleaver against it and found that there was give there.

No matter how it looked or what it did, this was basically paint on canvas, it had to be. Maybe it was also a damn wormhole or something, and if so, they were certainly about to use it.

That must not be allowed to happen. But he was in no position to steal it. He didn't know how it worked. He only knew that if he couldn't use it, they damn well weren't going to, either.

He went around behind it and positioned himself. He raised the cleaver, aiming for the center of the frame. With an easy motion, he cut the thing into two halves, which flew off in opposite directions. Where the painted area was slashed, tiny sparks flickered.

Again he slashed it, to the left, to the right, again and again, ripping and tearing and cutting until there was nothing left of it but smeared paint and scraps of cloth, and a tiny, shimmering corner not big enough for a finger.

He stood over it and smashed his heel into it and ground it and ground it until there was nothing left at all.

"Excuse me, what are you doing?"

He turned. He looked across the dark, flickering maw of the large recreation area. A shadow stood there.

"Hello, Doctor," he said, and advanced toward Marian Hunt.

When her eyes went to the cleaver, she took a step back, but he was on her then and before she could turn away he had grabbed her wrist and, with a swift upward swing of the knife, severed her arm.

Blood sprayed from her shoulder, shock and disbelief transformed her face into a gabbling mask, and he swung the severed arm at her and hit her in the side of the head with the ball head of the humerus bone, which struck her skull with a thick crunch.

She fell to her side, landing on the gushing shoulder with a sucking gasp of agony. He slammed her head with her arm again and again, hitting her skull until it was soup.

He didn't clean anything up, it was too late for that. He needed to get out of here because he didn't know why she'd suddenly appeared in the first place. He must have made too much noise, and that meant that others would be on their way. Plus, by now that guard had failed to report in and that was going to be investigated.

The painting represented science so advanced that he could not even begin to imagine how it might work, but two things were certain: first, it would not be doing its job now. Second, Light would tell him how it *did* work, and she would make one that worthy, decent people could use.

He tossed the arm into the air and slashed up as it came down, severing the forearm. Then he slit the flesh off the humerus and hefted it. A club could silence a man a whole lot faster than a knife.

As he headed for the patient suites, he heard a rise of voices all through the building—and realized that he wasn't the cause, because the windows were now as bright as dawn, but it was not dawn and the light was a bizarre, sickly violet.

He strode to the closest window and saw, rising on the northeastern horizon, the source of the earlier disturbance outside.

A new star was rising, and it brought a quote to his mind, "And a great star, blazing like a torch, fell from the sky on a third of the rivers and on the springs of water . . ."

The star Wormwood was here, and this was not only what the Book of Revelation foretold, but also the old calendars. It was what all the warnings from the past were about, and why they involved such exquisite calculations and precise dates.

The thing had only one meaning for him. Time was no longer running out, it *had* run out.

These bastards had known this, he suspected, right to the minute. That was why they had prepared their little escape hatch when they had. They would also realize that it was the most valuable thing in the world, or that had ever been in the world.

Well, they would do it all again, but not here. They would do it for him. He just very badly needed those people from the town to come up and create his diversion. Then he would take Light and Ford where he wanted to take them, and do with them what he needed to do.

16

MEMORY

As David watched the rising of the new star, the red star, he thought
of the Book of Revelation. What was the past, that it was so wise that it
could write such books? As he looked back from the world as it was
now, history seemed to him to be a long process of going blind.

He thought, *I am at stage two of the process of dying, I'm beginning to
accept the reality of what's happening, and that's changing my perspective.*

It meant accepting that he could not keep the Acton Clinic func-
tioning and he could not save the patients. Perhaps there had been a
mission. Of course there had. But he did not think that even Herbert
Action had been able to imagine the sheer scale of the catastrophe.

He tried to shake off the simmering anguish of failure, but that was
not going to be possible.

"David."

A shock went through him and he whirled around—and found himself confronting a large group of people who had entered his office so
quietly that he had not heard them.

"David," Caroline said again. He did not like that tone. He did not
like this crowd. On top of everything else, now he had a rebellion on
his hands.

Glen was there, Bev Cross and Sam Taylor, and a dozen or more patients, among them Susan Denman and a mysteriously recovered Aaron
Stein, who had been among the most profoundly psychotic. Katie was
nowhere to be seen.

Caroline said, "We're a delegation."

"May I know your complaint? I presume it is a complaint."

Bev brought out a disposable syringe. "David, we're going to do this." It was the substance—the gold.

"David," Glen said, "you need to let us."

Caroline's lips were a stern line, but her eyes were pale clouds, heavy with tears.

"We've all taken it, David," Sam said. "We all remember."

"I've taken it."

"How much have you taken?" Aaron asked.

"How much have you taken, Aaron? Any of you? I know the answer and so do you. Very damn little, just like me. So what does that tell you? *It doesn't work for me.*"

Glen asked, "Will you let Bev inject you?"

There was a stirring in the room.

"Look, I understand everything." He gestured toward the lamp. "I even understand how Herbert Acton saw into time. But I don't understand how this is going to help. Why would my brain require a megadose?"

"David," Caroline said, "once you wake up, you'll thank us."

"For injecting me with a heavy metal? I don't think so."

Glen said, "It isn't a heavy metal anymore."

"It's gold, for God's sake. If you think that's not a heavy metal, you missed high school science." He was thinking about the Beretta he'd been issued. If he could get to his desk, he could regain control of this situation.

Bev attempted to get behind him, but he turned as she did. "You can't put gold in somebody's veins."

"You can."

"What you made in that furnace is amateur chemistry. You can't inject somebody with amateur chemistry."

"It isn't amateur," Caroline said, "and it isn't chemistry." She gestured toward the glyphs above the door. "It induces the union of those two principles and results in an extension of consciousness beyond space and time."

"Look, I'm a doctor and I can only say that ingesting a heavy metal is bad, but taking one in an injection is going to be catastrophic."

"You're in amnesia—"

"I've remembered everything, Caroline! The class, all of it. So I don't need this—this attack. I do not need it." Again he looked toward the desk. The gun was in there.

"David, your amnesia is emotional. What the gold will do is open a door in you that's locked tight right now. The door to the heart."

"The heart has no place in this."

"David, the heart is everything! Without love to sustain us, we cannot make the journey."

"Look, folks, you need to face something, all of you. We aren't going to be making any journeys through time. Herbert Acton was incredibly accomplished, but he was also deluded. You can see into time. But actual, physical movement? Forget it."

He saw Glen's eyes flicker toward Sam, who came forward and was suddenly behind him with Beverly. Once again, David started to turn toward them, but this expert restrained him by immobilizing his arms just above the elbows.

Sam said, "Sorry, boss."

Glen said, "Either this happens with a struggle or without a struggle, it's your choice."

Part of him considered the provable skills of Herbert Acton and part of him the arrogance of these people—but then Bev removed the sheath from the needle and all of him felt anger.

"How dare you," he shouted, and he kicked at them.

"Hold him," Caroline said. "We need the neck!"

"Jesus God, NO!" But they swarmed him and immobilized him with their bodies. "Don't do this, this is insane!"

They forced him to the floor, they held his head so that he could not move it. He felt Bev swabbing the left side of his neck just above the carotid.

"Okay," she said, "you'll feel this one, hon."

The needle was fire and he bellowed; he twisted and writhed and tried to move his head enough to dislodge it but he could not dislodge it, and he felt the substance running like lava through the vein.

Then it hit his brain in an explosion of darting sparks, each of which seemed filled with information, and in the next instant he saw beyond words, beyond thought, beyond language itself, into the pure, wordless mathematics of hyperspace.

Which he understood—and with it, also understood more of himself than ever before, that they were, in one sense, right about him, that he contained an enormous past stretching across eons among the living and eons among the dead. He saw, also, that a living man and a dead man are simply two aspects of one creature. The living form moves through life in an active state; a dead man is the same creature in its contemplative form, looking at what has been done, and in so doing seeing the truth of the self.

There came next a burst of pure physicality—bodily sensation in its purest form, the agony of pleasure and the agony of pain mixed together.

"Oh, God, God, I'm . . . I think I'm having a stroke. You're giving me a stroke!"

"No," Caroline said. Her hand on his forehead was cool and firm, and the tears in her eyes gleamed.

Then something happened that he had not expected and could not expect. The rich, vivid sensation of his body seemed to concentrate until it was a single, burning point—and then his head, for want of a better word to explain total annihilation, exploded.

He had no eyes to see with, no ears to hear with, no sensation of the world around him.

He thought, *They killed me. They're all crazy and they killed me. This was a blood sacrifice.*

But the black that had enveloped him was not like the abyss he had glimpsed earlier. This darkness was vividly alive, and also changing, and it changed by degrees through all the colors that were on the Tiffany lamp, until it was a radiance, and suddenly he was no longer in a void, but back in his office.

He saw also within him another being who was not him but who occupied a place in hyperspace that was at once everywhere and was deeply, profoundly specific. He saw that this being, who had been called Osiris, who had been called Christ, who had been called Quet-zalcoatl and Viracocha, who had been called so many different names, was right here, right now, and he understood why the preflood ritual that was now known as communion, the sharing of the flesh, had been preserved, because to accept Him into your body was to accept Him into your soul.

He was looking up into a face. He reached up, and Caroline smiled, and kissed the tips of his fingers.

Around him was his class, his deep friends, his companions in the Great Work.

"I remember," he said, his voice faint. He tried again, attempting to speak more strongly. "I remember. I remember how I love you."

At first, he'd been afraid and embarrassed.

Dad had driven him into a world of Lamborghinis and Bentleys in an '88 Chevy Caprice. He had not understood then what he under-stood now, that he had been chosen not because his grandfather had happened to own a certain piece of land, but because he was, himself, exactly right for the role he was to perform.

"Mr. Acton didn't only see the future," he said, his voice faint. "We weren't chosen because of our lives, but because of our past lives. Nothing was an accident."

He had been a general, an admiral, he had led men and nations, and was an ancient being full of wisdom, and he *could* perform the role being offered to him. In fact, he was the only one who could do it, the good leader.

"I saw you," he said to Caroline, "you . . ." She'd been perhaps ten, he twelve, but she had shone like a child made of sunlight.

He remembered sitting side by side with her under the apple tree—for there was such a tree in the garden of every house of the Acton Group, including his own. The color of the apple blossom, he knew now, was a memory trigger. When that red blush came to the sky, it would be time.

The color of the new star was no longer frightening to him, for it was the color of the highest energy, and the auroras combined with it to make the sky the subtle pink of apple blossom.

He looked at Caroline again, and, softly, secretly, his heart opened—and he saw at once how necessary this had been. Without love, there was no reason to continue the species at all, and there was a great plan and there were rules, and without love they could not fly through time.

"I remember my promise to you, Caroline."

She met his eyes with the warmest gaze he could ever remember, and at once for him everything changed. They had held innocent hands as kids, but there had been a deeper bond, the entwining love of souls that has carried humanity across so many perils and divides.

They came together and he enfolded her in his arms, and it felt good, it felt so very, very good.

An instant later, he broke away. In his new role, he had new responsibilities.

"The painting," he said. "Who's guarding it?"

Glen and Sam looked at each other.

"Nobody? Is it *nobody*?"

"David, we didn't think that—"

He didn't listen to the rest, he didn't need to. He was already running. Please, God, that he not be too late.

17

THE TOWNSPEOPLE

"For God's sake, Glen, she's been dismembered! My dear God!" David felt as if he was watching himself from a distance as he stared down at the body of Marian Hunt. He knew that he was experiencing stress-induced dissociation, a symptom of shock. Claire Michaels, who had found her, sat slumped in a chair, her face in her hands.

If they had not needed to take the time to inject him, perhaps this wouldn't have happened.

Katrina said in a dull voice, "We need a blanket, David."

"Yes, of course. We need, uh, a body bag—Glen?"

"I'll get a couple of men to pull her out of here and clean up the blood. But we've got no communications, so this all has to be done with runners and my first priority is to locate and secure the person who did this, and I have to tell you that we've got perimeter issues. We had an incursion attempt earlier today, and there was one intruder injured."

"Where is he? Is he being treated?"

"They carried him off. I'm hopeful that it taught them a lesson." But then he stopped, listened.

David heard it, too, a chugging noise.

"What is it?"

Glen had gone pale.

"Automatic weapons fire," he said. "South wall."

"Ours?"

"That's an older-model machine gun, probably a Browning. The townies are back and my guess is that somebody's opened that back gate for them again."

There followed a sharp, rushing whisper.

"That's us. HK G40."

Then three cracking booms, sounding like a small cannon.

"Forty-five automatic. Civilian again. I need to get down there."

Cries echoed through the building. More chugging followed, and upstairs, glass breaking, followed by horrific screams.

"Somebody took a hit through the window," Glen said. The initial fear in his voice had been suppressed. In its place now was professional calm.

"We need to get everybody to safety," David said. "We need to bring the whole security team inside the building."

"David, begging to differ, you are telling us to begin our defense by retreating to our place of last refuge."

For a heartbreaking instant, David could see the boy in the man, the bright hope that had been there when they had been in class together. Glen was tired now, very tired. David's heart went out to his friend.

Feet pounded on the stairs and a patient appeared, Tom Dryden. He was naked, his face tight, a grin that spoke agony. Without a word, he ran past them and into the recreation area. An instant later there was a wet thud, and he was slamming himself against the windows the same way Linda had slammed herself against the door. All across his back there was an area so black that it looked more like a great hole in him than any sort of sore.

Shouting that the great ships were gone, David ran to help him.

But he kept on, just as Linda had, smashing himself to pieces against the thick, relentlessly resistant glass.

"Stop! Take it easy!" David got to the door and threw it open. "Here, you can go!"

Still, Tom hurled himself against the window, which, David saw, was starting to develop long, ominous cracks. He really did not need a point of easy access, not with a firefight going on a few hundred yards away.

"You can go, Tom," he shouted. But Tom didn't want to leave by the door, or at all. He wanted to break himself against the window and the wall.

"Mr. Dryden," a female voice called, sharp and high. It was Katie.

"Don't get near him."

"He's like me."

"What do you mean, Katie?"

Her eyes glittered like dark jewels, and he could see defiance in them. She held up her hair, and on her neck, spreading up from her back, was a gleaming spot of deepest blackness.

As a doctor, he might have thought melanoma, but not with borders that precise.

"On his back," she said. "He's dirty, they're never going to come for him." She laughed a little. "We're rejects."

Again Tom Dryden slammed himself against the window.

"We can't let him just do that," David said, attempting to pull him toward the door. As he did three more people appeared, all running to help, Amy Feiffer and Robert Noonan, both from the class, and Mack Graham. Robert was the youngest son of George Noonan of Web development fame.

The group of them manhandled Tom through the door and into the grounds. David hated to do it, but getting him out of here was better than having him slam himself to pieces.

As they returned, they shut and locked the door.

"How come you're out, Mack?"

"Nurse Fleigler released me."

"Yeah, well, okay, I can understand that." Under these circumstances, nobody could be left in lockup. But with this man, it was tempting.

"What can we do to help?" Noonan asked.

Now there was a thunder of gunfire, and greenish-blue flashes stuttered in the violet of the new star.

Under this new light, all the colors were different. The grass was a washed out pinkish brown, the new leaves on the trees yellow instead of green, the trunks black. As it raced toward the firefight, a white SUV, one of the security vehicles, appeared bright pink. The perimeter wall, visible in the distance, had gone from gray to rose, its razor wire gleaming an odd pinkish red.

Dryden stood where Linda had stood, his face raised, screaming rage at the sky.

David heard a cry from inside, and he recognized the voice instantly, and he forgot everything, and ran back in.

Caroline stood before her empty easel, her face in her hands. The easel itself was just a frame with tatters of canvas around the edges.

In the way that people sharing a tragedy will, Mack laid an arm on her shoulder. She shrugged him off, but he persisted, and finally she leaned against him and sobbed.

"There are more materials," Susan Denman said.

"Where are they?" Mack asked. "I'll help you."

"Caroline," Susan said, "why don't we go to the supply room together, you can pick out what you need."

When Mack started to follow, David called him back.

"Mack, I want you to remain in sight of staff at all times."

"Of course."

He was suspicious of Mack. Of course, there was no proof of anything, but when you added this patient up, you got a sum that was wrong.

Looking out across the bizarrely colored landscape, David knew that this new light would affect the human brain profoundly. Serotonin, dopamine—all the neurotransmitters—were light dependent, and this radically different wavelength—violet—would have the effect of intensifying and changing not only colors, but also the mind and heart. Colors you could see, but what it might be doing to brain chemistry he could scarcely imagine.

Again there were shots, but this time they were so close that David instinctively ducked. Mack hurried back to the door, and David followed.

"Katie," he called behind him, "get the patients upstairs, keep them away from the windows."

As Mack opened the door, David saw movement around the side of the house, and a figure backed into view. He was concentrated on whatever scene was unfolding before him. In his hands there was some sort of a gun, David did not know what sort. But a big one, certainly, oily black and complicated. David's own gun, the little Beretta he'd been issued by Glen, was in his pocket, but he dared not bring it out in the face of that monster.

The gun fired again, and this time the sound drew people out of the recreation area—and he saw that the patients—the real ones—had not gone upstairs at all, but were, in their panic, coming outside and straight into danger, with members of his class trying and failing to control them.

"No," he shouted, "get back!"

On hearing the voice behind him, the figure turned around, and David saw that this was a boy of maybe fourteen or fifteen, a towhead with darting, frightened eyes made red by the new light.

As he aimed the weapon, David threw himself against the wall. An instant later the heat of bullets seared past his face, and he saw the child's thin frame hopping from the recoil.

Silence followed, then a single, ripping shriek. Turning toward it, David saw that a crowd of patients that had come out the door had been torn to pieces by the bullets.

Many lay screaming, holding themselves, crying and gagging. One man capered wildly, blood as dark as a beet spraying out of his neck. Another bubbled foam from his chest, his hands fluttering around the wound, his eyes darting like the eyes of a trapped animal. Others were still, one of them kneeling and praying with his hands folded, gazing up toward the glow of the star.

The boy came a few hesitant steps closer. His face was a child's, but it contained the cruel shadows of fear and desperation.

Quickly, the boy raised his gun to his shoulder, a snapping, oddly military gesture. Pink fire burst from the barrel and the praying man came sailing backward, his arms thrusting out, hands spread.

Suddenly, there was movement beside David. The light was so bizarre that it was difficult to see some things, such as a fast-moving figure, but as she ran past him, he saw that it was Caroline and she was going to the boy.

"No!"

The boy kept the weapon raised, his face intent.

"Caroline, we need you!"

David ran, trying to put himself between her and the child, but she was well ahead of him.

Then she was standing before the child.

"Don't," she said to him.

"Mom got shot. You gonna help her, lady?"

"I can help her."

"She's dead." The voice was stark and cold. "What's wrong with the sun?"

"That's not the sun. It's a different star."

"It ain't the sun?"

"It's dangerous. You need to be inside."

David tried again. "Caroline, we can't afford to lose you."

The boy said, "I want a bowl of soup."

"You can have a bowl of soup."

"Caroline, get back. Let me do this."

"Get out of here, David. Son, come here."

"Fuck, no." The boy's hand moved and the rifle clicked.

Caroline took a step toward him.

David could smell the stark odor of cordite still coming from the rifle.

"Caroline, *please*!"

"Come here," she said, opening her arms.

The boy pushed the rifle into her face. David was behind her. He could not save her now.

"Son, no. No, please," he said, but his fear reduced it to a dry, barely audible murmur.

Caroline lifted her hand, palm out, as if trying to protect herself from the barrel of the weapon. The two of them remained like that, frozen. David could not see Caroline's face, but the boy's slowly changed, the hardness leaving his eyes and tears appearing at their edges.

"Ma'am, is this the end of the world?"

"It's a big change. Son, tell me, is there a black spot on you anywhere? Under your arm, maybe? On your leg?"

He hesitated. David took a step to one side, trying to get a clear run at the kid. Behind him, Mack was also in motion.

The boy said, "I got nothing like that."

Caroline said, "Give me the gun."

"No'm."

"Did the ships come over your house?"

"Yeah, they didn't stop, we got left here."

"Son, you have a chance to escape with us. Don't lose it now."

"I shot 'em all!" His voice broke. "I'm sorry." This was followed by a cataract of sobs and the boy ran into Caroline's arms. David had never seen anything quite like it.

Her arm around him, Caroline returned to the building. A security guard quickly scooped up his abandoned weapon.

Two staffers came out with sheets to cover the dead, of which there were four. The wounded, many more, had been taken to the infirmary.

Most of the remaining staff and patients were assembled in the recreation room. Caroline had gone back to her easel and set it up, Susan having supplied her with paint and a fresh canvas. Mack watched her, and Noonan watched him.

David got up on a chair. "Patients, you need to get upstairs with the others and stay away from windows. Our security team will get the situation under control, but we need to help them by staying out of harm's way."

As he watched, the others trooped upstairs, all except Mack and Noonan, and, of course, Caroline. He looked around for Sam, but didn't see him. Katie was still here, so he asked her to escort Mack to his room.

"Aren't we past that?" Mack immediately asked.

"I told you, I want you in the sight of staff, and I can't deal with you right now."

"I'm not being locked in any goddamn room! No way!"

"Just go upstairs with the others."

"What about her?" He gestured toward Caroline. "She can't stay down here."

"She needs to do her work."

"Let's take her somewhere safer."

"Mack, you go with the others, or I will lock you down at gunpoint."

"With what gun?"

He was about to produce it when Caroline whirled away from her painting.

"Stop it! Mack, stop being a fool. Go upstairs where it's safe."

"What is that thing, anyway? It's no damn painting." He advanced toward her, one aggressive step, then another. David took out the little pistol, which felt mysterious and awful in his hand.

"It's a way out," Caroline said. "It's a *chance*!"

"How does it work?"

"If it works."

"So you're not sure?"

"I'm sure I'm creating a portal. If nobody destroys it this time, maybe we can go through."

"To where?"

"Away from here."

"There's got to be more to it than that."

She shook her head—and Mack came yet closer to her. "Tell me how the goddamn thing *works*!"

David fired. Across the room, a painting of Amanda Acton, Herbert's wife, dropped to the floor with a resounding crash.

"The next one," he said to Mack, "belongs to you."

Mack still seemed ready to throttle Caroline, and David began tightening his finger on the trigger.

Mack's eyes were steady and unafraid. He was calculating odds, David could see that.

"All right," he said, "I'll go upstairs. Just don't goddamn well lock me down."

"Do it now."

At last he left, moving with exaggerated casualness, as if unconcerned about a thing.

When they were alone, David kissed Caroline's hair. There was such a strange combination of newness and old, assured love in the way he felt now about her, as if she was a settled lover who had mysteriously appeared in a fresh and sensual new body. It was all he could do not to embrace her, but she was working and he did not dare disturb a single line. He wanted to explore with her the wonder of adult love, in the innocence of childhood memory.

"How long will it take?" he asked.

"Too long."

"Then what happens?"

"Don't interrupt me!"

He stepped away from her. His stomach felt as if it would turn inside out. He laid an encouraging hand on his painter's slim shoulder.

She worked on, the steady whisper of her brush the only sound in the great room.

DAVID FORD'S JOURNAL: SEVEN

The substance they injected changed me profoundly. They were right to force me and I'm glad they did. In a sense, I suppose, it was my scientific education that made me so resistant—but it is this same education that has also enabled me to understand what we are trying to do.

For me, our hope is lodged in that woman hunched over the easel, in her concentrated face and long hands, and the ocean of love that hides behind her harsh exterior.

She is creating a true hyperdimensional object—the first one, I think, that has been created in a long time. The icons of the Russians are a degenerated memory of such paintings, in the sense that it is believed that they contain the actual, living consciousness of the saints they depict.

This is more than an icon, though, far more powerful. It is a bridge between art and science, fashioned out of the artist's love and creativity, and the scientist's patient attention to the laws of nature.

It is true alchemy, the transformation of base metal into gold—that is to say, the transformation of paint and canvas into a hyperdimensional portal.

I am humble before the alchemists, and especially before that one with her paints and the hyperdimensional colors out of which they have been made. For those are not mere oil paints that she applies to that canvas.

I don't know who mixed them or how, but I know this about those paints: they are a machine of the very highest order. The light reflected from the surface of paint she is applying not only penetrates this reality, it is visible in all realities.

I think one of those great physicists—was it Stephen Hawking, or possibly Roger Penrose?—said that a time machine would be the most visible thing in the world because it would necessarily exist in every moment. Well, that's true, for this painting, as she paints it, at once takes on the appearance of an old master, an ancient encaustic, a cave painting, and in every respect of line, it is perfect.

It is not meant to save just an elite few. It is meant to save all who need saving. The elect are rising, the judged sinking into the dark center of the earth. But the rest of us, we have to escape and we have to do it in our physical bodies. Of course, many of us won't make it. But many will, and I know this: when she is finished—when the moment is exactly right— this device will enter hyperspace and thus become visible to everybody with eyes to see it and the goodness of heart to use it.

It won't save just a few hundred here at the clinic. No, it is part of a much larger plan. When it is finished, it will indeed be the most visible thing on earth.

This thing being shuffled onto that fragile canvas is nothing less than light in a very dark time, our great chance and great hope.

And now I know that I am here not only to use it and guide others through it but to protect it.

We are few around her, and the enemy is very many—in fact, so many that he is legion and will certainly destroy us if he can.

I can sense the edges of a great plan that surrounds us with love and hope, but also another plan, equally powerful, that seeks the ruin of the world.

18

GENERAL WYLIE

In Hancock, Virginia, the convoy stopped to refuel, then reroute around the Hagerstown, Maryland, area. Recce ahead had identified an active uprising in Hagerstown, so they were going to need to bypass in order to reach Raleigh and the Acton Clinic fast, and speed was probably essential.

General Wylie had a small muster consisting of his command vehicle, a Stryker Mobile Gun System, three squad Humvees, and a fuel truck. He did not see the light defenses at the clinic as being able to stand up against twenty-one soldiers and the MGS, which could deliver a pretty fair punch, and he intended to take the place out and obtain whatever of value his agent was signaling him was located there.

He had received an urgent and promising communication from Mack Graham, which had convinced him that immediate action was essential. It had said, "Device located and understood."

That could not be more clear. There was a device and he knew where it was and he understood it.

So, fine. General Wylie was going to get it and take it back to Blue Ridge.

Over the past few days, one after another of the redoubts had reported over the fiberoptic network that the local situation was becoming critical. A number of them had since gone silent. Colonia Dignidad, with its reputation in Chile as having been founded by war-refugee Germans, had been an immediate target of the locals. Its last report was that the

Chilean air force was overhead using deep-penetrating bunker buster bombs. The center in England had simply gone silent. Destroyed? Over-run? No way to know.

There were no longer any satellites operational so it wasn't possible to get lookdowns. Also, there was no chance of deploying any sort of air power. That was all down due to electronics failures. How the Chilean air force had gotten up was anybody's guess. Old planes, probably, with-out sensitive electronics. But that had been three days ago. Because of the tremendous electromagnetic loading of all wiring, not even the sim-plest aircraft were going to be viable now. The only reason his own vehi-cles were operational was that they were diesel and they had been started inside the redoubt. They'd keep going as long as they weren't turned off and once again required their electronics.

General George Wylie sat in his command vehicle staring at an empty computer screen. He was back to Civil War–level intelligence. No eyes, no ears, except what a guy in a dusty diesel Jetta could bring back from his travels ahead.

"Device located and understood." After that, no further reports. Probably, Mack the Cat was dead. Mack took the extreme chance, always.

They'd put Mack in the Acton Clinic last year because it had become clear that the group who, as children, had been taught Acton's secrets by the son of his associate Bartholomew Light were assembling there.

A number of these children had been DNA profiled, and curious things were found, things that not even the most advanced genetics laboratories could decipher. Something—and it was extensive—had been added to their DNA. It was as if some sort of artificial evolution had been induced in them.

The redoubts around the world were full of members of important and very private societies, members of various fraternal orders and reli-gious organizations, all of them devoted to the same thing: maintaining and increasing the wealth of those who had it and deserved it.

But not even the most secret of them was as well concealed as Acton's group. They'd had their memories wiped, then experienced some kind of temporary psychotic induction process that was far in advance of any brainwashing technique ever developed. It had been this that had caused them to be so hard to find. Who would think to look among a bunch of psychotics? To all appearances, Mrs. Acton had left the estate to a favorite charity when she died, and it had used the money to found the clinic.

All very straightforward, and all a big, fat lie.

One of Mack's messages from last week had said, "group leaders now present."

So they were ready and whatever they were going to do, it was going to be going down pronto.

He tapped his driver's shoulder. "Get under way."

"Still fueling."

They had to anticipate fuel needs carefully. If a vehicle were to stop running, it might never be able to be started again.

"Snap it up!"

"Yeah, okay."

That sleazy response made his blood boil, but he sucked it in. The U.S. military had disintegrated. Who had ever imagined that regular soldiers like these would protect the redoubts effectively?

"We're rolling," his driver finally said as he increased power. Good. The sun was well up and that damn weird *thing* had set. What in God's name was that? Nothing good, no question there.

The convoy moved on, turning onto a side road. To the north, he could see tall columns of smoke rising from Hagerstown. Here and there along the road were burned-out cars, stripped cars, some kind of a cattle truck with half-butchered carcasses and flies around it, and bodies, always bodies, bloating, hacked, shot, burned, you name it.

The United States was gone. Long gone. All countries were gone. That whole thing was over.

He drove on through the slow morning and afternoon, stopping far too frequently to clear the road, or, where that wasn't possible, to do a slow workaround through the countryside.

At about two some asshole came running toward them with some kind of rifle in his hands. Before he could fire it, the general ordered him blown away. Then they moved on. The order of the day was, if it shows a gun it is hostile, and if it is hostile, kill it.

Here and there, you saw families on the road. Looked like Iraq during the invasion, or newsreel footage of World War II. Some of them even waved. Jerks. One time, incredibly, a Greyhound bus had passed going in the opposite direction. Now, that was amazing, but it was an old unit, looked like something from the sixties. No electronics, so all they needed was gas and they were in motion. There was a lot of gasoline around, too, if you could get to it. But pumps are electric and gas stations don't have generators. A bus company, though, probably would have some way of pulling up its fuel in the event of a power failure.

He liked to think about stuff like this. Keeping the world working. But the GODDAMN WORLD WAS NOT WORKING, WAS IT? Goddamn them, fine! FINE! What if this happened: this thing kept up until all the human garbage, the ragheads, the Chinks, the spics, the Mexes, the blacks, you name it, all of that trash perished? A few good Americans and Englishmen and Germans, too, of course, couldn't be helped. But ALL of that garbage—and then suddenly they opened the redoubts and here was a whole new world ready to start over again.

Except it wasn't going to be like that, was it? It wasn't going to be like that AT ALL.

Oh, he'd taken the fucking white powder gold. And he was a good man. Churchgoing. You had to be a good little boy, they said, to make that shit work. He'd goddamn well drunk it like a milkshake for days, and all he'd gotten out of it was bloody piss. Plus now there was this frigging black spot on his stomach that he could not get rid of. He tried scraping it, he'd even tried packing it in bleach. Would not go away. Cut at it with a razor. Whatever it was, the sucker went deep.

"General, we have an escort."

"What the fuck?"

"There's one'a them UFOs up there."

What in hell was this? He'd seen video of these things. They were kidnapping people all over the world. Well, hell, he had damn few soldiers in this unit and probably half of them would take off the second the sun set, so he did not need this. He popped the overhead hatch and saw this big goddamn thing up there. Should he shoot it? No fuckin' way, God only knew what kind of ordinance it had. These things had been around for years and nobody knew what they were. NASA maybe, the president maybe, but not this soldier. "Increase speed. Let's see if we can get out from under this sucker."

The radios didn't work, so they used hand signals, and it was about a minute before a signal came back from the fuel truck. If they increased speed, they would need to load more diesel fuel before they reached Raleigh. "Maintain speed!" And, goddamn it, what next?

One radio that was functional was the single sideband unit that was used for contacting Mack. It was kept powered down except when in use, and so far it was fine. In fact, he could hear his communications officer sending a burst right now. He did that every fifteen minutes.

But then, a screech of brakes, the screaming of tires.

"What the hell?"

One of the Humvees veered off the road and went over on its side in a cloud of dust and a crash of a kind he hadn't heard since Iraq— the sound of a whole lot of metal taking a hell of a beating.

A second later, a column of light as white as powder came down from the thing overhead, and two young soldiers floated out of the Humvee, their arms raised to the sky, and went up in it and were damn well gone. And so was the thing—whoosh, just like that. Steel-white sky, end of story.

He threw open the access hatch and ran to the Humvee. Nobody else had moved except one soldier, who had taken off across country and was going like hell. He was tempted to order the man shot, but that might bring outright rebellion, so he ignored the desertion.

When he looked inside the Humvee, he had a hell of a shock. What was in there was the driver, and he had literally ripped his own clothes off. His body was as red as a tomato and there was heat coming off it, a lot of heat. The eyes were open and staring and they were not glazed like the eyes of dead men, they were sharp with horror, like he was suffering somewhere deep inside himself. They were not dead eyes, and that was weird.

Whatever was happening to the guy, it was horrible and it just plain hit George Wylie right between the eyes. He was U.S. Army to the core, though, and the U.S. Army saved the lives of its soldiers. You got a man down, you did what was necessary to get all that training and that skill back to medical support. You did that. But here? "Hey, soldier, you hear me?"

Nothing.

Then he noticed on the kid's bare chest and around his side, one of those damn spots, black and gleaming. So what in shit's name was this stuff then, cancer caused by the fucked-up sun?

He went back to the Stryker.

"One KIA," he called out. "Driver. The other three are gone." He pulled himself into the vehicle and commanded them to get moving.

As they went on down the road the general found himself feeling kind of sick. There was something about the two guys who had gone up in that thing that he didn't like. Not the fact that he'd lost men, although that was a pain, for sure, but the way they had looked as they ascended, like saints or some damn thing. That was it, a couple of beautiful young saints. He was a Christian and all that. Damn right, and screw the opposition. You weren't with Jesus, you needed your heart cut out.

But he didn't like saints. You weren't gonna win a war with damn saints in your army.

He hit his driver on the shoulder. "What's our ETA?"

"We don't have any holdups, three hours."

That would be well after dark, such as it was with that violet thing, if it came back.

As the vehicle sped along, he found his mind going to his most recent wife, to Sally. Pretty, not beautiful, so why had he married her? Couldn't tell her no, was the main reason.

She went on and on, wanted this, wanted that. Expert in one thing: being disappointed.

He just got so damn mad sometimes, and leave it to a woman to bring out the worst in you.

So what happens when you're isolated in a survival redoubt and you command the security force and you off your wife? They put her in the freezer is what happens, and good-bye.

Too bad he hadn't brought a bottle on this little frolic. He needed a bottle. He always needed a goddamn bottle. Essential carry, soldier, forget it again, just blow your own head off.

One thing, the Acton Clinic meant maybe getting something that would get him out of this mess, and maybe the whole Blue Ridge group. Too late for the rest, probably. But the Seven Families were at Blue Ridge, plus the cream of America, so they were first in line, anyway.

"Any response from Mack?"

"No, Sir."

Never mind, they'd be there soon enough. If those bastards had offed Mack, though, there was going to be a slight change in plans. He would still kill them, of course, but slow. Damn slow.

19

STEALING PEOPLE

Mack had thought that he would kidnap Caroline Light and possi-
bly David Ford, but he had not anticipated that Caroline would start
re-creating the portal as immediately as she had, or move nearly so fast.
And he had not understood, until he saw them together, that they were
so tender toward one another. Now, he would definitely take Ford. Torture is a reliable form of interrogation in only one instance: when you
torture the lover and question the subject.

Because of the attack, Mack was no longer locked down, and he had
been able to slip out and watch her. He stood in the shadows on the
stairway that led into the recreation area.

Without knowing it, she had made this a race. Either her painting
got finished and they used it—however that was to be done—or the
townspeople invaded and gave Mack the chance he needed.

Except for one thing. They would not use it because he was going to
prevent it. He would destroy the painting again and this time he would
kill her as well. Far better, though, if the deserving got the benefit of the
thing.

In the darkness across the room, hidden in the red shadows, Katie
was also watching, and she felt every endearing touch between the
lovers like a knife skewering her heart.

As the new star had shone its baleful light through the high windows
of the rec room, her jealousy had festered into hate, and then into the

truth of her soul: the pathological, murderous rage that was her great hidden flaw.

Katrina had a secret. She had killed. She had killed more than once. First, when she was a child, she had killed a boy called Jerry Flournoy. It had happened during a celebration bonfire at Camp Oscalana.

They had just finished the musical, and parents and kids were sitting around in congratulatory mode. The show had been *Annie*, and Jerry Flournoy had directed and played Bert Healy, and he had been the one who had kept Katrina from being Annie.

She had slid a brand out of the fire, and let it fall against the leg of his costume. She had not realized that it was made of rayon, and he had burned to death. Nobody thought it was anything but an accident, and he should have rolled, he should never have tried to run down to the lake, he should have known that. But she had done it and she had never regretted it, because his agony and his death had filled a hole in her heart. His fire had cooled her jealousy. She had forgotten his cries, his racing, leaping death in a shower of sparks and flailing limbs. But the odor that had hung over the camp she would never forget, the honey stench of vengeance.

She had killed Jerry Flournoy and it had been a good thing to do, good for her soul, so when another cruel and hostile person—this one a man thief—had appeared in her life, she had killed her, too. She had backed over Patricia Dickerson while she was at the mailbox. What she remembered from that one was the crunch of the bones, and she enjoyed remembering it. Patty had taken her Tom. *Her* Tom. And this bitch Caroline, she had taken her David. *Her* David.

An accidental fire. A hit-and-run. Now, a slashing in a clinic full of psychotics—she would get away with this one, too. Both of them, the bitch and the ungrateful bastard.

For his part, Mack was quietly aware of her presence in the room, and watching her intently.

It was four thirty in the morning. The star would set before the sun rose, and there would be a period of darkness then. Things like night-vision equipment were all fried, so if the town was going to strike, that would most likely be when they came.

As he watched the drama unfolding below from the landing—the painting going on, the watcher preparing to strike—he began to hear sounds of movement from the patient area upstairs.

Worse, Katrina apparently heard it, too, because she started going closer to Caroline and David. Mack needed them alive—for a time.

Where in hell were those townies? God, if they didn't come, this was going to be a mess.

Katrina had gotten a knife from the kitchen, and if she could, she'd put it first in Caroline's spleen, which was full of blood. Puncture it and you had a dead body on your hands almost as fast as with the heart, and the spleen was more vulnerable. As a nurse, she knew that stabbing some-body in the heart was more difficult than it appeared, because of the breastbone in front and the spine in back. The body protected its heart. Going for the spleen was easier and just as efficient.

As she moved closer, she brushed the back of a chair. It made only the tiniest sound, but this was more than enough to make David turn around.

As he did so, she dropped to the floor. He looked out across the room for some time. The light coming in the windows from the new star was a little brighter than moonlight, but not so much that you couldn't hide in its shadows.

David came toward her. There was something in his hand—a gun, she thought. But first he'd talk, he wasn't going to shoot anybody except as a last resort, she didn't think . . . which somehow made her hate him all the more.

She could see his legs now. He'd paused just the other side of one of the bridge tables. All right, if he came around that table, she was going for him and hopefully she'd be fast enough to neutralize the gun.

In the distance, there was a ripping sound. A machine gun on the perimeter, she thought.

David heard it, too, and hurried back to Caroline and spoke softly to her, then sat down. His gun remained in his hand.

Carefully—very carefully—Katrina worked her way out from under the table. Rising just enough to get them in view, she saw that the bastard had not been distracted by whatever was happening outside. He still stared out into the room.

There was more machine gun fire, louder this time.

Then Caroline's voice rang out, "David! David, it's done!"

When he turned, Katie moved closer to them fast. He'd get his first, then her. She would rather have done her first and forced him to watch the bitch's death agony, but he had that gun.

She came up behind them and raised the knife, staring down at his back, looking at the place she would put it in.

As she started the thrust, something totally unexpected happened— it felt as if an iron cuff had gone around her wrist while at the same time a steel hand covered her mouth.

For a moment, she was too stunned to react. Nobody else had been in here. *Nobody.* Her heart flopped and her blood howled in her head.

A voice said, "Okay, David, drop the weapon, please." She was astonished to recognize Mack the Cat. He'd come up on her in absolute silence, and surprised the watchful David, too.

Mack saw that, once again, the painting looked like a window. In it, there were leaves moving on the trees, there was bright, normal moonlight, and the surface of a river could be seen shimmering in the distance. Except for one thing: the moon was different. More craters.

David said, "Mack, let her go."

"David, she's trouble."

All she could think about was bringing that knife down, and feeling the sliding resistance when it cut into him.

Mack could still feel the tension in Katie's body, so he wouldn't release her. She must not hurt either of these people, or that thing—the portal.

David took a step forward. "Mack, Katie is a good person, she's no danger to you."

Mack laughed. Then David followed his eyes and he saw the knife still poised in Katie's hand. When Mack increased the pressure on her wrist, Katie opened her fingers and it dropped to the floor with a clang.

"Katie?" David asked.

Mack uncovered her mouth and all of her rage and hate came spitting out in the form of one word, "*Bastard!*"

Surprise tightened David's face until the realization of why she was so enraged made his eyes go soft with regret.

"I'm sorry," he said to Katie.

Caroline said, "Let's get past this, because we have a miracle here." She looked from Mack to Katie to David. "A miracle—look at it!"

David said, "The others are waiting. We need to do this."

Unless he acted quickly and correctly right now, Mack understood that he was going to lose his chance forever. Before, he'd had no choice but to destroy the portal. He had not been ready, and they would have used it before he could get it away from them, and that must not be allowed to happen. If the right people didn't get the portal, nobody was going to get it.

But now they'd played into his hands by reconstructing it just as all hell broke loose around them. So now he could use the danger that was unfolding here to take the portal and the two of them off the clinic grounds and into some more private place. There, he would force them to teach him how to use it, and then he would slash their throats. Should he fail, he would kill them both and take the portal and just hope that somebody at the redoubt could figure out how to use it.

Reaching forward, he disarmed David, corkscrewing the gun out of his hand.

"Jesus, Mack!"

"Doc, please forgive me, but you have no idea how to use that, so let me do this." He said to Katie, "I'm gonna explain something to you. You need to do what I say. You need to help us and save your anger for later. When this is all over, beat the shit out of him, cut him, whatever you want. But *not now.*"

"He made a promise he didn't keep!"

David tried to reach her.

"It was just a night between us, Katie. A night together and it was lovely, but it wasn't love, and I think you know that."

Mack thought she might just leap on David and rip his throat out with her teeth.

"Katie," he said, "if you don't comply, I will kill you. I'm sorry, but you have no choice."

She nodded. In the distance, there was a faint *pop*, followed imme-diately by the sound of many high-velocity machine guns.

"Do you know how to shoot at all, Caroline?"

She shook her head. He didn't need to ask David. The way he'd han-dled the pistol so far told him all he needed to know.

"I know how to shoot very well," Katie said.

He gave her the pistol and produced his own.

David said, "Is that wise?"

"She's what we have, Doc."

"But she'll—she's liable to—"

Now came the chugging of a more primitive machine gun, but it was louder. There were screams, followed by a general outburst of firing.

"We need all the firepower we can get, David." Then, to Katie, "Don't even think about revenge right now." He thrust his gun into the small of her back. "Don't try me on."

"I'll be okay," Katie said. "I'll swallow it for now . . . what he did to me."

Mack gestured with his own pistol. "Let's get moving."

David hesitated, started to talk—and Mack shoved him, but gently.

"Let me protect you," he said. "I know what I'm doing."

"Security!" David shouted.

"They're busy, David. And we have to save this thing right now."

"Let's get it upstairs," David said, which was not what Mack wanted to hear. He had to play this very, very carefully. They didn't trust him, and that must not be forgotten for a moment.

"David, what if security fails?" he asked.

"They won't fail! Glen will keep us safe."

"IF, David!"

"He's right, David," Caroline said. "We can't risk the portal."

"We need to get it away from the clinic," Mack said, allowing his very real sense of urgency to enter his voice.

"But—it has to be here. It has to be where the people are!"

"When it's safe, we'll bring it back."

"But the class—you're saying the class could be killed. That must not happen!"

"David, all we can protect is the portal. We just have to hope for the best."

"Look, you know about firefights and such, I'm sure. Help me make my decision. Tell me what you think is happening out there?"

At last, a little trust. Mack moved to exploit it.

"Doc, I hate to tell you this, but it sounds to me like whoever's out there is moving closer to the house, which means that your security men are being defeated. The whole town is probably out there, and they are going to rip this place to shreds, and if you want to live and you want that portal to stay intact, you need to come with me right now."

"David, he's right," Caroline said.

"Cover us," Mack told Katie, "then follow us out the back." He had the portal. He had its designers. This operation was finally polishing up very nicely. The general was going to be pleased.

He gave David a reassuring pat on his shoulder. "Let's roll, Doc."

20

THE DESTRUCTION OF THE ACTON CLINIC

Just as Mack was ready to move them out, the gunfire rose to a chilling thunder. People began running downstairs, calling to David for leadership.

David went to the nearest one, Susan Denman.

"Get the class back upstairs." He looked past her to Aaron Stein and the others. "We're taking the portal to safety. We'll be back as soon as possible."

His words were swallowed by the cascading shatter of glass as rifle butts were used to smash the windows.

The sound caused the whole crowd to turn around and then to erupt into panic as men—strangers, not security personnel—began coming in through the debris. People ran everywhere, overturning tables and chairs, dashing for the doors, for the stairs.

"We need to move," Mack urged.

Bill Osterman appeared, greasy and exhausted, from the machinery room. "I'm the plant supervisor," he shouted to the armed men, women, and children. "I know what you want! I can show you everything."

A man walked up to him, raised a pistol, and fired it into his face. He rocketed back across the room, a flailing shadow in the blue-pink flash.

"Drop to the floor," Mack said to David and Caroline. "Katie, get that damn thing off the easel and bring it with us."

Katie looked at it. "Is it . . . liftable?"

"Just do it!"

More shots filled the room and people slammed against walls, flying into pieces as they did so. Modern high-velocity expanding rounds don't just injure people, they tear bodies apart.

Patients and staff scattered, running for the doors on both ends of the room. Mack noticed that the class—so very disciplined—had followed David's instructions and returned in a group to the temporary safety of the upper floor.

"Go out the back," he told Caroline and David. "It's our only chance!"

He had them now, he sure as hell did.

But David hesitated, so Mack gave him a slap to the side of the head—not hard, but hard enough to startle him.

"Sorry, Doc, but get moving! Right now!"

They scrambled toward the back doors.

Once they were outside, Mack told them, "We need to find a vehicle that works, otherwise we die here, now."

"We can't leave. We can't abandon the mission!"

"David, I'm on your side, so you listen to me. If you die, you abandon your mission. If you live, you still have a chance to come back here when it's safe and complete it. So *do this!*"

That seemed to reach him, and he began to follow Mack, and Caroline followed him. In the rear, Katie did a sort of guard action, not that Mack thought for a moment that she would be particularly effective.

Out in the grounds, dawn was just breaking across a running firefight between the security guards in their camouflage and the townspeople. The locals had some decent weapons now, too, not just deer rifles and shotguns. He heard the rasping whisper of an Uzi and saw one of the security guys turn to red haze.

"There's a lot of ordnance flying around," Mack said, "heads down."

Behind them, glass shattered upstairs and the body of Claire Michaels hit the ground, bounced once in a bed of blooming flowers, and was still.

"Claire!" David howled, rushing to her.

Mack grabbed him. "She's past help, but you're not. If I have to knock you cold and drag you, I'm saving you, Doc. You gotta understand that."

Ahead, the parking lot was jammed with derelict security vehicles, their electronics long since killed.

"We can't escape," Caroline said. "It's impossible."

"We have to," Mack replied, "because if we stay here, we are dead. No question. We get the hell out, lives are saved, and your thing that is so important to you—that is saved."

There was a voice raised, echoing across the broad lawn they were crossing, and then another, this one excited. Shots rang out—pistol, .22-caliber.

"Stop," the first man shouted. The other, right behind him, cried excitedly, "What is that? What've you got?"

Mack aimed, braced on his elbow, and squeezed off two rounds, dropping both men. Immediately, more townspeople came out of the house. They were cursing with rage, and letting loose a fusillade of bullets in their direction. No discipline but too many bullets to risk crossing the field of fire.

No choice now, they had to head for the garage.

"Move it! Fast!"

David and Caroline carried the portal.

Then Mack saw two more men coming from around the front of the house. They were not in a hurry. One of them raised a Benelli Riot Gun and blew away a security guard.

"Those two are trained," Mack said. "They know how to kill and we need to be out of their line of fire right now."

Moving among the disabled vehicles in the new parking lot, Mack led them toward the old garage. He knew this place as well as he knew every other corner of the Acton estate, and he knew that there were older vehicles in here, vehicles without sensitive electronics.

The garage was brick, built in the same grand style as the house, an incongruous place to store dusty trucks. The side door, as he knew, wasn't locked.

Taking no chances, he sent Katie in first. When nobody blew her head off, he followed with Caroline and David. Inside, the cars and trucks loomed, a silent row of angles and shadowy bulk. There were a couple of pickups, a Buick Roadmaster, a black Cadillac from half a century ago, a Chrysler convertible from even earlier, and a mid-seventies Pontiac.

Mack had previously identified the pickups with their simple mechanicals and magnetos as good bets. On his way back in from his visit to the town, he'd fueled one of them up and made sure its battery worked. He led them to it and opened the door.

"They went in there," a voice said from outside. Then the other: "They showin' any iron?" Then silence.

Mack whispered, "We have one chance. We start this and we blast out through the garage door. That's our chance."

David said, "We can't leave, the gate's closed."

"The power failed. Therefore, it opened automatically. That's the way it works." Mack replied.

"You certainly know a lot about this place," Caroline said.

"I know everything about this place." As he spoke, he watched David carefully. He had detected something there beyond the general level of mistrust of Mack Graham. Did David know anything more? Suspect it? Mack was watching.

"They came in this way," a male voice said.

Mack saw a shape appear at the door, so he got David and Caroline into the truck. There was room behind the seat for the portal.

"What about me?" Katie asked.

"Ride in the bed," Mack said.

"I will not."

He took Katie by the collar of her blouse and lifted her off the ground.

"You will. And you will provide covering fire or they will shoot our tires out, because these two know what they're doing. Do you understand me?"

The two shooters had opened the garage door and were moving carefully closer. Good soldiers don't hurry unless that's the only choice.

"Okay, folks," one of the men said. "We saw you come in here and we got the door covered. We want to see what you're carrying."

With an enormous rattling cough, the old truck's engine came to life. Mack jammed the gas to the floor and it shot forward, slamming into the garage door.

One of the men raised his rifle and fired across the line of vehicles, but the bullet hit a dust-covered Oldsmobile and went wild.

Mack backed up until the truck hit the back wall, then ground the gears into first.

"Is it fragile?" he shouted.

"Of course it's fragile!" Caroline responded.

On Mack's second try, the truck crashed through the door and out into the driveway.

Mack turned out into the grounds, avoiding the choke of vehicles in the drive and—he hoped—most of the marauders.

He drove down the driveway and through the gate into the outside world.

A view opened to the flaring dawn in the east, as to the north and west, the supernova set in purple haze. Mack headed toward Raleigh, from which he could see smoke rising. Was the convoy already there and raising a little hell? Fine, he'd deliver the portal, and with it Caroline and David. Let Wylie join him in tearing the information out of them, he was good at it. And Katie, too. She was going to enjoy sweet revenge.

DAVID FORD'S JOURNAL: EIGHT

I am writing this in my notebook as we drive toward Raleigh. There is little time, and I believe that this will be my last entry. After this, anything can happen. Herbert Acton offers no instructions for this period of extreme chaos.

In my last entry, I spoke briefly of the plan that I see, and with the appearance of the new star, its outlines are extremely clear. Also, it is already in our hands, in detail. The plan was expressed to a man half-mad with God, in a cave on the island of Patmos. The Book of Revelation was written in the reign of the Roman Emperor Nero, about a year before the great fire that consumed Rome.

In all probability, the Romans were right to blame the Christians. On one level, John's book is a coded message about the destruction of what was then the great Babylon of the world, the center of sin and oppression, Rome.

On a deeper level, though, Revelation is a document of the lost science, which describes very precisely what will unfold as time ends.

We are most assuredly being judged. Those who will not go forward are tainted with the mark of the beast; the elect are ascending. And the dead have indeed risen, in the sense that, statistically, there is a living body here on earth—or was, before this happened—for every single person who has ever lived in history. Reincarnation is real, and, as this disaster began, all human souls were in the physical state.

And now we see the final sign: "And there appeared another wonder in heaven; and behold a great red dragon, having seven heads and ten horns, and seven crowns upon his heads."

Seven is the number of completion. A dragon may be a comet or star. In this case, it's the lowering monster that is bringing the destruction of the world.

I have written of the elect and the condemned. Now, I turn to the matter of us, those who are going in neither direction.

I will not write down what is to happen to us, for two reasons. First, nothing is certain. Second, in doing so I would, perhaps fatally, betray a great secret.

I do not believe that the man driving this vehicle has our best interests in mind. I believe he means to harm us.

I sit here, writing and waiting. It is my belief that Caroline and I and the portal—all three of us—have fallen into the hands of the enemy.

21

REBELS

The farther they got from the clinic, the more disturbed Caroline became about the fate of the rest of the class. They were the core of the future, each one of them trained to carry out a fundamental task of governance. If all went well, there would be millions coming, and they would be urgently needed, every one of them.

Mack had been right, though. They could not stay where they were, and hiding the portal on the property—attempting to—was just too dangerous.

She just hoped that some of those carefully chosen people would be left. As David closed his little book and clutched her hand, she sensed that his thoughts were exactly the same.

As the invaded clinic disappeared behind them, though, she had to ask herself another question: had Mack captured them or rescued them? He was a subtle, skilled man, and she feared that this might go in a bad direction. She did not know exactly what he understood about the portal. He had watched her creating it, though, and had seen it in its finished state. He could not fail to recognize what it was.

It had come out of her mind and her hands, and existed at the vanishing edge between thought and reality. As she had painted it and the gold had done its work on her mind and body, she had remembered the lessons she'd taken about it in the class. She remembered being taught to paint, remembered the special state of surrender that allowed the colors to flow, and a new reality to emerge out of the art in her hands and the science in her mind. But the most critical part of the creation of the portal, the mixing of the colors, had been done by Susan Denman. Should they need to do this again—if by some miracle there was time—Susan would be needed.

But they were all needed.

The science that enabled the creation of the portal was not like modern science. It taught that reality is not the hard, immutable, inevitable structure that appears all around us, but rather an idea that only seems impossible to change. Brute force—the lumberman's axe, the builder's tractor—appears to be the only way, but it is not the only way. When science and art come into harmony, miracles become ordinary.

No miracles in the here and now, though. She sat jammed in beside David, with Mack driving and Katrina Starnes crouching in the truck bed.

She looked over at Mack, trying to see in his face some hint of his intentions. His eyes were as dark and dangerous as gun barrels.

"Where are we going?"

He didn't answer.

As they passed through the outskirts of Raleigh, the emptiness told her that the citizens who weren't attacking the clinic had probably left or been killed.

Here and there, untended wrecks lay abandoned in the road, and bodies in them and beside them. By the time they had reached the courthouse square at the center of the town, she had counted forty of them, most of them apparently the victims of gunshots.

They went around the courthouse square, turning, then turning again, until they were on the opposite side and once again facing out of town.

Finally, Mack stopped the truck with a scream of dry, old brakes. The three of them stared out the windshield, stunned silent by what they saw. From the bed behind them, Katie stifled a scream.

On the lampposts along the street, stretching at least a quarter of a mile to the entrance to the interstate, there were bodies hanging. Closest, a man dangled with his pants around his ankles. On the next lamp-post, a state policeman in uniform hung slumped and still, his wide-brimmed trooper's hat on the ground beneath him. On the next one was a woman wrapped in so much duct tape that she looked like a cocoon.

There were easily two dozen of them, stretching off into the distance.

But they were not the reason that Mack had stopped. She saw that he was indifferent to these bodies. Who knew why they had been hanged or who had done it? Perhaps they were a sacrifice to the old gods, or perhaps they'd violated some sort of jerkwater martial law that the locals had declared. Maybe they had refused to participate in the attack on the clinic.

In any case, it was all pointless. That final sign had sealed the matter, had it not?

Mack had stopped because of a great horde of people coming toward them, people filling the street and the sidewalk on both sides, inching toward them on their knees, their faces twisted with agony. They were singing tattered hymns. She heard snatches of "Amazing Grace," "How Great Thou Art," "What a Friend We Have In Jesus."

Running up and down among them were frantic children, their shrill voices adding an anarchic note of panic to the howled songs. The people closest were sliding slowly, their knees shredded to the exposed bone.

She thought, then, that the people who had been hanged were probably human sacrifices, and, since that had not worked, they were now torturing themselves to death in an effort to induce God—or maybe the old gods—to save them.

This was the fundamental error of history being acted out in these desperate streets. The gods to whom they offered sacrifice did not exist and never had existed, and cosmic disaster was not the fault of man and never would be. Earth's history was not about gods at all, but rather a very large-scale scientific program that was aimed at creating a harvest of souls. Who the designers were, Caroline did not know, but she believed in their work with all her being, for vast numbers of the good were being freed every day, every hour, and taking the human experience up into a higher level of reality.

The end of the world wasn't a disaster at all. It was a huge, resounding, amazing success.

Mack sat staring at the crowd. His profile was granite. He had taken on the stillness of determination, and Caroline knew that he was about to drive right through them.

She said, "Mack, don't."

There were hundreds of them, it seemed, maybe thousands, filling the street, the sidewalk, and the side streets feeding into this one.

"This is human behavior we do not understand," David said. "This is beyond what is known about stress response."

Mack gunned the motor, and Caroline writhed in her seat.

But David, who was closest to the door, jumped out.

"You can't do this," he said.

The leading edge of the penitents or whatever they were had now reached the truck's front bumper.

David faced them. "Wake up, wake up, all of you!"

He went to one of them, a man with the bones of his knees visible as he dragged himself along. He leaned into the man's face, calling on him to stop. Robotically, he continued on.

Mack said to Caroline, "Stay here." He also got out of the truck. "We have to keep moving, David, we can't stay here!" Then Katrina came up to them. Her—or rather, David's—gun was at the ready.

Caroline had had enough. Why would Mack, if he had good intentions, ever give a gun to somebody as obviously murderous as Katie? And why go so far from the clinic, and why even enter the town? No, this was all wrong, all of it.

The crowd had surrounded the truck, men, women, and children moving past them with the indifference of a flooding river. Mack was in front, struggling to push people aside.

Katie saw that he was having trouble and fired into the air.

He turned. "Help me," he shouted.

She went toward him, firing a second time, this time into the face of a woman, who pitched back amid her screaming children.

Caroline saw their chance. "This isn't right," she said to David.

"I know it."

They got out of the truck. David reached in for the portal.

"Stop!"

Mack was blasting through the crowd toward them.

"David, run!"

"The portal!"

"*Run!*"

She turned toward a nearby alley, and David followed her.

Mack had gotten in the truck and was gunning the motor, Katie hanging on the running board of the old vehicle. Honking the horn, they drove through the crowd, the engine snarling as the truck bounded and crunched over people.

David and Caroline ran hard down a side street, but the truck was faster and it was on them in moments, and suddenly it was beside them and Katie was pointing her gun straight at David's head. He angled away, heading into the alley.

At that point, Mack hit the brakes, Katie jumped off the running board of the old vehicle, and Mack got out, caught up to David in a few strides, then dragged him farther back into the alley.

"Come on," Katie said to Caroline, motioning with the gun.

"Katie, I understand your anger. I'd feel the same way. But you have to accept the fact that David and I go back—"

As David struggled with Mack, Katie slapped Caroline so hard that she reeled and fell to the sidewalk—which also brought David to a stop.

Mack kicked in one of the doors that opened onto the alley.

"Bring her," he said to Katie as he dragged David inside what turned out to be a restaurant kitchen. "Lotta useful stuff in here," he explained to Katie.

When he had his gun on both David and Caroline, he told Katie, "Go out and get the portal. I want it in my sight at all times."

Caroline and David both understood immediately what was about to happen here, and exactly why Mack had chosen a place full of the tools you find in a kitchen.

"Mack," David said, "we can't help you. The time for that is over."

"What in *hell* kind of bullshit is that?"

"If you have a black spot on your body, Mack, you've been judged and you can't go through. The portal is part of a science we know only in legend. It's not a science of inanimate matter, but of the soul—and so it's alive, in a sense, and it won't allow you through unless you are chosen."

"I am damned well chosen! I am one of *the* chosen!"

At that moment, Katie returned with the portal.

"A Humvee with soldiers just pulled up out there," she said. Then, as she leaned it against the wall, she added, "My God, Mack, look at this."

As she held the portal up and moved it, the image within it also moved. Trees appeared, then, as she continued to move it, they slipped away into a riverbank dotted with flowers and thick grass.

"It's a window," she said in wonder.

"I know what it is," Mack snapped. "I promised you your revenge and now's the time. We need to find out how they made this and how in hell to get through it."

She was completely entranced with the portal.

"It's soft," she said. Pressing a little, she pushed her fingers through.

"Jesus," Mack said, "Jesus, can you go farther?"

She pressed until her whole hand was inside.

"I can feel it! Oh, it's sort of cool but I can feel the sun on my hand."

Mack was right beside her now.

"That grass," he said, "can you reach down and—"

Katie crouched, taking the portal with her.

"Sure—oh, I can feel it. It's grass. Oh—God—" Smoke, fast and thick, began coming out from under her T-shirt.

She snatched her hand back, and blood came gushing out of the neatly sliced stump of her wrist. Flailing, she screamed, then flames shot out around her midriff, melting the shirt and causing her to twist and turn in agony, then to run to the far end of the long kitchen and smash into the wall.

All the while, Mack watched with the coldest eyes Caroline had ever seen. He did not try to help Katie at all, but kept his gun trained on the two of them.

Katie struggled in her death agonies, her pealing screams dropping to choked gargles as the room filled with a sickening stench of charred flesh and the overwhelming stink of burned hair.

The portal lay flat. Pressed into the grass on the other side of its surface was Katie's hand and most of her forearm.

"What in hell happened to her?" Mack snarled.

"She was marked," David said quietly.

Mack thrust the gun into his stomach.

"What is this about these marks?"

"You get them from the life you've lived. A life beyond redemption, and you—"

Mack slammed him with the pistol and sent him sprawling and spitting.

"All right, shut up with that bullshit! You listen to me, both of you, and listen close, or you will die slower and harder than you can imagine. That Humvee out there is a recce unit. Behind it is a strike force. They know what you have and these are your choices. Either tell us how to work this thing right now, or we will torture the life out of you until you do, then go to the clinic and waste whoever there is left to waste. Choose, children. Now."

"Mack, listen to me," Caroline said, putting all the urgency she could into her voice. "We can all go together. We can be friends. Partners!"

With a speed so sudden that it was in itself terrifying, Mack lunged at her and slammed her against the wall so hard she slumped, momentarily stunned. He shook her back to consciousness.

"I tried it before and it hurt so much I couldn't do it. Then this woman—Goddamn! But this fucker works and there's a secret to it, and you *will* tell me that secret."

She remained silent. What else could she do? If he couldn't get through, it was because he was judged.

"Okay, Doc David, then you tell me how it works."

He had something in his free hand that was not a gun, then she heard her clothes ripping and felt coldness and tightness against her skin. It was a point, she knew, and a little more pressure and it would penetrate.

"I swear to you, I will take every inch of skin off her, every *fucking inch*, unless you tell me the truth."

"There's nothing to tell," David said. "It's a sort of filter, it only lets certain people through."

"Then you're gonna change it."

"We can't."

The knife began sliding along her skin. She forced her pain to remain silent.

"You will hold her skin in your hands and she will still be alive, David. She will be in agony unlike any either of you have ever known. The only way you will be able to stop her pain will be to kill her with your own hands!"

"David—"

David turned on her. "Shut up!" Then, back to Mack. "Mack, we can change it. For you. You can go through."

"Where? Where is that place? It sure as hell isn't anywhere on this Earth."

"It is, Mack. It's on this Earth."

"*Where?*"

"Mack, it's right here. It's where we're standing right now. It's what the Earth will become after . . . after what's going to happen."

"And what would that be?"

"The end of this cycle."

"And the Earth is totally destroyed?"

"The cycle is over. Those of us who enter the new Earth start the new cycle there."

Caroline felt the pressure of the knife lessen.

"And who decides?"

"We decide," David said. "We can change the portal for you."

He lifted it from the floor. Caroline wasn't sure what he was doing, and remained silent. But one thing she did know. He could not change the portal in such a way that it would let someone with the mark through, because that mark identified them as being below the human level, lacking higher morality, compassion, and judgment. This is why it was called the mark of the beast. It meant, simply, that your life had left you more animal than human.

From outside, there came the snarling of big vehicles, then the squealing of brakes, followed by voices.

"That's the general," Mack said. "He's seen the truck."

"He knows about your truck? How?"

"We have communications. Just enough."

David looked doubtful. "May I ask—"

"Just fix the damn portal. Do it now!"

Caroline realized that Mack did not know how General Wylie had found them. A lucky guess, perhaps.

David picked up the portal. "Caroline, we have to do this."

There wasn't a thing she could do to change it. All she could think was that he was buying time, so she took it from him. Up close like this, it was indistinguishable from a window. It was marvelous, just the most extraordinary thing she'd ever seen. But what would she do to make Mack think she'd changed it?

"It has to be tuned to the people who're going to use it," David said. "It works like a fingerprint reader. Let us—Caroline, print Mack to it."

Dear God, he was going to trick Mack into doing the same thing that Katie had done.

She had no choice but to go along. "Give me your hand, Mack," she said. Touching his damp skin was horrible. There was a sense of the corpse about it, not like the skin of a living person.

The judged were still moving and breathing, but they were already outside of life, in a state where no further change could take place. They just didn't know it yet.

She positioned her hand in his, so that her palm faced the portal and his hand enclosed hers. She had no idea what she was doing, she was just trying to make something up that he would believe.

"This is doing what?"

"Imprinting you," she said. "Then you can go through."

"What about my people?"

David said, "You imprint them. Do it the same way."

"Do you feel anything yet, Mack?"

"Yeah, actually, the same thing I felt before. Warmth."

"You tried this before?"

"It nearly burned me like it did her. Jesus!"

Caroline drew his hand away. "Okay, you're imprinted."

He addressed himself to David. "There's a general out there. I am going to imprint some of his men and send them through your portal. If all goes well, we will take it and put it to good use. But if not, you are going to experience hell firsthand, both of you, until we are told the truth about how to make it work."

"I don't know what else to tell you," David said. "You just imprint and step through. That's all."

"You are a poor liar, David."

Outside, the snarling of the big vehicles was joined by a ferocious thunder of weapons.

"Those praying crazies," Mack said pleasantly. "He'll kill 'em all just to tidy the place up."

He picked up the portal and went to the door. He opened it. "I need a guard in here right now."

"Mack," came a gruff voice. "How the hell are you?"

The door closed.

"Come on," David said softly.

As David led her toward the front of the restaurant, the kitchen door was opening again.

They went through into the wrecked dining room, with sunlight glaring in through the shattered windows, tables smashed, chairs up-ended, and a great splash of blood across one wall.

Behind them, they heard a curse. The young soldier sent to guard them had discovered that the room was empty.

"Quick!"

She followed David into the street. The door by which they'd entered the restaurant opened onto the alley beside it, but this one faced directly into the street where the convoy was parked. Closest was an enormous machine with a slanted front. It was bigger than a truck, emblazoned with three stars, flying a general's flag, and painted with a lurid image of skeletal Cimil, the Mayan god of the underworld. Atop the vehicle was a remote-controlled .50-caliber machine gun—which immediately moved toward David and Caroline.

"Down!"

But then it whirled, its motors screaming, spinning upward toward a huge silver object that was just appearing overhead.

Caroline felt washed by the sacredness that these silver objects seemed to carry with them like a sort of force field. The urge, when they were near, was to drop to your knees.

The heavily armed soldiers looked extremely uneasy, clutching their weapons, looking up. Around the convoy, in piles, sprawled, twisted, and bloody, were hundreds of bodies, the remains of the people who had been on their knees. Piled among the dead adults were their dead children.

There was a huge sound, a hissing thud, and light shone down from the silver device, flooding the convoy in powder white. A moment later, one of the soldiers cried out, leaped from his vehicle, and throwing off his helmet, began rising.

"Stop that man," General Wylie shouted. "Shoot him!"

The machine gun fired, bullets streaming toward the rising soldier . . . and then sparks appeared in the light around him, a pattern that grew as the gun continued to fire.

"The bullets are stopping," Caroline said. She gripped David's hand as they both watched, awed by the magnificent and flawless display of technological power they were seeing.

Then the convoy command vehicle's hatch flew open and three young soldiers piled out, also throwing aside their helmets and leaping, then rising into the light. General Wylie emptied his pistol at them, but with the same lack of effect that the machine gunner had experienced.

"Launch grenades," the general roared, and another soldier pulled a bulky-looking item out of one of the vehicles, loaded it with a large projectile, and fired it upward.

With a clap of thunder and a burst of flame, it shot into the light and exploded—or started to. The projectile cracked apart in slow motion, the burning gasses and shrapnel oozing into a mushroom shape and stopping, the explosion frozen like a flower dotted with bits of steel. As if it was as light as the air itself, the frozen explosion drifted away on the breeze.

As this was happening, there came from the bodies all around the convoy a stirring and a groaning, and, at the same time, from the great machine above waves of what could only be described as directed emotion—waves of love, in fact, that made David and Caroline draw closer together, and made them both wish the same wish, that they, also, could join the mysteries unfolding above. Except . . . they didn't, actually. They were workers and needed elsewhere, and—if they could only reach it—an important task was waiting for them.

The heaps of dead began coming to their feet, their wounds disappearing, life returning to their bodies. For an instant, David found himself looking directly into the eyes of one of them, and in the instant that he was connected to this man, David relived his whole life, not in linear memory, but as a compressed, stunningly poignant, and fragile instant of pure emotion, and it was good, so good that it hurt and he sobbed aloud, unable to contain his emotion.

Beside him Caroline also sobbed, and the dead began to rise into what at first seemed to be a great, round opening in the bottom of the craft. But as his eyes followed them, he saw that this was not an opening in the ship, but in the universe itself, for its velvet, living darkness was spread with a spectacle of stars.

Around them, more and more of the slaughtered rose upward, disappearing into the star garden at the heart of the machine.

He saw, at the very top of this perfect sky, the constellation of the Pleiades, the Sailing Ones, so clear that the vivid colors of the stars was clearly visible, the magenta of Pleione and the faint red of its blazing hydrogen ring, the white of Alcyone, and the iridescent blue of Electra.

As he watched, the people ascended in increasing numbers, rising one after another, and he saw them go sailing upward, and transform as they did into bright points of light.

Then the last of them were swept up into the fountain of stars. As suddenly as it had opened, the gateway in the sky closed. He was left watching the leaping death of the auroras' return, and he bowed his head and fell to the ground crouching, and covered his face, so great was the pain of losing touch with that beauty.

"And so the dead rise," he said, "and now to follow there will be great earthquakes."

Caroline, weeping also, clutched at him, and their love—so essential to maintaining one's humanity in dark times—enabled them to help each other, and give one another the strength they needed to go on.

But the convoy remained in chaos, with men screaming and leaping on the vehicles, trying to somehow jump into the sky, tearing at one another, bellowing and cursing and fighting to get to a door that was already closed.

Mack and General Wylie strode among them, their pistols in their hands. When a soldier clambered onto a vehicle, Mack or the general would shoot him and he would lurch off, hitting the ground with a thud.

Taking advantage of the confusion, David pulled Caroline into a shattered drugstore, and they were going through to the rear when they both saw it at the same time—a flash of green in the street outside.

Two soldiers had come into view. Between them they held the portal, which now contained an image of a sweep of meadow that ended on a riverbank. Beyond this stretched an enormous view that faded into blue hills.

Corralled at gunpoint by Mack and the general, soldiers shuffled toward the portal. They were eager at first, looking at it in wonder.

Mack held the first man's hand against it until he snatched it away, pulling at his tunic.

When the man hesitated, the general lifted his gun as casually as he might a spoonful of soup, and sent a bullet through his head.

"This fucker works, at least," he said as the young solder dropped.

The next soldier stepped right into the portal.

Caroline gripped David's arm. On the neck of the man going through, they could see a telltale shadow.

Then this man also hesitated. His body jerked and he seemed to stop, his front half in the portal. Mack kicked him in the small of the back, shoving him forward.

For a moment, he seemed to go deeper.

"Jesus, it's working," Mack exclaimed. "We have got it, General!"

They were congratulating one another when the soldier, still only halfway through the portal, burst into flames. His writhing became frantic, his head jerking from side to side, his midriff lurching and squirming, and suddenly the man was out, falling back, hitting the ground as he was consumed, screaming in agony as the fire engulfed him.

In the air there was the same horrifying odor of cooked flesh and hair that had filled the kitchen when Katrina had burned.

General Wylie glared at Mack. David could see the veins standing out on his neck.

"You stupid asshole! Fuck you! Fuck you!"

Mack stood at attention, taking it.

"Get those freaks," Wylie muttered. "I want them front and center."

"Get them," Mack snapped.

Soldiers looked at each other.

Mack pointed directly at the store—at them, at the precise spot they had imagined that they were hiding.

"DO IT NOW!" he roared.

Caroline and David ran for their lives.

The portal remained where they had left it.

22

DEATH BEYOND THE END OF TIME

For a moment, their pursuers lost sight of them in the alley and David understood very clearly that these seconds were their last and only chance—whereupon they came up against a chain-link fence.

"David!"

He grabbed it and shook it with frustration—and then saw that it was loose along the bottom. "This way," he said, lifting it, ignoring what the jagged metal was doing to his hands.

She went through and he followed, pulling it back into place behind him.

They found themselves in a yard with a greenhouse, with their pursuers close behind.

Almost certainly, it was going to be a trap, but their only hope of not being seen was to duck into the structure.

They found themselves in a steamy and exotic world of vivid yellow and blue and red orchids. They went deep among the vines and crouched there, hiding, barely breathing.

They did not hear Mack the Cat approaching, and David was almost ready to move to a broken window he had noticed when he suddenly realized that this master stalker was three feet away from them. From here, he could just see the side of Mack's head, and his nostrils were dilating as he smelled the air, trying to catch a scent of his prey.

The humid air was heavy, though, and the way he moved his eyes, flicking them from place to place with the suddenness of the expert predator, David knew that he could not smell any faint perfume or sweat that would betray their presence.

He turned, and now he was so close that David could have reached out through the vines and touched the gun in his hand.

Absolute stillness. Absolute quiet. Except . . . what was that rustling? A glance at Caroline revealed that she was flushed with effort, both hands clapped over her face. Something in here had triggered an allergy and she was fighting a sneeze.

Mack sighed, then looked toward the door. He started out and David's whole body shuddered with hope—but then he stopped. Slowly, the long, predatory face turned his way. He seemed to be looking directly into David's eyes. But no, then he turned away again. When he moved, it was like watching a dancer, swift and lethal . . . but, in this case, making an error.

A moment later, low voices came from the front of the greenhouse. There was a curse, sharp, urgent, then the clatter of the door.

Caroline started to rise, but David gripped her arm and she froze. And saw what he saw—Mack, still right there, listening, sniffing the air, his eyes darting. And so he remained for long minutes, so still that he was almost impossible to see through the vines. And then there would be another dance step to another part of the greenhouse, and another long silence while he tested the space for presence.

Eventually, though, he was gone. They never saw him slip away, but his absence was signaled in a way that felt surprisingly like love: a cricket began chirping, and soon the greenhouse was splendid with their song.

Warily, David slipped out of the deep tangle and lifted his head above the edge of a broken window. His view was across a short lawn to a bobbing flower bed full of impatiens and petunias, and beyond it a cottage, and that, he thought, was where Mack might yet lurk.

Overhead, a meteor appeared, falling gracefully through the pink plasma that dominated the sky. The new star had set, and to the east, down low where the sky should be glowing pink with the blush of predawn, there lay instead a line of deep bloodred. David estimated that they would have about an hour of semidarkness before the sun rose once again.

It was during this brief night that he intended to make his move. His plan was to return to the Acton Clinic, hoping that the class would still be there, or enough of the class to still carry out some part of their mission.

Soft voices came to his attention. He looked up and down the lawn. Then he saw them, three men. One was dressed in ill-fitting military fatigues, the other two in sweatsuits. None of them were Mack, and that worried him. Their young faces were tight and their eyes were hunter-quick as they came into the yard. One of them went up to the back door of the house and tried it. He drew it open and looked back at his friends.

An instant later, he exploded—not as if he'd been blown up with a bomb, but as if he was literally ripping apart as he lurched backward. His head shot up and hit the doorjamb with a thick crunch, then came rolling through the air, hit in the petunias, and didn't bounce. The face, expressionless, stared. Even as this was happening, a flash of black and steel appeared under the right arm, which flew up as if in surprise, then tumbled out into the grass. Slowly, the fingers closed.

The body buckled, and as it did, he could see a shadowy form just inside the house, wielding an axe.

Not Mack, though, not that humped figure.

Whoever was in there was long past rescue, hiding in psychotic rage and despair, in the state of savagery that would be emerging now in all the judged.

The survivors poured gunfire into the house, creating a cataract of noise and a fury of flashes.

David grabbed Caroline's arm. "Come on," he said

Together, they leaped through the glass wall of the greenhouse. As they dashed down the driveway, passing the two survivors just ten feet away, one of them shouted and wheeled his gun toward them, and David saw a red laser telltale bouncing on Caroline's back, and the bullets passed so close they felt surges of air.

But then there was another cry, this one choked with horror, then dropping to wet gabble as one of the two remaining men looked down at the axe handle protruding from his stomach. Somehow, the defender of the house had survived their fusillade and once again used his ferocious weapon.

The last of the soldiers ran so frantically that he lost control of himself and fell in the driveway. Screaming again and again, he went off down the street, his cries echoing away into the distance.

"Let's move," David said. There had been too much shooting here not to attract more of the soldiers.

"Not so fast."

Whirling, David saw Mack standing in the middle of the street.

"Quick," he said, and leaped a low rock wall, Caroline close behind.

They ran into a thin woods behind the house. David had no idea where they were or where they might be going, just that they had to get out of here.

He could hear Mack moving fast to close the distance.

Then the woods ended. They came out on a two-lane highway, one that he recognized immediately. It was Maryland 1440, the road that passed the small private airfield that the clinic had used.

It was suicide to stay exposed like this, so they went to the far shoulder—and saw here a field just sprouting young shoots of some sort, the life of the past still unfolding. Beyond it, perhaps half a mile away, was the roofline of a condo complex—shelter, certainly, but they could not survive an attempt to cross that field.

For a few moments, David ran down the middle of the road, looking for something that would afford them more shelter than the field. All he found was a concrete bus stop plastered with Celebrex and McDonald's ads. He drew Caroline to it and crouched beside her, shielding her with his body.

Not hurrying now—not needing to—Mack came toward them. As he walked, he moved first into the center of the highway, then angled to the far side. As David and Caroline tried to keep the bulk of the shelter in front of them, Mack tried to widen the angle.

"We can make a deal," he said. "I bring the portal and you take me through. That's all I need now. Forget the rest of them."

Behind Mack, David saw an unlikely sight—headlights. A vehicle was coming. Mack kept moving closer to the two of them. Either he didn't see it or he didn't care. David watched, trying to see what it was, waiting for it to overtake Mack.

What the hell was that thing? It was big, not a car or an SUV, or even a military vehicle, which had been David's initial fear. A big truck, perhaps. No, he saw more lights. A marquee. But—holy God, it was a Greyhound bus. A *bus?*

Mack stepped easily aside as it passed him, but David ran out into the middle of the road, waving his arms frantically. Caroline joined him.

On the marquee, David saw the word "Baltimore." Inside, there was a driver, there were passengers, and it all looked astonishingly, impossibly normal.

Now the bus was a hundred feet from them. Fifty feet. They could see the face of the driver. Behind it, David was aware that Mack had started running.

The loud *phew* of its air brakes sounded. The driver leaned forward over his steering wheel. *Phew. PHEW.*

It stood there, engine rattling. With a quiet hiss and a click, the door opened. He went around it—and saw Mack not fifty feet away, coming up beside the back of the bus. A huge knife brought from the kitchen left his hand like a lightning bolt.

As David and Caroline threw themselves onto the steps, it slammed into the door, embedding itself in the vinyl and insulation. They scrambled into the cabin, David shouting, "Close the door!"

The driver didn't need to be told.

Outside, Mack commenced hammering on it with a fury unbound, the sound of his assault filling the bus, the power of it making the big vehicle shake like a leaf.

"Jesus!" the driver said.

"Get moving!"

He threw the bus into gear and pulled out onto the road. As they drew away from Mack, he emitted an inhuman roar of anger.

But now, very suddenly, David and Caroline were in a different world. Other passengers filled the seats, people with bundles, people with kids. Some seats empty, most not.

"Hey," the driver called.

"Yes. Thank you."

"How far?"

"Excuse me?"

"This is a bus, buddy. You buy a ticket. That's the way we do it."

"Oh, Baltimore. Baltimore . . ." He gave the driver a twenty and got back a dollar and change. Stuffing the money in his pocket, looking down at his receipt, he almost wanted to cry.

How had they ever kept buses running? But of course, they were old vehicles, many of them forty and fifty years old. They didn't contain the kind of electronics that would be fried. So, even this deep in death, life went on.

"Behind the white line," the driver said, "thank you."

They went down the aisle, finding seats across from an older woman, prim, her eyes keen with a light he hoped was not madness.

"May we sit here?"

"I don't own it."

When they sat, David realized just how deeply, deeply tired he was. The star having set, it was full dark now, and the windows reflected the interior of the bus. Distantly, he could see blood in the east, getting brighter. The old woman saw it, too, and began to chew her gums.

"I will not taste of the bitter water," she said.

He knew the reference, of course, to the water ruined by the star Wormwood in Revelation.

It would happen that way, too. There would be deuterium in the debris of the supernova, and the water of the world would be absorbing it, turning it into heavy water. It wasn't in itself radioactive, but when half the water content of a larger animal's body was replaced with heavy water, the animal died. Or the man.

She said, "I am saved, hallelujah."

The bus would pass the Acton Clinic in a few minutes, and it was there that they must get off. David squeezed Caroline's hand, then returned to the front.

"Do you know the Acton Clinic?" he asked the driver.

"Yeah, it's a couple of miles on. I pass it four times a day."

"We want to get off there."

The driver glanced at him. "It's been burning for hours."

His heart heaved in his chest. He forced his voice to a calm he did not feel.

"You can make a stop, though?"

"Sure. But there ain't no refund. No refund here."

"Fair enough."

"You got that man's name? 'Cause he damaged this bus. I gotta write that up and the company's gonna want to go to the cops. Vandalism. They don't like it."

"Your company?"

"Maryland Trails Bus Lines," the driver said, ignoring the passengers. "I been drivin' their rigs for thirty years. Never got a citation, not one, not never."

"It's still operating?"

Again, he glanced at David. "What does it look like?"

A hand grabbed David's shoulder. He turned to face a woman whose face had been made pink by too much exposure to the supernova core.

"You a doctor? My baby got fluid. You a doctor?" She held up a baby as bloated as a stuffed toy and gray with death.

Ethically, he could not deny his profession. But he'd barely touched pediatrics in medical school. He was not qualified to help.

"We thought it was God's light, we slept him in it, my husband did. My husband was a fool."

David did not know how to tell her that this was a sunburn of a new and terrible kind.

"I'm sorry for you," he said.

"They nothin' you can do?"

"That is not God's light," another passenger shouted. "You have laid your baby in Lucifer's light."

This lovely, ignorant young woman raised a long hand to her cheek, and with a gesture of surpassing grace, wiped away her tears.

"I'll put him in the ground," she said. "Very well. Thank you."

She went swaying back to her seat, the other passengers looking straight ahead.

"We all told her," a man said. "She's got a dead baby."

The bus's brakes hissed and it lurched to a stop.

"Acton Clinic," the driver intoned. "Acton!"

David and Caroline got off, stepping out into the dew of morning.

Above the sun, in the purity of the eastern sky, hung a full moon, its face the red of blood.

As he watched, he saw a brief flash on the lunar surface, then another and another.

The driver closed the door of the bus and pulled out. What would happen to it, and to the people aboard? Nothing good, that was certain.

The great iron gates of the Acton estate still stood open. At the end of the curving driveway, the building loomed, still and silent. He could see jagged edges in the line of the roof where the fire had burned through. The windows were dark.

"It's destroyed," Caroline said.

David did not reply. He could only think that, even if they did find the class, what would they do without the portal? He had been counting on finding the supplies here for Caroline to re-create it a third time, but that did not look possible now.

"Come on," he said. They proceeded into the grounds, moving quickly but carefully.

As they drew closer to the house, he watched the door and the rows of broken windows for any suggestion of activity inside. They would have done well to look behind them, but they did not do that. Instead, they responded to the deep animal instincts that drive all men in times as terrible as these, and went toward the concealment that the house offered.

Thus they did not see who had dropped off the back of the bus as they had come through its door. Mack moved swiftly to the gate, then slipped into the grounds, then to the apple tree, now naked, where he had spent his afternoons.

He watched them enter the house through the sprung front door. He went closer, listening, and heard the scuffling of their clumsy movement through the ruins inside.

When he saw that they had gone through to the patient wing and all was quiet, he slipped into the house.

23

THE RISING OF THE SOULS

Mike and Tim Pelton and Delmar Twine were in terrible trouble because their general had gone crazy, and in just a minute, it was going to be Timmy's turn to get himself burned alive in that damn mirror or whatever it was.

The three of them had been friends all of their lives, growing up on the same street in Sandusky, going to the same schools, finally joining the army together, all three intent on getting the education they could not otherwise afford. Mike and Tim were identical twins, and they had joined up on the condition that they would stay together.

But instead of the training they'd hoped to get, they'd come out the other end of boot camp as infantrymen, and spent two years in 'Stan. Then, as the U.S. withdrew from that country, they had been reassigned to General Wylie's specialist brigade, guarding some sort of supersecret underground facility deep in the Blue Ridge Mountains.

The guard unit hadn't been allowed inside, but instead had been billeted in tents near the entrance. They'd seen the people coming, though, famous faces glimpsed as they got out of their vehicles and went through the thick steel doors into what appeared to be a luxurious interior. For weeks they'd come, the masters of the world—congressmen and senators, big-time preachers and Catholic hierarchy, TV personalities, movie stars, hundreds of them. Some of them had the black spot disease big-time, with the weird pigmentation almost covering their skin. Others, you couldn't see if they had it or not.

Mike and Tim and Del didn't have it, and they wouldn't bunk with people who did. You didn't want that, no way.

There were burned bodies all around the portal now, the remains of guys they'd worked with in the unit for the better part of a year. Behind them there was just Colonel Manders with his pistol, and at his feet the bodies of the seven men who had refused even to try.

Mike and Timmy and Del had talked about this thing. Whatever it was, it belonged to that man and woman who that CIA guy and the general had tried to kill.

The point was, those two people were the ones who knew how to make the sucker work right and stop burning guys. Everybody in the unit knew they were from the Acton Clinic, which was another secret installation of some kind.

"Okay, look," the general said. "You—" He pointed at Timmy. "You just make one smooth, easy movement. The problem is, guys keep trying to pull back—"

Timmy vomited.

"Shit!" The general thrust his gun into Timmy's face. "Do it!"

Timmy gagged and raised his hands flat against the sublime view of an orchard, its trees dripping with tiny, blushing red apples.

"Do it!"

And then the next thing Mike knew, the gun was in *his* face.

"Do it," the general shouted at Timmy, "or I blow your fuckin' brother's fuckin' brains out right now!"

Timmy went to the portal. He stood before it.

"I love you," he said without turning around. The tears in his voice broke his brother's heart. He was gonna burn, Timmy was gonna burn, and Mike and Del, they would be next. What a shitty goddamn way to go, how stupid was this?

"Sir," Del said frantically, "we need to take this thing up to the clinic. That's a secret installation! They know how it works, they can tell us."

"Move!"

There was a click. The cold of the gun barrel nestled against Mike's neck.

Suddenly Timmy just very smoothly stepped forward and went right into the thing. He seemed to walk forward, but also to get smaller and smaller, until finally he just disappeared.

Silence. Nobody moved. "Jesus . . ." the general whispered.

Then he seemed to climb out of something, and there he stood as clear as day in the grass on the other side, facing away from them. He bent down on one knee and ran his hands through the grass. Then he stood up and raised his eyes to what looked like a summer sky, floated with soft white clouds. Mike could practically hear the birds singing.

"Timmy," Mike shouted.

"Shut the fuck up!" The general removed the gun from Mike's neck and stepped closer to the portal. "Can you hear me?"

Timmy came close to the portal. Inclining his head to one side, he peered back at them. Could he see in this direction?

"Come back, Timmy," Del shouted. "Come on back, man!"

"Stuff it, soldier!"

"Yessir. But, Sir—"

Timmy held out a hand. He flattened it against his side of the portal—and instantly pulled it away.

Then Timmy was looking past the portal, seemingly into the sky above his side of it, or maybe at the portal itself, it was hard to be certain.

His face changed, moving into a wide-eyed expression of disbelief, then amazement.

He turned and went the other way, disappearing in among the trees of the orchard.

"*TIMMY!*" Mike went toward the portal. "*TIMMY!*" But as he tried to follow his brother, the general shoved him aside.

"Get outta there," he said.

"Where's my brother?"

"Eating goddamn apples, looks like to me."

"He was running. Something was wrong."

"Yeah, what's wrong is he's a fucking dumbass not to come back."

General Wylie stepped into the portal, using exactly the same decisive motion that Tim had used. Except . . . he stopped. For a moment, there was silence. This was followed by a stifled cry that quickly became a howl of agony as flames burst through the fabric of his uniform, accompanied by a sound as if of frying bacon.

"Help him," Colonel Manders shouted, shielding his eyes as he tried to get near the general, who was flopping like a fish, his body enveloped in flames.

Then, just as the others had done, he fell backward off the portal and lay kicking and spinning on the ground in burned agony.

Aside from the colonel, Mike and Del were the only members of the unit near the portal—alive, at least. Most of the ones who hadn't gone up into that machine or been killed like the general was being killed, had deserted by now. Maybe someone was still hanging in a Humvee here and there, but nobody who was willing to come anywhere near the portal.

Overhead, another meteor roared past, a thick streak of light accompanied by an ominous rumble. Somewhere below the southern horizon, it exploded in a flash.

"Fuck this," the colonel muttered. He swung into a Humvee, started it, and went back down the road, heading out toward the interstate and the Blue Ridge.

Mike and Del watched him go.

"Well, shit," Del said into the silence that had enveloped the convoy. "Anybody home? HELLO?"

Mike went to the portal.

"Timmy," he shouted into it. "Timmy!"

What was in there that had so upset him? Timothy Pelton did not scare easily, and Mike was in a position to know that. Even as kids, Tim had always been the bold one, the first one up the tree, the first one to ride the Top Thrill Dragster in Cedar Point, the first one to ask a girl out, the first one in to save Momma that time they had the fire.

Mike slumped. He felt Del's arm come over his shoulder.

"Del, I feel like he's on the other side of the moon. Farther."

"What the hell is this thing?"

"Some kinda classified stuff, has to be."

"They ain't got no problems over there," Del said, "'cept them crab apples don't look real worth eating."

"He's not eating crab apples! He run scared, man." A sudden burst of pure hate overcame Mike, and he kicked the blackened rubble of the general hard a few times. "Fuckin' bastard! BASTARD!"

"Hey. HEY!" Del pulled him away. "That ain't gonna do nothin'. That guy was headed for a court-martial, anyhow, the way he's killing people. I mean, I saw about five murder ones go down here today."

"Time of war." He went close to the portal. "Timmy! TIMMY, damn your eyes, come back here!"

Then he saw, across a far hill, a small dot in motion. For some moments, he watched it as it moved steadily up the grassy hillside. Del also watched.

At some length, he said, "Could be him."

"Or some caveman who ate him. We gotta find out how this thing works."

Del went to a Humvee and opened the door. Inside was Ken Freitag, a gun in his mouth and the back of his head spread across the cab.

"Occupied," Del muttered.

He went to the next one down the line and got in. There was a click, then the engine started. Hardened military electronics were not so quick to fry, fortunately, but there was going to be more than one vehicle in this convoy that wasn't gonna move. "Got forty miles left in this," Del said.

Without speaking—they didn't need to bother, the three of them always understood one another's thinking—Mike picked up the portal and slid it into the back of the Humvee, where it fit nicely . . . or had it gotten smaller when Mike tried to put it in?

Everybody knew the way the image in it changed as you moved it, and Mike didn't want to lose the spot where Timmy had gone in.

"We get this thing working right, we need to bring it back right here," he said.

"It's a countryside over there. If we get through safely, we're gonna find him sooner or later. Looks like southern Ohio, matter of fact."

"Southern Ohio is God's country."

"So is the rest of the world."

They were silent for a moment, each contemplating in his own way the enormity of what was happening.

"Why don't we just go in now?"

"You think we should?"

They both looked at it, then at each other. At last Mike said, "I think we need to find out more about it."

"I hear you," Del said. He pulled the Humvee out of the line and proceeded toward the town square. Plasmas so intense that they outshone the dismal sun now flashed across the sky without ceasing. Instead of the empty streets that had followed the passage of the penitents, they soon found that Raleigh was crowded with people who were pushing and pulling anything they could that was on wheels, trying to take supplies with them as they headed west toward the interstate. It looked like something out of a World War II movie.

People stared hard at the Humvee as it trundled east. They'd been shot at one too many times when trying to approach the convoy. They gave the soldiers their distance.

Up and down the street, buildings were burning. Molten insulation was dripping off overhead wires. "Spontaneous electrical fires," Del said. "Must be a whole lot of solar juice in the air to cause this."

Mike knew that the sun's energy would concentrate in wires if it became intense enough. There were weapons that could do that, too.

Up and down Main Street, the same street lamps from which the victims of the penitents were hanging were now exploding, sending sparks down into panicky crowds of refugees. Sheets of fire flared along electric lines, and columns of smoke rushed up from the roofs of buildings.

"It's everywhere," Mike said. "The whole world is burning."

When Del was forced to slow down, people began coming up to the Humvee. "This could get ugly," he said, and jammed the gas to the floor.

"Easy on the clutch, man."

"I know it, but I gotta not hit these folks."

In the sky, a huge plasma danced, a long electrical body writhing, its appendages sweeping the horizons like great snakes.

Soon, they were through the town and onto the highway that led to what had been the convoy's original destination. Like the town, the road was filling with refugees, a few on horseback, more on bikes, most on foot. Mike held a weapon in sight, making sure it was visible to the angry eyes and the mad eyes that watched them pass.

These poor damn people—somebody had to save them. If this darn portal would work, they could go through. Given enough time, maybe the whole darned country could go through.

What a damn miracle it was, but probably not for ordinary folks. Only people like the ones in the Blue Ridge would be allowed to use a thing like this, you could bet on it.

His heart just literally felt like it was tearing in two. He could feel his twin wanting to be with him. He could feel Tim being scared and being alone, and maybe knowing that the portal was in motion, that it was disappearing like a summer cloud or whatever it looked like on that side.

The farther they got from town, the fewer people there were on the road, and Del began to run the Humvee harder—until he saw someone ahead of them.

"Damn," he said as they drew near the person standing in the middle of the road. It was a woman with a baby stroller filled with fishing equipment, rods, reels, poles, hooks and lines in packets. She wasn't going anywhere, either. She held her ground right in the middle of the two-lane blacktop.

Del stopped, leaving the Humvee idling.

She came around to the window. "We're moving our stock," she said, "and I'd be willing to pay you twenty dollars for an hour of the truck." She glanced around. "There's looting. The cops are gone."

"Lady, we'll all be dead in a few days."

"What in the world is the matter with you? How dare you say such a thing."

"This is the Last Judgment, lady," Del said. The Twines were Church of Christ, big-time. Not the Peltons. Their dad had steered clear of religion altogether. But Mike knew about the Last Judgment, of course, and from where he sat, Del could damn well be right. What if that black stuff on people was sin showing up right through their skin?

"I need to move my stock. We're in hard times and we're planning a sale next week. We need inventory."

Mike leaned over to Del. "She's blown," he said. "Totaled."

"Christians can't just leave people," Del snapped.

"So let me drive. I ain't one. Anyway, you left all those people back there."

"Yeah, they weren't askin' for help."

Mike had to get this portal working. He had to get over into wherever the hell it was and find Tim. Mom and Dad were gone now, but this is what they would've wanted him to do, and it was what his blood wanted him to do. You lose your twin, you lose half your soul. But how to convince Del?

"Lady," Mike said, "we need to get on. We got a mission."

"There's no mission, Mike!"

"My brother is my mission!"

"Fellas, if you need to go—"

"We need to go!"

Del did not move, and it shocked Mike to realize just how strongly he felt about this. He was going to push Del out of that seat and drive away without him if he didn't get this vehicle moving again.

But, in the end, Mike had to admit that he couldn't bust up with Del, let alone make him eat a fist or something. So the next thing he knew, he was loading fishing tackle into the Humvee.

They did six miles to a just plain pitiful little house, sad and tired and full of kids. An older boy and his dad came out and quickly unloaded the Humvee. Helping them and seeing the way they treasured this stuff that nobody would ever buy, Mike was almost moved to tears. It reminded him of being in Afghanistan and having cold families come up to camp in the night, to huddle against the warm sides of tents and fill them with their ripe stink and the reek of 'Stan food.

Guys would kick the shit out of them through the canvas, but Mike and Tim didn't, and Del would go out and feed them, which would draw more, and he'd feed them until he ran out of damn loaves and fishes or whatever.

These were Americans, though, but it no longer felt much different.

They finished, then Del went out and got their well going by osmosis using garden hoses, which is the kind of thing he always knew how to do.

Mike let the boys look at his weapon, but not fire it. Who knew if those rounds would be needed. He kept the portal covered. No use in having to explain that damn thing, and he knew as well as any soldier that desperate people can turn nasty real fast, if they see something they think might save them.

When he had a chance, though, he looked into the portal. He was sort of hoping to see Tim, but he only saw the day over there getting slowly older, just like it was here.

Del reappeared. "Done and done," he said, satisfaction in his voice.

"Let's just get rolling, man. It's already sunset damn near, so it's sunset over there, too, and my bro is gonna be feeling mighty needful."

The first thing they saw of the Acton Clinic was a big wall topped with razor wire. There was a huge iron gate that was wide open, and as they went through it, there appeared what Mike knew at once was the most beautiful house he'd ever seen. But as they drew closer, he saw that it was partially burned out. Windows were broken. There was an ugly silence of a kind he knew all too well.

And now, as the sun set, the violet star that Colonel Manders had told them was a supernova appeared low in the northeastern sky, flooding the world in its creepy light.

When they arrived at the front of the house, Del stopped the Humvee and cut the engine. He turned to Mike. "What now?"

Mike had no idea what now. The windows of the old house were dark. It looked pretty ruined in there. But it didn't look real classified. No government warning signs, a wide-open gate, and no lights or guard units didn't exactly suggest this.

"What now is, we take a look around."

"Weapons?"

"You carry and cover, I'll take the portal."

"We can't leave a weapon uncontrolled."

"Then we pull the ammo outta mine and I'll hold on to the bolt."

"We might need that firepower."

So Mike strapped on his rifle and carried the portal. The thing wasn't heavy, and from the back it looked like a piece of canvas. But on the front, it was as slick as glass and you could go in it and run off in there, which Mike did not have the guts to do. He wanted his brother, though, and worse every minute.

The darker it got, the brighter the light from the portal appeared. Now it was looking over a glade full of grazing horses. The sun was a glow in the west, the sunset rich with gold at the horizon, then orange and yellow above it, and finally pale green fading into the blue of night. You could see plenty of stars, and Mike knew a fair amount about stars, thanks to their dad, who had a Celestron and had taught them the sky.

"How weird," he said. He held the portal directly overhead and looked up into it, then brought it slowly down to the eastern horizon.

"The constellations are out of place."

"Useful to know. Let's go inside and see if we can find out why."

Mike was transfixed. "Let me tell you . . . this sky is not right."

"Okay! Now let's move our asses. This can't be safe out here, man."

He kept moving the portal, trying to find north based on the glow on the western horizon. From the foliage he had seen when it was light there, he knew that the season was the same—early summer. So . . .

"What the hell is Draco doing *there?*"

"Dray-who doing where?"

"The constellation Draco . . . it's way north. There's Eltamin, and . . . Thuban. Thuban is the North Star!"

"Goddamn it, will you get your ass in gear?"

He lowered the portal. "Del," he said, "this is just a damn amazing thing."

"Well, *duh!*"

"No, you don't understand what this is. Because this isn't just some kind of window, like, into China or somewheres. Some kind of worm-hole or whatever. Del, the polestar in that sky—" He tapped the edge of the portal, being careful not to touch its lethal surface. "The polestar is not Polaris, it's Thuban. *Thuban*, man!"

"Look, do you remember how interested I was in the telescope, which was not at all? So I am not going to know what the fuck that means, am I?"

"What it means is that this thing is a damn time machine!" He held it up. "Thuban won't be the polestar for another twenty thousand years. When Timmy went into that thing, he crossed thousands of years into the future, Del. It's the future in there!"

"Oh, yeah, what about the little matter of the fact that Earth is gonna be a burned-out cinder in the future?"

"The dinosaurs got torched, and we're here. So it's not gonna stay, like, a cinder forever."

"Oh, man, somebody is gonna be very pissed off at us, because this thing is unbelievably classified, it has to be. The general was taking it back to the Blue Ridge for, you know, the Family, the politicians, all those rich people, the senators—"

"I know who's down there, I seen 'em go in same as you."

"Okay, then, we are criminals. Big-time. The whole fucking army is gonna be after us, plus the FBI, the CIA, and all'a that shit."

"Except that doesn't matter a shit anymore and I am not gonna stop until I get my brother back, and that is the line in the sand here, Del, so if you want to go back, that's fine by me. Personally, I wouldn't sell those scumbags shit on a platter, much less give 'em this thing. Find me some good folks—decent, you know—and let's get 'em through. And get us through, and find my brother."

Del ran a hand along the top edge of the thing, which now gleamed purple as the supernova spread its rising light.

"It's gonna be a brave fucking guy goes through this thing first. I mean, it's a damn miracle your brother didn't do like the rest of 'em."

"Drop the gun and step away from it, please."

Del did exactly as the voice from inside the house instructed. To Mike he mouthed the words "told you."

"Now face me. Come up onto the porch, please."

Mike started to lift the portal, but the unmistakable snicker of a bolt being thrown on a very proficient-sounding weapon froze him. Turning slowly, he held up his hands. Side by side, he and Del walked onto the porch. After a moment, a flashlight shone in their faces. It lingered on their patches. Whoever this was wanted to identify their unit, obviously.

"PFC Twine, please come forward."

Del took another step closer to the door. Behind them, Mike heard movement. Somebody was taking the portal! He reacted immediately, turning to stop them.

"Freeze!"

Which Mike did. But he had seen a woman in the violet light, her long legs striding, her hair flowing back, carrying the portal like the damn thing was her own personal possession. But Tim was in there. He had to get his brother back!

"Hey, look, we come here to bring it to you," he said. "But you gotta understand, my brother's in it. He's lost in there!"

There was no reaction. He could hear the woman's footsteps fading away. He dared not try again to look. He focused his attention on the flashlight.

"We're twins, see. So we are real close and I gotta get him outa there or go in—go over—with him. That's what I gotta do." He said nothing about the time machine part of it. That was probably the most secret thing about it. Guys were getting shot right and left these days. Forget the court-martial, the brig. Nowadays, you got your head blown off by a psycho general and nobody gave the slightest shit.

"Okay, Specialist Pelton, please come forward."

Del was shaking like a terrified Chihuahua or something, which was not like Del Twine, who could chew the beard of a Taliban for lunch.

"Now what's going to happen is I want you to come into the building. I am going to be standing aside. You will not see me. Then you will go where you're directed."

Del was shaking so much he looked drunk, and Mike was about to wet his pants. Maybe there was another Blue Ridge here, full of even more rich shitkickers, and they were gonna end up getting their asses tortured.

Then a match was struck ahead of them, and Mike saw that they were in a ruined hall that had once been really, really beautiful, with a sweeping staircase that led up to a mass of blackened beams where part of the roof had come in. Delicate fingers touched the match to a candle, and Mike saw a beautiful girl in the yellow light, with big eyes that looked him over dispassionately and frankly.

"Hello," he said.

She turned and went through a dining room full of upended tables and toward a big black door. So this was it, the inner sanctum.

The windows were draped with blankets, and there were many candles. And, in their light, many faces.

Mike's first thought was, *These are civilians.* His second was that they were hurt, some of them. Then that there were a whole lot of them, maybe over a hundred, and they had to be the quietest people he had ever seen in his life.

Then, from the back, the woman who had taken the portal came in.

Del sucked an awed breath, and even in flickering candlelight, Mike could see why. There was just very little question—this was about the most beautiful woman in the world. She carried the portal, which was glowing softly with starlight from the other side, and put it on an easel.

Mike said, "Lady, my brother is in there. I want you folks—" He looked around the room, tried to smile, but his smile collapsed and he was all of a sudden not a soldier. That all just went out of him, all the hardness, the long, cold nights ducking Taliban mortar shells and hating the bastards, all of that and all the misery he had endured as a virtual slave guarding the Blue Ridge, and the terror of this day—all of it just melted away.

What was left was his truth—he was a scared nineteen-year-old boy in an impossible situation, who had lost his twin brother and with him half of his own soul. He let out a long sob, then choked it back.

A man came to him, a guy in his thirties, the kind of guy who was born to command. When the guy's arm came around his shoulder, he wasn't embarrassed, not even in front of all these people. He was just tired and scared and alone.

"Come on, you two, I want to introduce you to our head of security. There's work for you here."

The two young soldiers went with David Ford, watched by many eyes, and in the candlelight, there gleamed many tears. Before them, the portal, back where it belonged, glowed with soft and beautiful light.

From his careful place of hiding, Mack also saw this. As he calculated his odds, he fingered the safety on his gun. He was sick and his burn hurt like nothing else he had ever known, but mostly he was filled with a rage that was beyond any emotion he had ever felt, a great, fiery darkness that boiled up from the center of his soul, and would drive him, he knew, both to feats even beyond his own great skill, and to death if it was necessary to fulfill his aim, which had become very simple.

Alone, he could not get the portal to Blue Ridge, which meant that the people who deserved it were not going to get it.

So nobody else would, either.

24

THE MOON

As soon as he'd disarmed the two young soldiers and assured himself
that they meant no harm, Glen had gone outside to run the perimeter.
He'd lost six of his sixteen men, but that still left enough of a force to
reestablish a presence on the walls. They were a lot better off with a
deeper defense, even if it had some light spots.

It was as he was crossing the broad lawn that led to the front gate,
which was stuck open and thus guarded now by three men, that he
noticed the moon.

He stopped, then focused his full attention on it. Over millions upon
millions of nights, the moon has risen in peaceful splendor. But there is
a reason that her face is marked by craters so enormous that they define
her very form. They are a reminder and a warning that what has happened in the past can happen again.

He decided that he needed David to see this, and returned to the rec
area where the survivors were assembled.

David could see by Glen's expression that something was very
wrong.

"You need to come outside."

"What's the problem?"

He nodded toward the door, and David followed.

"My God," David said as soon as he saw the moon.

"What do you think it means?"

The face of the moon was unrecognizable. That strange, shocked expression that had fascinated human beings from time immemorial was turned in a new direction.

"It's in motion," David said, "the moon is rotating."

Del and Mike had followed them out.

"Does this mean the end of the world?" Del asked.

Hardly hearing him, David watched in awe as this enormous cosmic event continued to unfold. Another object appeared in the sky, this one perhaps a tenth the size of the moon itself. As it crossed the face, it became a black irregular shadow. Size was impossible to judge, of course, but it was easily visible, so it was huge.

Once it crossed the face, it was lost to view because it was too black to reflect sunlight.

David knew what it was. It was an immense mass of debris of some sort from the supernova. He said, "I think if it strikes the moon, we're going to see gigantic boulders thrown off. Some will fall back, but some won't and the ones that don't are headed here."

"Which means . . . what?"

"Mike, it means devastating earthquakes. Tidal waves. Maybe worse. Much worse."

As Del backed away from him, David saw a trapped animal come into his eyes.

"You think you know it all but you don't know a damn thing!"

David did not challenge him, what would be the point? His fear and his anger would mean nothing, not in the face of what was coming.

The object reappeared, dark again as it crossed the moon's face. With deceptive slowness, it arced downward. On the moon's surface, then, there was a flicker of light. A moment later dust rose in a cloud so huge that it could be seen clearly as a haze spreading across the whole face, making it go out of focus.

Then a rain of gleaming specks emerged from this haze, some of them big enough that they could be seen to be tumbling, others nothing more than additions to a star field made faint behind the endless auroras and sick, purple-pink light.

David knew that these were actually huge stones, and that they would reach Earth in the next few days. But even before then—long before then—others were going to strike, and that could start happening at any moment.

"We got a problem," Glen said. He wasn't looking at the moon, and David followed his eyes toward the distant front gate.

"This is just the beginning," David said.

"I can't stop them this time, David."

"We can dust 'em," Mike said. "Give us back our guns."

"No," David said. "You need to let this happen. Just be sure they're orderly, because there're going to be more."

The people began to hesitate, then to cluster in uneasy groups, when guards on the perimeter showed themselves.

"Go in and retrieve your weapons," Glen told the two soldiers.

David saw men, women, and children, he saw dogs on leads, cats in carriers, people hauling suitcases and straining under heavy backpacks.

As people flooded into the compound, it became possible to observe great, long columns of them stretching off along the road as far as could be seen.

Glen called to his men, "Pull it in, stay in front of them!"

As the guards on the gate began backing up, the others came in off the walls.

Del fired his gun into the air.

"NO!" David said. "Not that."

A woman tried to settle a barking dog, but other than that, there was silence from the whole enormous and swelling mass.

A man came forward, his hands in the air, a white handkerchief in one fist. "Please," he said, "let our children come with you."

"They know about the portal," David said.

"How?" Mike asked.

"A lot more people are going to know about it. It's going to be seen all over the world by the ones who need to see it."

"Seen? How?"

"As time passes, it becomes more . . . I guess the best word is 'focused.' And the more focused it is, the more people see it."

Mike shook his head.

"It's hyperdimensional. It's outside of space-time as we know it. What's happening is that it's growing in hyperspace, like a gigantic crystal made of time. Does that make sense to you?"

"No, Sir, it does not. But I assume it means that a whole lot of people are going to go through it."

David drew on his now clear memories of what he'd learned in the class. "Around a million worldwide," he said. He called to the crowd, "You're welcome on the grounds. But the building is off limits, do not attempt to enter the building."

To emphasize this, the security guards moved toward them in a line, arms linked. The crowd spread into the broad front garden, but there were still many more coming.

"Man, look at the moon," Mike said. "Look at it!"

The orb was dark red from dust, and the familiar face was now gone.

What had been the dark side was now facing earth.

"Man, that sucker could be about to come out of its orbit," Mike said. "If it hits us, we're done."

The last time the moon had rotated was four hundred and fifty million years ago, before even single-celled life-forms trembled in the waters. It had been struck, then, by an even larger asteroid—actually a small planet—and a huge piece of it had crashed to earth. The crater it had left remained the largest landform on earth. It is called the Pacific Ocean.

Now the whole crowd was watching, and people were coming out of the house, all looking up at the greatest cosmic spectacle that any man had ever witnessed.

From within the mass of them, there arose a female voice, clear in the cathedral silence of the moment.

" 'Yea, though I walk through the valley of the shadow of death, I will fear no evil.' " And although her tone was filled with fear and even the ragged edge of desperation, a chorus took up the lines, until by the time the final verse was uttered, it was a solemn chant, clear and determined, from many thousands of throats.

In the silence that followed, they watched as bright sparks flickered in waves across the new face of the moon.

"Jesus, it's the fishing tackle lady," Del said. He went into the crowd to the woman who had spoken out.

David saw that she and her husband and kids carried an extraordinary variety of angling equipment, and he thought that it might prove very useful if where they were going was as undeveloped as it appeared. So far, no matter what direction he had pointed the portal in, he hadn't seen a sign of any sort of structure. He feared that a great many people were going to be thrown into a very primitive environment, and that was going to be a very hard situation for them to face, especially after the hellish conditions they were enduring here.

"It's beautiful," a voice said from behind them. David did not need to turn to know that Caroline was there. Suddenly and with great intensity, he remembered her body close to his, and her gentle, insistent ways.

"David," she said, "I'm having a problem with the portal. It's flickering. It looks like it's failing somehow."

Terror like lightning shot through him. He looked out at the crowd. "Don't tell them," he said, and followed her back into the building.

25

THE OMEGA POINT

Looking at it on its easel, David could see at once how it was chang-
ing. There was something dim and grainy about it now. He touched it.
"It looks like a painting again," he said.

The class was clustered around it. As it turned out, they had survived
the worst of the assault by hiding in the attic and ductwork of the patient wing. They had been clever about hiding, and only two lives had
been lost.

"Before we moved, I thought we should wait for dawn over there,"
Caroline said. "I didn't expect this."

David did not say that he thought that Caroline had made a mistake.
How could anybody be blamed for anything now?

He addressed the group. "We need to start getting people through.
We need to do it right now."

Nobody moved.

George Noonan said, "All those people, one by one? Through this?"
He shook his head.

"I don't see how we can help them," Aaron added. "Not with such a
small opening."

"I think we have to," a voice replied. It was Peggy Turnbull, who had
been a tomboy in the days of their class, interested only in hunting
and horses. In recent years, she had become a poet. Her false psychosis
had been depression. He regarded her narrow face, pale in the candle-

light. How long would this delicate creature survive in the wilderness that they would soon be entering?

At that moment, there was light so bright that it glared in through the blankets that had been hung over the windows, and from outside there came a howling uproar of terror.

There followed a clap of thunder so enormous that it shattered the few remaining windows.

"Bolide," Mike said. "Big one. Hit just below the horizon, so better hold on."

The world began shaking.

He grabbed David. "If we can go through that thing, we need to *do it*!"

The shaking got rapidly worse. Caroline and others staggered, then she fell to her knees. As David went to her, there arose from outside a clamor of shouts, followed by the chatter of an automatic weapon.

"NO!" David shouted, but his cry was lost in the thunder of the earthquake, as the whole patient wing trembled and cracks raced up the walls. Still, though, the earthquake increased, and David threw his body over Caroline, and could practically feel the ceiling above them getting ready to give way.

"We have to get it outside," she shouted above the din of crackling plaster and collapsing window frames.

Again light, so intense this time that heat came with it, searing, burning, their exposed skin.

The air was sucked out of David's lungs, and he thought that he must die.

"It's coming down," a voice cried, and then Glen and Mike were there, and everyone was running for the doors. Glen helped them up, and Caroline took the portal.

As they went toward the door that led into the side garden, the wall collapsed before them.

"The front," George Noonan shouted. "It's our only chance."

They picked their way through the rubble of the front of the house, moving in a fog of dust almost too thick to navigate at all, but then there were lights ahead, bobbing closer. There came a girl of perhaps twenty, her tired face full of sadness. David remembered her from the bus, and thought, *She has lost her future, that's what a child is.*

An agony deeper than blood filled him, because he thought not only of her and the others outside, but all the millions who were suffering this without even the slight hope of survival represented by something like the portal.

"Help us," the girl said, reaching out and taking David's hand. "I buried my baby just a while ago. But I want to live. I want to live for him."

In his heart, David felt that the baby had ascended, but he would explain it to the mother later. He found himself being led onto the front porch with its now teetering colonnade. Behind him, Caroline brought the portal and the class came with her, struggling, covered with dust, some of them nursing injuries. But nobody was screaming, and the house still stood, and the quake was subsiding into a series of more and more distant shudders, and thuds as if a giant was walking off into the forest behind the house.

Caroline raised the portal up before the crowd. "If we stay calm," she shouted, "if we get in line and take our time—"

Susan Denman said, "Isn't it holographic? I remember your dad taught us that it would be."

"I know what he said, but look at it! We need to deal with what we have."

"But this is all wrong, then! We didn't give our lives to save a couple of hundred people. This is supposed to be about millions!"

Had they been lied to? Were they, in fact, the most elite of the elite?

She returned to the crowd. "Let's start now, and nobody rush forward. Just take it easy—"

Without warning, a shock passed through the earth with such force that it hurled people flat, causing the whole crowd to drop in a confusion of possessions, pets, and terrified, screaming children.

The power of it caused trees to leap out of the ground as if they were being fired from buried cannons, and the Acton mansion itself, as strongly built as it was, shuddered and kept shuddering.

People were unable to stay on their feet, and David was no exception. Struggling, falling, clawing the heaving earth, it was like being in a nightmare where you ran but went nowhere.

"Get away from it," he cried—but then Caroline pointed, and he looked up to the great roof and saw a figure there, a man with a rifle. "Glen," he shouted, "get that man to come down off there!"

"He's not one of mine, David!"

But David didn't need to be told. He had recognized Mack the Cat. Despite the gigantic shaking, Mack remained absolutely still and steady as he raised the rifle and fired down, at first, David thought, at him and Caroline. But he was not shooting at them, he was shooting at the portal, and David understood instantly that he cared only for one thing now: if he couldn't use it, nobody would.

It took all of his effort and all of his strength, but he managed to get to his feet and to stagger along the heaving ground and throw himself onto it, pressing it against the earth beneath him. The front of it was to the ground, and the back still seemed like nothing more than canvas stretched on a frame. But then he saw a bullet hole in it, and something like starlight leaking out onto the backing, as if the tear was oozing the blood of time.

Behind him there was a sound that was almost human, a great, grinding sigh, which for all the world sounded like the death rattle of a very old man. He turned in time to see the great mansion implode, the figure of Mack disappearing into the dust and chaos of its disintegration.

One after another, the great columns fell, and when the collapse had ended, David was struck by how very much the place resembled the rubble of an ancient Roman palace, and he felt the echo of ruins.

The dust grew as thick as the air in a cave. Around David there was now no more movement, nothing except material falling from the sky, stones, bricks, bits of furniture, and red-hot scraps of what he supposed must be a meteor that had struck close by. To the west, violet light swam in blackness. The supernova was setting. In the east, there was blood on the horizon. But the northern sky was different. The northern sky was glowing, then going dark again, then glowing more brightly.

"David, it's damaged!"

Caroline's eyes were fierce with panic, which surprised David. In these past few moments, he had stopped struggling. Too much was wrong, and his heart was telling him that they must fail.

"It's clear," Caroline cried. "Oh, my God, look at it!"

As the crowd drew closer, people coming tentatively up through the grounds, families, pets, children, the portal not only became clear again, the rip made by the bullet simply faded into the image itself.

But then something else happened, that made David's mind go blank with amazement, as the portal also began to get larger, as if curtains were spreading or clouds parting.

Caroline no longer held it, but only stood beside it. The portal had taken on an existence of its own, spreading wider and wider until it was ten feet wide, then fifty feet, then filling the whole grounds.

Tears streamed down her face, which was transfixed with joy.

David grabbed her shoulders and looked into her blazing, triumphant eyes.

As the portal grew, it looked like a gate into heaven, leading away from the roaring, dust-choked catastrophe that surrounded them.

Like ghosts, people came out of the dust clouds, moving tentatively toward the crystal predawn that spread before them.

But they did not enter it. Instead they began throwing themselves to their knees, pleading.

"They don't understand," Caroline said. "David, help them."

He tried to raise his voice, but the dust that choked his throat made that impossible. Finally, he took a man by the shoulders and guided him toward the portal, but he shrank back.

"Don't be afraid," David said. He did not think any of them would be here if they bore the mark. By now most of those—the ones who were not hiding in bunkers—must surely have come to their ends. But what if he pushed this man and he burned, then what?

Before he could decide how to proceed, the light from the north came soaring above the horizon, an immense, flaming mass, the largest thing that any creature for the last half a billion years had seen in the sky of earth.

David called to the class, "Help them," he shouted. "We have to help them!"

As a glare brighter by far than the sun flooded down from the object now speeding overhead, David tried to speak in the man's ear, but he pulled away and ran. David knew that he must look mad, covered as he was by dust.

Still, there was no choice now, no time to waste, so he ran to a cowering family, the children so panicked that they were beyond control, the mother screaming, the father trying to shield them from the thing passing overhead. He picked up a girl of perhaps ten.

"Come on," he said, "come with me."

"What's that thing?" the father shouted.

What did he mean, the thing in the sky or the portal? No time to find out. David grabbed him by the collar. "Come on, follow me!"

As he went toward the portal with the screaming girl trying to pull away from him, he felt once again heat from above, but also saw that the light was getting less bright. The gigantic meteor was not going to strike here, it was going farther south. But he couldn't think about that now. He had reached the portal where Caroline stood with her arms outspread, calling to the crowd, telling them they could go through, in a voice that was lost in the roar of voices and the wind that had followed the meteor, and was now shaking the few trees left standing, and drawing dust up like a massive cloud of roiling smoke from the ruins of the mansion.

And now, as suddenly as it had come, the great light was gone, disappearing beneath the southern horizon, which glowed briefly with white light, and then was once again dark.

Mike said, "It hit in the ocean."

"I know it." And they both also knew exactly what, therefore, would be coming. The elevation here was six hundred feet, which would not be nearly enough.

"What's in there?" the father asked him.

"A new world," David said, and did the only thing left for him to do, which was that he thrust the screaming, writhing little girl through the portal.

"Jesus God," the father cried, and the mother and younger brother both screamed in terror as they saw the girl inside the portal. She turned and put her hands to her head as if she was going to pull her hair out, and her face twisted into a scream that they could see but not hear. She came to the portal and threw herself against it, pressing herself and clawing at it, her face grotesque. From this side, she looked as if she was pressing herself against glass, and David understood for the first time that there was no return, and he remembered what had happened to Katrina's arm when she had tried to pull it out.

"Do not stop, do NOT try to come back," he shouted to the people crowding toward the glory of it, a sparkling dawn, enormous across the whole expanse of the lawn, concealing behind it the ruins of the house.

He took the father by the hand and said to him, "You need to help your daughter," and the father took his wife's arm and she held her son, and the three of them stepped through. A big old springer spaniel with gray dewlaps barked twice after they had gone, and jumped through behind them.

So far, none of these people showed the slightest sign of the mark, but God help any that did, should they try to go through.

Dawn was gold and clear in the east of the portal, and the family, now hand in hand, walked a short distance. The father bent down to feel the grass beneath their feet, then turned and spread his arms wide.

Along the southern horizon in this world, though, there had appeared a shimmering line, and David thought he knew what it was, and Mike certainly knew. "We just got a few minutes," he said.

Inside the portal, David saw other people appearing, coming from other directions, and realized for the first time that this place was indeed not the only one where the portal was present. Just as they had been promised that it would in the class, it had appeared all over the world.

"Your father was right," he told Caroline. "It's holographic."

David thought, at this point, that he understood the mechanics of judgment. Over the many lifetimes that come and go during a great earthly cycle, we are born and born again, making choices as we go along, each time locked in physical bodies that remember little of the soul's past and its aims, where we enact lives that either add to the weight of the soul or reduce it. Evil makes it heavy, good makes it light, and the vast number of people die, each life, a little lighter than before.

Then, as the cycle's end approaches, the chance to be reborn anew ceases. The changes become permanent and most people are harvested to higher life. Some, who have ruined themselves, sink away, and a few remain to take the wisdom of the last cycle forward into the next.

"We got maybe ten minutes, man!" Mike said.

So David believed he understood these sacred mechanics, which was lovely, but this was no time to stand watching the spectacle and indulging his inner professor.

He raised his voice. "Get moving, everybody! Everybody! NOW! NOW!"

People stirred but were still unwilling.

"They're scared," Caroline said. "They still don't understand."

"There's no time left!" He knew that this scene was being repeated all over the world, and many would fall by the wayside, and also that this was intended, that it fit the gigantic plan of life, and for just an instant he sensed the presence of the mind that had conceived the universe . . . and felt as if he was in the presence of a child.

Caroline stepped to the center of the portal. "We can go through," she shouted. "Look, we can all do this!" But then she was absorbed in the milling, panicky crowd.

"Caroline!" He waded after her.

Ahead, he saw her hair, then he saw a tall, ghostly figure come to her, and she was lifted by her hair, her face distended with pain, her eyes bulging.

Against her throat, Mack held a jagged blade that had been broken off an electric hedge clipper.

26

THE LAST BREATH

Across the world, as the gigantic event reached its climax, all the trea-sures and wonders of history were being swept away. Some of the boulders that had broken off the moon were the size of islands, and they had begun striking Earth mercilessly. Those that hit the oceans generated waves unlike any that had been seen even during the climax of the Ice Age, black mountains of water that were now sweeping away whole nations.

London and Rio and Tokyo and Amsterdam were among the first to disappear in the maelstrom. A boulder the size of Bermuda slammed into the central Ukraine, releasing the equivalent energy of a billion hydrogen bombs and instantly vaporizing every living thing from St. Petersburg to the Black Sea.

The shock waves of the meteor impacts were so great that they completely disintegrated cities from Casablanca to Paris, and the gigantic explosions they generated made millions instantly deaf.

Whole species of animals died in an instant, herds upon the prairies, fish in the sea, and the bodies of great schools drifted to the ocean floor where they would become fossils. In millions of years, very different hands would raise them as human hands had raised the mats of fish skeletons that had died exactly the same way in the Permian extinction over two hundred million years before.

There is, indeed, nothing new under the sun.

Everyone who was not near a portal was afflicted with the stain, and they had come to understand their fate, and they cut themselves to pieces and burned themselves and ripped at themselves to remove the stain, but they could not remove the stain, and in their billions they lay writhing from their mutilations, or they ran in doomed streets, or tried to end their agony with suicide, only to discover that the death of the body was what sprung the trap. Their darkness also grew and grew, until they were reduced to a state that is darker than darkness itself, for this new skin reflected no light at all. They were shadow people now, sweeping through the streets in despairing packs, their cries like the wind wailing on a winter night.

A series of more than fifty objects struck the Pacific, including one that sent a tsunami slamming into the coasts of Washington and Oregon, drowning Vancouver and Seattle and Portland, inundating San Francisco, and sweeping across the entire Los Angeles basin with such energy that it gushed through the mountain passes to the east, finally expending itself a hundred frothing, foaming miles into the high desert.

The people who had come to the Acton Clinic were streaming into the portal in a more orderly manner, as the members of the class moved among them, urging them forward.

Mack had dragged Caroline into the leafy shambles of some trees, and David had gone with them.

"We're going through together," Mack said. "The three of us."

"Mack, it can't work." Mack's body was almost entirely a shadow now, as if he was becoming a living darkness.

"Then I rip her throat out."

Surely he could not be deceived another time. Surely he understood that the portal would not let him through.

David did the only thing he could, which was to lead Mack to the portal, which was now busy with people crossing, moving easily and quickly, ten and twenty at a time walking into what was becoming a great, wondering crowd on the other side.

There came a rumbling sound that quickly deepened, soon trembling the ground.

"Hurry," Mack said.

David pushed a pregnant mother through. Until every one of them was safe, he would not himself go through.

On the distance, the horizon began shimmering.

"Hurry, goddamn you!"

"Go without me," Caroline shouted against the rising thunder of the oncoming tsunami.

David pulled at people. "Everybody," he shouted, "GO GO GO!"

As he cried out, yet another enormous light appeared in the north, this time striking the ground below the horizon. Immediately a great, bright swarm of objects rose from where it had fallen—and David thought that this was ice dislodged from the polar cap just as it had been dislodged twelve thousand years ago by a strike on the Laurentian glacier. The icebergs would probably fall as far south now as they had then, when they had hit from the Carolinas to New Mexico, leaving, among other artifacts, the hundreds of thousands of craters of the Carolina Dells.

Finally, the last of the people were through, except for Mike and Del and Glen, who stood with him and with Caroline.

"So how do I do it?" Mack asked. Embracing Caroline tightly, he moved toward the portal. "If I burn, she burns," he cried against the enormous, echoing thunder of the onrushing water.

David did the only thing he could think of, he exploded into Mack's back, throwing himself against the larger man—and Del and Mike and Glen joined him, kicking him and shoving him—and then, suddenly, he was lighter and David saw, on the other side of the portal, that Caroline had come free and crossed.

Slowly Mack turned. He no longer had the blade. In fact, he no longer had the hand that had held it, but his open wrist did not pump blood. David could see in the eerie wells of his eyes the reason for this: Mack was dead. He was still moving and still thought himself alive, but this was not a living creature anymore, this dark, shifting form was a corpse.

The air began to scream and to suck them back, and even the edges of the portal trembled.

Glen turned and jumped through it, followed by Del and Mike, and Mack groaned to see them do it, and gargled deep rage in his throat, and if a corpse could utter a sound, this was what it would be like.

Mack's remaining hand grabbed David's throat—but David managed to twist away and half jump through the portal. Mack still held him, though, and began to pull him back, and he felt moving through the part of his body that was between the future and the past a churning coldness, as if the absolute waters of death were flooding into him.

Laughing now, Mack dragged at him, and the coldness turned to fire, and he knew that he was being sliced apart—but then felt hands grab the arm that was flailing on the far side of the portal, and felt himself being pulled.

Mack's eyes, a moment ago empty with death, now sparkled with hatred. Despite his injuries and the shadow that had enveloped him, he remained strong. In fact, his grip was like iron, and David thought, *This is what a demon is.* He struggled with all his might, but he could not overcome Mack's steel strength.

Behind Mack, though, he saw what appeared to be a great, dark cliff, and he knew that this was the wave, and it was here, now.

They were both swept up in it and smashed as if by the fist of a giant against the portal—and suddenly, there was silence.

David scrambled to his feet. The wave was hitting, and he braced himself. He did not understand why this had happened to him. Was there some sort of mistake? He had not judged himself evil, had not marked himself . . . for it is always a choice, to accept the mark of the beast. We are our own judges, but we always choose correctly.

David now found himself face-to-face with something that was no longer even a human form. Mack had disappeared entirely, into the deepest darkness he had ever seen or known possible, a darkness as deep as all the sins of the world, radiating evil like brutal heat. Embedded in it he could see the billions of faces of those who had lost their souls, the faces distended by what must have been truly terrible screams, but the screams were silent.

They seemed to be taken up, somehow, into the wave, but it wasn't affecting him, he was watching it as if through glass—and then he understood: he was looking *back in time*, through the portal.

Then he was racing through the portal, and the old Earth, the ruined Earth, was becoming smaller and smaller, dwindling faster and faster, disappearing so totally that it was as if it had never been.

What had hit the portal was not only a gigantic tidal wave, it was also a wave in hyperspace, capturing in its dark waters all who had made the commitment to evil. Him, it had simply pushed away—and through the portal.

And then he saw a face appear, much closer than the others, the eyes terrible in their desperation, the mouth distorted by great agony, the hands clawing through time, clawing and burning, and despite all his effort and the will of a demon, Mack the Cat became outlined with fire and then became fire, but still the face screamed, still the agony went on.

As David watched in sorrow and loathing, Mack transformed from the dark-cloaked figure he had been on the roof of the clinic into another person entirely, a man wearing the uniform of some sort of officer, black, the chest spread with medals. And then David saw the red armband with the black swastika, and then the body changed again, this time wearing the splendid suit of a wealthy nineteenth-century businessman, and then it wore the flowing robes of a cardinal, and then the changes flickered past so fast that it was impossible to see anything except that David knew that he was actually watching Mack's whole time on Earth move past, lifetime after lifetime of evil.

Seeing this caused stirrings of memory from his own long-past time, but the memories were not evil, they were haunting and wonderful and full of nostalgia, loves, and hard work; they were lives he would be proud to live again.

Mack was washed away into the blackness then, a spark instantly absorbed into what was at once a tidal wave containing a whole ocean, and a wave of purest evil.

The darkness itself began to recede, until there was nothing left of the past in the portal, which itself shuddered, then faded, and slipped into memory.

David found himself looking out across a broad meadow that ended in trees, and beyond the trees, the vine-choked pink debris of a city, its ruined towers glowing in the dawn.

The ruins were very, very old, and they looked dark and haunted with the terrors of the last cycle. But they must be filled with useful materials, even with shelter.

But where was everybody else? In fact, where was he?

"David?"

Her! He'd come through the portal backward, that was all, and he whirled around and there she stood, her body framed by the golden light of dawn, as the sun, now placid again, rose behind her.

All across the meadow, sitting silently and watching the new sun rise, were the people they had rescued, and more; in fact, there were thousands upon thousands in this verdant new world.

There was a man with her, and they were hand in hand, and a knife cut to the frightened heart of David's love.

"David, don't you remember your old teacher?" the man asked.

Flushed with relief, then with the joy of meeting again after all these years, he took the shoulders of Charles Light, looked into his eyes, and the happiness of those days came flooding back, and with it all the memories that had remained lost, not the important things, which he had already remembered, but the less important ones, the way the desks were arranged, how exciting it was to understand the marvels they were being taught. And, above all, he remembered Caroline.

They had not been lovers in any adult sense, but in an instant he recaptured all the innocent happiness he had known with her, and remembered the promises they had made.

She stood before him, her eyes cast down, the sunlight flaming in her hair, a picture of dizzying sensuality and innocence all mixed together, and in that moment he truly understood how perfectly the human spirit is paralleled by the personalities of the old gods, and he saw her as the Lady of the Starry Skirt, at once an earthy, sweaty, soft woman and a star keeper, her body belonging to youth and the promise of the womb, her soul to the heavens.

He could not speak. He was beyond speech.

She came into his arms, and when he embraced her, she felt as soft as a cloud. Her eyes regarded him, looking in amazement at his face, then fluttering closed in the cathedral of their kiss.

For a moment, the kiss was the center of the universe—and then there came a hand to his shoulder.

They slipped away from one another. Charles Light was smiling, but then his expression became more serious.

"We have to organize them," he said. "We have to get this thing rolling."

Arm in arm, he and Caroline headed back toward the great crowd, where children were now running and dogs cavorting, and people were relaying down to the nearby river to get water.

"There's a lot of work to do," David said.

"That's why we're here," a voice replied. It was Del, and he and Mike were arm in arm with a third soldier. They had found Tim.

Tim was appalled by the magnitude of the situation. All these people without food, without shelter.

"I don't know where to start!"

Caroline squeezed his hand. "Of course you do."

Which, he realized, was true. All of them did. They knew in their blood why they were still here on Earth, because they had wanted to participate in the building of the next great cycle.

But they weren't the sort of people who were likely to think on such things. If you put one of them in a room, they would clean the room. Give them a file, and they would organize it, or an empty field on a summer morning and they would think ahead to winter, and start a house.

They were already stirring among themselves, seeking aim and direction, looking for work to do.

The immeasurably conscious presence that is the ascended wing of mankind was never wrong and could not be wrong. These were the ones who would put their shoulders to their task, and create the foundation of a new and better world, that would emerge out of the compassion that was common to all of their hearts, and it would be better than the old world, because in it there would be no more souls devoted to greed and all its cruelties. The last phase of history had been designed to cause them to reveal themselves, so that they could be removed forever. Mankind was not going to experience another cycle of evil and ruin, but this time would work on ecstasy, so that, somewhere along the vast halls of time, when this age ended, everyone would ascend and the species, finally, would leave the physical world entirely behind.

Eventually, other earthly species would gain intelligence, but that would not be for a billion and a half years, and by then even the least trace of human works would be gone, and mankind would have joined the journey into ecstasy which, like heat, has no upper limit.

In the deep redoubts that Mack had striven so to save, death had been slow, for they had been built to last, and to the people imprisoned within there came bitter hatred and violence, and finally madness, and they all sank away, all of those people, into the same darkness that had consumed Mack.

The god with whom David had been identified from his childhood, the great plumed serpent Quetzalcoatl, manifested in him not as a grand presence, but rather as a practical one, concerned less about the mysteries of time and the grandeur of its cycles, and more about making sure the water was fit to drink and shelter could be found, and food gathered during the plenitude of summer.

As some got water, others were already scouring the shrubs for berries, others heading in groups toward the ruined city, to find what might be of use there.

From across a far hill, another group appeared, people waving, and here and there joyous reunions took place, wife running to husband, child to mother. Over the whole of the restored Earth of all those thousands of years in the future, this same scene was being repeated.

But it would not be all joy. There would be struggle and suffering here. This was going to be hard.

David would do his best at his job, and become famous among them for his tirelessness, but time would wear on him as it does on us all, and one day he would leave them, and his beloved Caroline, and the family that they would make in a small house that was yet to be built, in a village that was not yet, on this first day, even an idea.

The secret of Quetzalcoatl's power is that he is a humble god.

In many stories and religious traditions, and even in the science of the lost world, this time had been predicted. But there was one statement about it that turned out to be the clearest and the most profoundly true, which had been made over two thousand years before the old cycle had ended.

It had been uttered on a little hill in Palestine, by a tired man with a matted beard, the last public practitioner of the lost science. He was an itinerant Jewish carpenter and sometime preacher who had met an old Egyptian priest, who had given him white powder gold of the true form, confected at one of the great time temples, all of which were dedicated to Hathor. This one was in the Sinai, and it was here that he was taught the secret laws of reality, which enabled him to raise the dead and heal the sick, and see clearly along the dim halls of time.

He had gone far in his studies, and seen much. And so it was that there came a day when he saw a chance to speak a sermon that would contain the deepest human meaning that there is. So he set forth, in a few hoarsely shouted verses on a hot afternoon, the whole journey of the human soul, and the inner meaning of mankind.

In that sermon was contained the most important prophecy ever made—ten words shouted out while people ate and chatted, and listened with the same casual wonder they might give to a bird of surpassing voice, or a street-corner mountebank with a deck of cards.

After he had been speaking for a while, he saw that he was not gaining their undivided attention, and he therefore tried this: "Blessed are the poor in spirit: for theirs is the kingdom of heaven." He had shouted it at them, but still there was little attention paid. What did it mean, anyway? They did not understand that he spoke not of the spiritually impoverished, but of those who share in spirit the suffering of the poor, and give of themselves to lift others.

He tried again, crying out, "Blessed are they that mourn: for they shall be comforted." This had immediately regained the attention of the crowd. In that hard era, when the Jews were chained to the Roman yoke, there was not one of them who did not have reason to mourn.

So he had what he needed, the crucial moment of attention into which he would utter words that would define a future that was still over twelve thousand years away.

He then cried out, "Blessed are the meek: for they shall inherit the earth."

That had brought silence and questioning glances, then a confused murmur.

Soon after, he had gone down and taken a meal of bread and oil, and some thick wine. Nobody had recorded the words, but they had stayed in many hearts, and, in time, were given to the ages.

Today, though, those of whom they had been spoken had no time to think on them. And they weren't thinkers, anyway, most of them. They were workers, and the sun was full up and the day was growing warm, and there was a very great deal to be done.

AUTHOR'S NOTE

THE WORLD OF *THE OMEGA POINT*

What if the world really did end? What would we do? How would the human species come to a close — in terror and chaos, or according to some sort of hidden plan?

If there is a plan, there will also be chaos, that's clear enough. No matter how sublime the plan, people are likely to be quite upset, so I am happy to report that I don't have any specific information that the world will end in 2012, 2020, or, for that matter, anytime soon. But I can assure you that, one day, for one reason or another, planet Earth will become unable to sustain human life, and there are people, or will be people, who will face this distressing inevitability.

So, what happens? Is it all simply random or is there some sort of meaning? Is there an afterlife, perhaps, or some other place we can go, or is our species condemned to join all the others who have emerged here, lived for a while, then died out and been forgotten?

Or, put another way, is the universe essentially random and chaotic, but so large that the emergence of conscious life here and there is more or less inevitable?

Modern science says that human beings are biological machines and that we emerged out of a long period of evolution that is mechanical and random. To make matters even more dolorous, the fossil record demonstrates with terrifying eloquence that gigantic, devastating extinctions are the norm on our innocent-seeming little planet. Add to that the fact that modern science says that death is the end of everything, and a pretty dreary picture emerges.

However, modern science's vision is quite a new approach to the meaning of life, and there are reasons—a few—that enable legitimate speculation that it may not be correct. My own life has unfolded so far outside of what science tells us that we should expect, I really do wonder if we might not be having, as we live, quite a different experience from what appears to be the case, and one that is only partially explained by a mechanistic view.

Over the course of this little essay, I'll tell some of the stories from my own experience that suggest—at least to me—that life may be much more than it seems, and there may be good reason for our inability to perceive the whole truth of it. Of course, I would be the last person to assert that I'm right and the entire scientific establishment is wrong.

In fact, I'm more than a little embarrassed at ending up so far outside of the mainstream. In terms of getting things like book reviews, for example, it's been quite inconvenient. But I love quiet, and being an outsider certainly brings plenty of that. It also brings undeserved opprobrium and spittle-hazed rage. In my career, I have encountered many pumping carotids, and I confess to taking an evil pleasure in inducing bluster and outrage.

I'm annoying and, unfortunately, I enjoy this. But there's a larger reason. I don't think that I'm wrong about the marvels that have filled my life, and I do want others to enjoy them, as well, and to find the same delightfully light and deep meaning that they have brought me.

It is incredibly freeing to know—as, in my heart, I do—that human life is indeed part of a vast continuum of consciousness that persists after death, and that is woven into the extraordinary glory that is intelligent life in the universe.

So I'm full of joy, because I have had, and am having, a marvelous adventure that suggests that the secular and essentially mechanical vision of ourselves that has become a shorthand and core belief in scientific and intellectual circles, is not true, and that what is true about us is so far beyond even the most optimistic imaginings of the ancients that we actually live on a hidden frontier. Just beyond the lowering clouds that choke the present horizon lies a world of wonders, and the electrifying discovery of what we truly are.

I don't think that, at any time in recorded history, we have been right about our true nature. Certainly, the old Western theocracy that arose out of the dismal Council of Nicaea in A.D. 325 is wrong, and probably even more wrong than modern science.

I suppose that leaves me more or less out on a limb—or, more properly, a plank. Without science or religion, I certainly have no established allies. Maybe secret societies could take up my cause, but so far, no cigar.

It's quite fun on my plank. Out here, if you jump you may just fly. Out here, we are a delicious mystery that goes far beyond the intricacies of physical life, but is also divorced from the guilty weight of conventional religion.

I do not think that we live in the highest civilization ever known, and I think that the modern intellectual enterprise has failed in two fundamental ways. It has been unable, or unwilling, to look at the past objectively, and it has been unable to devise any means to detect the existence of the soul as a part of the physical universe—a measurement that, I think, must be possible. If I am correct, it must also be the foundation of a much truer science than we now know.

I think that the modern failure to realize that energy can itself be conscious is as fundamental to our progress as was the failure of the ancient world to understand the potential of steam power.

Around A.D. 120, Heron of Alexandria invented a device called the aeolipile, a simple steam engine, which was used to open the doors of a temple, and also showed up in Roman playrooms as a toy. The potential of the technology was never understood by the Roman world. Without any ability to see the soul, and penetrate into its reality with technology, modern science is at least as far from understanding the truth about human life as the Romans were from understanding steam power.

If the experience gained from lives like mine is at all true, then we have two forms, one that is active and embedded in the physical body, and another that is contemplative and lives on when the body dies, in an energetic state. I believe that consciousness cycles back and forth between the two, but both are essentially part of physical reality. The soul is not in any way outside of nature, but human death is a transformation into another form, in the same way that a caterpillar becomes a butterfly.

To me, the physical world is far richer than would be suggested by a mechanistic model of reality. I do not believe that religious traditions such as that of resurrection, which emerges in earliest times in the form of the story of Osiris, and continues to the promise of Christ, involve the supernatural at all. They are about living in the physical world in a way that leads to the preservation of individuality when the body dies and consciousness enters the energetic state.

From Osiris to Christ, I wonder if the resurrection stories might not reflect an ancient science of the soul that was lost as our increasing focus on the material world caused us to become soul-blind and thus god-blind and therefore also blind to the most vividly alive aspect of our own being?

As a result of this change in focus, we no longer live to die, we live to live. On the surface, this seems nicer, of course. But that's only on the surface. In that it assumes that death has no meaning, it also assumes that life has no meaning.

I think that it has led to a situation where most of us are completely unprepared for death. So we enter the other world in confusion, clinging to the residue of our physical lives. It has also led us to our fantastic obsession with material existence, and our addictive habits of consumption.

It's interesting to contemplate just how awkward it must be for some people when they arrive on the other side. Christians who find no Saint Peter, or Muslims who are not greeted by dancing virgins—except, perhaps, for the women. Or people like Jean-Paul Sartre or, say, Nietzsche, whose embarrassment must have been quite fantastic. The truth,

I suspect, is that on dying we enter another kind of life, but it is, also, ordinary life. Chiefly, it offers an immeasurably detailed reconstruction of our physical experience that can enable us to rise above the whole process altogether and, seeing ourselves with true objectivity, ascend into unimagined realms.

This is what is happening in *The Omega Point*, to the vast numbers of people who are ascending into the enigmatic higher reality. David Ford never quite understands what is happening to them, or why it doesn't happen to him, so he soldiers on in his elegantly unsure way, trying to find the sense of his own very different mission.

Certain parts of the Bible, and traditions such as the ancient Egyptian religion, suggest that there may once have been more objective understanding of this other reality, and that it may have been addressed with the lost science of the soul. Among the relevant documents in the Bible, the Gospels are a chronicle of how to live to die in a state of compassion and forgiveness that enables us to let go of the concerns of physical life and ascend, rather than cling to them and end up eventually returning to this state—a fate which cannot possibly be considered as other than a pretty mawkish outcome, once one has become aware of the greater potential that one might have realized.

This is why, in *The Omega Point*, Christ is seen as a scientist. I think that's exactly what he was, and his miracles reflect not supernatural powers but scientific knowledge of the way the energetic world actually works, and an ability to apply its principles to physical reality, thus effecting cure and defying death.

Developing this assertion, it would therefore be probable that he learned his techniques during the time he spent in Egypt, and that he was specifically chosen because of his Davidic heritage, by practitioners who understood that their own world was coming to an end, and were seeking to bequeath their knowledge to the future. When the Romans tacked that sign on his cross, KING OF THE JEWS, they weren't just being sardonic but also stating a fact: he was the heir to the House of David and thus the mortal enemy of Rome's client-king Herod.

If this knowledge still existed in Jesus' time, it must have already been quite isolated from the central and public stream of Egyptian culture. For example, what we know of Egyptian religion suggests, in its elaborate use of magical implements and ritual, that it was enacting something that had lost its true meaning, somewhat like what happens when children who have observed an adult drive a car play at doing the same thing.

As a child I did this—unfortunately, though, with a real car. I was no more effective at driving down the street at the age of ten than the Egyptians were, I suspect, at engaging conscious energy with their rituals.

During World War II, natives in the mountains of New Guinea were exposed to Western technology for the first time when the U.S. Air Force began building bases in the area. When they saw planes landing and disgorging an unimaginable cornucopia of supplies, they responded by using sympathetic magic. They cleared jungle air strips. They built airplanes out of bamboo and leaves, and wove objects that looked to them like the refrigerators the airmen had. Then they devised ritual movements and sounds that to them mimicked the movements of the U.S. personnel back and forth between the airplanes and the refrigerators.

But when they opened the doors to their "refrigerators," no beer came out, and I speculate that this could be what was happening when Egyptians concluded their rituals, which mimicked the operations of a much older lost science, but were no more functional than bamboo airplanes.

All was not lost, though, not entirely. Here and there, some traditions had retained at least some of that knowledge, and later in the discussion we will speculate about who and where.

Nevertheless, for the most part, the science that once gave these rituals potency had been lost, I believe, in a phenomenal upheaval that swamped the world thousands of years before Egyptian civilization even appeared.

Around twelve thousand years ago, the last Ice Age ended. And, as is not uncommon on planet Earth, this was a violent event. As the Laurentide glacier melted, sea levels around the world rose precipitately, and other upheavals caused further chaos.

There is enigmatic evidence—necessarily ignored by modern science—that a much more potent human presence existed then, probably hugging coastlines which are now submerged to a depth of hundreds of feet, and in some cases actually swept into the abyssal deep.

At the same time that this civilization was flourishing in the lowlands of the late Pleistocene, in the highlands of that world, human life was primitive. But go into a mountainous region today. Almost everywhere, you will find there the poorest people in the world. And where are our greatest cities? Hugging the coasts. If the future had only the remains of life in the Himalayas and the Andes to tell us about this world, it would not realize that our civilization had even existed.

Many books have been published about the evidence of a lost civilization, but I would like to mention here just one telling piece of it that is rarely referred to, but which I find fascinating. It is that there are seventeen ancient ritual sites and cities around the world, all situated on the same great circle, with a southern axis point that falls about five hundred miles from the coast of Antarctica, and a northern axis in British Columbia roughly fifteen hundred miles from the present geographic North Pole.

In itself, it is remarkable that places as diverse as the first Sumerian city, Ur, the Giza Plateau, Easter Island, Nazca, and the ancient Indian city of Mohenjo Daro would all be on the same great circle, but they are.

Modern science has no real explanation for this, except that it must have been just random happenstance. But surely that isn't enough of an answer. It's satisfactory only if you want to cling to cherished theories and ignore evidence.

I no longer ignore evidence. The last time I did that, I ended up being dragged out of my house by aliens. The evidence that such things could happen was abundant, but I assumed that it was absurd. So what might have been a fascinating meeting turned into a screaming confusion for me. It could have been more civilized, surely, but I will never forget the ghastly shock that coursed through me a few days later when my doctor said, "You've been raped." It was so humiliating that it took me twenty years to actually utter those words. To this day, I suffer pain from the injury I sustained on that night, which I mentioned only in passing in *Communion* as the "rectal probe" that has made me such a laughingstock. Rape and laughter don't actually go together all that well, though, at least not to the victim.

Had I been aware that such things could happen, I would certainly have been more calm, and perhaps the experience would have been less chaotic. Over the eleven years of contact that followed, I ended up in a sort of school, the lessons of which were glimpses into the greater reality in which we actually live. In short, what started out pretty badly became the most precious of treasures. Even the fear became entertaining and profoundly instructive, especially when I realized that the outré little beings I have called "the visitors" found me every bit as terrifying as I did them.

It's too bad that science has not acknowledged their presence, because, even without direct contact with them, there is a wealth of physical evidence available for study. But they don't fit our theories of the cosmos. According to modern theory, it is impossible for there to be physical travel across the universe because the distances are too great. But there is also no evidence of where they are from. Maybe they are far stranger even than aliens from another planet.

As our rational culture has matured, it has also become, as is inevitable, more decadent. In science, this decadence finds expression in the fact that we've slipped into the trap of putting theory before evidence, which is the core reason that we are missing so much of what is real all around us.

Given the evidence of all the sites along that great circle, for example, it is also likely that, in very ancient times, somebody knew that the Earth was round, had an awareness of its size, was in planetwide communication, and intentionally built these sites on a great circle measured from the physical North and South poles, which, during the cataclysm, moved when the earth's crust shifted on its mantle.

If such a movement were to have taken place, as Charles Hapgood first postulated and Rand Flem-Ath developed in his book *When the Sky Fell*, the consequences would have been fantastic destruction, a catastrophe beyond imagining.

But what's so unusual about that? This is planet Earth, where catastrophes beyond imagining happen pretty darned frequently.

An earth movement that great and that sudden would have changed the planet's coastlines—as, in fact, it did. But underwater archaeology is in its infancy. We have barely explored the ancient coastlines of the planet, but what we have explored, as Graham Hancock demonstrates in his book *Underworld*, seems to be populated with enigmatic ruins.

Great catastrophes are ordinary events on Earth, and even mass extinctions are relatively common. Much more common are the smaller disasters that are not classifiable as mass extinctions, and there have been at least two of these just in the past fifteen thousand years.

My story refers to the infamous upheaval that ended the Ice Age 12,600 years ago.

Whether or not a sequel to that disaster is building now is unknown, but certainly something is causing persistent changes in our solar system, and has been for about forty years, and possibly longer.

A Dr. Alexey Dimitriev allegedly published an article in 1997 suggesting that charged particles were entering the solar system from the outside, resulting in changes to all bodies within the solar system. I say "allegedly" because I have been unable to contact Dr. Dimitriev, and there is some evidence that the paper may be a fabrication.

But, in this case, that isn't important. *The Omega Point* is fiction and, frankly, I would be flabbergasted if the world in 2020 was anything like what appears in the book. At the same time, though, more than one ancient calendar points to the immediate future as being a time of great change.

Whether Dimitriev's paper is real or not, there is evidence of increased planetary heating not only on Earth, but also on Mars and Jupiter. Planetologists observed an approximate 1 degree Fahrenheit warming on Mars between 1970 and 1990, and in recent years the Martian polar cap has retreated. An increase in the number of red spots of Jupiter, and other signs on various planetary bodies and moons in our solar system, point to the widespread presence of this phenomenon.

As of this writing, the sun is also acting in an unusual manner, but rather than increasing solar activity, which would be expected if it was being bombarded from the outside, it has become unexpectedly quiet.

At the same time, the amount of observed cometary and asteroid activity in the solar system may have been increasing. Because the amount of observation and the sensitivity of instruments is also increasing, it's difficult to be certain. But when the Shoemaker-Levy comet struck Jupiter in 1994, it was thought to be a thousand-year event. Just fifteen years later, though, another large object struck Jupiter, surprising astronomers. It would never have been noticed, except that the scar it left was photographed by an amateur astronomer. A day before the object's scar was seen on Jupiter on July 20, 2009, a similar scar appeared on Venus. Whether this was the result of an impact is not known, but if it was, then the object that produced it was a large one. Had it struck Earth on July 20 instead of Venus, it would have resulted in a massive planetary catastrophe very much like the one that overtook us 12,600 years ago.

So, are we more than ordinarily exposed to an asteroid strike right now? Truthfully, nobody can be certain, but observation does suggest that there is more debris in the solar system just now.

In my story, by the time 2020 has come around, the amount of material entering it has increased exponentially from where it was in 2012, and as a result the sun has begun to be affected by it.

It is difficult to imagine the scale of what is happening, certainly for those living through it in the story, but as author and readers, we can visualize matters more clearly. A supernova emits two forms of material. The first is a radiation burst that moves at about 90 percent of the speed of light. This generally spreads through space as a gigantic expanding ball of energy. The second is a mass of debris, which moves much more slowly and unevenly, with the densest parts expanding most slowly.

As a result, this expanding cloud has an irregular front, and it is this fact that gives rise to the fundamental premise of the story, that our solar system passed through one node of it 12,600 years ago, and is now entering another.

While there is no certain evidence that this is actually happening, something must be causing the changes we are seeing in the solar system at the present time.

One thing has become clear in the past few years: 12,600 years ago, there was indeed a tremendous upheaval on planet Earth. It hit North America the hardest, and was responsible for the mass extinctions that took place then, including the destruction of the entire human population of North America that existed at that time, the Clovis culture, and the extinction of no fewer than thirty-five animal genera, including most large animals in North America, such as the American horse, the mammoth, the mastodon, the American camel, and many others.

There are dozens of myths about a time of flooding and upheaval in the world, some of which may date to this very early period.

On May 23, 2007, in the General Assembly of the American Geophysical Union in Acapulco, Mexico, the work of a multiinstitutional twenty-six-member team proposed the theory that just such an impact caused the upheaval that ended the last Ice Age.

They presented substantial evidence of the event, and three of them also published a popular book on the subject, *The Cycle of Cosmic Catastrophes*, which lays out their evidence for the nonscientific reader.

But the event that took place 12,600 years ago was hardly unique in Earth's history. In fact, it is simply one of a continuum of such events.

Approximately 5,200 years ago something extraordinary caused the collapse of Mediterranean civilizations from archaic Greece to Egypt. Terrible drought struck the area. At the same time, in Peru, leafy plants were frozen so quickly that they did not wither—in other words, in a matter of seconds, like frozen food. Subsequently they were covered over by glaciers that remain intact even now.

The climate there went from temperate to extremely cold in a matter of minutes or even seconds, and has remained extremely cold ever since in the area where Professor Lonnie Thompson of the Byrd Polar Research Institute studies these glaciers, in the Andean highlands.

During the same period a man running through an alpine meadow in the Tyrol was overtaken by a blizzard and frozen. He—and the meadow—were then covered by a glacier that melted enough to expose his remains only in 1991, when the mummified form of Otzi the Ice Man was discovered lying in the frost of the retreating glacier.

What sort of event would cause changes this sudden and yet long lasting across the globe? The simple answer is that the universe is a very messy place and even though Earth happens to be packed with a mind-boggling mass of sensitive, intelligent creatures who urgently seek to survive, it is still subject to arbitrary and random catastrophes, and—in terms of geologic time—they are relatively frequent.

This book started with a thought: what if it happens? What if the world really does end for us?

Teresa McDonald of the University of Kansas Natural History Museum says that 99.9 percent of all species that have ever lived are extinct right now, so extinction is certainly the norm—and, in fact, unless we happen to establish ourselves somewhere else in the universe, our time on planet Earth will sooner or later run out. And not only that, there is, in fact, no way at all to determine when this might happen.

If an object that we happen to be able to see collides with the planet, we might have some warning, but there are many perils on Earth and in space—in fact, most—that will come as complete surprises.

But was that always true, and need it still be true?

Conventional modern wisdom asserts that time is immutable, reality is limited to what we can measure now, and that both evolution and civilization display rigid progressions occasionally punctuated by unanticipated changes, which are entirely unpredictable.

However, that may not be entirely true, and it could be very far from true. As an example, there are buried in our past suggestions that somebody understood the world very differently from the way we do today, and perhaps saw a structure in the development of human civilization to which we have become blind.

One of the oddest facts about our past is the number of very long-term calendars that exist, the most famous of which are the Zodiac and the Mayan Long Count calendar. The reason that this is odd is that our modern understanding of the ancient world leaves no room for the need for such calendars, let alone any ability to create them. For example, creating the Zodiac required understanding the precession of the equinoxes, which must necessarily involve thousands of years of observation as the Earth slowly gyrates and the stars its poles point at gradually change. Who could have made such long-term observations and recorded them? No civilization in recorded history has lasted long enough to create such a record.

But then again, our understanding of the past does not have any room in it for the building of cities and sacred sites along the same great circle around the planet, either.

One bit of evidence that cannot be disputed is that the authors of both the Old and New Testaments knew very well which signs of the Zodiac the books were being written under, and wove this knowledge into their texts.

The Old Testament was written under the sign of Aries, the ram, and the ram is mentioned seventy-two times in it, more than any other animal. But, of course, that could be dismissed as a coincidence.

But not when one realizes that the New Testament was written at the beginning of the next 2,300-year astrological cycle, Pisces, and its primary symbol, even more than the cross, is that of the fish. Jesus is the Fisher of Men. He gathers his apostles from among fishermen. Among early Christians, the universal symbol of recognition was the fish.

The Old Testament that was written under Aries also reflects the demanding, stubborn characteristics of that sign, the exemplar of which is the dour personality of its governing deity, Yahweh. Similarly, Jesus with his message of compassion is characteristically Piscean. In addition, Pisces the fish swims in nurturing, supportive water, so if we are Pisces, then Earth is our water, providing us with everything we need to live.

But not always. At present, we are leaving Pisces and entering Aquarius, and the water that has sustained us so long is being poured out. And indeed, Earth is already being plagued by droughts. In 2008, the southeastern United States came close to a catastrophic drought. In 2009, droughts afflicted much of Asia, parts of Europe and Africa, Mexico and the American Southwest, and the potential for catastrophic drought was reaching an extreme in Australia.

In the February 28, 2009, issue of *The New Scientist*, it was suggested that a 4-degree Centigrade rise in planetary temperatures is likely by the end of the century, with the result that huge areas of Earth, including much of the United States, Africa, India, the Middle East, and most of the Amazon, are going to become much too dry to sustain the populations that now live in those areas. According to James Lovelock, the author of *The Gaia Hypothesis*, the situation is likely to lead to something approaching a 95 percent reduction in the human population of Earth, and, given present worldwide temperature changes, the predicted increase is probably already inevitable. In addition, as ocean currents slow, there could be serious and unpredictable shorter-term weather events, such as ferocious storms and, as the temperature of the planet becomes more even, the slowing and eventual stopping of essential air circulation.

Were air circulation to stop, dozens of cities across the planet would become unlivable in a matter of weeks.

Obviously, this is a horrific prognosis for the future of man, but there is a different way of looking at it, and in *The Omega Point*, the journey of David Ford, Caroline Light, and the class expresses the importance of ways of thinking that are completely new, and bear no reference to the entire system of values and way of life that have led us to the peril in which we now find ourselves.

The first signs of human industrial activity on Earth become visible during the middle centuries of the Roman Empire, when residue from smelting activities in Britain and Spain was deposited on glaciers in Greenland.

This is also when there was a fundamental change in the way human beings conceived of their lives. For the first time, material well-being became more important to a large social class that also became divorced from spiritual awareness. Previously, material opulence had been part of the ritual presence of leaderships that were both temporal and spiritual. During the great Roman peace, however, there came into being a class of people who were more or less irreligious, and whose interests focused primarily on material wealth. This secular class was focused on material consumption and longevity, not on preparing for an afterlife in which they no longer had any belief. And the more devoted to the material world they became, the less real the soul seemed to them.

After Rome collapsed, the Western world returned to theocracy, but it was not a healthy theocracy. Christ taught the triumph of resurrection, but in A.D. 325, the Council of Nicaea changed the focus of the church from joy at Christ's triumph over death to guilt at our—probably entirely fictional—birth into sin. Prior to Nicaea, Christ had often been portrayed as carrying a magician's wand that promised new life. Now, he was portrayed as suffering on a cross that was our fault.

This change was made for political reasons, because guilty people can be controlled by those who claim the power of forgiveness. As a result Christianity sank into the long trance of guilt and retribution from which it is just beginning to emerge.

Growing wealth in the fifteenth century caused the reemergence of a secular community, followed by a revolt against the oppression of the church. This, in turn, led to a second and more formidable rise of materialism. And now we are at the climax of material civilization. Most of us are either soul blind or passive to the idea that our lives may matter in some larger way. Most of us live to live, and struggle against death as if it was an absolute and final end, whether we have cherished beliefs about an afterlife or not. We have, in short, gone soul blind, which is another of the core themes of the book.

Largely because of extraordinary, unstoppable population growth, we find ourselves in a situation where only the most heroic efforts, probably already beyond both our capacity and our will, would enable the planet to continue to sustain us.

We are almost exactly in the place anyone watching the stately movement of the Zodiac would expect us to be, and whether anything unusual happens precisely on December 21, 2012, or not, the Mayan Long Count calendar has also been uncannily accurate in predicting vast change during this period.

It is strange enough that these calendars even exist, but far stranger is the fact that they are in any way at all accurate. Even stranger is the fact that there exists knowledge of a great plan of some sort concealed in the Bible.

If modern perceptions of the human past did not make it seem impossible, there would be no question but that people in earlier times possessed deeper understanding of the human situation than we do, and recorded their understanding in long count calendars that can have no purpose other than to mark great cycles of life that are hidden to the modern mind.

In fact, somebody in the past did understand. The Maya understood. The creators of the Zodiac understood. The authors of the Bible understood. But we no longer understand.

But what did they understand, and why did they understand it? Is it possible that they had skills that we no longer possess, such as the skill that is recovered by Herbert Acton and Bartholomew Light in the book, in the jungles of Guatemala?

This gets us to one of the central elements in the story: white powder gold. The existence of this substance was first brought to my attention by an old friend, Laurence Gardner, in his book *Lost Secrets of the Sacred Ark*, which basically asks the question, was the Ark of the Covenant an artifact of an ancient science now lost, and, if so, does it have any relevance now?

Gardner describes a substance the Egyptians called *mfkzt* and the Hebrews *shem*. It was believed to confer great powers of concentration and physical health, and to enable users to enter the world of the gods and confer with these higher powers. It is depicted in reliefs as a conical white substance, and was apparently created under extremely high heat. A quantity of it was unearthed at a dig on Mount Horeb in the Sinai peninsula by Sir Flinders Petrie in 1904.

Sir Flinders found this substance while excavating the only Egyptian temple ever found outside Egypt. In the 270-foot-long temple he discovered a metallurgist's workshop, and hieroglyphs indicating that the site had been in active use for fifteen hundred years, up to the reign of Akhenaton in 1350 B.C. Most of what Petrie found of the white substance was abandoned at the site and blew away, and both the sample he returned to England and his notes have been lost.

The actual formula for this substance remains lost to history, but it may have been accidentally rediscovered by a farmer called David Hudson while he was attempting to restore some land to arability in Arizona. He was a wealthy and politically conservative man, and had no interest in or awareness of ancient alchemical formulations. The soil was full of salt, so he was using sulfuric acid on it when he noticed that black and red material was appearing in the soil that he could not identify. When it dried, it exploded with a silent flash and disappeared, taking the paper on which he had put it with it.

Naturally, he was intrigued. He soon discovered that the flash did not cause a change of air pressure. So it was a release of light, not an explosion. After crucible reduction, he was left with beads of gold and silver that shattered like glass. But there is no alloy of these elements that is that brittle. So what did he have?

By heating, he eventually created a substance that was a white powder, which was 56 percent lighter than the original material. This could be explained by the material partly volatizing away, but when he heated it to the point that it fused into the glass container where it was being tested, all of its weight returned.

He had found a very unusual substance, one that Dr. Hal Puthoff, of the Austin Institute for Advanced Studies, said "bends" space and time.

Interestingly, there is some evidence that colloidal gold does help people with rheumatoid arthritis, and can even raise I.Q., but this is different from white powder gold.

Because the modern substance doesn't seem to be as dramatically efficacious as the ancient one, in *The Omega Point* some of the ancient substance must be acquired first before the material that is used in the story can have its full effect.

This effect involves the ability to see events outside of time, before they have actually happened, as well as the ability to physically move into the past and the future.

Now, one would assume that such things are fiction. My problem with that is that I have actually done them. I've gone into the past and into the future both, and have often had physical experience of events before they happened.

From time to time I've read things in newspapers, only to look again a moment later and find them gone—and then to discover them weeks later in the latest edition of the same paper. Sadly, these little visions have not involved the stock market tables. An annoyance, to be sure.

The first of these involved the Claude Chabrol film, *A Girl Cut in Two*. I saw a listing of it in the *Los Angeles Times* in June of 2008, looked up and said to my wife, "There's a new Chabrol movie. We've got to go." I then turned back to the paper to find out where it was playing, and the listing had completely disappeared. There was no mention of it in the paper at all. So I went online and discovered that it had not yet been released.

Six weeks later, in August, I saw the same listing again. Naturally we went to the film.

But what had happened? Well, truthfully, I'm not at all sure. It was as if I read a listing from August in June. Since then, this has happened to me three or four times.

It is far from the most extraordinary thing that has ever happened to me involving time. The most amazing of these events took place in March of 1983, when we lived on LaGuardia Place in Manhattan. One rainy Saturday morning, I was crossing Houston Street on the way to the bank when I suddenly heard a terrific creaking and sloshing and clip-clopping in front of me. This symphony passed me and turned the corner, and I turned with it, to see an immense wagon come into view as if out of nowhere. It was stacked with barrels and there was a strong smell of pickles. High atop it sat a man wrapped in a black leather apron. It was being drawn by a huge horse, I assume a dray horse.

Of course, I thought that it was one of the Budweiser Clydesdales, but it was worn and dirty, and the smell was very clearly not beer.

As it passed up the street, I found that LaGuardia Place had changed entirely. Gone was the street I knew, with modern co-op towers on the northeast side of LaGuardia and Houston. Instead, a man in a derby stood across the street, much closer and in front of a row of smaller buildings. He shouted something, and at the same moment, there was movement to my right, and I turned to see a small woman dressed entirely in black go skittering away from me. Then I saw, coming up what in 1983 was West Broadway, a group of five or six riders on gorgeous horses, looking like some sort of equestrian team.

I became aware of the fact that this was no longer the New York of 1983, but that, somehow, I was seeing the same street corner in the past. I noticed an odd, curved curb at my feet, then a bit of paper in it. I thought, if I get that paper, that'll prove what's happening. But as I bent down, something that felt like ice-cold water seemed to pour right through my body, and with it came a loneliness so intense that, had it persisted for more than a few moments, it might have driven me mad.

The thought came that, if I touched that paper, I would remain here forever, and I froze. Slowly, the sharp smell of coal and the denser stench of manure dissipated. Then the sound of cars returned. When I looked up, everything seemed normal.

Forgetting about the bank, I rushed home, frightened that something was terribly wrong and I might never see my family again. This was before my 1985 close encounter, so I was totally unprepared for anything in the least unusual.

It never happened quite like that again, but I never forgot it. I went to the library and read endless microfiche records of old newspapers, looking for classified ads that might have been placed by people trapped in time. I didn't find anything.

These experiences, though, have led me to think that we are not fixed in time, and that we don't really need any technology more exotic than the human body to move through it.

In *The Omega Point*, movement through time has been developed to an art and a science, and the time machine involved is a mixture of both. It is a scientific device, in that the colors mixed for it contain chemical properties that enable movement through time. But it is also created with love and artistry, and it is the combination of science and art that confers its amazing properties on it.

This is because it is constructed using not the arid principles of modern science, but those of the lost science of the soul, which combines, in my novel and perhaps in reality, a rigorous physical technology with a carefully controlled and immeasurably potent emotional state, the love that Caroline Light needs so badly to succeed, and gets, after a struggle, when her beloved David finally remembers what they shared as children.

Christian principles of love, compassion, and forgiveness are explored throughout the book, and it is love, in the end, that confers on mankind the ability to move on into time, and reestablish our presence in the physical world.

I am not a conventional Christian, but I am certainly a believer in the intelligence and compassionate insights of Jesus, and the meaning of his resurrection. I reject the idea that it was done to free us from some sort of sin. It was an example of what happens when a person lives an ethical life that feeds the soul, and dies without attachment to life's hungers.

One of the most ancient of all human ideas is that there is a judgment after death. The Egyptians saw the soul as being weighed, and in my story, greed, cruelty, and arrogance weigh souls down to the point that, when the body dies, the soul literally drops out of it and ends up imprisoned in the depths of the earth, remaining there, presumably, until the end of time. Other souls—the great majority—which are light enough to rise, ascend into a state that is never described in the book, because its mystery has never really been explored, and perhaps cannot be explored.

So far, the plan described in *The Omega Point* mirrors the one in the Book of Revelation. But then it takes a turn in another direction. In the Sermon on the Mount, which is probably the most profound statement ever made, there is mention that the meek will inherit the earth.

To me, this is promise of some surcease from the ages-long torment that the ordinary human being has experienced at the hands of the more aggressive and powerful. In my story, the great of the world are left hiding in their holes to die, I suppose, a lingering death. The innocent majority ascend, as well as those chosen for the special work of constructing a new home for mankind to move forward in time and continue our ages-long journey toward ecstasy, but this time without the cruel, the avaricious, and the arrogant, only with those who are fully human.

When I was a young man, I had the extraordinary privilege of being an occasional student of P. L. Travers, who was deeply involved in esoteric work. She taught a powerful ethics of the meek, whom she used to call "the little cottagers," and this ethic was present not only in her talks but also in the letters I received from her. It affected me profoundly, and I have never forgotten that it is, in the end, the humble man at the bottom of the world, the one who is entirely overlooked by the grand and the powerful, who is forced into war, starved, left to die, ignored, and broken on the wheel of the avarice of the great, who emerges into immortality while, as Jesus put it so succinctly, those who display their excellence receive their reward in life.

Is there really a plan for us, one that brings justice to this unjust world? When one thinks of all the ages of oppression and injustice that define our history, one can only hope that, somewhere in time, the promise of the Sermon on the Mount will indeed be fulfilled. If so, then the earth will wind up in the hands of those who will cherish her, riding her in joy and respect, into the reaches of time.